Coming Home Again

A Novel of Nova Scotia by
Peter H. Riddle

Best wishes,

PublishAmerica
Baltimore

Photo of sailing yacht by Robert E. Rushton. Used by permission.

First printing

At the specific preference of the author, PublishAmerica allowed this work to remain exactly as the author intended, verbatim, without editorial input.

ISBN: 1-4241-2010-1
PUBLISHED BY PUBLISHAMERICA, LLLP
www.publishamerica.com
Baltimore

Printed in the United States of America

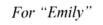

For "Emily"

Acknowledgments

The author is indebted to representatives of Family and Children's Services of Nova Scotia for their assistance in navigating the convoluted legislation involving the protection of children in the Province, and the rights they enjoy under the law.

The large coastal town of Bournemouth lies nestled along the South Shore of Nova Scotia, not far from the capital city of Halifax, but only in the author's imagination. Farrell Island and the characters portrayed are also fictional.

Do not let it grieve you,
No one leaves for good.
You are not alone.
> Stephen Sondheim, *Into the Woods*

We may take something like a star
To stay our minds on and be staid.
> Robert Frost

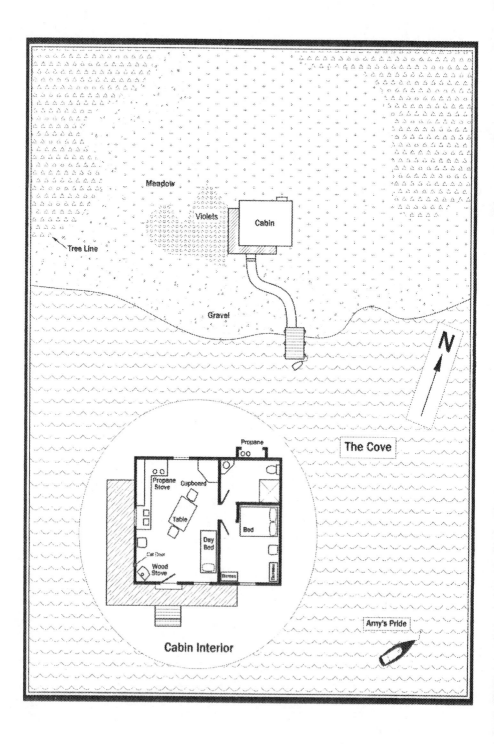

Meadow

Violets

Cabin

Tree Line

Gravel

N

The Cove

Propane

Propane
Stove

Cupboard

Table

Bed

Day
Bed

Cat Door

Wood
Stove

Bureau

Cabin Interior

Amy's Pride

1
Monday

Sunshine. Wind steady offshore, eight to ten knots, filling the sails and urging *Amy's Pride* gently toward Farrell Island. A bottlenose dolphin breaks the surface a dozen yards to port, scattering brilliant diamonds of sun-drenched droplets and grinning his pleasure at a perfect day in late July.

Once, when Amy was alive, such a sight would have brought me immense pleasure. Now I no longer give a damn. Sailing down the most beautiful stretch of Nova Scotia's Atlantic coastline, I should be feeling content, at ease, even joyful, not bleak and purposeless. Instead, the loss of her has wiped away such simple pleasures and reduced the myriad colours of the world to shades of muted grey.

The wind drops almost to dead calm as I round the leeward side of the island and coast into the shadow of its craggy headland. The sails wilt, sapped of their energy as I am of mine, and the boat comes about to face the receding tide. She slows and settles into the trough of her own wake. It takes but a few minutes to winch the jib onto its roller furling and release the main halyard, a few more to fold the mainsail against the boom and snap the cover in place. Such routine tasks are now the sum and substance of the aimless, unproductive rhythms of my long and pointless days.

My condition is not an uncommon one: clinical depression. But knowledge is not necessarily wisdom, and simply pasting a label on my situation does nothing to relieve its debilitating effects. To restore oneself requires not merely the recognition of a disorder, but the innate desire to heal, which I lack. Without some defining purpose, simply to live day by day is an endless procession of meaningless repetitions, oppressing the soul.

Amy is gone. Where once just being together made us so much more than two, alone I am so much less than one.

With no other boats in sight, it seems safe to put the engine in gear and head for the sheltered cove deep within the core of Farrell Island. I'm jealous of my privacy, and never enter the inlet when there is anyone nearby who might discover that it exists. From the sea the craggy coastline appears impenetrable, but there is a hidden channel. A trio of tiny barrier islets conceals the entrance, and the steep and rocky coastline discourages almost anyone who might approach them.

The S-shaped channel weaves sinuously between densely grouped pine and spruce groves and is strewn with rocks and debris, a treacherous passage forbidding enough to discourage any boat owner who values the safety of his craft. It had taken my brother and me many cautious explorations to determine a safe route through the hazards. Only a very few strangers had ever penetrated deeply enough to find my cabin, none recently.

With the engine barely above idle, *Amy's Pride* picks her way among the partly sunken logs and jagged rocks that make a low tide approach so dangerous. When I was younger, I relished the challenge of completing a safe passage, a welcome test for a competent seaman. Later on, when Amy sailed by my side and lounged in comfort against the rail in complete confidence of my expertise, her approval had nourished my ego. Now alone, I find the slow pace annoying, an impediment to my swift return home.

Home! The word has taken on a different meaning over the past six months.

I should sell the boat, a big CS 30 with a six-foot draft. It's a fine yacht, but unwieldy in close quarters and expensive to maintain. A simple outboard skiff would make entering the island much easier. It's also a difficult craft to sail in rough seas or high winds without an extra crew member to keep the sails in trim. I no longer cruise for pleasure, making only infrequent trips to the mainland to do laundry and for supplies. When Amy was aboard, the boat seemed hardly big enough to contain our joy. Now its empty recesses mock my solitude.

The channel gives way suddenly to the sheltered cove that fronts my cabin, deserted as always except for the mooring buoy anchored off shore. My boat tender lies still and serene in the almost motionless water, its painter hanging slack from the bow, waiting for me to catch the buoy with my boat hook and tie off the yacht. The wake swings the dinghy wide and it comes to rest against the starboard side, ready to take me to shore.

It takes a while to offload my supplies over the gunwale. Groceries. Laundry. The boring necessities of life. Heaviest are two full propane tanks that provide the fuel to cook my meals, and the little pram settles low in the water as I step aboard and unship the oars for the short haul to the dock.

The supply run to the mainland means two more weeks of freedom from want, fourteen days during which I can avoid having to deal with other people. The clean laundry is a matter of habit, ingrained by a civilized upbringing and hard to ignore. All told, the chores have cost me more than half a day in Bournemouth, including two tedious hours spent feeding coins into the washer and dryer at the laundromat.

The line-up to pay for food in the crowded supermarket seemed interminable, but at least I had been spared running into anyone I knew, and the necessity for meaningless polite conversation. The only bright spot had been a solitary noontime meal in a secluded waterfront café, and the enjoyment of freshly caught halibut steak and vegetables that had never seen the inside of a can. Aside from the waiter no one spoke to me, nor did I talk to anyone else. I would have been poor company.

Am I a hermit? I suppose. But the world has little use for me now, and I for it.

It takes another five minutes to offload the supplies from the dinghy onto the dock and carry them to the deck of the cabin, five uneasy minutes. There's something out of place, some anomaly that sets my nerves on edge. The door to the cabin is closed, just as I left it that morning, and the clearing that surrounds the building is deserted. But something…

The two propane tanks go around back to the small lean-to that protects them from the weather. Nothing unusual to be seen there. A slender copper pipe emerges through the wall, coupled to a third tank. Although it's nearly empty, I suspect there's enough reserve for one more evening meal, and perhaps to heat water for tomorrow morning's coffee. I can replace it after that.

Back on the deck, I manage to lift all three grocery bags at once. As I depress the door latch with my elbow, something disquieting catches my eye. A vague trail winds through the meadow that separates the cabin from the forest to the west. Someone has tramped among the violets that Amy's love and care once nurtured into a rampant blaze of purple, blanketing almost half of the clearing on that side. Johnny-Jump-Ups, she always called them, her personal, anthropomorphic friends.

After placing the groceries on the table inside, I return to the deck for a closer look. Where the carpet of violets gives way to wild grasses, the reeds and fronds are pushed aside in a definite pathway running parallel to the shore. It's too wide to have been made by small wildlife, the raccoons and skunks and assorted rodents that call Farrell Island home. Nothing else lives here that could have made so significant a trail.

The dense, dark woods lie silent and opaque, possibly concealing a mystery. Other than the dinghy at the dock and *Amy's Pride*, there is no other boat in sight. But someone has definitely come ashore, and I'd like to know if they're still here.

I bend to retrieve the duffle bag full of laundry and shove it through the open door, then leave the deck to follow the path across the meadow. The violets are recovering, their small faces gradually springing up amid faint impressions of running shoe treads, curiously small. Stepping carefully among the blossoms, I finally reach the forest's edge where the footprints vanish in sun-baked earth and gravel, but scuff marks in the dust and downtrodden undergrowth beneath the trees suggest which way my visitor has gone.

A slight movement deep among the trees catches my eye, a pale flicker quickly extinguished, possibly my imagination but more likely an intruder. A couple of dozen yards into the woods the trail vanishes completely, and the closely spaced tree trunks and brambles block my way. After another few minutes spent trying to see through the gloom of the dense forest, I give up and return to the cabin, only to find signs that the trespasser has invaded my home.

A dishtowel hangs slightly askew over the edge of the sink, and a cupboard door stands somewhat ajar. I never leave it that way myself, bullied into an almost compulsive habit of neatness by a stern and proper live-in grandmother. But what disturbs me most is not seeing Jenny, she who almost invariably greets me at the door with a loud meow when I come home.

The cabin seems deserted. Having made at least some noise when coming through the door, I figure that anyone still inside would have heard me and shown himself. But someone could be holed up somewhere in the back.

"Hello?"

Silence. I walk quietly into the back hallway and find the tiny bathroom vacant. The bedroom is also empty, the door wide open, but the blanket on my bed is rumpled as if someone has sat upon the edge.

"Jenny, you in here?" I call soothingly. "It's okay, you can come out."

A pitiful wail tells me where she's hiding. I approach the bed and drop to my knees to lift the edge of the blanket. The cat crouches against the baseboard in a far corner, her long dishevelled hair flowing out around her and her eyes huge and luminous.

"Come here, stupid. It's only me."

Reluctantly and with great caution she uncoils just enough to slink along the wall, and finally emerges by the foot of the bed. She stretches forward to sniff my extended hand. Finally she begins to relax, letting me stroke her fur gently, and settles into a soft rhythmic purr.

"Had a guest, did we?" I say to her. She arches her back and leans against my leg. Surely the world's most cowardly cat, she might have been crouched under the bed for hours, or whoever frightened her could have been inside the cabin much more recently. There's no way to know for sure.

Why the hell can't people just leave me alone?

Once Jenny is reassured, I go back outside to stand on the deck and survey the cove. Nothing has changed. The dead low tide laps the shore gently, and *Amy's Pride* lies absolutely still in the heavy warmth of late afternoon. There's nothing out of place along the shoreline on either side of the dock, no skid marks in the gravel where a craft might have landed. This is no surprise, for if someone had come by boat, they surely would have tied up at the dock instead. But if so, where is the boat now? Has the invader come and gone? Mystery upon mystery...

Behind the cabin to the north the land slopes steeply upward, the terrain rugged and inhospitable. The vegetation there is too sparse to offer anyone a hiding place. To the east, scrubby evergreens grow thinly among a jumble of glacial rocks. If someone is still on the island, he's most likely concealed among the densely packed trees to the west.

After a wet spring the foliage is thick and lush, and I can barely see beyond the first row of trees. The sun is dropping toward the tree line on the ridge of the westward hill, and the shadows are growing long and increasingly diffuse. There's an uncommon silence on the west side of the cabin. Not a bird sings, nor is there any sign of the ubiquitous squirrels that multiply geometrically in the almost predator-free safety of Farrell Island.

Time to eat. I re-enter the cabin and open the cupboard to put the groceries away and choose my evening meal.

Someone has raided my supplies. The half dozen cans of beans and soup that were there in the morning haven't been touched, but a box of crackers is missing and the top gapes open on a box of shredded wheat. It had been nearly half full, and now just two biscuits lie in the bottom. Whoever took them must have needed them badly. There couldn't have been much pleasure in eating the straw-like cereal with neither milk nor sugar to make it go down easily. Both items had been on my shopping list.

Well, bon appetite, whoever you are.

It takes just a few minutes to stow the groceries. Still somewhat full from the seafood lunch, I don't bother to cook anything for supper, opting for a simple sandwich instead. I light the propane stove and measure coffee into my ancient percolator, then open a loaf of bread and a small can of processed chicken.

Not having any sort of icebox or refrigerator to preserve perishables, I don't enjoy the luxury of butter or mayonnaise, but eating has become more a matter of necessity than enjoyment anyway. I spread a slice of bread with half of the meat from the can and add a thick layer of lettuce. Jenny will appreciate having the remainder of the chicken later in the evening.

While waiting for the coffee to brew, I put the sandwich on a plate and carry it out through the door. The air has cooled a bit and the humidity is low, and it's pleasant to sit on the rudimentary bench that overlooks the forest to the west. The woods are still unnaturally hushed. Behind me on the opposite side of the cabin, the normal sounds of insects and an occasional birdcall embellish the clear air, but in front of me nothing stirs. Something, some foreign presence, has intimidated the fauna, which means that my visitor is still hanging about and for some reason is hiding from me.

As I finish my meal, a fleeting glimpse of white flutters among the darkened trunks within the dense forest. I jump down from the deck and start across the clearing and the phantom vanishes abruptly, leaving me to wonder if I've imagined it.

The hell with it!

Back in the cabin the coffee is ready, and I turn the flame down low and fill a mug, a soothing aid to contemplation. Seen through the open window over the sink, the blue of the sky has given way to a rich and vibrant pink above the hills, shadowing the distant trees to a muted and colourless blur. An owl calls softly somewhere off to the right, and something rustles in the undergrowth across the clearing. The flash of white appears again and lingers for a moment, then evaporates once more, a pale and insubstantial ghost that could be hallucination, but isn't.

Without doubt I'm not alone, but since there's no boat, it's a puzzle. In addition to a rugged coastline, Farrell Island is protected by offshore reefs that prevent any approach by water other than the channel into my cove. Even

16

a boat with a very shallow draft cannot land elsewhere, and it seems highly improbable that an intruder can have swum so far from the mainland. Had there been a boating accident, the survivors would hardly be hiding out. They would instead be asking for help.

There's always the possibility of drug smugglers, not uncommon among the many islands of Nova Scotia's South Shore, but such unsavoury characters would hardly be avoiding me. They would more likely be lounging about in plain sight, guns at their sides. There has to be some other explanation as to why someone is hiding in the woods.

If the intruder is hungry but reluctant to ask for a meal, he might be planning another raid on my cupboard, and I want to forestall that. Once my mug is empty I light a lantern against the gathering dusk and retrieve the loaf of bread from the cupboard, along with the lettuce and the half-full can of chicken.

Sorry, Jenny. Next time.

It takes only a couple of minutes to make another sandwich, and I retrieve a bottle of water from the cabinet next to the sink and head outside to place them both on the bench. The woods are now completely dark, and it's unlikely that anyone hiding there can see clearly as far as the cabin. It's best to help things along.

"There's some food here on the deck," I call out loudly, "and some water! You're welcome to it!" There's no answer, but I'm not expecting any. I may just be feeding the racoons.

Inside the cabin another cup of coffee tempts me, and I sit at the table and click on my battery-powered radio to listen to a news recap while I drink. At the conclusion of the weather forecast—clear overnight and unseasonably cool for a midsummer evening—I take my mug and the coffee pot to the sink. I pump enough water to wash them and set them on the strainer to dry. It's full dark by now, and I can't see much through the window. My flashlight shows the sandwich still untouched; no mysterious visitor and no racoons, at least not yet.

Time for a bath. The makeshift gauge on my overhead shower bucket shows it still to be almost full, and I strip off my clothes and stand under the cold spray, washing off the day's sweat and dirt. I dry myself and pull on a tee shirt and a pair of shorts, then pick up the flashlight and leave the cabin to check the bench once more.

The empty plate stares up at me, nothing left but a very few crumbs, confirming that the intruder is human. An animal would have scattered some remains about, and whoever has taken the sandwich apparently needed every bite. More significantly, the bottle of water is missing. I flick off the flashlight and wait a few moments for my eyes to adjust to the dark. The woods are opaque against the starlit sky.

If the unseen diner poses a threat to me, it will probably come during the night, but somehow that seems unlikely. If he were armed, I doubt that he would still be in hiding after seeing me without a weapon. It seems probable that something has caused him to fear exposure, but whatever the reason can be, I have no idea.

What to do? I can ignore him. I can threaten him. Or I can try to meet him on my own terms. The latter seems to be the most reasonable approach.

I raise my voice once more. "You're welcome to come inside."

Nothing stirs. I wait a bit longer but no one appears, and finally I pick up the plate and head back to the cabin, pausing with my hand on the latch.

"It gets cold here at night," I call out again. "I can put a fire in the wood stove for you."

More silence. With a shrug I go through the door, closing and bolting it behind me. I crank the lantern wick down to a soft glow, ready for bed but worried about the flimsy hardware that can hold the door closed against the weather, but not against a determined invader. I don't want any surprises, and assemble a stack of empty tin cans against the door to serve as an alarm.

Sleep comes eventually, light and uneasy.

2
Tuesday

Only the barest hint of early light touches the edge of the clearing when I climb out of bed the next morning and look through the west window. The clearing seems deserted. The tin cans of my alarm system are undisturbed by the door, and after lighting a lantern, I gather them up and put them in the cabinet under the sink, hoping not to need them again. Once the coffee is under way, I return to the bedroom and pull on a light sport shirt and a pair of jeans. Lazy Jenny lies stretched out at the foot of the bed, eyes barely slits, playing possum.

For breakfast I crumble the two leftover shredded wheat biscuits into a bowl and mix some powdered milk with cold water from the pump. A little sugar makes them palatable. By the time I finish eating, the sky has begun to brighten as the sun creeps slowly toward the eastern horizon.

Sunrise on Nova Scotia's South Shore can be very special. On a morning such as this, a luminous stillness blankets the sea. Tendrils of mist await a rainbow's touch as the first thin crescent of the sun steals out of the water to launch a highway of shimmering gold racing toward the shore. Amy and I watched it many times from the deck of the boat, wrapped in each other's arms, in each other's lives. Now alone, I can no longer bear to see it.

By now there is enough daylight to reveal something unfamiliar across the meadow, little more than an amorphous shape among the bushes at that distance. In the gloom beneath a massive oak tree someone seems to be sitting on the ground, visible only by the contrast of light-coloured clothing against the darkness of the forest beyond. I'm tempted to cross the clearing to investigate, but chasing an intruder through the underbrush is an unpleasant option. Better simply to renew the previous night's invitation. The earlier I can coax him out of hiding, the sooner I can be rid of him.

"You're welcome to some breakfast," I call out through the window. "I've got cereal and powdered milk, and some coffee if you want."

There's no response, and I try again.

"How do you like your coffee? I drink it black, but I've got sugar too, and milk."

Silence. The distant figure seems rooted to the ground, motionless as if part of the forest itself.

"Suppose I leave it out here on the deck, okay?"

More silence. I take a fresh box of corn flakes from the cupboard and pour a generous amount into a clean bowl. I mix more powdered milk and pour some of it over the cereal, then sprinkle on half a spoonful of sugar, leaving the spoon in the bowl. The coffee has finished brewing, and I pour a cup and take it and the cereal out onto the deck, leaving it in plain sight on the bench. The shadowy figure under the tree sits as before, still as death.

Dawn is well under way as I return to the cabin, the first rays of sun filtering through the trees just above the low hill east of the cove. I douse the lantern and stand by the sink, far enough back to be invisible from outside, and watch the clearing. After several minutes the figure rises and steps warily into a leaf-dappled patch of sunlight.

A child! A girl!

Nothing could have surprised me more. Closer inspection reveals a slight and very young teenager, dressed in skimpy shorts and a bare-shouldered, bare-midriff halter top, no protection against the bite of an Atlantic coastal night. She takes one tentative step forward, then another, hesitating anxiously at the edge of the forest. With her arms tightly crossed over her chest, she huddles into herself against the lingering chill of early morning. Finally she begins to pick her way across the clearing, and stops at the edge of the deck and peers intently at the window, unable to see me in the shadows.

Hunger overcomes fear, and she levers herself up onto the deck and reaches for the bowl. She hops down again quickly and takes half a dozen steps away from the cabin, wolfing down the cereal as she goes. Then she returns furtively to the deck to get the coffee.

She looks somewhat the worse for wear. Traces of heavy makeup smear her eyes and lips, in strong contrast to her pale, almost translucent skin. An immense amount of thick, dark brown hair falls well below her shoulders, tangled and unkempt, dwarfing her slender, immature body. Her clothes, what little there is of them, are soiled and wrinkled. Streaks of mud stain her arms and legs.

Once more she retreats into the clearing and stands staring at the window as she tastes the coffee. Her mouth curls down in distaste. Moving slowly and cautiously to avoid frightening her, I step forward to the window. She looks close to panic, but stands her ground.

How the hell do you talk to a kid? I hadn't even the experience of dealing with a niece or a nephew to guide me. Amy, a teacher, had been the expert.

"I bet you'd like some milk and sugar with that, right?" I ask her. She looks down into the cup, then raises her head and nods.

"I'm sorry I forgot it. I always drink mine black. Why don't you come inside where it's warm and drink it in here?"

She shakes her head vehemently.

"Okay, your choice. I'll put the milk and sugar out on the deck for you instead."

She's poised to run, gripping the coffee mug tightly. I turn to the table and pour the leftover milk into a small pitcher and take the sugar bowl out of the cabinet. I find another spoon and carry everything outside and set it down on the deck. My bedraggled guest has backed off another dozen yards and is watching me suspiciously. Her shoulders are hunched, and she's shivering. I could invite her inside again, but it would probably be a waste of breath.

"Wait there," I tell her as I head for the door. "I'll get you something warm to put on."

Deep inside my duffel bag of clean laundry is a fleece-lined sweatshirt, far too large for her but promising some relief from the cold. When I carry it out onto the deck, she's still standing in the same place.

"This is pretty big," I say, trying to sound conversational and unthreatening while placing the sweatshirt on the edge of the deck, "but it should help you warm up. Sure you don't want to come inside?"

Another head shake. So much for hospitality.

Once I'm back inside the cabin, she wastes no time in approaching the deck. She sets the mug down and snatches up the shirt, thrusting her arms into it and pulling it down over her head. It hangs loosely from her thin shoulders and covers her shorts, trailing more than half way to her knees. She hugs herself, then reaches onto the deck and picks up the mug again. She pours some milk into the coffee but ignores the sugar, and retreats from the deck to drink it.

I lean forward over the sink to speak to her again. "So you don't like sugar in it. I'll remember that next time."

She stares at me over the rim of the mug as she drinks.

"It's nice and warm in here," I continue. "There's more coffee, and if you're still hungry, I can…"

She shakes her head violently, cutting me off.

"Listen, do you need a lift somewhere? I can take you to the mainland in my boat."

She seems not to hear me, or is deliberately ignoring me.

"You're trespassing, you know that?"

Her head jerks up in alarm, sheer desperation filling her huge dark eyes. Her mouth sags open, and her lower lip trembles. Something seems to have scared her to death, leaving her too skittish to accept the help she so obviously needs.

"Hey, I'm sorry," I say. "I didn't mean to frighten you. But you can't just stay out there like this. Right? You'll get sick, sleeping outside in the cold."

She shrugs.

"At least talk to me. I can't help you unless I know what's wrong, or what you want to do."

She drains the mug and looks down into it morosely as if wishing for more of its warmth. It dangles from her hand as she turns to go back toward the woods.

"Okay," I call out, "if you don't want to tell me, that's all right. But if you're going to stay out there again tonight, I've got a sleeping bag you can use. I'll put it out on the deck for you later."

She looks back over her shoulder and seems about to reply, but changes her mind and merely stares, neither nodding nor speaking. I have never before seen such sadness in anyone's eyes. Slowly she turns and shuffles through the violets to the woods, then vanishes in among the trees once more.

As I stand by the window, trying to imagine how someone her age could have come to my island alone, Jenny strolls indolently out of the bedroom, her beautiful green eyes languid in silent protest against the daily necessity of waking up. She stretches luxuriously and sidles over to be stroked, fully recovered from her fright the day before.

"You're a first class coward," I tell her, "scared of a kid like that. Come on and I'll get you your breakfast."

She arches her back as I stroke her, and twines herself in and out between my legs as I replenish her water and food. As she begins to eat, I glance out the window again. The empty coffee mug is back on the deck, sitting between the pitcher and the sugar bowl. There's no sign of the child. The sun-washed forest stares back at me blankly, no trace of white among the variegated greens and browns.

* * *

I spend the morning in various time-filling ways, reading, cleaning up the cabin and folding the laundry from my duffel bag. The problem of the lost child—for that is how I have begun to think of her, as lost—nags at me. I can't ignore her, can't simply leave her to live in my woods. I have to take some sort of action, get her off the island somehow. In the more than four months since I moved to the cabin, she is the first to invade my space, and I want my solitude back again. I have to be rid of her, get her back somehow to safety, but I can't very well take her to the mainland unless she decides to let me. For that I have to gain her confidence.

The prospect of a bath and some clean clothes might coax her into the cabin. I pump enough water to replenish the shower barrel and put out a clean towel and a fresh bar of soap in the dish beside the basin in the bathroom. In the bedroom are a pair of battered but serviceable bureaus where Amy and I kept our things when we stayed on the island. I haven't looked inside Amy's drawers since coming to the cabin in early March. I don't really want to now, afraid of the memories they might hold, but finally I cross the room and pull the top one open.

It's nearly empty, just socks, some panties and a well-worn, soft cotton bra. In the next one are tee shirts and shorts—just a few items, and all too big for a child. But maybe not by much. Amy had been a small woman.

I take all of the clothes out of the bureau and spread them on the bed so the girl can choose among them, provided I can lure her into the cabin. At about eleven o'clock I gather up another can of chicken, a can opener, the bread and lettuce, and a knife and plate. I add a bottle of water and take everything outside, spreading them under the bench out of the direct rays of the sun.

"Lunch is here on the deck," I holler toward the tree line. "And if you want to get cleaned up, there's a shower in here. Some clean clothes too, on the bed. You're welcome to anything you can use. I'll be back in a couple of hours."

I stride purposefully and ostentatiously around the corner of the deck to the front steps and down into the yard. Without looking back I mount the dock and cast off the tender's bow rope, then step in and fit the oars into the locks. It takes only a few minutes to reach *Amy's Pride*, tie off the tender on the buoy and climb over the rail.

The wind is light in the shelter of the island's core, but I can hear the distant sound of waves crashing against the coast. A powerful current surges from the mouth of the inlet and sets my boat rocking. Once the mainsail is up, I take a single reef and let it hang loose. The jib stays rolled up.

The little Volvo diesel coughs to life, and I cast off and point the bow toward the pass, resisting the temptation to look back. I'm hoping the child will trust my absence and take a chance on going into the cabin. I decide to give her plenty of time.

The sea is surprisingly rough, a forceful and erratic wind blowing onshore from the southwest. I clear the channel and secure the wheel with a makeshift bungee cord to take a second reef in the sail. Needing the jib to steady the hull, I haul it off the roller and winch it in tight, then adjust the traveller on the main and return to the console.

Freeing the wheel once more, I point up into the wind and the sails snap full with a solid thump. *Amy's Pride* heels hard over and digs in, spray soaking her bowsprit and forward deck. Even with two reefs in the main she's overpowered, and she dips and plunges uncomfortably between the crests of the waves, keeping me busy. Single-handed in a two-man yacht—not fun.

The child's unexpected arrival puzzles me, as does the fact that she seems to be completely alone. Farrell Island lies about two nautical miles from the mainland amid rocky shoals on all sides and shifting sandbars seaward. It has no coastal beaches, the headlands rising steeply and abruptly out of the sea. Naval charts show it as inaccessible, and except for the treacherous inlet and the cove where I shelter *Amy's Pride,* that's true. Had the child come by boat, I certainly should have found it, unless it sank. Her grubby appearance suggests she spent some time in the water. Had she been sailing alone and fallen overboard? If so, why wouldn't she tell me so, and accept my help?

As I round the southern end of the island the wind shifts to westerly. The boat sheds its erratic motion and settles into a more rhythmic rise and fall, demanding less of my attention. I relax against the stern rail and enjoy the warmth of the sun, feeling the power of the capable hull under my feet. It's the first time in months that I've sailed her without some specific destination, and it feels good.

Off toward the southeast two container ships make their way toward the commercial harbour at Halifax. Less than half a dozen pleasure craft dot the bay off Bournemouth, well away from Farrell Island in deference to its reputation for perilous waters. It's not a day for serene and effortless sailing.

The north side of the island, toward the mainland, rises like a huge

24

inverted cone. It's bare and windswept summit thrusts upward through a thick collar of stunted deciduous trees, a gigantic monk's tonsure. In winter there is little colour to be seen, there being so few evergreens in the higher elevations. As a result the soil is alkaline, encouraging the growth of thick underbrush. Most of the interior is steep and impassable unless one carries a machete. That fact alone makes it almost certain that, by whatever means the girl arrived, it must have been on the seaward side and most likely by way of the evergreen groves surrounding the cove.

Amy's Pride clears the northern tip of the island and enters the strait that faces the mainland. The wind is now directly over the stern, and I let the boom cross over to port but leave the jib in place to starboard, sailing along wing and wing. She fairly flies along the coast. A scant twenty yards off the starboard bow, whitecaps churn and break over the tops of jagged rocks, a beautiful but intimidating sight. Although I know the depth beneath me to be well below the keel, I ease the wheel cautiously to port. Better safe than sorry.

After some readjustment of the sails, I bring the boat about to charge down the north-eastern end of the island and out to sea, pounding along on a broad reach at better than six knots. I'm surprised to discover I'm enjoying myself. It would be a perfect day, perhaps a balm for my tortured soul, if not for the problem of the child nagging at me. But it's also strangely satisfying to have something concrete to occupy my mind, some problem to solve after four months of barren solitude.

It's more than two hours later when I head once again for the cove, drop the sails, and motor onto the mooring, close to mid afternoon when I finally tie the tender up at the dock. The meadow is deserted, but inside the cabin there is ample evidence of the girl's visit. The plate and knife and can opener, and even the empty meat can, have been thoroughly washed and dried and arranged beside the sink. The leftover lettuce is carefully wrapped in perforated plastic. Only the water bottle is missing.

In the bedroom I find Amy's clothing slightly disarranged. It takes only a glance to see what's missing: one pair of camp shorts, a tee shirt, and a pair of panties. Everything else remains. My sweatshirt lies neatly folded beside the pillow. There are a few items tumbled on the floor at the foot of the bed, the child's own shorts, midriff top, socks and underwear. Reaching down to gather them up, I find them stiff with salt from the ocean.

The little bra and panties are brief and filmy and seductive, oddly inappropriate for one so young. The shorts, made of a shiny satin material and with a zipper up the back, seem hardly likely to be a child's choice. But what do I know? With the influence of the media and the ever-present commercialism of sex, especially on TV's pop music channels, maybe such provocative clothing is what all kids wear these days. Not having children of my own, I'm somewhat out of touch.

Jenny is nowhere to be seen. I bend down to look under the bed and find her once again tucked into the far corner, looking spooked. In the bathroom the gauge on the shower barrel stands below the halfway mark. The soap is wet, and the damp towel is neatly arranged over the edge of the sink, almost as I left it. The lid on the chemical toilet is down, an uncommon position in my exclusively male hideaway.

I wander back to the kitchen to look out through the window. On the far side of the clearing the girl sits motionless on the grass, canted over on one hip with her legs tucked beneath her. When I walk out on deck and come around the corner, she doesn't move. I sit down on the edge of the deck with my legs hanging over the side and lean back, spreading my palms on the boards behind me.

I wait patiently. After about five minutes she gets to her feet and hesitates among the trees, scuffing her feet indecisively in the dirt. Amy's tee shirt hangs loosely from her shoulders, bloused out where she has tucked it into the oversized shorts, which are riding low on her slender hips. She has sneakers on her feet, no socks.

A waif.

Finally she steps out into the sunlight and starts walking north along the trees, circling the meadow until she's opposite the back of the cabin. She takes a few tentative steps into the clearing, eyes glued to me, possibly expecting me to jump up and chase her. I stay where I am, casually relaxed and feigning disinterest.

What can have happened to her to make her so fearful?

She makes her way slowly toward the cabin, stopping warily every few paces to observe me. It takes her a full five minutes to cover the short distance between us, until at last she's standing close to the far end of the deck, still many yards away from me.

"Hi." Her voice is tiny and uncertain.

"Hi, yourself," I say. "This morning, I thought maybe you couldn't talk."

My feeble attempt at humour falls flat and I sit still, trying to look harmless and hoping she will open up.

"Thanks for the clothes and stuff," she says at last.

"You're welcome."

"I'll give them back when I leave."

"That's fine." I put on my gentlest, least threatening smile. "Or you can keep them as long as you need them. You could sit down and talk to me for a while, too."

She tilts her head to one side and rotates her shoulders, as if to ease the stiffness of a night spent sleeping on the hard ground. Then she hoists herself up onto the deck and sits side-saddle, still watching me closely through distrustful eyes.

"Thanks for the lunch, too. And the shower."

"The clothes don't fit you too badly," I say, just trying to make conversation. "I hear baggy is the style now."

"Who owns all that stuff?"

"My wife."

"Is she here too?"

"No."

She shifts uneasily on the deck, turning to face me more directly. "How come?"

"More important, how did you get here? Where did you come from?"

She ignores my question, as I had hers. "Can I still borrow that sleeping bag?"

"Sure. But you can come inside tonight instead if you want. Or I can take you home right now, in the boat. Whatever you want."

She looks down at the deck and traces the grain of the wood with her finger. I try again.

"How about that? It's only a short distance to the mainland."

"This is an island?" she asks. She apparently has no idea where she is.

"That's right. You like to sail?"

She shrugs.

"It's fun. You'll like it. And you'll be home with your folks in time for supper if we leave right now." I start to get up.

The girl hops down off the deck, her huge brown eyes wide like those of a panicked deer, and I sit down again. "Okay, so I guess that's not such a good idea."

She looks at me forlornly, rotates her shoulders again in that odd, distracted manner, and turns toward the trees once more. She crosses the meadow, enters the forest and disappears.

So far I'm batting about two-fifty, succeeding with the clothes and food but not much more. If I'm going to get rid of her soon, I need a plan.

3

Tuesday, Late Afternoon

I'm sitting at the table with a mug of coffee in front of me, listening to the radio, when I hear faint scuffling sounds on the deck, followed a few moments later by a soft knock.

"It isn't locked," I call out. "Just push down on the latch."

Nothing happens for several minutes. Then I hear the soft scraping noises again, and the latch rattles. The door swings slowly inward, but no one is standing in the opening. Eventually the child appears, edging along the far side of the deck. Her eyes are wide and wary, darting back and forth as if trying to spot any sort of trap I might be planning to spring.

"Want some coffee?" I ask.

"I don't like it much," she answers.

"Some milk then? It's not too bad if I make it with water fresh from the pump. It's colder that way."

"Okay." The odd shrug again, as if her shoulders hurt. Tension.

I rise from the table, moving slowly to avoid scaring her off, and go to the cupboard for the package of powdered milk. After measuring a generous amount into the pitcher, I take it to the pump at the sink and fill it and stir the mixture energetically. She watches me suspiciously as I take a glass from the cupboard, pour the milk into it, and set it down on the table.

She approaches the threshold, lingering on the deck and looking at me distrustfully. I smile and try to look unthreatening.

"If you don't want to come in, I can set it outside for you."

She frowns, then crosses the sill, stopping just inside the door and poised to flee. I sit down on the opposite side of the table and reach out to slide the glass toward her, then lean back. She crosses the floor one slow, careful step

28

at a time and reaches out to pick up the glass. She backs up almost to the door, takes a long drink and grimaces, then drains it.

"It tastes funny," she says.

"Powdered milk is a poor substitute for the real thing," I tell her, "but it's all I've got. No electricity, so no fridge to keep the good stuff."

She looks around the inside of the cabin. "Your cat's scared of me. She ran under the bed when I came in."

"Jenny is scared of everyone. She hasn't seen anybody but me in a long time."

"Where is she?"

"Probably still hiding. Shivering and shaking."

A delicate smile touches her lips, the first I've seen. It's a pretty smile, very young. Her tiny heart-shaped face is nearly buried within a mass of thick, flowing hair, freshly combed after her shower into casual neatness. The oversized clothes emphasize her delicate frame, too little flesh, too little substance. She looks hungry.

"Want some supper?" I ask. She hovers between the table and the door. "If you don't want to stay, I can bring it out to you like last night."

Still mistrustful, she finally makes up her mind and pulls out a chair to sit down, stiffly perched on the very edge.

"What's your name?" she asks.

I tell her. "And what's yours?"

She looks down. "Bambi," she says, very softly.

I wait. She looks up at me shyly.

"That's a nice name," I venture, but her mouth twists in disgust. "Or not."

She drags in a deep breath, and then sighs. "My real name is Emily."

"That's even better," I tell her. "Is Bambi a nickname?"

She squirms in her chair. "Are you gonna take me back to Lucas?"

"Who?"

"Don't shit me!" she flares abruptly. "Lucas sent you here to bring me back, didn't he?"

Her sudden eruption startles me. "I have no idea who you're talking about."

She jumps up and shoves the chair back so hard that it falls over. "He's gonna get me again, just like the last time. He always finds me, and I bet you're his friend too, and you're just being nice so you can grab me!"

She backs up toward the door and trips over the fallen chair. She scrambles to her feet, terror dilating her eyes.

29

"Emily," I say, as calmly as possible, "do I look like I'm trying to grab you?" I sit relaxed on the opposite side of the table, my hands folded in front of me.

She stumbles against the door and gropes for the latch. "He's coming..."

"Calm down a minute. No one is coming. In fact, I doubt if anyone knows you're here. I'll bet *you* don't even know where you are."

She clings trembling to the door frame, panting hard in short gasps, her face ashen and her legs wobbly.

"This island is way out in the ocean," I tell her. "It's all mine, and nobody lives here except me. I own the whole thing. There are no roads or bridges, and nobody else knows how to get in here, even by boat. So no one is coming after you."

She heaves a deep, shuddering sigh, and her knees buckle. I take a chance and get up slowly to walk around the table. I pick up the chair and set it back on its feet, then turn deliberately and sit down again on the opposite side.

Emily looks at me and then at the chair. She picks her way warily toward the table and edges onto the seat. "How do I know you aren't lying to me?"

"I can show you on a map."

"What's this place called?"

"Farrell Island, named after my great-grandfather on my mother's side. His name was Perley Farrell.

"Weird name."

I smile at her. "Not so strange a hundred years ago, just out of style now. It's not like Emily. Your name was popular then, and it's just as pretty now."

She ignores the compliment. "You own this whole place?"

"Not only that, I built this cabin myself. It was one of my first projects, back while I was still in high school, my own design. I wasn't much older than you then. After that I went to university and studied to be an architect."

She looks around at the rough-hewn walls, the substantial pine mouldings and the open beam ceiling. I suddenly see it through her eyes, as if for the first time, and feel an unbidden surge of pride.

"You did this all by yourself?" she asks.

"My brother and I. He's five years older. It took us two years."

"So maybe you're telling the truth, then. But that still doesn't mean Lucas won't come and get me."

"Who is this Lucas?"

She looks away.

"Okay, whoever he is, let's think about this for a minute. Up to now you didn't even know where you were. And I still don't know how you got here."

"I swam."

"What? From the mainland?"

"From a boat..." Her voice trails off. I wait for her to go on but she slumps in the chair, fidgeting and looking down at her hands.

"Let's leave that for now," I continue. "Somehow you got here, and there's no one on this whole island except you and me. The only way anyone can get a boat in here is to know exactly where the channel is, and how to get through it. Besides my brother and me, no one else does, and he lives far away now, in Winnipeg. So can we just agree that nobody is going to come after you?"

Her eyes grow narrow, her mouth a thin straight line; Natalie Wood distrusting Santa in *Miracle on 34th Street.* "Prove it!" she demands.

"Jesus Christ!" My patience is wearing thin. "Prove what?"

"That you built this place. That it's really yours, and that you didn't just come out here after me to take me back to Lucas."

I lean back, exasperated. "Look, you're a bright kid. Figure it out for yourself. When did you get here?"

"Two nights ago."

"And what did you do then?"

"I hid out in the woods overnight, and then I found this place, and when you came I hid again."

"So you saw me come home?"

"Uh, huh."

"And what did I do?"

"You tried to get me to come to the cabin."

"Not at first! Damn it, Emily, what would you expect me to do? You're just a kid, and it looked like you were in trouble. How old are you, anyway?"

Her eyes drop. "Eighteen."

"Oh yeah. Me too."

Her head snaps up. "I am!" she bristles.

I'm getting nowhere. "Fine. There's the door. Go sleep in the woods if you're so scared to be in here with me."

She glares back defiantly. "You said I could use your sleeping bag! And I'm hungry!"

"I'll put it on the deck. Your supper too, when it's ready." I stand up and stride to the cupboard, ignoring her. I begin to sort through the canned goods on the shelf, rattling them unnecessarily. She mumbles something behind me.

"What?" I ask roughly.

"I said, what have you got to eat?"

"Worms and ground glass!" I bark.

"What're you so mad at?"

I don't really know, just that I'm trying to help her and she's getting under my skin. It takes a lot of effort, but I manage to regain control.

"How about some pheasant under glass? Or caviar? Calamari, maybe?"

"What's calamari?"

"Squid."

"You mean like an octopus? Gross! You're kidding me, right?"

"Not about the squid. It's supposed to be a delicacy. But I don't really have any. All I've got is basic camp food."

"Like what?"

"How about beans and franks? And corn, maybe?"

"Okay."

"So are you staying for supper, or are you going to eat in the woods with the squirrels?"

She squirms and frowns, her eyes searching the room nervously. "Staying, I guess."

"Good. You can set the table. The plates are up there," I point to the cabinet beside the window, "and the knives and forks are in the drawer next to the sink. Get yourself a clean glass, too, and a mug for my coffee."

She stands up cautiously, watching me carefully out of the corner of her eye. I cross to the stove to light it and open the cans of food, dumping the contents into two saucepans over the burners. Then I sit back down, well away from the table to give her plenty of room as she lays out the dishes and silverware.

"You forgot the napkins," I tell her brusquely.

"You didn't tell me where they are."

"You could have figured it out!"

"I don't live here, you do!"

"Right," I say gently. "That's what I've been trying to tell you."

"Shit!" she mutters, and flops into her chair.

"Nice talk for a pretty thirteen-year-old."

Her eyes widen. "How did you...I'm eighteen, I told you."

"And you just gave yourself away."

"Shit, shit, shit!" She glares out the window. She catches sight of me grinning at her and smiles in spite of herself. Then she bursts out laughing.

32

Perhaps we're making progress.

"Okay, so I'm only thirteen. But I'll be fourteen next Monday. So what?"

"So where's your family, and why are you out here all alone? And how did you get here? How about the truth this time?"

"Got any dessert?"

I shake my head. "You're some piece of work."

* * *

The light begins to fail as we finish the meal. We stand side by side at the sink, washing the pans and dishes and staring together out the window as the setting sun paints scalloped bands of blue and orange across the western sky. It's the closest she has dared to come to me. She dries the plates and hands them to me to put up in the cabinet.

A slight shudder shakes her small frame. "Cold?" I ask.

"A little."

"I can put a fire in the wood stove," I tell her, pointing to the cast iron monster in the corner near the door. "Or you can go get my sweatshirt. You left it on the bed."

She pads to the bedroom. Several minutes later, as I'm measuring some more coffee into the percolator, I realize she hasn't come out again.

"What's the matter," I call out, "get lost in there?"

"Shhh!"

Curious, I enter the bedroom and find her bundled in the sweatshirt, kneeling beside the bed and holding up a corner of the blanket. She's making coaxing noises.

"You'll never get her out that way," I say.

She raises her head and looks at me over her shoulder. "She doesn't trust me, I guess."

"That seems to be a common problem in this house right about now."

I move to the head of the bed and slide it out away from the wall, where Jenny is cowering against the baseboard. I bend down and pick her up, and she digs her claws into my shoulder and yowls pitifully. I carry her out into the main part of the cabin and sit down at the table, and Emily sits opposite me.

I begin to stroke the cat's fur slowly and rhythmically, and gradually she lets herself be comforted, not quite relaxed but less tense. She starts to purr quietly, but never takes her eyes off the child in the other chair.

33

"I had a cat once," Emily says softly. I ask her what happened to it, but she just shakes her head sadly.

"Now," I tell her, "get up very slowly and walk around the table."

She eases herself off the chair with exaggerated care, and I keep petting Jenny as she approaches. The cat kneads my leg painfully through my jeans, but doesn't try to run.

"Make a fist and hold it out to her, real slow."

Emily does so. Jenny regards the offering suspiciously, then stretches her nose to sniff. She yowls again.

"Just doesn't like me, I guess," she says.

"Give her time. You can't always win someone's trust right off. It takes patience."

She regards me seriously. "You really don't know Lucas, do you?"

"No."

"I had to be sure."

"That's okay. Who is he, anyway?"

She ignores the question, turning her attention back to the cat. Jenny pokes her hand and she giggles. "Her nose is wet!"

"Try rubbing under her chin."

She extends one finger and Jenny lets her touch her, at first suspiciously, then with greater abandon as the child's finger caresses the long silky fur. "Hey! She likes me!"

"Told you. It just takes time."

The cabin is nearly dark and I put Jenny down and stand up to light the lantern. I go into the bedroom to light another one, with Emily following close behind.

"Where am I gonna sleep?" she asks.

"In here," I say, inclining my head toward the bed.

She looks past me, frowning. A strange expression crosses her face, a mixture of pain and disgust and what seems almost to be hatred.

"Figures!" she spits out, and storms out of the room. I follow along, baffled.

"What's the matter?" I ask. I can't understand the abrupt change in her.

"I thought maybe you were different!"

She spins around and disappears through the bedroom door, leaving me bewildered by the sudden and violent change of mood. After a few minutes she reappears, still buried in my oversized sweatshirt. She won't look directly at me.

34

"I need to brush my teeth," she says, her voice flat and toneless.

"There are a couple of new toothbrushes in the little cabinet over the toilet. Take your pick."

"I need some water."

"You know where the glasses are. Pump away."

She approaches the cupboard and takes down a glass.

"Emily," I try again, "what's wrong?"

Her face is a rigid mask, blank and emotionless. She stops pumping and leaves the room without another word, disappearing into the bathroom.

"There's one blanket on the bed," I call out. "If you need another one, it's in the bottom drawer." She doesn't answer.

What the hell has turned her off like that?

I decide that the sooner I can get rid of her, the better. If she's any example of what kids are like today, I'm not equipped to deal with one.

After a few minutes I hear her soft footsteps creep across the hall from the bathroom to the bedroom, followed by the creak of the bedsprings. Then silence. I turn up the lantern and pick up a novel, trying to remember where I left off reading the last time. I find the appropriate page but can't recall the plot elements, and put the book down again. The cabin suddenly feels stuffy and confining, and the cool night beckons me out onto the deck.

The air is fresh and clean and the winds calm. Soothing sounds, insects and the soft murmur of the water around the dock pilings, play like a Mozart sonata on the strings of my frayed nerves. The few clouds of sunset have dissolved before a brilliant, moon-free sky, and the stars shine with uncommon clarity. I scan the heavens, waiting for inspiration, but can't fathom what could be bothering this annoying child. Finally I conclude that any decisions can wait until morning. Maybe after a good night's sleep she'll be more amenable to going home and leaving me in peace.

Half an hour passes, giving me respite from the emotional turmoil of the evening, and my eyes begin to droop. Back inside the cabin, I'm starting to make up the daybed when Emily appears in the bedroom door, rubbing her eyes and only half awake. The sweatshirt is gone, replaced by one of Amy's light tee shirts, and her hair is gathered at the back of her head in an impressively full ponytail.

"So are you coming, or aren't you?" she says in a small, toneless voice.

Now what?

"Coming where?" I ask her.

"Let's just get it over with so I can go to sleep."

And suddenly it hits me. The sexy clothing she came in, all that smeared makeup, the fear and panic. Someone named Lucas. *Her pimp!*

I stand there stupidly, unable to think what to say. She rubs her eyes again. Absently she reaches for the hem of the tee shirt and begins to lift it.

"Emily!" I shout harshly.

She drops the hem, startled. "Don't you like me?"

"Of course I like you."

"So let's do it, then."

"No. *No!*"

She looks genuinely puzzled. "Why not?"

Nothing in my life has prepared me for anything remotely like this, and I have no idea what to say. "Because...Because I don't like you that way. Look..."

My confusion mounts, my brain refusing to believe what my own eyes and ears tell me must be true. This thirteen-year-old, this barely-a-teenager, this *child*, is a prostitute.

Her face crumples. "Have I done something bad?"

"You haven't done anything wrong," I tell her.

"Because if I've been bad you can punish me, if you want to. Or anything else you want to do. Just don't make me go back to the woods, okay?"

That galvanizes me. "Come out here!"

She enters the room shyly and I point to one of the chairs. She sits down. I haul out the chair opposite her, the table a barrier between us. Her eyes drift downward, staring vaguely at the floorboards.

"What made you think I wanted to...to sleep with you?" I ask softly but firmly.

"You sent me to your bed," she says quietly.

"Not my bed, *the* bed. The *only* bed. I just wanted you to be comfortable." I gesture toward the daybed in a corner of the room. "I've got this couch thing for me."

"Oh. Anyway, Lucas says..."

"I don't think I'd like Lucas very much."

"I have to do what he tells me. If I don't, he hurts me."

"He isn't going to hurt you any more."

"Yes he will," she says lethargically. "He'll find me again. He'll get me, just like the last time I ran away, and he'll beat the crap out of me." She lifts her head and stares into my eyes, her own dulled by the sheer hopelessness of the inevitable. "He owns me."

36

Her eyes fill, and huge silent tears course down her ravaged face. I have no idea what to do. Finally I stand up and retrieve a washcloth from the bathroom and dampen it under the pump. She takes it from me and wipes her eyes with it. She puts it down and stares at me morosely. A tremor shakes her, and a quick, gasping breath catches in her throat.

"You want me to go away?" she asks timidly.

That's exactly what I want, but I can't tell her so. She has nowhere to go, and like it or not, the responsibility for her safety has been dumped in my lap. I head for the bedroom and pull the blanket off the bed, and when I return to the main part of the cabin, she's staring listlessly toward the darkened window. I drop the blanket onto the table.

"That's for you if you get cold," I tell her. "Now let's just talk about this for a few minutes."

She slides off the chair, but instead of reaching for the blanket she approaches me, standing close. She puts her hand on my arm and rotates her narrow hips in a small seductive wiggle, tilting her head forward against my chest. I recoil and shake off her hand.

"Stop it!"

She looks up, nervous and fearful and confused.

"Just...Just go sit down over there."

She hunches her shoulders and shuffles over to the daybed, collapsing into the corner. I scoop up the blanket and toss it over beside her.

"You'll get cold," I say curtly. "Put this around yourself."

She stares at me miserably, then pulls the fabric around her shoulders and sinks back into the cushions, her eyes drifting toward the door. I sit down at the table again. Long minutes pass.

"Feel any better?" I ask finally.

She nods her head slightly.

"Are you sleepy?" A brief shake this time.

"Then how about giving me a few answers, okay? First, where are your mom and dad?"

"I don't know. I'm pretty sure they're dead."

I wait for her to go on. Finally she fills the silence.

"I was only nine the last time I saw them. I don't remember them much. Aunt Margaret told me they were in some kind of accident, my grandma and grandpa too, and had to go away. I figured out that meant they were dead, but I didn't really believe it."

"Who do you live with?"

"Aunt Margaret and Uncle Frank. Until last winter, anyway. They took me to their house out in the Valley, someplace west of Windsor."

"What happened?"

Loathing colours her voice. "Uncle Frank happened."

Again I wait patiently.

"He was always so mean. Everything I did was wrong. Nothing I did was ever as good as his own kids."

"They have children of their own?"

"My two cousins. Boys!" she spits. "Anyway, Uncle Frank used to hit me. Said I had to learn to behave myself better. He used to smack me really hard." Tears begin to flow, and she wipes her eyes on the sleeve of the tee shirt. "He never hit his own kids like that."

She shrugs with that odd rotation of her head and neck and turns away from me, eyes dull and hopeless.

I try again. "How come you aren't living with them any more?"

"I ran away."

"Why?"

"Uncle Frank started getting really weird. I didn't know much then, and I didn't know how to stop him. It got so he was after me all the time. The minute Aunt Margaret was out of the house, he'd try to get me to sit on his lap, and mess around with my clothes. Then he'd try to put his hands...He'd try..."

"Never mind," I say. "I get the idea."

"So I figured anyplace was better than his house, and I ran. Boy, was I wrong!"

"How did Lucas get hold of you?"

"I was really dumb." She lapses into silence, slumped in the corner of the daybed, tiny and defenceless.

"You're only thirteen." I say. "Everybody's kind of dumb at that age."

She rallies a bit. "Anyway, I took the bus into Halifax. I guess I was sort of hoping my mom and dad weren't really dead, and I was going to try to find them, you know, like go where we used to live. But when I got to the city I didn't know what bus to get on next, and Lucas came and sat down next to me and offered to help me. Some help!"

"It wasn't your fault."

"Yes it *was!* If I hadn't been such a *kid*, I could have figured out what he wanted." She sits tense and rigid. She won't look at me, her eyes fixed on a point on the floor halfway to the table. "I went with him, and instead of finding a bus for me, he took me to this place where there were all these girls.

Older than me. They..."

Her breath catches in her throat. I wait for her to begin again, not really wanting to hear any more, sickened by what she's saying but trying not to show it.

"Anyway, I told him I wanted to leave, and he said I couldn't. He said stuff like, he was going to teach me how to make a lot of money. I said I didn't want to, and he slapped me across the face, so hard I fell on the floor. Then he said I was going to do what he told me to from then on."

"Didn't anyone try to help you?"

"The other girls just laughed. Then Lucas took me into a back room and he... He..."

She swallows and drags in a deep, rasping breath. When she speaks again, her voice is raw but controlled.

"He says I'm his now, for always."

"You don't have to go back to him," I tell her.

"He'll find me," she says sadly. "He did the last time."

"Look, I don't know much about this kind of thing, but there are people who can help you, social agencies..."

"Like the one that made me go live with Uncle Frank? No thanks!"

"Okay, so that was a mistake, but you can't just stay here. Maybe if we talk to the police first..."

"You think they care?" she says wearily. "They know what Lucas does, and they've seen me and the other girls on the street. They don't do anything about it."

"They will if I say so."

"You think?" she says sarcastically.

"We have to try. I'll take you back to the mainland in the morning, and we'll find someone who can help you."

She levers herself up and wraps the blanket tightly around her shoulders. "I'm going back to bed."

I swing around in the chair as she heads out of the room. "Emily..."

She disappears around the corner, and the bedsprings complain again. I sit bewildered, unsure that I can do anything to make her future any less horrible than her past, and not really sure I want to try.

39

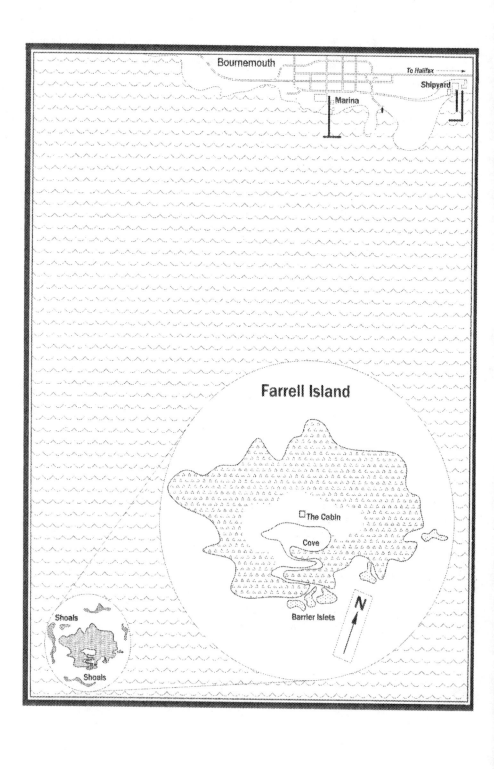

4

Wednesday

After a restless, wakeful night I'm up with the first light. As soon as the coffee is under way, I check the bedroom and find Emily still buried beneath the blanket, face down with her hair splayed out across the pillow. Surprisingly, Jenny lays curled up next to her, plastered against her side.

I back out and make myself some breakfast, then tackle a few inconsequential chores while waiting for her to wake up. At eight I catch the CBC news, hoping to hear something about a missing child or anything else that might give me a clue as to where the she came from. Nothing.

At nine o'clock a thump echoes from the bedroom, Jenny's stocky body hitting the floor, and she wanders out looking for something to eat. Otherwise everything is quiet. I consider waking Emily but decide she probably needs the extra sleep after spending several nights in the woods. Once Jenny has her breakfast in front of her, I mix some fresh powdered milk and set out the box of corn flakes, a glass, and a bowl and spoon. Then I leave and row the dinghy out to *Amy's Pride* for a little marine housekeeping. It's close to ten-thirty when I return to shore.

Emily is sitting bleary-eyed at the table, looking hopeless and dejected and very small within the folds of my sweatshirt. She's spooning corn flakes into her mouth lethargically, and doesn't look up as I enter.

"Find enough to eat?" I ask.

She ignores me. I pull out a chair and sit down.

"I cleaned up the boat a little," I tell her, just making conversation. "We can go whenever you're ready."

She finishes the cereal and stands up to take the bowl to the sink, avoiding my eyes.

"I've been thinking about your problem," I continue. "Where to take you, I mean. Any ideas?"

She shrugs. "Whatever."

"I think Family and Children's Services then. If they don't have an office in Bournemouth, I can take you into Halifax. Okay?"

She lingers by the sink, staring out the window across the meadow. "Doesn't matter."

"Sure it does. You said the police wouldn't help, and I suppose you're right. But…"

She whirls around, her eyes flashing. "Look, I told you last night, no matter who you take me to, they'll just send me back to Uncle Frank."

"Not if you tell them what he did to you."

"I'm so sure! You think they'll believe me instead of him?"

"Emily…"

"Never mind! Let's just go and get it over with!" She stamps off toward the bedroom. She disappears through the door and I give up trying to talk to her. A few minutes later she reappears, dressed in Amy's clothes once more. She still won't look directly at me.

"You want anything more to eat before we go?" I ask gently.

She shakes her head and trudges over to the door, flinging it open so angrily that it slams back against the wall. I gather up my wallet and the boat keys and follow her. She's standing beside the dinghy when I reach the dock, and I hold it steady for her as she climbs over the gunwale and drops into the stern. She sits sideways and stares out over the transom at the cabin as I row toward the centre of the cove.

Five minutes later we're aboard *Amy's Pride*. I open up the hatchway and reach inside to turn on the electrical system, then start the engine to let it warm up a bit. Once it's running smoothly, I untie the bow rope and put the transmission in gear.

Emily sits huddled on the starboard locker as I guide the boat out of the cove. In her present frame of mind there's no point in trying to talk to her, and I concentrate instead on navigating between the various hazards of the inlet. When we reach the small barrier islets that shield the mouth of the channel, I throttle back and kill the engine.

She stirs. "Why are we stopping?"

"Shhh," I caution, listening carefully for power boats, voices, or the quieter sounds made by nearby sails and riggings. "I'm just making sure no one will see us come out."

"How come?"

"So nobody will know I live here."

"That's weird."

We drift slowly into open water to find no other boats close by, and I restart the diesel and swing the bow eastward to head for Bournemouth. Well to the east of Farrell Island the sea is dotted with two dozen or more pleasure craft, three quarters of them sailboats of various sizes and the remainder outboards or cruisers. The wind is light and erratic out of the south, and it seems as if the sailors are having trouble finding enough air to maintain headway. I decide to leave the sails furled and use the diesel all the way to the mainland.

Emily's mood is dark. She takes no pleasure in being on the water and pays little attention to the other boats as we approach them. She toys with the starboard jib sheet and glances occasionally toward the bow, pointedly ignoring me.

A sleek vintage Kirby 25 crosses our bow, sails aloft but barely filled and making less than two knots, and I back off on the throttle to give her plenty of room. Off to starboard a Hunter 33 heads for the seaward side of Farrell Island, a Yarmouth Charter Service logo painted on the hull just aft of the bowsprit. A small runabout, overpowered by a big Honda outboard, slaps the waves of the charter's wake, its crew of teenagers shouting and laughing.

Emily seems barely to glance at any of them, then suddenly exclaims "Holy shit!" and throws herself off the hatch. She sprawls onto the cockpit deck, her head below the rail.

"What's the matter?" I ask her.

"Turn around! Go back! Go back!"

"What for?"

Her eyes bulge, panicked. "Quick! Please!"

"Emily…"

Her head spins wildly, a trapped animal hunting an escape route, and she spies the open hatchway. She scuttles across the deck and clambers over the sill, nearly losing her balance as she fights for footing on the ladder inside. She disappears from view and hits the floor heavily.

The Kirby has moved well clear of my bow, and I push the throttle forward again. The big Hunter changes course slightly and approaches me to seaward, under power with her sails down. The helmsman stands high beneath a canopy over the cockpit, dressed in a white uniform shirt with official-looking stripes on the sleeves, a charter captain's hat on his head. He gives me a once-over and I wave to him, but he doesn't respond.

A similarly dressed crew member stands by the forward stay, coiling a line as he searches the surface of the ocean. As the yacht passes by I spot a burly, rough-looking man in a hooded sweatshirt standing in the cockpit. He looks my way, then gestures to the helmsman. Both shake their heads. Strange...

The teenagers in the runabout roar between our two boats, and I turn the wheel to starboard to cross the turbulent wakes. Once the sound of the outboard recedes I call to Emily, but she doesn't answer. Traffic thickens as *Amy's Pride* leaves the open sea and enters Bournemouth Bay, and I thread my way cautiously among nearly becalmed sailors and some heedless power boaters to come up on the dock at the public marina.

As I throttle back, Emily's head appears in the hatchway, eyes darting nervously from one side of the boat to the other. I put the boat in reverse to bring it to a stop and toss my stern line to a marina employee who comes out to meet us. As he snubs the line around a cleat, Emily vaults out of the hatchway and scrambles over the gunwale. She drops down and hits the dock running.

Jesus Christ!

I shut the engine down and hurry forward to pick up the bow line. By the time I climb over the side and flip a quick half hitch onto a piling, Emily is already out of sight.

"Rig a spring line for me, will you?" I call out to the dock hand. He nods and I take off at a fast trot, passing the marina office and several other seaside buildings to come out onto the coastal road.

Swarms of tourists mill around the restaurants and gift shops, and I search the crowd for any sign of Emily, paying special attention to the young people. Her distinctive mass of hair is nowhere to be seen outside, and it's hopeless trying to decide where she might have gone. She has a good head start, and there are too many places to hide, too many shops to disappear into.

Son of a bitch! Now what?

I'd prefer to wash my hands of the whole affair and let her go back to whatever sordid life she's been leading, but her strange behaviour on board the boat troubles me. Something spooked her, although I suspect she was planning all along to take off as soon as we docked.

There's a pay phone outside the marina office, but no directory. Information gives me the number of Family and Children's Services in Halifax. I place the call and a businesslike but pleasant-sounding woman answers.

"Family and Children's Services, Florence Pineo. How may I help you?"

I give her my name, then hesitate, not quite sure how to explain what I need. Finally I say, "Do you people keep track of runaway children somehow?"

"Are you calling about someone in your own family?" the woman asks.

"No. There's this girl…Look, I ran into a child, a thirteen-year-old, who seems to be in some kind of trouble. Her name's Emily."

"Last name?" she prompts.

"I have no idea."

"It's a common name. I could go through the files if you give me some idea what you want us to do."

"She's apparently a runaway from an abusive family, and afraid of the police. And of your agency, too. I was trying to bring her to you when she took off."

"Where are you?"

"Bournemouth."

"The RCMP handles policing for the town," she says. "Have you contacted them?"

"Not yet. Should I do that?"

"I'd advise it if you want an official investigation. We don't have the manpower to search for children ourselves, but if you can give the police a good description, maybe they can run her down."

"Ms. Pineo, if they do find her, what happens next?"

"That depends on the circumstances. If she's just a runaway they'll most likely refer the case to us, but if she has a juvenile record, any past or current offences, they could hold her."

"And if they send her to you? Does she go back to her family?"

"Not until we've investigated the home conditions. We'll want to know why she ran away, and if there are any health or safety issues."

"Where would she live until then?"

"Temporary foster care, or a group home."

"And if the allegations of abuse…"

"Please believe me, we're very thorough," the woman assures me. "If a child is returned to a family, and that only happens if we're absolutely sure there's no danger, we keep close watch from then on. But the first step is to locate her, and you'll need the police for that."

She gives me the number of the Bournemouth RCMP Detachment and I thank her and promise to call them, but after I hang up something stops me. *Run her down*, the woman had said. The police top the list of things Emily seemed to be most afraid of, and I find myself wondering if they would handle the situation well. It's hard to imagine the Mounties having much compassion for a prostitute, even one so young.

Watching for any sign of her, I wander off the dock and mix with the summertime crowd along the quay. A row of souvenir shops and food kiosks fronts the town's sand beach, and I peer through every window, although not really expecting to see her. As far as I know she has no money to buy food. I try to imagine where a kid like her might go to hide, but come up empty.

Checking the time and finding it well past noon, I buy a lobster roll and a paper cup of bad coffee from a mobile canteen and sit down near the far end of the quay to think things over. The problem of street kids and juvenile prostitution is far outside my personal field of experience. Conventional wisdom seems to be that rootless kids like Emily are throwaways, and probably unredeemable. I've done all I can for her. When she rejected my help and ran off, she stopped being my problem any longer.

Right?

I finish the food and dump half of the coffee into the bay, annoyed with myself but not quite sure why. Some residual guilt, I suppose, thinking I should have done better. The beautiful day has attracted large numbers of visitors to the area, and I'm suddenly anxious to get away from them and back to the solitude of my island. I dump my trash and head for the boat.

As I pass the marina office, the big Hunter yacht that passed me east of Farrell Island drifts into the charter company's slip. The captain manoeuvres her in close to the dock and the crew ties her up diagonally across the dock from *Amy's Pride*.

The man in the sweatshirt watches the action from the cockpit. I assume it's his charter, and wonder about his mode of dress on such a warm day. The hood is now pushed back, revealing thick, jet black and heavily-gelled hair and a single gold hoop earring that catches the sun. Not your typical sailor.

They watch me approach, and as I come abreast of them I nod my admiration and call out, "Nice boat."

The charter captain regards me for a moment, then turns to the dark-haired man and asks a question, too softly for me to hear. The other man nods, and the captain turns back to me.

"You live around here?" he asks.

"Yes," I tell him.

"Bournemouth?"

I nod, not exactly a lie. I still own the house that Amy and I shared until her death, although it's now closed up and empty, awaiting my decision to sell it.

"What do you know about that island out there?" he continues, waving in the direction of Farrell.

I consider a *Why do you want to know?* or *What business is it of yours?* response, then decide to avoid any confrontation that might arouse suspicion.

"Not much," I answer. "It's just rocks and trees."

"Know how to land on it?" he asks.

"You can't. There are shoals all the way around, and no way through the woods even if you managed to get ashore."

He mutters something to the man next to him, and they turn away from me and look out over the water. Other than Farrell Island, there are no sizeable offshore land masses within a dozen kilometres of the town, just tide-swept sandbars and tiny cays. The men seem to be arguing, and the captain keeps shaking his head.

"Anything I can help you with?" I call out. The captain glances at me over his shoulder but doesn't speak, then returns to the debate.

You could at least say thanks.

I cross the dock to release my boat's lines. A few minutes later I have the diesel fired up and underway, out through the channel that separates the coastline from my island. I plan a bit of evasive action, an approach from well to the south once I'm out of sight of the marina, just in case those aboard the Hunter 33 are watching me.

* * *

Sometime after seven I sit at the table in the cabin over a third cup of coffee, watching the sun drop toward the western tree line and trying to put Emily out of my mind. It's a struggle to convince myself that she isn't my responsibility. I had tried to take her somewhere safe and turn her over to someone who knows how to deal with street kids. It wasn't my fault that it hadn't worked out.

Not my fault...

As I drain my cup and carry it to the sink, I hear a faint scuffling sound on the deck outside. Thinking of raccoons, I ignore the noise, but a moment or two later the latch clicks and the door swings open slowly. Emily stands just beyond the threshold, the baggy shorts and tee shirt soaked and drooping. A drowned rat.

"Can I come in?"

I stare at her in amazement. "How did you get here?"

"On your boat," she says, and steps inside and closes the door behind her. She hugs herself as if cold, salt water dripping from her clothing onto the floor.

"You were below decks the whole time?" I ask. I hadn't looked into the galley or any of the berths during the trip back from Bournemouth.

"Uh, huh. I was gonna stay there, but I got hungry, so I swam ashore. Are you mad?"

"No, I'm not mad," I tell her, surprised to feel only relief. "Go get yourself dried off. I'll find you some fresh clothes."

She steps out of her wet sneakers and pads toward the bathroom. I take an extra towel out of a cabinet and hand it in to her. She shuts the door, and I enter the bedroom and search through the drawers in the chest for something of Amy's that she can wear. The shower starts, making me wish I had thought to heat some water for her. She emerges five minutes later, wrapped in the towel and shivering.

"Clean clothes on the bed," I tell her, and turn to light a fire in the wood stove as she disappears into the bedroom. By the time she comes out in shorts and a tee shirt, the stove is beginning to give off some heat. She crosses the room to stand in front of it, her arms folded tightly against her thin chest.

"How does some chicken stew sound?" I ask her, and she nods. I open a can and pour the contents into a saucepan, and light the propane stove to start it heating. Emily squats down, her back just inches from the fire. She looks pale and bedraggled, damp hair clinging to her shoulders. I take her a chair and she climbs onto it, clearly exhausted.

"Why did you run away from me?" I ask her. "I was only trying to help you."

She shrugs, not looking up.

"Look, I know you're frightened, but you can't just go off on your own like that. If this Lucas guy is really looking for you..."

"I know," she murmurs.

I stir the stew, then turn to the pump and mix some powdered milk into a glass. I set it down on the table and take a bowl from the cupboard.

"Spoon or fork?" I ask. She shrugs again. I decide on a spoon and drop it beside the bowl, then put a couple of slices of bread on a plate and slide everything across the table.

"The stew's almost hot enough," I tell her. "Want to sit here or eat it by the fire?"

The wood stove has warmed the room quickly, and she rises wearily and drags the chair across to the table. I scoop a generous amount of stew into the bowl and she begins to eat. When the stew is gone I offer her some canned fruit for dessert, but she refuses it. She carries her bowl to the sink, then crosses the room and sinks down into one corner of the day bed, forlorn and miserable.

"Why did you come back to the boat?" I ask.

"I was scared," she says softly.

"Of what?"

"Some guys I know…"

I decide to let that pass. "I was worried about you."

"Yeah, sure."

"Whether you believe it or not, I was. And I did some checking while you were gone. I called the child protection agency."

"I don't need protecting."

"Just listen for a minute, okay? I spoke to a very nice lady named Ms. Pineo, and she told me how they handle cases like yours."

She sits bolt upright, eyes wild. "You told her all about me?"

"No, just that you were a runaway who needs help. That's all."

"Did you tell her my name?"

"Your first name, sure. I had to. But I got the impression they run into lots of Emilys. She didn't know you."

She subsides back into the cushions.

"Anyway," I continue, "she said you wouldn't have to go back to the family you ran away from, at least until they check everything out."

"I told you before, they won't take my word against Uncle Frank's. He's a salesman, a good one. They'll believe him."

"I don't think so. She seemed pretty sure. And they can find a safe place for you to live. A group home or foster care, she said. You'll have a place to sleep, maybe even your own room, and enough to eat. Clothes. That kind of thing."

"Won't matter. Lucas'll find me and take me back anyway."

She turns away and stares out through the window at the gathering dusk. The sun has dropped below the top of the tree line, and heavy shadows criss-cross the broad expanse of gravel that separates the meadow from the shore.

"How about telling me what spooked you on the boat?" I say. "Was it one of the boats out there? The big yacht maybe?"

She ignores the question. "So you're gonna take me back again tomorrow?"

"I think the guys on that boat were looking for something," I persist. "Or someone."

Bulls eye! The panicky, hunted expression on her face tells me I'm right. "I told you, you'll be safe from them. The agency will look after you from now on."

"I'll never be safe," she says miserably. She stands up and heads for the bedroom, and I let her go. There will be time enough in the morning to try to bring her around.

5
Thursday, Very Early

It's well after midnight, and I'm still wide awake. Jenny lies beside me on the day bed, curled warmly into the hollow behind my knees. More than two hours have passed since I turned in, and my mind is still churning with maddening impotence, trying to solve the unsolvable.

There are faint rustling noises in the bedroom and a single protesting creak from the springs. A few minutes later Emily's shadowy form crosses the room, and the door opens and closes softly. I throw off the blanket, pull on my shirt and jeans, and stuff my feet into shoes. By the time I reach the door and step out onto the deck, she's down on the dock trying to untie the boat tender in the dark.

"Don't try to stop me!" she shouts defiantly, as I make my way down the steps and approach her. There's just enough light from the stars for me to see that she is once again wearing the skimpy clothes she came in, dirty and wrinkled and little protection against the chill of the night.

"I won't," I tell her. "But there isn't anywhere for you to go."

"I left your wife's clothes on the bed. I'm taking this boat, but I'll leave it somewhere so you can find it."

"Not a good idea," I say calmly.

"Why not?"

"Look, let's just go back inside where it's warm and talk about this."

"No!"

"You can't leave here in that little boat," I tell her.

"Want to bet? I got here by myself, didn't I?"

"Yes, and I still don't know how. But you'll never find your way through the channel in the dark. You'll hit the rocks and sink. Can you swim?"

"Damn right I can swim!"

"And even if you make it out to the ocean, you can't row to the mainland. The tide and the wind will carry you out to sea."

"Leave me alone! I'm not going back with you tomorrow!"

"All right. Fine. I won't try to take you back. We'll find some other way to handle this."

"You say that now!" She struggles with the line, unable to loosen the knot in the dark, and finally drops it in frustration. Her legs fold beneath her and she collapses onto the dock, sobbing.

"I *can't* go back," she cries piteously.

"I said okay. Just please come back inside so we can figure out what to do next."

She drags herself upright and stomps angrily to the end of the dock, staring out toward where *Amy's Pride* lies glistening in the light from the stars. She stands tense and rigid, her fists balled and her shoulders hunched.

"Please?" I say.

She spins abruptly and pushes her way past me, up the path to the cabin. When I catch up with her, she's fumbling with the door latch in the dark, sobbing bitterly. When I let her inside she sinks down onto the daybed, scaring Jenny off onto the floor, and pulls the blanket tightly around her.

I light a lantern and place it on the table, then sit on the opposite end of the daybed and turn to face her. The silence drags on for several long minutes as she gazes across the room at nothing, her eyes red-rimmed and angry. Sadness chases terror across her tear-stained features. Finally she twists her head and glares at me, defiant but badly frightened.

"What are you staring at me like that for?" she challenges.

"Just trying to think of some way to help you," I say lamely.

"Yeah, right! Turn me over to the police or some stupid damn social worker."

"Look, I'm trying to understand what's happened to you, that's all. Until then, I don't know what to do. You're only thirteen, you've got your whole life ahead of you..."

"Some life."

I don't know how to answer that, but since sympathy isn't working, I decide to try another approach.

"Okay, fine, throw it all away! Life screwed you over, so just give up! Tell me, tell *everybody* to piss off and leave you alone! That'll fix things, right?"

I make no effort to conceal the fury building within me, rage against a world that allows children to be victimized, their innocence stripped away far too soon. Her eyes widen and she shrinks from my outburst, huddling back into the cushions.

"Or," I say, trying to adopt a more reasonable tone, "you can pick yourself up off the floor and try again. Maybe even let someone help you. What's it going to be?"

She turns away and buries her face in the cushion, crying softly. So much for my amateur psychology. I'm in way over my head, but I have to keep her from trying to leave in the dinghy again. If she makes it out to the Atlantic she's as good as dead, and if by some miracle she manages to reach the mainland she has nowhere to go, no resources whatever. Somehow I have to calm her down before I can reason with her, and then find a way to convince her that she has to accept help from someone in authority.

Amy would have known how to get through to her. My mind drifts back to a day in late May, just a few years after she and I were married.

* * *

We had escaped to the island for a weekend away from our troubles, and Amy was wrestling with the kind of problem that should have filled her with delight, but instead demoralized her with undeserved guilt. Neither of us could sleep, and we left the cabin with an armload of blankets and rowed out to the yacht. The temperature was barely above freezing, one of those full-moon, frost-threatening nights that Nova Scotian gardeners fear so much, and the heavens blazed with light. We made ourselves a nest in front of the mast and cuddled together under the stars.

"Just tell me what to do," she whispered in my ear. "Whatever you say, that'll be it."

"I can't do that," I told her. "I know what I think you should do, but you have to come to it yourself."

"Take the job, right?"

Amy was short-listed for an assistant professorship in the English Department at St. Mary's University in Halifax, an unusual honour for a very young Ph.D. candidate with less than two years of teaching experience. The previous day the department chair had called her with an offer, giving her barely a week to decide whether to accept.

"It's a great opportunity," I told her. "Another one might not come along for years."

"But how can I do that to my kids?"

By *"my kids"* she meant the classes she taught in the local middle school, her first job and a source of great satisfaction. She was not merely good at it, she was extraordinary. Her outgoing personality captivated the children. She had a gift for cloaking her lessons in the kind of fun that stimulated the students' intellectual curiosity, so much so that the boys and girls barely realized how hard they were working.

"Look at it this way," I reasoned. *"If you take this job you're moving on, but they soon will too. First to high school, then who knows where. You've given them two good years, and even if you stay, they won't be there."*

"But there will be others coming up. Don't I owe them something?"

"You do if you think you do. But university students are kids too, just big kids. They need good teachers as well. Some of them will go on to be teachers themselves. If you show enough of them how, they'll reach more children than you ever could by staying in the public schools."

"You're just rationalizing."

"Maybe..."

She turned away, lost in her own indecision. We stared up through the crisp, clear air at an astonishing display, constellations painted on a massive velvet canvas and pulsating as if alive. As always, the immensity of the universe overwhelmed me.

"How many stars?" I asked Amy at last.

"Forty-two billion and six."

"Funny. And wrong."

She burrowed into my neck and nipped my ear lobe. *"I suppose you have the right answer, mister know-it-all."*

"Nope. No one does. Think there's anybody up there?"

"Has to be. We can't be the only ones."

"How many kids in your classes?" I asked her.

"Uh, oh. Object lesson coming up, I suppose."

"It's a big world, honey. You have the potential to make it better. You just have to choose how best to go about it. But don't lose yourself while you're doing it. It's not a sin to do what satisfies you the most."

"But how do I decide what that is? And how do I know I'd be good at it? Teaching university, I mean. Some of the students will be almost as old as I am."

"But not half as smart. You'll never know if you don't take the chance. What did Robert Frost say? 'Choose something like a star...'"

"'Take ', " she corrected me. "'We may take something like a star to stay our minds on and be staid.' "

* * *

In the end, Amy decided to accept the appointment. All it had taken to convince her was a little perspective, a sense of our place in the enormity of the universe. Perhaps some of the same magic could work for Emily.

"Tell you what," I say to her finally. "Let's go outside for awhile."

"What for?"

"I want to show you something. Go put on something warmer. My sweatshirt too."

"Where are we going?" she asks suspiciously.

"Not very far. I just want to show you something."

She casts the blanket aside and gets to her feet. When she reaches the bedroom door she pauses, looking back over her shoulder at me, still indecisive.

"And wash your face," I say, hoping some light teasing may ease the strain between us. "You're a mess."

It doesn't work. She glares at me and disappears through the doorway. A few minutes later she comes out dressed in Amy's clothes once more and approaches the pump. She splashes water on her face and towels it dry.

"Now what?" she asks, pulling on the sweatshirt.

"Come outside with me." I pick up the blanket and carry it to the cabin door. She follows me out onto the deck and down to the shore, dragging her feet. The water lies almost perfectly calm, and the tender's bow rope hangs slack around the piling. I cast it off and hold the gunwale steady.

"All aboard," I tell her.

"Oh, no!" She backs up defensively.

"We're just going out to my boat."

"Yeah, and then we're *just* gonna go for a sail, right? And then we're *just* gonna stop off on the mainland. Well, screw that!"

"It's the middle of the night. I told you before, nobody can go through the channel in the dark."

"How do I know you're telling me the truth?"

"Look, you can swim, right?"

She gives me a tolerant look.

"So if I try to move the boat you can jump overboard."

"You're gonna tie me up or something!"

"Emily…"

We stare at each other, me helpless and her defiant. Stalemate. I try another approach.

"You can go back inside then. I'm going out to the boat to sit and think." I step into the dinghy and take up the oars, about to pull away from the dock.

"I don't want to stay here by myself," she says quietly.

"Why not? You slept out in the woods."

"And I was scared."

"So come with me, then. I just want to show you something that might make you feel better."

"What?"

"It's hard to explain, but I promise, it's really neat. Beautiful, in fact."

She hesitates, then climbs down off the dock and settles into the stern, tense and ready to bolt, arms folded across her chest and chin thrust out. I haul on the oars and a few minutes later we pull up alongside *Amy's Pride*.

She sits nervously, pressed back against the transom, as I tie the tender to the buoy. "I changed my mind," she says. "I'm not getting on that boat!"

"Why not?" I ask.

"You're trying to trick me."

"For Christ's sake, Emily, we're not going anywhere. Horatio Hornblower himself couldn't find his way through that channel in the dark."

"Who's that?"

"Never mind. Will you just this once try to trust me a little? Take a chance!"

Take a chance, I had once told Amy.

Leaving her behind, I climb the transom ladder with the blanket rolled up under my arm. The little boat drifts around and comes to rest against the side of the yacht. Emily sits stubbornly in the stern.

"Well?" I say.

She tosses her head in annoyance, then stands up and grips the gunwale. I reach out to help her over the rail into the cockpit, but she shakes off my hand and manages to scramble aboard. The starlight is strong enough to reflect off the boat's brilliant white fibreglass deck, and she looks around suspiciously.

"I'm not going anywhere with you," she says. "I really will jump overboard if you try to take me someplace."

"We're just going to sit for a while." I point to the top of the cabin. "Up there."

She thinks it over, and finally boosts herself up and clings to the mast. I climb up beside her and head forward to where the cabin roof slopes gently down toward the bow, beckoning for her to follow.

"Can you see where you're going?" I ask.

"Sure. It isn't as dark as I thought."

"That's your night vision kicking in. The pupils in your eyes get bigger to let in more light."

"I didn't know that."

"That's why cats like Jenny can see so well in the dark. They have really big pupils that can open extra wide."

I spread the blanket out and sit down, then stretch out on my back, patting the space beside me in invitation. She joins me, anxious and edgy, plenty of distance between us.

"Now what?" she says testily.

"Lie down and look up."

"What for?"

I ignore the question. She heaves a dramatic sigh and leans back, and I stare up at the sky, knowing she soon will, too.

"Wow." Soft, almost a whisper. "So many stars…"

"Amazing, isn't it?"

"How come I've never seen this before?"

"They don't show up like this in towns or cities. There are too many lights on the ground. They block out most of the starlight."

"I never knew there could be so many."

"Guess how big they are."

"I don't know."

I point north toward Polaris, prominent in its isolation against the velvet blackness, cold and stark among the fainter glow of lesser and more distant stars.

"See that big one, almost all by itself? That's the North Star, the one sailors once used to navigate by. It's huge, much bigger than the Earth and even than our sun, and really hot. But it's so far away, it looks tiny and cold. And look how many more there are, billions and billions. The whole universe is so large, we can't even begin to comprehend the whole thing."

"Do they all have names?"

"Names or numbers, most of them. Astronomers discover new ones all the time. The brightest ones make pictures in the sky, constellations they call them. You know what a dipper is?"

"Like a big soup spoon?"

"Uh huh. But the one up there is more like a sort of square ladle. It's shaped like this." I draw a rough diagram with my finger against the palm of my hand, just visible in the dim light. "Now can you find the North Star again?"

She points upward.

"Right. Now follow my finger." I trace a line in front of her face from Polaris to the lip of the Big Dipper. "See that one? Now find the stars that make a shape like the one I just showed you. Down, across, up again, and some stars in a row that make the curved handle. See?"

"No."

"Look again." I slide over a bit closer and take her hand, expecting her to resist, but she doesn't. I trace the design into her small palm, stopping briefly at each point where a star would be. "Now try to find the same pattern up there. Look for the bright ones."

She raises her arm and points, moving it down and up, and suddenly exclaims in excitement.

"I see it! I didn't think it would be so big!"

"Now look away."

"Huh?" She turns her face toward me.

"Can you find it again?"

She grins and spots the constellation immediately. "Sure. Right there."

"See how easy it is when you know what to look for? That's called the Big Dipper, and people have been using it to find the North Star for thousands of years. There's a smaller one, too. The Little Dipper."

"Where?" she asks eagerly, her distrust of me dissolving in the face of her enthusiasm.

"See if you can find it."

She props herself up on her elbows and concentrates fiercely. "There are too many of them."

"I'll give you a hint. It's over this way a little." I wave my hand in the right direction, and she bounces up onto her knees and searches the sky.

"There!" she cries triumphantly, one small hand tracing the pattern at arm's length. "Only it's tilted differently."

"Good work."

"That's the *Little* Dipper, huh? Still pretty big."

"Immense. In the fastest rocket ship ever built, you couldn't live long enough to travel between even two of those stars."

"You know a lot."

"I know one thing," I say calmly. "Even this one world we live on is big enough for you to have your own space in it. Safe space."

"I don't get it."

"Lucas."

"What about him?" That dead, toneless voice again.

"There are lots of other places for you to be besides with him."

"He won't give up until he gets me back."

"Suppose we can convince him to forget about you?"

"How?"

"I don't know yet. But I'll help you if you let me."

She turns her head to look at me, still disbelieving. She grimaces and looks back at the stars. After what has happened to her, she seems to have lost the ability to hope.

She stretches out on her back once more, and we lie quietly for several minutes.

"What difference does it make to you?" she says finally.

Damned if I know.

The last thing I need in my life is a throwaway kid from the streets. She should be someone else's problem, anyone's but mine, but I seem to be the only person around right now. I'm stuck with her, at least for a while.

"Do you like the way you've been living?" I venture.

"I hate it!"

"Then we have to do something about it."

The stars capture her attention again. She seems to be thinking about what I've said, and when at last she speaks, her voice trembles. "Like I said, why do you care?"

"You've got trouble. I don't like trouble. Anybody's."

She takes a deep, sighing breath and rolls over onto one hip. She hitches herself up on her elbow. Propping her chin on her palm, she searches for my eyes in the darkness.

"Your turn," she says bluntly.

"What?"

"I answered your questions, and you haven't answered any of mine."

"Not all my questions, you haven't," I argue, "but you're right. Fire away."

"Where's your wife?"

That old involuntary stab of pain again. "Like your mom and dad…"

"Car accident?"

"Uh, huh."

She lies quietly for awhile. Then: "You have any kids?"

"No. We decided to wait. We thought we still had plenty of time."

"How old are you, anyway?"

"Thirty-seven."

"And your wife? What was her name?"

"Amy. She was ten years younger. Look, that's enough about that, okay?"

"I told *you* a whole lot. How come you're living out here on this island?"

"Just a kind of vacation."

"All by yourself?"

I don't want to talk about it, especially to a child. "Ready to go back to the cabin?"

"No. I want to stay here. And I bet you ran away, just like me."

That startles me. I haven't thought about it quite that way, but she's right. After Amy's death the previous November I had gradually let my business slip away, refused new contracts, half-heartedly completed old ones, given my small staff notice. And when my desk was clear I came to the island, alone except for Jenny.

Again I try to change the subject. "We have to figure out what to do about you tomorrow. Do you have anybody besides your aunt and uncle you can stay with?"

She flops down on her back again and gathers the edge of the blanket around her, covering her bare legs. She points toward the sky. "What's that one?"

I follow her finger toward a bright speck on the rim of the Milky Way. "I don't know most of their names. There's one famous one, though, called the Dog Star."

"Where?"

"I have no idea. Off chasing cats, I suppose."

She giggles.

"There are other pictures in the sky besides the dippers too, more constellations, but you have to use your imagination to see them. There's a hunter named Orion with a sword, and a goat and a ram. Even fish, and a dragon named Draco. Want to look for some?"

"Sure."

For the next ten minutes we discuss the basic principles of stellar organization. Then I help her to trace Aires and Capricorn and the few other constellations I can identify. She has trouble imagining the fanciful designs the stars supposedly make, Pisces and Libra and the others, but the concept intrigues her. When I show her Cancer, she decides to call it the Old Crab, and Capricorn becomes the Old Goat.

"It's like a horoscope," she says.

"Astrology, right. Some people think the stars control our destiny."

"My aunt says that's crap. I know my sign, though. I'm a Leo. How about you?"

"Capricorn."

She giggles again. "Old Goat." Her laugh is infectious, and I'm relieved to see that we've gotten past at least some of her mistrust. But we still have a long way to go.

A brilliant point of light flares high in the southwest and plummets across the sky.

"Hey!" Emily shouts. "What's that?"

"A shooting star. Make a wish."

"What for?"

"It's an old legend. If you make a wish when you see a shooting star, it comes true."

"Too late," she says. "It's gone. Was it really a star?"

"No, just a meteor. A space rock on fire. They burn up from friction when they come near the earth's atmosphere. And it's not too late to make that wish."

"Okay," she murmurs. "But I bet it won't come true."

"Maybe it will if we help it along."

She squints her eyes tight, concentrating. "Want to know what I wished?" she says at last.

"Better not tell me, or it might not come true."

We hunt for a few more star patterns, and finally her voice begins to blur. She trails off in mid sentence. I shake her shoulder, and when she stirs I help her to get down off the cabin roof, intending to row back to the island. She slumps down in the cockpit, eyes closed and arms slack at her sides.

I manage to rouse her enough to climb down below decks, and put her into the forward berth. She falls deeply asleep almost instantly, and I climb back up on deck to get the blanket. Once she's covered, I retreat to the narrow bunk next to the engine hatch.

Sleep doesn't come as easily to me as to her.

6

Thursday

Night passes too quickly. At the first faint hint of dawn I'm sitting in the cockpit listening to the lines tick against the mast, and wondering what the hell to do next.

It would be easiest just to accept her as nothing more than a teenage hooker and turn her over to the police, except that she didn't choose that life style herself. On the contrary, she's apparently managed to escape from the worst kind of abusive slavery. With her captors out looking for her, most likely she'll just end up back in their hands unless someone figures out a way to help her.

By default, that someone seems to be me.

When her face appears at the top of the ladder, her eyes are still bleary from sleep. She blinks in the sunlight. "What time is it?"

"A little after six, I think. I didn't bring my watch."

"I have to pee."

"The head's down there," I tell her. She looks puzzled. "The bathroom. Little door the other side of the galley."

"The what?"

"Galley. The kitchen."

"Why don't they call it that, then?" She disappears from view, and I get up and reach inside the hatch to turn on the power switch so the pump will work. A couple of minutes later the water starts running, and soon she comes back out on deck. She checks out the cove, her gaze lingering on the cabin.

"We're still here," she says, suspicious but surprised. "You didn't try to take me anywhere."

"I promised, didn't I?"

She regards me distractedly, considering. "I'm hungry."

"Me too." I point toward the hatchway. "Reach in there and shut off the battery for me, and we'll row over to the cabin."

She leans in through the hatch. "How do I do it?"

"There are some switches on a little panel next to the ladder. It's the one on the left. Watch for the pilot light to go out."

"Got it!"

She backs out again and heads for the rail. I reach over the side and draw the tender in close, and she clambers over and drops down, taking her place in the stern. She's quiet but a bit agitated, almost eager, as we row back to the dock. She seems to be planning something.

As soon as we reach land she runs up to the cabin door and vanishes inside, leaving me to ship the oars and tie the tender off. Remembering the almost-empty propane tank, I circle the cabin to install a fresh one. As I'm tightening the nut on the pipe, I can hear the creak of the water pump handle through the walls.

She already has the table set by the time I arrive inside, with napkins prominently displayed. A pitcher of newly-mixed milk stands in the centre, along with the box of corn flakes and the sugar bowl.

"I was going to light the stove," she says, "but I wasn't sure how."

"I'll show you." I twist the valve to start the gas flowing and touch a match to each of the burners.

"I've never made coffee, either," she tells me.

"It's not hard. Watch."

She stares intently as I take the percolator from the drain board by the sink and assemble the parts. I show her how to measure the grounds and add the water, and she puts it on the stove. I pump some more water into a kettle and set it on the other burner.

"That's for washing up later," I tell her.

"I can make the coffee next time," she says brightly. "Anything else I forgot?" Having something to do, some chores to perform, has lightened her mood from the night before.

"I've got some powdered orange juice around here somewhere."

"Any better than the milk?"

"Not quite like the real thing, but it tastes okay. It's full of vitamins, too."

I rummage through the cupboard and find the packets of crystals. She takes another pitcher from the cabinet and pumps it half full of water.

"Is this enough?" she asks.

"Pretty close, I guess. I never bother to measure it exactly. Just dump in the powder and stir it up."

She mixes the juice carefully, focussed on doing it just right as if she has something to prove to me. We sit down at the table and she pours herself a glass of juice, another one of milk, and then fills her bowl with corn flakes. She adds milk and some sugar and takes a bite, then another. Then the spoon stops halfway to her mouth.

"What?" I ask.

"Funny…" A small, sad smile plays across her lips.

"What is?"

"Aunt Margaret never let me help make breakfast or even set the table. She was afraid I'd break something. But I could have done it, because Mom taught me."

"When you were eight or nine?"

"No, before, and I still remember how. She was gonna teach me how to make scrambled eggs, too, just before she…"

The words trail off and she takes another bite of corn flakes.

"Some stuff stays with us," I offer. "Sounds like you had a pretty good mom."

"I can hardly remember her," she says, almost too softly for me to hear.

I pour myself some cereal and we continue eating in silence. Halfway through the meal, Jenny jumps up on the table and inches her way toward Emily's bowl. She extends her chin, nose and whiskers twitching.

"Hey, cat!" she says. "This is mine, not yours."

"When you're done, save her just a little milk in the bottom. That's what I always do, and she expects it."

"Why don't you give her a bowl of milk for herself?"

"Believe it or not, milk isn't the best thing for cats. They like it, but it can upset their stomachs. A little won't hurt, though, and she likes the sugar in it."

Emily spoons up the last of her corn flakes and Jenny takes that as a signal to move in, poking her nose over the rim. Her little pink tongue flashes in and out.

"Congratulations," I say.

"What for?"

"She's accepted you. You're family now."

I would take back those ill-chosen words if I could. Her mouth turns down and her eyes cloud over with memories of the family she lost so long ago. Unsure of what to say to ease the strain, I finish my meal without speaking, then lift the coffee pot from the stove and fill my mug.

"Want some?" I ask her.

She shakes her head. Moving quietly, she collects the dishes and carries them to the sink, stacking them neatly to one side. She opens the cupboard beneath the sink and finds the dishwashing soap. Cinderella, being good so she'll be allowed to attend the ball.

I stop her as she's about to use the pump. "Come back and sit down for a minute."

She looks at me over her shoulder.

"Come on."

She turns and sits down again, but won't meet my eyes.

"We can't avoid this any longer," I say.

"What?" Barely a whisper.

"Where to take you."

"Why can't I stay here?"

"And do what? You need to get on with your life."

"I can make breakfast for you," she says, leaning forward eagerly. "Lunch and supper, too, if you want. And I can clean up and do laundry and stuff."

"That's not a permanent solution. We have to find a safe place for you to live. Get you back to school in the fall where you can make some friends again. Find some nice folks to look out for you."

She sinks back on the chair and toys absently with her crumpled napkin. "Nobody'll want me," she says softly.

"There are foster parents..." I begin.

"Yeah, right! I know how that works. They keep a kid they don't want just to get a cheque every month."

"Hey!"

She looks up, her eyes wet.

"It won't be so bad," I tell her. "It has to be better than what you've been doing up to now, right?"

She shrugs and gets up from the table. She goes to the sink and puts the plug in the drain. She squirts some soap over the dishes and starts working the pump handle, then collects the kettle from the stove and adds some hot water.

"Want some help with that?" I ask her, and join her at the sink. She washes each piece lethargically, handing them to me one by one to dry. When she finishes the last one, she pulls the plug and watches the water go down the drain. Outside the window, bright and welcoming sunshine streams in as I put away the last of the bowls.

It's time to resolve matters somehow. I want this strange, sad child off my island and out of my life, but I can't let those men on the charter yacht catch up with her again. There has to be some authority that can deal with kids like her, and find some caring people to take her in and get her straightened out somehow. An institution of some sort, perhaps.

"What's em-*path*-y?" she asks suddenly as I close up the cupboard.

"You mean *em*pathy? The emphasis is on the first syllable."

"Whatever. What is it?"

"It's being able to understand and sympathize with what somebody else is feeling."

"Huh?"

"Suppose you were sad, and I could tell and wanted to help somehow. That's empathy. What made you think of it, anyway?"

"It's in a book I found in the other room."

She hurries into the hallway and disappears into the bedroom. A few seconds later she's back, clutching the journal that I began a month or so after moving to the island.

"This one," she says. "It's got poems and stuff in it."

"That's private," I tell her.

"Then you shouldn't leave it around where people can find it. This one that's got 'empathy' in the title, it's called *The Empathy of Cats*, and it's about Jenny, right? Did you write it?"

I nod distractedly.

"So what's it mean?"

"You can read, can't you?" I say, unaccountably annoyed and not sure why.

"Of course I can read! I read good!"

"Well."

"Well what?" she snaps back.

"I meant you read *well*, not good."

"What's the difference?"

"It's like...Look, never mind."

"I want to know what the poem means. It's got some words in it that I don't understand." She traces a line of my handwriting with her forefinger. "Like what's this one, e-n-n-u-i?"

"Ennui," I reply. "Being tired of everything, or bored. Fed up."

"You're kidding, right?"

"What do you mean?"

"E-n-n-u-i is pronounced 'on-wee'?"

"It's French."

"How about this one, then? Supine."

"Emily…Oh, all right, it means stretched out, sort of. Like the way a lazy cat lies down."

"So why didn't you just say 'stretched out'?"

"Because then it wouldn't be poetry. Look, one thing that makes a poem different from ordinary prose is the language you use. Sometimes that's even more important than what it means. You try to choose words that are as beautiful as possible."

She puzzles over the lines for a minute. "It doesn't seem so beautiful to me."

"Damn it, give me the book." She hands it over timidly. "Now listen."

I let my eyes drift over the lines. I had written them months before, while the pain of losing Amy still haunted my nights.

"Jenny knows," I begin, and the words catch in my throat. My eyes begin to fill, and I look up to find Emily staring at me intently. My gaze drops to the poem again, and I suck in a deep breath.

Jenny knows.
She knows when I'm not well
or lost in Hell,
or simply in a spell
of self-involved ennui.
She lies supine against my spine
in silken, furry drowsiness,
and purrs her song of comfort
'til comes my healing sleep.

The journal falls shut in my lap. Emily's eyes are glowing, her lips forming a tiny, pursed letter O.

"Understand it now?" I ask.

"Not really," she says. "But it *is* beautiful. It's different when you read it out loud. Can I hear it again?"

"Emily…"

"Please?"

The second time the words flow more evenly, the emotional torrent I had felt a moment before now somewhat muted, a bit less painful. She sits perfectly still until I finish.

"It means you're sad, right? And somehow your cat can tell, so she keeps you company. And that helps you go to sleep. Am I right?"

"Yes, you're right."

"Only the poem says it better than I did."

That surprises me. Somewhere inside this irritating child there seems to be a sensitive human being.

She takes the journal from me and sits still for several minutes, lost in thought over the lines. Finally her head comes up, her gaze keen and penetrating.

"You don't have any, huh?" she says.

"What are you talking about?"

"Empathy. You don't have any. If you did, you'd know why I don't want to go back."

How can I answer that? She's hurting. Even with my total lack of experience with children I can see that, and the fact that, worst of all, she's afraid. She needs some time to heal, some safe rest period away from the horror her life has become, before I consign her to the system again. It won't hurt me to give her one more day.

"Tell you what," I say. "How about a little adventure? We could take the boat out for a while."

"And go where?" she asks suspiciously.

"Nowhere. Anywhere. And then come back here to stay the night. I promise. Just for fun."

She eyes me coldly.

"Listen, my small friend, we made a lot of progress last night. You started to trust me, and I'm not going to do anything to spoil that."

"You won't try to give me to the cops?"

"I promise. Scout's honour. You can stay here for at least one more day. Maybe more."

More? Did I really say that? Oh, well...

"But I want you to talk to somebody later on. On the telephone."

"Who?"

"The lady I spoke to yesterday, the one at Family and Children's Services. Her name is Ms. Pineo, and she sounded really nice."

"Why do I have to talk to her?"

"You don't *have* to. I'm just asking you to, okay? Just let her explain what she can do to help you. Then you can make up your own mind whether to let her try."

68

"Where is she?"

"Halifax."

"So just on the telephone, right?"

"Right. We won't tell her where you are, not even your name if you don't want to."

She thinks it over carefully. "Okay. I believe you."

I'm trapped. If I violate her trust now, she may never believe anyone again.

"No, you don't," I tell her. "But after today maybe you will."

7

Thursday, Late Morning

The Atlantic coast of Nova Scotia can be a sailor's delight, or his worst nightmare. When the seas are calm and the weather warm, no pleasure compares to a cruise out of St. Margaret's Bay, or down among the islands that litter the sea between Chester and the rugged peninsula that stretches eastward from Lunenburg.

Offshore the icy waters once ran deep with cod and mackerel, tuna and swordfish. The seabed teemed with lobsters, at one time so plentiful that the poorest families ate little else when the price of meat and vegetables was beyond their reach. Generations of fisherman have wrested a living from the banks and shoals, but many also lie beneath the waves, victims of careless navigation or the abrupt vagaries of storm and tide that still conspire to catch the unwary too far from port.

I never leave Farrell Island without checking the weather, and rarely venture beyond the cove unless the forecast is reasonably favourable. Single-handed sailing in a thirty-foot yacht is tricky enough without the added complication of high winds and rough seas. On this day, despite the brilliant blue of the morning sky, the high winds of the night before have almost certainly churned the Atlantic into a froth of swells. *Amy's Pride* is a stable and forgiving craft, but I feel a little apprehensive when the radio confirms my suspicions. We might have to stick close to home, unless Emily shows some aptitude for crewmanship.

"You don't get seasick, do you?" I ask her as we rummage through Amy's left-behind clothing for something to protect her from the harsh rays of the sun.

"Don't know."

"Car sick, maybe? It's the same thing."

"Nope. Hey, what's this?" She hauls a broad-brimmed yellow souwester from the back of the bottom drawer and smoothes it out. She plops it on her head, back side front, and it falls forward over her eyes.

"Turn it around," I tell her. "The shorter brim goes in the front. The long one is to keep rain off your neck."

She twirls it and grips the sides, pulling them down over her ears and crossing her eyes. A baggy-pants comic in a vaudeville sketch.

"Better?"

"Not much." I can't help laughing.

"Where's the mirror?" she squeals, jumping up and running into the bathroom for a look. She comes back with a grin a mile wide.

"This'll keep the sun off me, right?"

"You'll scare the hell out of the seagulls in that thing."

"Well, *I* like it!" she bristles, hands on her hips, and the hat slides forward over her eyes. "But I guess it's too big, huh? What else is in here?" She digs through the chest of drawers again. "No more hats."

"We can make that one do. Use your hair to fill it up."

"Hey! That'll work!" She loops the strands into a fat skein and piles it on top of her head, holding it in place while tucking the loose ends into the souwester. This time it rides high enough above her eyes to let her see clearly.

"This'll be fun," she says, getting to her feet. "Come on, let's go." Then she pauses, the serious expression back on her face. "As long as we come right back here. Nowhere else."

"We have to go ashore to find a phone."

"No!" She tears the hat from her head and clutches it in front of her, the hunted look back in her eyes.

"I thought we agreed you'd talk to Ms. Pineo."

"I thought you meant on a cell phone or something!"

"Haven't got one."

"Don't you get it?" she cries. "If I go back there, they'll *get* me!"

"Who will?"

"Lucas!"

"Did you see him yesterday?"

"No. But I saw that boat."

"You mean the big sailboat that passed us yesterday? Why did that scare you?"

Her face shuts down. Her hands wring the souwester into a crumpled, wrinkled mass.

"That was a charter boat," I tell her. "It doesn't belong to Lucas. The company that owns it is in Yarmouth, and they just rent dock space down here for the summer."

She shakes her head violently.

"Listen, you can't spend your whole life scared of your own shadow. Did you see Lucas on board?"

"I didn't see anybody."

"But you've seen that boat before?"

She nods.

"When?"

She looks away. I'm getting closer to learning how she ended up on the island, but it's too soon to try to force it out of her.

"Whatever it is about that boat that frightens you," I tell her, "you'll have to deal with it sooner or later. But if we see it again you can go below, just like last time, until it's out of sight."

"I want to stay here!"

"Come on, sit down for a minute."

Reluctantly she perches on the edge of a chair, stressed and apprehensive. I join her on the opposite side of the table.

"Now look. Two minutes ago you were excited about going for an adventure. Now all of a sudden you're going to miss all that fun just because you might—*might*—see some boat that you're afraid of. Does that make sense?"

No response.

"I won't let anything happen to you. I promise."

Her shoulders droop. "You don't know them."

"No, but I'm not afraid of them either. There are ways to deal with dangerous people, criminals like Lucas. We avoid them if we can, and if we can't, we get help to fight them."

"He'll take me back," she says again.

"Not if you're with me. Now how about it? We take the boat out, have some fun, then go ashore at the marina for just a few minutes where there are lots of people around, just in case we need help. We'll make that phone call and then go right back to the boat. Okay?"

She slumps in the chair, staring at her feet.

"Last night turned out okay, didn't it? I made you a promise and I kept it. All I'm asking is that you trust me just once more."

72

Long minutes pass as she twists the hem of her tee shirt and scuffs her sneakers on the floor. At last her eyes come up, still wide and anxious, but she nods almost imperceptibly.

"Good. But you're going to have to work. The radio says it'll be a little rough out there. Unless it's calm, I need a crew member to help keep the boat under control."

"I don't know how," she says forlornly.

"Are you willing to learn?"

She rallies a bit. "Is it hard?"

"You mean hard work? Yes. You'll have calluses and sore arms by the time we get back. But I think you'll catch on pretty quickly."

"Okay."

"We'll need a lunch too, in case you start having fun and don't want to come back too soon."

"I'll help." She slips off the chair uncertainly, still anxious and fearful. We load a grocery bag with bread, canned tuna, lettuce and bottled water, say goodbye to Jenny, and row the tender out to *Amy's Pride* to begin her sailing lessons.

She watches me uncover the sails, and I show her where the main halyard attaches and how the roller furling works. She masters the winches after a couple of tries, and practices over and over as I start the engine and head for the channel.

She's beginning to relax, still apprehensive but distracted by trying to learn about the boat's equipment, and gradually becoming a bit more animated. I give her sentry duty at the bow, telling her to watch for rocks and sunken logs as we motor out of the cove. It's an unnecessary job, given my experience in those waters, but I don't tell her that.

She stretches out on her stomach near the bowsprit, the souwester planted firmly on her head, taking the responsibility seriously. She calls out every rock, every submerged log, every sandbar, no matter how far off the rail they might be. Once I approach a hazard a little too closely to see how she'll react, and she jumps up and screams a warning, sure we're about to run aground. Pretending to be alarmed, I spin the wheel and narrowly miss a branch-strewn sandbar.

"Nice work, first mate," I call out to her. She beams at me. I have to fight to keep a serious expression, letting her think she's saved us from sinking.

A funny thing... Her pleasure is rubbing off on me a little. I had forgotten the joy of having someone to sail with. The last time had been the previous

October, with Amy. Nine months ago. A lifetime.

After a brief pause to check for other boats in the area, we clear the mouth of the channel and face the open Atlantic. Gouts of spray erupt across the bow and soak her face. She scampers back over the cabin roof and drops down into the cockpit, losing her balance as a turbulent swell slaps us on the starboard side and rolls us to port. I catch her arm and keep her from falling onto the locker.

"Wow! Thanks. Is it safe out here? This thing won't sink, will it?"

"Not a chance. And it won't be too bad once we get away from the island. The tide and the wind are a little at cross purposes, so we'll have some waves, but that's what makes it fun. That is, if you can learn how to handle the sails so I can stay at the helm."

"What's that?"

"The helm? This wheel. That's what controls the rudder, so we can turn the boat."

"What do I do?"

"Are you sure you want to? We can turn back if you're scared."

"Of what? You said we won't sink. Anyway, I told you I can swim."

"Okay. Remember which line raises the mainsail?" She nods. "Pull on it as hard as you can until the sail goes up. Then put it on the winch and crank it in tight until I say stop."

She locates the halyard and falls to work, and we soon have the main and jib set. I shut down the diesel and point up, and *Amy's Pride* digs in and races off at an acute angle to the coast, cleaving the swells that wash her rails with spray. Emily stretches up on tiptoe, clinging to the rim of the protective canvas dodger that overhangs the companionway and traveller. She strains eagerly to see beyond the mast. Her oversized hat conceals the masses of hair, dwarfing her slim body and emphasizing her youth.

"This is *way* better than a motor boat," she squeals excitedly. She's a little kid again, eager for something new and exciting. Christmas morning...

And only a week ago, she was doing God-knows-what.

"Time to turn!" I shout to her, and she jumps down and joins me behind the console. "It's called 'coming about,' and *you* have to do most of the work."

She listens keenly as I explain the principle of tacking against the wind and show her how to release the jib on one side and crank it in on the other. Her concentration is fierce as she memorizes each step.

"Keep your head down," I caution. "The boom will come across the

cockpit and take off your hat if you're not careful. Maybe your head, too."
She's too short to be in any real danger, but I want her to stay alert.

"What's the boom?"

"You'll see. Just keep your head down. Ready?"

"I guess so." Nerves and excitement have her bouncing on her toes.

"Take the line off that winch," I tell her, pointing to the port side, "and keep it taut. Be ready to let it go when I tell you and pull in the one on the other side."

"Which?"

"Here," I say, holding up the starboard jib sheet. "When I yell 'coming about,' let go of the line you're holding and grab this one. Haul it in as fast as you can and throw it on the winch and crank it in tight. Okay?"

She nods apprehensively, a quick study.

"Coming about!"

I spin the wheel, and she drops the sheet and fumbles to take the other one from me. She turns toward the winch, and as the hull rolls to starboard she loses her balance and tumbles against the rail. She shoves herself upright and pulls in the line, and manages to get it around the winch just as the boom crashes over her head.

"Wow!" she hollers. "What was that?"

"The boom!" I yell. "Crank, don't talk!"

She slaps the winch handle home and hauls away, and the jib stiffens and begins to fill.

"Tighter! Turn it the other way! It'll give you more leverage. Put your back into it!"

She braces her feet and yanks on the handle, and *Amy's Pride* catches her balance and races off on the opposite tack.

"Enough," I call out. "Nice work."

She stops cranking and collapses heavily onto the locker, breathing hard. "My God..."

"That wasn't bad for your first try," I tell her. "Really. It just takes practice, that's all."

"Does the big sail always do that? Smash across to the other side like that?"

"Usually I catch it on the way past and slow it down, but I missed that time. Scared you, did it?"

"A little."

"Good!"

She sticks her tongue out at me and grins. Cute.

"Want to do it again?"

"No!"

"Hey, it's the only way to learn how."

She struggles to her feet, faking exhaustion. "What now?"

"Same thing, only in reverse. Take the starboard line off the winch and hang on to it. It's called a 'sheet,' by the way. When we come about, let it go and pull on the other one until you can get it on the winch."

"A rope is called a sheet?"

"Right."

"What do you call those things on a bed, ropes?"

"Very funny. Understand what to do?"

"I think so."

"Coming about!"

She learns fast. We tack twice more and the final turn flows smoothly, with barely a loss in forward speed. As she hauls the jib in close and tight she looks to me for approval, and I give her a big thumbs up.

"You're a sailor now," I tell her.

She flops down on the port locker with a big grin on her face and leans out over the rail. The wind catches the brim of her souwester and flips it onto the gunwale, and she squeals and lunges for it as it slips over the side, just missing.

"Sorry," she says.

"It was too big anyway. We'll get you one that fits."

She stands up on the locker beside the dodger and leans forward to peer over the bow. The wind lifts her plentiful hair and it streams out behind her, a rich brown cape that shines in the sunlight. A normal, happy kid, having fun.

She turns and finds me watching her.

"What?"

I smile at her. "Just thinking."

"Thinking about what?" she persists.

"You're doing my wife's job. She always ran the winches for me."

"So how am I doing? As good as her?"

"Pretty close," I concede.

Emily's face turns serious. "What was she like?"

I don't want to go there. "Coming about!" I shout, and crank the wheel hard. She jumps off the locker and releases the jib sheet in one fluid motion. She grasps the starboard sheet and hauls it in rapidly, hand over hand, and wraps it around the winch. *Amy's Pride* sprints onto the opposite tack with no loss of headway.

"Now *that* was great!" I praise her. "I couldn't have done it better."

Emily flushes with pleasure. She climbs up beside the dodger again, stretching sideways to see around the jib toward the distant horizon. I can hardly believe the change that learning to sail has made in her. She's gone from a fearful emotional cripple to a lively, enthusiastic young adolescent, all because of a fast boat.

She glances over her shoulder and catches me looking at her again. "What is it this time?"

"Nothing."

"Come on, you keep staring at me. How come?"

"I was just thinking that if I had been lucky enough to have a daughter, I'd have wanted her to be just like you."

"I'm so sure!" She grimaces and turns away in disgust. "Everybody wants a kid who's a whore," she mutters under her breath.

"That may be what you've been doing," I say calmly, "but that isn't necessarily what you *are*. There's a big difference."

"Not to me."

"Maybe we can change that. Anyway, you won't be doing that any more."

She whirls around, eyes flashing. "What makes you so sure?" she says sarcastically.

I consider my answer carefully. "Because by now I know what kind of person you are. That's why."

She glares at me. "You're kidding me, right?"

"Do I sound like it?"

She glowers sullenly for a few moments, then turns away abruptly and boosts herself up on top of the cabin. Hanging on to the boom to steady herself against the cant of the hull, she makes her way forward and sits down just aft of the bowsprit, as far away from me as she can get. *Amy's Pride* plunges onward toward the open Atlantic, leaving Farrell Island and Bournemouth harbour far behind.

Just when I thought we were making real progress, her sudden mood swing troubles me. Her emotional state is still fragile, her self image badly damaged by the freaks who've been molesting her. It will no doubt be a long time before she can accept even the smallest expression of praise or affection at face value.

Ten minutes later she wanders back to the cockpit somewhat subdued, her forehead wrinkled in a frown. She skirts around me, morose and uncommunicative, and slides onto the stern locker.

"You're like the stars last night," I tell her.

She won't look at me. "What do you mean?"

"You're an Old Crab."

She smiles before she can catch herself, and ducks her head so I won't see. Then she shrugs and stands up beside me at the console.

"I'm sorry I got mad," she says.

"That's okay. It was mostly my fault."

"And I'm sorry you never had any kids of your own."

I don't have an answer for that.

"You're going to have to tell me sometime," she says.

"What?"

"About your wife. About what happened to her."

"I told you, an accident."

"What kind?"

"Listen…"

"No, *you* listen. You keep going on about me trusting you and everything, but you don't even trust me enough to answer my questions. It's not fair!"

I swallow painfully and gaze out across the top of the cabin. "Like I said, it was an automobile accident."

"And…?"

Her face is expectant and strangely sympathetic, belying her immaturity. I concentrate on the wheel, then the billowing mainsail, making minute and unnecessary corrections in our heading. Remembering…

* * *

The police report reconstructed the scene in stark, official language, leaving me to read between the lines. Hurrying to an early morning conference in Middleton on Highway 101, Amy topped the crest of a hill south of the town of Kentville. Her small sedan gained speed slightly as it coasted down a gentle incline, approaching the underpass beneath Highway Twelve. In the dim light just before dawn, tendrils of frost sparkled on the matted, uncut grass beside the road, a luminous blanket turning winter's brown to silver.

Her lane lay clear ahead. On the opposite side a lone car and a delivery van climbed eastbound and passed her halfway up the hill. In the distance a heavily loaded eighteen-wheeler bore down upon the underpass. The road curved gently, and Amy touched the brakes as she approached the bottom of the hill.

The car drifted left. Too late she sensed the slippery and invisible black ice that coated the road surface. She jerked the wheel abruptly, overcorrecting, and when the tires touched bare pavement again, the car spun into the oncoming lane, broadside to the huge front bumper of the speeding semi.

Crushed instantly to half its width, the car rebounded around the truck's fender, caught by its own bumper, and slid under the trailer. The truck driver slammed on his brakes, and both vehicles careened off the road and ploughed into the soft shoulder. Metal screeched and grated, spewing fountains of sparks into the sky. A fuel tank ruptured and ignited, and as the twisted mass ground to a stop, both car and truck exploded in an oily cloud of horror.

* * *

The memories fade slowly and I find my cheeks wet, the unbidden tears cold against my skin in the freshening wind. I turn my face away and wipe at them with my sleeve.

"I'm sorry I made you cry," she whispers. "You don't have to tell me if you don't want to."

I try to smile at her. "Some time maybe I will. I just can't right now."

"That's okay." She concentrates on the small precise movements of my hands that are keeping the sail taut, the bow pointed up into the wind.

"How about teaching me to steer, then?" she asks at last.

"You don't steer a boat. You man the helm."

"Whatever." She pushes in beside me playfully, and for the next half hour I show her the finer aspects of reading the wind, flying the ticklers, and that tactical error that causes the sails to luff and the boat to lose headway: pinching. That earns me a sharp tweak on the arm and her infectious giggle.

I'm sensing a subtle change in our relationship. Her cautious detachment is giving way to a first few tentative gestures of physical contact that say "I trust you." My mind strays to the poem about Jenny. Empathy is a quality that Emily shares.

"I'm getting hungry," she says as we tack eastward for the fourth time. The mainland is a distant blur off the port rail. "When are we gonna eat?"

I check my watch: after eleven. "Any time you're ready."

"Out here?"

"Why not? You aren't seasick, are you?"

"Nope. Guess I'm tough, huh?"

"Oh, yeah. How about you dig the grocery bag out of the galley while I slow us down a little. There's a can opener in one of the drawers down there."

"Got it." She skips over to the hatch and braces her hands on the rails on either side of the opening. She lifts both feet and thrusts forward, plummeting down the ladder without touching a single step. She lands with a solid thump.

"You okay?" I call out.

"Sure."

Youth! They think they're invincible...

I let the boat fall off the wind, easing the main and resetting the traveller. The knot metre drops below three. I engage the autopilot as Emily reappears on deck, clutching our lunch bag.

"I found some cans of Coke in the cupboard down there," she announces. "They'll be warm."

"Doesn't matter. Where can I put them?"

I point to the starboard seat. "Flip open that locker." She does.

"See those wire things, the green ones?"

"What are they?"

"Seagoing cup holders. They hang on the rail."

Once the Coke cans are swaying in the breeze, we spread out the makings for lunch and are soon enjoying fat tuna and lettuce sandwiches.

"You were right," she says between mouthfuls. "This is hard work, but it's fun."

"You're pretty good with the winch," I tell her. "Are your hands sore?"

"Kind of, but I don't care. What's next?"

"We're a long way out. It'll take us close to an hour to get back, so we'd better head for town."

"Just to make that phone call, right? Then back to the island."

"If you want. But there's lots to do there. We can leave the boat at the marina for the rest of the afternoon. There are some gift shops and a museum, and when we get hungry again we can eat in one of the seafood restaurants. We'll have time to go back to the island before it gets dark."

"No!" She shoves away from me, spilling the remains of her meal on the cockpit floor. "You promised! You said you wouldn't make me stay there!"

"I just thought...Look, we can't live on sandwiches all the time. We could both use a good meal later on. And do you really want more of that powdered milk again?"

The old suspicion is back in her eyes. "You're gonna try to take me to the cops."

"No. We'll go back to the island any time you want."

"What if we see that boat?"

"So? I told you, it doesn't belong to Lucas. It'll probably be tied up at the wharf, or out on some other charter."

"Are you sure?"

"Absolutely. What scares you about it anyway?"

She turns away and sits down on top of the port locker. I decide not to pursue it.

"What'll it be?" I ask her. "Shall we go back, or snoop around the dock and have supper ashore? You decide."

"How do I know you won't double-cross me?"

"You don't. That's why I'm giving you your choice right now. If you want to, we can even skip the phone call. When we get back you can see whether Jenny still trusts *you*. Maybe you'll have better luck with her than I'm having with you."

Her face softens a little. "What's this restaurant like?"

"You can't be hungry again already."

"No, but I will be later."

"My wife and I used to go there a lot when we went sailing. It's got a dumb name, Mussel Beach, but the food's good. It's built out on the dock, and we can sit inside by the window and watch the other boats go in and out."

"Is it anywhere near downtown?"

"About three blocks away."

"Suppose Lucas is hanging around?"

"Does he live in Bournemouth?"

"No. Halifax."

"So why would he be around here?"

She ducks her head. "Maybe he's looking for me there."

"Why would he? How did you get here, anyway? Isn't it time you told me what's going on?"

She stares out across the bay toward the distant harbour, her lips a tight thin line and her spine rigid.

"Okay, so you won't tell me. Anyway, forget Lucas. You're free of him now."

"That isn't how it works. There was this girl my age who…"

"Never mind. I don't want to hear about it. Whoever she was, she doesn't

81

have anything to do with you any more. Besides, Lucas won't mess with me. I guarantee it."

She scuffs her sneaker on the deck.

"Okay, if you're still not sure, I've got another idea." I take a step backwards and stroke my chin, looking her up and down in false criticism. "You're still a mess. Your shorts are too big and your tee shirt won't stay tucked in. I'm embarrassed to be seen with you."

"Stop it! Why are you saying that?"

"There's a shopping mall just a few blocks from the dock. What do you say we stop in and get you a little camouflage? When we're finished, Lucas won't even recognize you. Maybe I won't either."

"What are you talking about?"

"Some new clothes. Something that fits. And a new hat."

"You'd do that for me?"

"Why not? Are you game?"

"I'm really scared to go ashore."

"I know," I say softly, "and we have to work on that. You can't hide out for the rest of your life. You have to face what frightens you, and this can be a first step in that direction. I'll be right beside you the whole time, so you won't have to face it alone."

Fear and hope play tag across her face, and hope wins. She slides off the locker and joins me at the helm. She hip-checks me aside and takes the wheel again.

"Hey!" I complain.

"I'm getting blisters," she says. "You pull on the ropes for a while."

8

Thursday Afternoon

After leaving *Amy's Pride* docked at the marina, within sight of Mussel Beach, we leave the wharf and walk up Holland Avenue. Emily clings to me as closely as she can without touching me, her head swivelling nervously to look down each side street. Her eyes search every face that passes by. She doesn't begin to relax until we enter the mall.

An escalator takes us to the second level. Bright sunshine through a skylight illuminates the word "Sears" on an archway at the far end. We make our way to the store entrance, and I check the directory for children's and teens' wear.

"I've never been in a store like this before," she says, craning her neck like a first-time tourist in New York. "It's big!"

"Not likely to find Paris originals here," I tell her, "but they have good, middle-of-the-road stuff."

"I don't have any money. Lucas always pays for whatever I need."

"Will you accept a present from me? No strings attached."

She smiles sadly. "I guess you know how *that* works."

"Not between friends."

"Are we friends?"

That catches me off guard. I'm letting myself be drawn farther and farther into a situation that I'm not sure I can handle. After cutting myself off from everyone and everything, suddenly I'm beginning to care about someone again. It scares me, but I don't know what else I can do. Right now she doesn't seem to have anyone else.

I should simply offload this problem child at the nearest police station and relieve myself of any responsibility. She's trouble, a major distraction and an intrusion into my carefully built shell of self-pity; an annoyance to be rid of as soon as possible.

But on the boat... How could I have known that with the wind in her hair and her sturdy legs braced against the cant of the racing hull, the cynical teenage hooker would vanish before my eyes? She was a child again, a happy, excited, innocent participant in one of the great joys of life.

Someone to protect.

Then came her surprising compassion when the memories of Amy brought tears to my eyes...

She misinterprets my long silence and her face falls. "I guess we're not."

"What?"

"Friends."

"I'm sorry. I thought it was obvious. Of course we're friends."

She rewards me with a shy grin, a not-quite-believing but hopeful expression that brings me unexpected pain. A lot of people have already let her down, and she's afraid I will too.

"Come on," I tell her, "let's go down this way."

We set off along the main aisle, then turn right to wander among rows and rows of bright summer clothes, lined up all the way to a bank of huge windows on the outside wall. Emily seems overwhelmed.

"You've been to a mall before, haven't you?" I ask.

"Just strip malls in the Valley, and the one in New Minas a couple of times. Little stores compared to this one."

"Well, let's get going. You need some stuff that fits, and supper won't wait forever."

For the next half hour I trail along as she picks her way through the racks. Most of the shorts she chooses to try on are in muted colours of beige or light blue, traditionally styled in a loose fit. Finally, after working her way through six pairs and putting them all back on their hangers again, she returns to one of the first ones.

"I guess I'll get these, if that's okay," she says.

"Sure it's okay. That's what we're here for. Don't you like any of the others?"

"Uh huh. I like them all. Most, anyway." She fingers the cloth and examines the label. "These best, though."

"You can have more than one, you know."

She looks up in surprise. "I can?"

"Why not? You can't wear the same clothes every day."

84

"I thought… Aunt Margaret never let me get more than one thing at a time."

"I'm not Aunt Margaret," I tell her. "Let's get you a whole bunch."

"That'll cost a lot."

"So?"

"I'll feel bad, spending all your money."

"No reason to. I have more than I need, and I haven't had anyone to spend it on in a long time. Besides, I'm sick and tired of having a scruffy kid hanging around."

"Hey!"

"Scruffy!"

"I am not!"

"You will be if you don't listen to what I'm telling you."

She pretends to be offended, hiding a grin, and snatches another pair of shorts off a hanger.

"That's better," I tell her. "From scruffy to stylish in less than two seconds. Now get busy and make some more choices. I'm getting really hungry again."

She picks out two pairs of shorts and some jeans, then moves on to the tops. She shows surprisingly good taste, but her selections are almost painfully conservative, the antithesis of a hooker's wardrobe. She leans toward loose and simple designs, nothing too bare or bright or flashy. Her most adventurous choice is a cute tiny skirt with wide box pleats, hiding a modest pair of shorts beneath, and I have to talk her into that.

Finally we accumulate enough to give her at least a week's worth of changes: the jeans for cool evenings and the shorts, a sweatshirt with a cat embroidered on the front and, despite her protests over the expense, half a dozen simple tops. She'll have things of her own when she goes to a foster family or group home. Wherever she ends up, she won't look like a neglected orphan or, worse, a street kid.

Strangely enough, although I expected to be bored and restless while she shopped, the whole experience has been fun. Her youthful enthusiasm is contagious. It's been too long since I've had any reason to smile, and it almost feels good.

I haven't been in a mall for a long time, nor anywhere else of consequence. Not since Amy. After the accident I shut everyone out and retreated from friends and work and life itself, and now this waif has wormed her way inside my defences. A sailing lesson and a few dollars spent on new clothes has wrought a wonderful transformation in this half-pint, sorrowful stray. I feel as if I've done something worthwhile, and regained some purpose to my life.

Amy had been an enthusiastic shopper too, but, like Emily, overly anxious about the cost. It had been my delight to see her looking beautiful, happy and confident inside her own skin. I always tried to brush aside her concern about money. My architectural firm was attracting the kinds of prosperous customers for whom quality was the first priority, and turning a substantial profit. Adding in her salary from her teaching position, we had no financial worries at all.

I enjoyed teasing her with feigned impatience as she tried on outfit after outfit, vicariously enjoying her pleasure. She'd often spent hours putting together just the right image that, with a perfect blend of dignity and femininity, would enhance her status as the youngest Assistant Professor in the English Department at St. Mary's University. She'd been so proud of that achievement, so dedicated to her classes, and understandably insecure about the impression she made on students and colleagues alike.

As if clothes really mattered… Amy was a magnet. She made friends instantly, everywhere she went.

Emily folds her choices neatly into a pile. On the way to the checkout counter I tap her on the shoulder and point to the lingerie aisle.

"Forgotten something?"

"Geez, yes. You stay here and hold this stuff, okay?"

She leaves me standing alone in the centre of the store. Fifteen minutes later she reappears clutching some boxed bras, a bundle of white sport socks and two plastic bags of panties, three pair to a bag. They're cut from plain cotton, white and pastel, not skimpy and sheer like the ones she had on when she came to the island.

"What have you got?" I tease.

She blushes appealingly. "Mind your own business." She pushes past me and dumps the packages on the checkout counter, and I place the rest of the clothing beside them.

"Quite a selection," the clerk says brightly as she scans the price tags into the register. "Birthday or special occasion?" Not knowing how to answer, Emily looks to me for help.

"Growth spurt," I fib. "Woke up one morning and almost nothing fit any more. And she does have a birthday coming up in a couple of days."

"Maybe you need something for dress-up, then?" she asks.

"I didn't think of that." I turn to Emily. "What do you think?"

She shrugs. "I'm not going anywhere special."

"You never know," I tell her. "Somebody might take you out to dinner tonight." Then, to the salesgirl, "Can you put these aside while we look around a little more?"

She smiles at me and nods. She clears the register and motions for the next customer to come forward. I take Emily's arm and lead her toward a mannequin in a sundress at the end of the next row.

"Remember what I said about camouflage? How about if we give your image a really big makeover?"

She stares sceptically at the dummy. "What, a dress? Come on!"

"Why not?"

"I haven't worn a dress since…Well, I can't even remember when."

"See what I mean? A change of image, something more grown up. Besides, since we're going out to dinner, you might want to look extra nice."

"But a *dress?*"

"What's wrong with that? Look, just try a couple on. If you can't find anything you like, fine."

"Which one?"

"Hey, what I know about kids' fashions you could write on the back of a postage stamp." I lift a ruffled blue and white, cap-sleeved creation off the rack. "How about this?"

She bursts out laughing. "I'm not ten!"

"This, then." I pull out a bright red sundress with a low squared-off neckline and a wide white belt. Images of Amy prod my memory again. Red had been her favourite colour, setting off her golden skin and the soft tendrils of her cornsilk hair.

Emily eyes the dress dubiously. "I don't think so…"

"Why not? You could at least try it on."

"Too bright," she says decisively.

"What's wrong with that?"

"Might make people look at me."

So *that's* it! She's searching for a sort of anonymity, a way to hide in plain sight. It can't possibly work, not with her heavy mane of dark brown hair and those huge, round eyes. I sort through the hangers and come upon a striped shirtwaist in light green and white.

"That's not so bad, I guess," she says.

"Try it."

"This is a waste of time. And it's not even my size."

She hangs the dress back on the rack and searches through the ones next to it, finally coming up with a duplicate two sizes smaller.

"This one's better."

She disappears into the fitting room, and I find a couple more that seem right for someone her age, at least to my untrained eye. She's out again in less than three minutes, the dress slung over her arm.

"You didn't show me," I complain.

"Makes me look fat." She hangs it back on the rack. "Too long, too. I felt like a dwarf walking in a ditch. Let's just go."

"You give up too easily. Look at this one." I hand her a pale yellow sundress, sleeveless but with wide shoulder straps and a short flared skirt. "Better?"

"I hate dresses."

"Okay, if you want to look like a scruffy little kid all your life…"

"Not that again!"

"Humour me."

She scowls, yanks the hanger out of my hand, and stamps over to the fitting room.

"And you have to show me, okay?" I call after her.

She takes a little longer this time, and when she emerges at last I can see it's the right choice. The simple lines of the dress give her an innocent, youthful look, so much so that it's as if I'm seeing a different child. Gone are the hard, brittle edges, the careworn remnants of a captive life in Lucas's world.

She pirouettes in front of the mirror, the skirt swirling gently several inches above her knees. She cocks her head and makes a face.

"Well? Satisfied? Can I take it off now?"

"Turn around," I tell her.

She twists back and I point to her image in the mirror.

"Who's that?" I ask.

"Damned if I know."

"Watch your mouth, young lady. Swearing doesn't fit your new image. And I know who that is."

"Oh yeah? Who?"

"Emily. Nobody else. The Emily I know, and she's brand new."

For a moment she looks bewildered. She stares at the mirror for a long time, and I hear her mumble something.

"What was that?"

I can still barely hear her. "I said, am I pretty?"

"No. You're beautiful."

She turns from the mirror and her eyes are glistening above a radiant smile. I dab them dry with my handkerchief.

"Come on, let's settle up. You can wear this to dinner."

The salesgirl rings up each item, and when she finishes, Emily motions for her to lean down close so she can whisper. The woman listens, then nods with a smile, and Emily grasps the bag of purchases and disappears back into the fitting room. I look to the clerk in question.

"The new underwear," she tells me.

I nod as if I had known it all along.

9
Thursday, Late Afternoon

Emily's salt-encrusted sneakers ruin the effect of the new dress, so we make one more stop in the shoe department for a fancy pair of sandals. The salt-damaged sneakers are unsalvageable, and we replace those too. We leave Sears toting two huge shopping bags and two shoeboxes tied together, and find a pay phone in the main lobby of the mall. The receptionist at Family and Children's Services in Halifax connects me with Florence Pineo, and I give her my name and remind her of our earlier conversation.

"The young lady I told you about is here with me," I tell her.

"In police custody?" she asks.

"No, I found her by myself. She isn't in any trouble with the law. She just doesn't have any place to live, and I thought perhaps you could tell her what you told me yesterday. About what you can do to help her."

"Why not just bring her here?" she says.

Emily clings to every word I'm saying, nervous and apprehensive and shifting her weight from one foot to the other.

"I don't think that will work," I say evasively. "It's a confidence thing, you understand?"

"She's listening to you talk to me?"

"Yes."

"All right," the woman says, "put her on the line and I'll do my best."

Emily takes the phone and I move a few steps away. She listens in nervous silence, broken only occasionally by one-word answers, mostly the word *no*. After a few minutes she hands the receiver back to me. She stays close, anxious to hear whatever comes next.

"She wasn't very responsive, was she?" I say into the phone.

"She wouldn't tell me anything besides her first name," Pineo tells me. "I tried to be as positive as possible about where we could place her. I know of a good family that would probably take her in, at least for the short term. But she wouldn't agree to it."

"I'll have to work on that."

"Is this child a relative of yours?" she asks.

"No. I've only known her a few days."

"Then you really shouldn't be involved. You should hand her over to the police and let them take it from there. Just give them my name..."

"I can't do that," I interrupt. "It's the thing she's most afraid of."

"Why?"

"I'm not entirely sure." Emily's eyes are wide and fearful, and I smile at her reassuringly. "But she's just beginning to trust me, and if I turn her in she'll just run away again, first chance she gets. I have to go at this slowly."

"You have no legal standing, you know. You could end up in trouble with the law yourself."

I haven't thought of that. "You've been very helpful, Ms. Pineo, and I'll be in touch." I put the receiver down.

"You won't make me go, will you?" Emily asks plaintively.

"It doesn't sound so bad," I answer evasively. "She says she's found a nice family that you can live with for a while."

"I'll just run away. Like you said."

"And go where? Look, let's drop it for now. You can come back to my cabin for tonight and we'll talk some more."

She shrugs and looks down.

"Hey, come on. We've had fun so far today, right? You've got some new clothes and we're going to eat out. Let's not spoil it by worrying about tomorrow before it comes."

She raises her eyes again. "She wanted you to call the police, didn't she?"

"She suggested it. And you heard me say I wouldn't, just like I promised. Are you ready for supper now?"

"I guess."

"A little more enthusiasm would be nice. Mussel Beach won't serve Old Crabs. Except on a plate."

"Gross!" She manages a weak smile. We find the mall exit, Emily carrying the shoeboxes in her right hand and me hefting the shopping bags in my left. It's just after five when we reach Holland Avenue and head down the hill toward the marina.

Two blocks from the harbour, Holland slopes gently toward the water, presenting an unobstructed view of the dock and an array of colourful yachts and cruisers lined up against the pilings. Dozens more swing from the buoys in the centre of the harbour, a scene of indescribable beauty in the afternoon sun. Emily's worried face softens with pleasure. She steals a glance in my direction, then looks away deliberately. Her small hand snakes upward to grasp mine, surprising me into an involuntary flinch. She clings stubbornly, her face resolute, and we walk hand in hand the rest of the way to the entrance of the restaurant.

I've apparently gained her confidence, but I'm not sure what to do with it.

The waiter finds us a window booth overlooking the boat slips. He produces two irregularly shaped menus that open like the halves of a mussel shell, and asks if I want a drink before the meal. I decline, and he leaves us to read the menus.

"Look near the top of the second page," I tell Emily.

"Where?"

I reach across and tilt her menu toward me, pointing to one of the appetizers.

"See? Calamari. That's what you should order."

"Yeah, right! Besides, I bet it isn't really squid. You were kidding me, weren't you?"

"Ask the waiter when he comes back."

"You ask him."

"If I'm right, will you promise to eat it?"

"Not if it's squid!" She wrinkles her nose. "No way!"

"There are a lot of other choices," I tell her. "Caviar, escargot..."

"What's that?"

"Caviar is fish eggs. Escargot is French for snails."

She grins at me. "What kind of a sick place is this? I want a hamburger."

"You can't order hamburger in a seafood restaurant. It isn't civilized. How about fish and chips?"

"Okay. I like that."

The waiter reappears with a small notebook in hand.

"Two orders of fish and chips, please," I tell him. "And could you please explain to the young lady what calamari is?"

"Of course," he answers formally. "Only the very finest, delicately sliced squid, imported from Cape Cod and served in its own ink."

Emily's eyes grow large and I stifle a laugh. "Thank you. Maybe next time."

"Something to drink, sir?" the waiter asks.

"Coffee, please. Black."

"And for your daughter?"

Emily's astonished eyes fly to mine.

"A Coke, sweetheart?"

She gulps and nods, and the waiter makes a final notation and backs away from the booth. She leans forward.

"You let him think I was your daughter," she whispers.

"Why not? It was easier than trying to explain who you really are. Which I don't happen to know anyway."

She sits back, her eyes still wide. "But then you called me..." She can't say the word.

"That just seemed to come naturally, I guess. I told you on the boat that if I had a daughter, I'd want her to be just like you."

"I didn't think you really meant it."

"Well, I did."

She squirms in self-conscious silence, eyes cast down to her hands in her lap. Outside the window a big catboat is gliding along the pier and approaching *Amy's Pride*.

"See the boat with the twin hulls?" I ask her conversationally, hoping to ease her embarrassment. "It's called a catamaran. Really fast."

The helmsman gestures to his young crew member, a boy about Emily's age, who is straddling the rail near the bow. He fends them off against my boat's bumpers, and the cat drifts almost to a stop. The boy jumps onto my deck, holding on to his own bow rope.

"Hey!" Emily says, sitting up alertly. "He's on your boat."

"That's okay. He's just using it to get to the dock so he can tow theirs forward. It's pretty close quarters, and a wide boat like that is hard to manoeuvre with a little outboard motor."

"Is that allowed?"

"Sure. If we'd been aboard he'd have asked permission first, and I'd have said okay, so what's the difference? He won't hurt anything."

The boy crosses my deck and jumps down onto the dock. He hurries forward, towing the catamaran until its starboard hull is parallel to the last remaining slip. Then he pulls it in close.

"See how it works?" I tell her. "Sailors respect each other's property, at least most of them do, and nobody minds if they need to cross over. Sometimes they even tie up alongside other boats if there isn't enough room next to the dock."

She continues to stare out the window in wonder. In her limited experience, such mutual respect is probably in short supply.

The food and drinks arrive and we dig in. The people from the catamaran enter the restaurant and take a booth across from us. The man looks to be about my age, his son perhaps fifteen, and both are tanned and hard muscled, no doubt experienced sailors. Unlike his father's darker colouring, the boy's sandy hair and deep blue eyes suggest northern ancestry, perhaps Scandinavian. They share tall stature, however, and a squared-off jaw line that leaves little doubt that they're related.

I gesture to them as they sit down. "Nice boat."

"Thanks," the man replies. "Which one is yours?"

"That one." I point toward the dock. "The CS 30."

"Oh. Sorry my son crossed your deck. I was afraid we'd bump her if he didn't."

"Not a problem."

The waiter arrives with their menus and Emily and I return to our meals, but I soon become aware of some interest from the other booth. I catch her eye and waggle my head from side to side, raising my eyebrows dramatically.

She looks across the aisle and sees the young teen checking her out. He turns back quickly to his menu, and a bright red flush creeps up his neck. Emily hunches her shoulders and giggles softly.

"Told you that dress was a good choice," I whisper.

"Stop!" she hisses. Her cheeks brighten to a rosy pink.

For the next five minutes the two of them exchange furtive glances, interrupted only by the waiter bringing the newcomers' order. I catch his attention and ask for refills of my coffee and Emily's Coke, and we linger over them. By the time we finish, the boy has wolfed down his fish burger, and looks as if he's trying to get up the courage to speak to her.

"You could say 'Hi,' you know," I whisper across the table.

Emily blushes again. Her head swings away from the other booth, toward the window.

"Coward," I tease. I stand up and cross the aisle.

"Mind if we take a look at your boat?" I ask the man.

"My pleasure," he replies, getting out of his seat. He sticks out his hand. "I'm Art MacKenzie, and this is my son David." He inclines his head toward the boy. David offers his hand too, and I introduce myself to them both.

"And this is Emily," I say, smiling at her. "Don't hurry with your meals.

94

We can wait until you're finished."

"We're done," MacKenzie tells me. "We're going to skip dessert."

He signals for his bill, and I do the same. I leave payment on the table, and we pick up our purchases and walk outside into the warmth of a perfect midsummer evening.

At first David and Emily skirt around each other like wary cats. Finally they begin to talk and drift away down the dock. MacKenzie and I chat about the catamaran and its advantages and disadvantages, the speed of its twin hulls and the lack of space below decks. He asks about the specs on the CS, never having been aboard one, and we agree to a mutual inspection tour. We're about to go below when David trots up to us, Emily lagging uncertainly behind.

"Dad, can we go get some cones?"

"Sure. That is…" He glances at me.

"Is that okay with you, sweetheart?" I say to Emily.

She can't answer, her eyes huge and excited.

"Come on," the boy says. "My treat."

"I'll put all your stuff on the boat," I tell her, reaching out and taking the shoeboxes from her. "Take your time."

David grabs her hand and they hurry off the dock, heading toward an ice cream vendor at the intersection of Holland and Lower Water. Emily glances back over her shoulder, her expression unreadable, mildly panicked over an event as simple as having an ice cream cone with a boy her own age. After what she'd been through…

"Lovely daughter you've got there," the man says, interrupting my thoughts. "Want to see below decks?"

I nod my thanks and toss the shoeboxes and shopping bags over my boat's rail. MacKenzie leads me along the dock to the cat and we climb aboard. He answers my questions about the elaborate rigging and the neat canvas sling that bridges the two hulls, and asks if I want to go below. He pops the hatch and I start to follow him, but with an apprehensive glance up the pier toward the street. There's no sign of the children, but there are crowds wandering about the dock and going in and out of the shops. I try to convince myself that nothing can happen to her with so many people about, but demons cavort in my gut.

After a tour of the catamaran, MacKenzie accepts my offer of coffee in my boat's lounge. It takes only a few minutes to heat the water on the galley's propane stove, and we're sitting over steaming cups and discussing the relative merits of single versus twin hulls when we hear a voice outside.

"Dad, where are you?"

"Aboard the CS," MacKenzie calls out to his son. "Come on down."

The boat rocks as they climb over the rail, and Emily's head appears in the hatchway, a half-eaten ice cream cone in her hand. "Can we stay out here?" she asks me softly.

"Sure."

"We're just gonna sit on the end of the dock and finish eating."

"That's fine," I tell her. "Don't fall in." She disappears from view, and we hear light footsteps cross the cockpit. The boat sways once more as they drop over the side.

"Just the two of you?" MacKenzie asks.

"Today, yes," I tell him evasively, and then add quickly, to avoid the next obvious question, "You, too?"

"Always. David's mother has neither sea legs nor stomach. She turns green just getting into a full bath tub."

"That's tough. They've got motion sickness patches for that, you know."

"Tried them. Didn't work. But it wouldn't matter anyway. She's an avid cross-country skier in the winter, but when it's hot, her idea of a good time is sitting poolside with a tall glass and a bestseller."

"It sounds to me like she's got her priorities straight." I'm feeling apprehensive, and slide off the bench. "I think I'll just take a look and see where the kids are."

I climb topside and spot them at the very end of the pier. They're sitting on the edge, shoulder to shoulder and almost but not quite touching, their legs dangling above the water.

"They okay?" MacKenzie asks as I come down the ladder.

"Getting along fine." I pour him another cup of coffee. "Ever race your boat?" I ask conversationally.

MacKenzie's face lights up. As he launches into his passion for offshore racing, my thoughts keep drifting to Emily, to her recent past and the faceless men who've abused her. It should have hardened her beyond redemption, and yet, involved in an ordinary flirtation with a good-looking boy, she's shy and uncertain, very much a child. Maybe it's not too late for her.

Maybe it's never too late.

It occurs to me how strange it feels to be sitting and talking with this man, a simple social occasion after months of isolation on the island. If not for Emily I wouldn't be here, but it had seemed the right thing to do. She needed some ordinary human contact, and she'd never have gotten up the courage to speak to David on her own.

I drain my cup and am reaching for the pot when we hear footsteps pounding along the dock, and David screaming his father's name. I spring toward the ladder and throw myself up on deck. The boy is trying to boost Emily over the starboard rail, and she catches her foot on the jib sheet and sprawls into the cockpit. David hauls himself over the side and spins around.

"There! Him!" he shouts, gasping for breath. He points wildly at a bulky figure limping toward us from the seaward end of the dock. I've seen him before, his black styled hair and gold earring, standing in the cockpit of the big Hunter 33 a day earlier. Our eyes lock and he slides to a stop a dozen yards from the stern.

"Who the hell is that?" MacKenzie says.

"He tried to grab Emily!" David blurts. "He chased us."

MacKenzie hauls out a cell phone and flips it open.

"Wait," I say quietly.

"The police…" he begins.

"No, give me a minute." I advance toward the rail. The man on the dock is examining the stern, reading the name off the transom. He starts forward again and comes abreast of the starboard rail, staring at me and memorizing my face as I am his.

"Next time," he growls, and lumbers toward the landward end of the dock, dragging his right foot slightly. I watch until he disappears into the crowd on Lower Water Street.

"You know him?" MacKenzie asks, still clutching the cell phone.

"No."

Emily huddles in a forward corner of the cockpit. I cross over and help her up. "It's okay, he's gone," I whisper. She's breathing hard. She smoothes her dress and sits down nervously on the port locker.

"Should I call nine-one-one?" MacKenzie says.

"Won't do any good. He's gone."

"We should report it, give them a description."

"I'll do it later," I tell him. "David, what happened back there?"

The boy is still excited, and the story spills out rapidly. "We finished our cones, and we were just sitting there talking. Then that jerk came up behind us and grabbed Emily by both arms and yanked her up."

"Did he say anything?"

"He called her 'Bambi,' I think. She was trying to get loose and he raised his hand like he was gonna hit her. That's when I did it."

"Did what?"

"Stamped on his foot. He yelled something awful and dropped her, and I grabbed her hand and we ran."

"My God!" MacKenzie exclaims. "Damn perverts are everywhere these days."

"You did all right," I tell David.

"Scared the shit out of me!"

"I believe it. And we owe you." The boy is getting over his shock enough to look a little bit proud, a brave Sir Galahad facing down the dragon for his fair lady.

"I think we'd better push off," MacKenzie tells me. "Unless I can do something for you?"

"I'm just very glad you were here. David is one hell of a kid."

"I know." He turns to Emily. "Nice to meet you, young lady. I'm sorry you had such a scare."

She manages a tiny smile and a "Thank you," and the man and boy climb over the rail and head forward to their own boat. I sit down beside Emily and wait until they're out of earshot.

"Who was that guy?" I say at last.

She hunches her shoulders, close to tears. "His name's Ben. He's Lucas's pal."

"He was on that big sailboat we saw yesterday."

"I *told* you. That's Lucas's boat."

"No it's not, but he could have chartered it. Where did you see it before?"

Her eyes slip away and she doesn't answer.

"That settles it," I tell her. "You have to go someplace where no one knows you, like a foster home. That's the only way you'll be safe."

"No I won't. They'll find me anywhere."

"Emily, if I'm going to help you, you have to come clean with me."

"Let's just go, huh? He might come back."

"All right, but when we get to the cabin, you have to tell me everything. How you got to my island. Who these people are who are after you, and anything else I should know about. Deal?"

"Okay." Reluctantly.

"Good. Now help me cast off, and we'll get going."

10
Thursday Evening

We sail back to the island in the gathering dusk, the limited visibility making our entry into the cove a bit tense. Emily is warm in her new jeans and sweatshirt, the yellow sundress now carefully folded and stowed away with her other purchases. Granite-coloured clouds are sweeping up the coast, and once we moor the boat to the buoy, she helps me cover the sails and secure the hatches against the possibility of rain overnight.

Jenny greets us as we enter the cabin, accepting Emily as if she belongs there. As I light a couple of lanterns, the cat jumps up on the day bed and Emily sinks down on the cushions beside her, exhausted but mostly recovered from her fright. She scratches Jenny's chin.

"Feeling any better now?" I ask her. She nods. "You were getting pretty good with the sails. Was it fun?"

"Duh!"

"Got a limited vocabulary, have you?"

"I do okay. How about, 'I had a most pleasant day, thank you.' Is that better?"

"Well, except for the sarcastic tone of voice, that's a lot more civilized."

"I really did. And thanks for all the clothes. I've never had so much new stuff all at once."

"You're very welcome."

Jenny curls up next to her and begins to wash, and Emily strokes her back. "What's gonna happen to me now?" she asks.

"With that guy hanging around the marina, we have to find someplace far away from Bournemouth for you to stay."

"A foster home," she says sadly.

"It's the only thing I can think of. And wherever Ms. Pineo finds for you to live, you have to promise not to run away again. It's not safe for you to be wandering around by yourself."

"Why can't I just stay here with you?"

"You know that's not possible."

"Not even for one more day? Please?"

"Putting off going won't do any good."

"I suppose…" She pets the cat absently. "If I promise to stay wherever they send me, can we at least take another boat ride before I have to go?"

"All right, just once more. But it'll cost you."

Wrong thing to say, of course. Her face shuts down.

"Hey, come on. No hidden meanings. If I have to analyse every word I say before I say it, we're not going to get anywhere."

"I'm sorry," she says softly.

"Apology accepted. What I meant was, we have work to do first. We have to clean up the boat. The deck is getting grungy, and there's salt spray all over the hardware."

She brightens. "I can help with all that." I suspect she'll do anything to forestall being left with strangers.

"Something else, too," I tell her.

"What?"

"Information."

"I've already told you everything."

"Oh no, not even close. For example, how did you get here in the first place?"

"I'm too tired."

"Tough. I need to know. If you found this place, other people might too, and I don't want that."

"Why?"

"That's a long story."

She grins at me impishly. "I've got time."

"Okay, we'll make a trade, your story for mine. Go brush your teeth and get in bed. Then you'll be all set to go to sleep. *After* you tell me what I need to know, that is."

Something occurs to me. "Damn…"

"What?"

"We forgot to get another hat, and we should have bought you some pyjamas."

"That's okay. I can wear one of your wife's tee shirts to bed like last night. But I need a shower first. My hair's all salty."

"Fine. While you brush your teeth, I'll heat some water to add to the shower barrel. Now scram."

Twenty minutes later she's feeling fresh and clean, snuggled under the blanket with her damp hair wrapped in a towel. I sit on the edge of the bed.

"No more stalling now. Spill it."

She frowns. "I don't like to think about it."

"I know you don't. But I need to know what happened if I'm going to be able to help you from now on."

"If I tell you, are you gonna tell that social worker?"

I'll probably have to. In order to ensure her safety, the agency will want to know as much as possible about her situation. They'll undoubtedly require a medical exam too, and that might turn up any number of sexually transmitted diseases. If we try to conceal her background, she might not get the treatment she needs.

I decide to stall. "Why don't we wait and see how it goes? Maybe they won't ask about that."

She sighs dramatically. "Okay."

"Start with where you've been living."

"Halifax." She burrows down and pulls the blanket up tight under her chin. She stares at the far wall and her voice softens to a dull monotone. "Lucas has this place just off Gottingen Street, kinda like a rooming house, only it's a whore house. Me and six other girls live there."

"So how come you ended up way down here?"

"Lucas set up this party thing on that big boat, me and two other girls and four guys. It was the first time he ever let me go anywhere."

"What do you mean?"

"He kept me locked up in the house most of the time. I only got away once before, and he found me right away and beat the crap out of me."

"They never let you out?"

"Not by myself. The other girls were supposed to keep track of me on the boat, too."

"Girls your age?"

"No, older."

"Who was running the boat?"

"One of the guys."

"What did he look like?"

"He had on some kind of uniform, and a hat."

That had to be the charter captain. "Did he put the sails up?"

"Nope."

If they just used the engine, he wouldn't have needed any other crew members. Part of the captain's charter fee had probably been free access to the girls.

"Then what?"

"It was really like a party. We left from the Northwest Arm about noon and had lunch out on the ocean, someplace where there was this real pretty lighthouse stuck up on some big grey rocks."

That was probably Peggy's Cove. Remembering the boat, she became more animated, and her eyes found mine. "At first it was really fun. Most of the afternoon they just ran up and down the coast. Finally they stopped and put the anchor down."

"Where was that?"

"Pretty close to here. Out in the ocean, I mean, but close enough so I could still see land. Anyway, we sat out on the deck and ate sandwiches and chips and stuff, and the rest of them drank beer and wine. They wouldn't let me have any, but they gave me Cokes. Every so often one of the guys would take one of the other girls down below for a while, but they left me alone. I couldn't figure out why they even wanted me there."

"I take it you found out."

"You've got that right! When it was almost dark, one of them said something like, 'Now we're gonna play a little game.' Everybody was looking at me, and I figured out I was the main event."

"What happened?"

She turns away from me again, and her voice fades.

"Most of the sex stuff doesn't bother me much any more," she says quietly. "You know, what they make me do."

"I don't need to hear about that," I say. "Just tell me how you got away, and why."

"Things got really weird. They started calling me 'little girl,' and then 'naughty little girl' and 'bad little girl.' They said I had to go change my clothes. I had on my hooker shorts and top, and they told me to go down in the cabin and put on what was on the bed. I started to go, and this one guy was giggling, sort of high like a girl, you know? I turned around and looked at him, and he had a big wooden ruler in his hand. He started slapping it against his palm."

She squirms under the blanket, tense with the memory of terror.

"Then the guy in the uniform took this great big paddle out of a locker. It was *huge!* Scared the hell out of me. I went down into the cabin and I heard them all laughing, the girls too. There was this weird dress on the table, about my size but like something a five-year-old would wear, you know? Real short, and lots of lace and ruffles. Ruffled panties too. I didn't even touch them. I was scared to death."

"What did you do?"

"There was this wide window up near the roof at the other end of the cabin. I got it open far enough to squeeze through, and climbed up and crawled out on the deck. They were making so much noise they didn't hear me. It was dark by then, and I ducked under the rail and dropped down and started swimming."

"Weren't you afraid of the water? How far off shore were you?"

"I'm not sure, pretty far. But I can swim real good. And even though I couldn't see much in the dark, I knew which way land was. A couple of minutes later I heard them yelling, and I figured they found out I was gone. Anyway, I kept swimming and ended up here, and you know the rest."

"Did they try to come after you?"

"Nope. I was hoping they'd think I drowned."

"You could have, you know."

"Not me!" She grins. "I'm like a fish."

"Scaly and slimy, right?" She kicks me through the blanket. "You're amazing," I tell her honestly.

"Huh?"

"I mean it. That's the bravest thing I ever heard a kid do."

"Those freaks were gonna *hurt* me!"

"I know. And you saved yourself. That took real courage."

"I should have stayed. It couldn't have been any worse than what Lucas is gonna do to me when he finds me."

"You still don't get it, do you?" I pull the blanket slightly away from her chin and smooth it out. "You're never going back to him."

"He found me the last time I ran away."

"This time you've got help."

"You're just gonna dump me in some foster home," she says.

"I'm not going to *dump* you. When we get to Halifax, I'll make sure the agency takes you to an okay place. I promise. That's the best way."

103

"How are we gonna get there?"

"You can have that boat ride first. Then we'll catch a bus into the city."

"Don't you have a car?"

"I sold it. I haven't needed one since I moved out here."

She rubs her eyes, sleep beginning to overtake her. "Where do we get the bus?"

"In Bournemouth."

"No!" She sits up straight.

"Hey, it's okay. It's a big place, and we won't be there long. Even if we run into that Ben guy again, I won't be more than two feet away from you the whole time. I won't let him get near you."

Her eyes bore into mine, and for the first time I can read real hope there. On impulse I lean forward and kiss her forehead lightly.

"Are you sleepy yet?"

"Not any more."

"You will be. Want to hear a story?"

"Oh sure. How about Goldilocks? Or Jack and the Beanstalk?"

"Sarcasm is not pretty, smart aleck. I was thinking more along the lines of how Amy and I got Jenny."

"Okay, yeah!" She brightens and sits up, unwinding the towel and shaking her head. Her hair swirls about her ears, almost dry.

"She's not just any ordinary cat, you know," I continue. "The vet told me she's a Norwegian Forest Cat."

"What's that?"

"Just what she looks like. Lots of long hair, short front legs and a big, solid body. And very sweet and gentle."

Her eyes crinkle. "And you went all the way to Norway to get her? Did you swim there?"

"Do you want to hear this story, or not?"

"I'm sorry. Go on." She settles back, propped up on her elbows, and pulls the blanket up to her shoulders.

"We found her stranded on a floating branch in the middle of the Gaspereau River when she was just a kitten."

"You're kidding!"

"Nope. We were out hiking near the hydro station one day in early spring. The water was high from the winter runoff, and some of the riverbank had washed away, taking a couple of dead trees and debris with it. We were crossing the bridge upstream when Amy spotted a pile of brush heading toward the dam. Jenny was hanging on to a branch right in the middle of it, meowing at the top of her lungs."

"Where did she come from?"

"We never found out."

Emily tries to stay awake as I embroider my kitten-rescuing tale, but after a few minutes she droops and her eyes sag shut. I ease her down on the pillow and turn the lantern down low. I'm nearly out of the bedroom when her voice brings me up short.

"You broke your promise."

"What?"

"You said we'd trade. About why you're living all alone and won't let anyone come to your island."

"I'll tell you tomorrow. Go to sleep."

"You'd better..." Her voice trails off and I creep out of the room and sit down at the table.

The weight of the problem rests like a black cloud over the day. Now that I know how she got to the island, everything is changed. It's only a matter of time before the pimps figure out where she escaped to, and I have to head them off.

There aren't many options. I could report the prostitution ring to the police, but they probably already know about it and tolerate it. I've heard the sex trade called a "victimless crime," impossible to stamp out and best just simply contained as much as possible. The only real victims are the girls themselves, and the prevailing attitude seems to be that they get what they deserve.

I keep coming back to the same conclusion: foster care, shifting the responsibility for protecting her to people with more resources than I have. After the episode with the man on the dock, I can't afford to underestimate the opposition. To them, Emily is just a piece of property, and I can't put her beyond their reach permanently without official help.

11
Friday

It rains in the night and the world feels new in the morning, cleanly scrubbed and smelling fresh. The eaves drip musically, and the first rays of the sun are painting the eastern end of the island with gold as I rise and make up the daybed. After starting the coffee, I mix plenty of fresh milk and juice and eat a bowl of cornflakes. Once the percolator finishes its work, I pour a mug full of coffee and take it out on the deck.

The sun is well above the horizon when I hear the door creak open, and Emily sticks her head out.

"What's for breakfast?"

"Same as yesterday, same as tomorrow. Corn flakes and powdered drinks."

"Boring."

"We'll stop somewhere on the way to Halifax and have lunch. Something special."

She freezes in the doorway, then backs up and lets the door swung shut. A few minutes later I find her inside seated at the table, finishing the last of her cereal. She won't look at me.

"I know you don't want to go," I tell her, "but there just isn't anything else we can do. You can't hide out here forever."

"Why not?" She fixes me with a hostile glare. "You do!"

"That's different." I grasp a chair back and reverse it, straddling the seat with my chin resting on my folded arms.

"How is it different?" she challenges me.

"You have your whole life ahead of you."

"And yours is over, I suppose. Thirty-seven is *so* ancient."

"You're a rude kid, you know that?" I'm suddenly unaccountably angry, and my voice shows it. I shove the chair away and stride into the bathroom, slamming the door behind me.

By the time I shower and shave and get dressed, Emily is gone. Through the window I see her sitting on the end of the dock, hunched forward with her legs dangling. She swings them slowly back and forth.

I'm angry at myself for letting her get under my skin. She can't possibly know what I'm feeling, or why I retreated to the island after the accident. She has no idea what it's like to lose someone, as I had lost Amy.

Or maybe she does.

She doesn't look up as I wander slowly out onto the dock. "May I sit down?"

"Why would you want to? I'm rude, remember?"

I lower myself down beside her.

"Well, you are."

"I'm sorry, but you make me so *mad* sometimes."

"Why?"

She thinks it over. "I don't know."

"That makes two of us."

Time passes. A fish jumps in the middle of the cove, and wavelets spread in wide concentric circles, finally touching the pilings of the dock. The sunlight sparkles on the ripples. Too pretty a day for what I have to do.

"Anyway," I tell her, "you were sort of right, rude or not."

She doesn't respond.

"Maybe I have been hiding. A little."

More silence.

"Hey, are you in there?"

She turns a serious face toward me. "When are you gonna tell me what she was like?"

"Why do you want to know?"

"Because then I'll know you a little better."

"How old *are* you, anyway? Kids aren't supposed to think about things like that."

"I'm a genius."

"That reminds me, how much school have you missed?"

"Half a year. I ran away from Uncle Frank right after Christmas. Some Christmas *that* was!"

"Okay, you can make that up pretty easy. Where did you go to school?"

"I'm not going back there!"

"I didn't mean that. The agency will need your records so you can start again somewhere else."

"Where?"

"I don't know yet. Did you like school?"

"It was okay. I got good marks."

"That'll be the first step to becoming a regular kid again," I tell her. "And pretty soon what happened to you will just be like a bad dream."

She toys with the end of the tender's painter. "What was Amy like?"

"Don't change the subject."

"That's what you just did!"

I take a deep breath, trying not to get annoyed.

"Okay. She was wonderful. She looked a whole lot like you, except her hair was much lighter, and you've got a lot more of it. She had deep brown eyes, just like yours, and really fair skin. And when she laughed, the sound of it made everybody happy. She was…"

Suddenly I can't go on. We sit quietly for several minutes. Then she slides over close to me. She reaches out shyly and touches my hand, and I turn it over and take hold of hers gently. She leans her head against my shoulder, and I feel strangely comforted.

Who's the adult here?

"When are we going to clean up the boat?" she asks at last.

"We can start any time." There's a large tin can floating in an inch or two of rainwater at the bottom of the tender. "First we have to bail this thing out."

"I'll do it," she says, getting up. She climbs into the dinghy and balances on the middle seat. She squats down and begins scooping the water out and tossing it over the side.

"I'll get the rest of the stuff we need," I tell her, getting up to return to the cabin. I gather up some sponges and a mop and dig out some detergent from under the sink. When I reach the deck again, she's working hard at bailing, oblivious to me.

Busy. And safe, at least for now.

I still have no idea what I'm going to do.

* * *

The little diesel bubbles energetically as we head for the mouth of the cove, the first leg of our trip to Halifax. I throttle back as we come to the first bend in the S-shaped channel. Emily is perched on the bow, trying to enjoy the boat in spite of what awaits her at the end of the voyage. She has on a new pair of shorts from our shopping expedition, pale blue with wide cuffs. The tails of her loose cotton top are tied together high above her flat little belly. She looks about eight.

"There's rocks down there," she calls back to me. "Want me to be lookout again?"

"You can if you want, but I know where most of them are."

"I thought so. You weren't really gonna hit that sandbar yesterday, were you?"

"I might have. You warned me just in time."

"Yeah, right." I hadn't fooled her after all.

"I always go pretty slow through here," I tell her. "With the tide low like this, we could tear the bottom out of the keel."

"How do you remember where all the rocks are?"

"Experience. And a little bit of good luck. It's easier when the tide is high. I was in a powerboat the first time my brother and I came in here. It didn't draw much water, so we went right over the worst of the rocks. A few more times in and out, and I memorized where the bad ones are."

We glide around the top of the backward S, and the open ocean comes slowly into view. Unlike the previous day the sea looks dead calm, and there's no wind at all from any direction as we emerge from the narrow channel. Among the pleasure boats plying back and forth across the bay, there's no sign of the distinctive outline of the big Hunter 33.

"We travel by stinkpot today, I guess," I tell her.

"What's that mean?"

"There isn't any wind to drive the sails, so we have to use the engine."

"Why did you call it a stinkpot?"

"Real sailors don't think much of engines. Noisy and smelly, they say, whereas sail power is quiet and completely clean. Therefore, stinkpot."

"Less work, though. All you have to do is steer."

"How many times do I have to tell you?" I draw myself up pompously, trying to make her laugh. "It's 'man the helm.' 'Steer' is for cars."

"Steer," she mutters under her breath.

"I heard that!"

She grins up at me. "What happens if you shut the motor off?"

"It's an engine, not a motor. We'd coast a bit and slow down. The tide's just starting to come in, so we'd drift in the general direction of the shore."

"What's the difference?"

"What do you mean?"

"Motor. Engine."

"Motors run by electricity. Engines run by heat."

"Who says?"

"Everybody who knows anything."

"Motor," she mumbles.

"Engine!"

The surface of the water is almost mirror calm. *Amy's Pride* cuts a frothy wake through the gentle swells as we clear the eastern end of the island, close to her top speed of six knots.

"Let's do it," she says.

"What?"

"Shut the *engine* off."

"Why?"

"We aren't in a hurry, are we?"

"Not really. We can get the last bus at three and still be in Halifax before the agency closes. I can call ahead and let them know we're coming."

"So let's coast a little."

I shut the ignition down, and the soft rush of water under the hull replaces the noise of the diesel as we lose way. Sails down and stern to the tide, *Amy's Pride* floats serenely on the glassy surface.

"Can I go in?" she asks.

"What, swim?"

"Uh, huh."

"Sure, if you want to."

She starts to take off her tee shirt, then stops. She looks around at me, blushes, and pulls it back down again. She sits on the port locker and plays with the halyard that hangs down under the forward panel of the dodger. I busy myself with inconsequential jobs, stowing a stray bumper and coiling the jib sheets around the winches, checking the wheel periodically to keep the boat stern on to the tide.

"Decide not to go in?" I ask gently.

"There might be sharks," she says quietly.

"They don't eat Old Crabs."

She makes a face, then squints her eyes against the glare of the sun and gazes morosely out over the bow. I sit down next to her.

"Want to take another quick shopping trip before we go to Halifax?"

110

"What for?"

"Swimsuit, maybe?"

She turns to look at me. "You don't miss much, do you?"

"I'm a genius, too."

She twists the lines. "I don't know why it bothered me. With all those guys Lucas made me undress for..."

"Stop."

"Huh?"

"I said stop. That was a different Emily, somebody named Bambi, and she's gone now. The new Emily is modest and shy, and I like that."

She looks away.

"So how about it? Shall we stop at Sears again before we catch the bus?"

"No."

"Why not?"

"This is my last boat ride with you. I won't need a bathing suit after that."

"Maybe your new foster parents will have a pool."

"Yeah, right. Rich people take in little sluts like me all the time."

I decide to let that pass. The boat dips a bit to starboard, and I gesture over the rail at a series of gently undulating waves.

"See those ripples?" I ask. She nods. "Know where they came from?" A side-to-side shake. "Some big ship probably, way out over the horizon, out of sight."

"You're kidding. Waves can't travel that far."

"Sure they can. Energy never disappears. It just changes, and it has to go somewhere. That's a principle of physics."

"But..."

"A boat makes waves, and the waves push against the water and make more waves, and so on all the way to shore. They keep going in a straight line unless they run into something along the way. Then they get deflected and go somewhere else."

She puzzles over the concept. "You're trying to teach me something, aren't you?"

"Am I?"

"Like yesterday. All that stuff about what I am isn't what I do. And the stars the other night. You're always doing that."

"So what am I teaching you this time?"

"I don't know."

"Are you like a wave?"

"Me?"

"Uh, huh."

"I don't get it."

"What's been pushing you along this past six months?"

"Lucas!" She spits out the name.

"And what did you run into?"

She thinks about that for a moment. "You?"

"Me. And now you can't keep on going along the same way. You've bounced off me and changed direction. Now look out at the water again."

She gazes over the rail at the still surface.

"Where's that wave?" I ask her.

"Gone," she says quietly.

"Not really, just somewhere else. And who can tell, maybe somewhere better. Like you will be soon."

Several long minutes pass. Then she slides over close and tucks her hand into the crook of my elbow, and we sit quietly looking out over the motionless ocean.

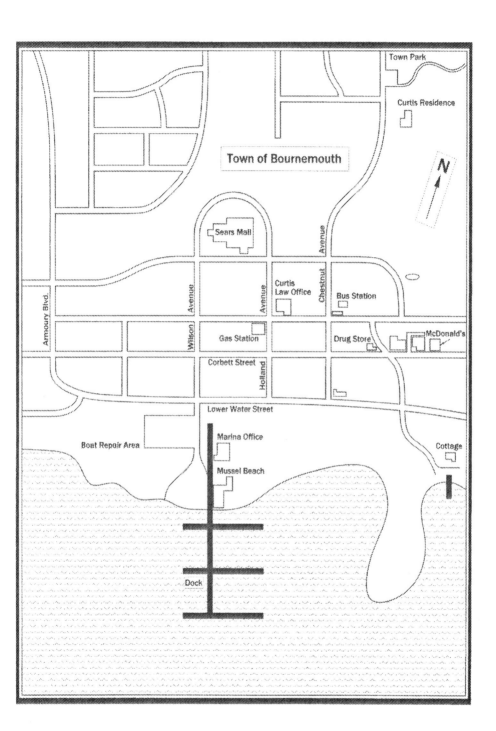

12
Friday Afternoon

E mily sticks to my side like a Band-Aid as we leave *Amy's Pride* at the marina and head for the Acadian Lines bus station several blocks away. I'm lugging a duffel bag, half filled with her new clothes. It contains everything she owns, the only things she has to take with her into her new life.

"Want some lunch?" I ask her.

"Can't we just go?" she pleads. "I don't like it here."

"Okay. The next bus comes at two o'clock. We can take that one and have a late lunch in Halifax."

That satisfies her, and we hurry uptown and reach the station five minutes later. Emily sits nervously on a bench in one corner while I find a pay phone and call Florence Pineo once more.

"I'm glad you decided to do the right thing," she says after I explain that we're coming. Her tone irritates me, but I manage to keep my annoyance from showing.

She's just doing her job.

"Where can we meet you?" I ask.

She gives me the address. "Does the child have any possessions?"

"Just clothes," I reply.

"Good. That will make things easier. I have a home lined up and waiting for her."

"Where is it?"

"We don't give out that information."

"Ms. Pineo, I have a certain responsibility to this child. As I told you before, she trusts me, and I promised to make sure she'll be going somewhere

114

safe."

"She will be. This home is one of our best; the family's been working with us for over ten years. Forgive me, but I know nothing about you, and since you're not the child's relative, we must ask that you end your involvement when we take over."

I'm not likely to make any more headway over the phone, and decide to renew my argument when we get to Halifax. It will be easier to plead my case when I'm face to face with her.

"All right," I tell her, "we're going to take the two o'clock bus into the city. We should be at your office by about four."

"We'll be expecting you," she says, and as I hang up I'm beginning to feel uneasy about the whole process. Emily is about to disappear into a bureaucracy, one no doubt staffed by some caring people but bound by rules and regulations that don't always make room to take the human element into account. I would somehow have to make her understand that I wasn't just abandoning her.

Emily stands up and follows me as I walk to the ticket booth. "Well?" she asks.

"It's all set. They have someplace for you to live."

"Where?"

"I don't know yet. We'll find out when we get there."

I hope.

We buy two tickets for the run to Halifax and leave the cramped office to sit down in the outdoor enclosure and wait, shielded from the sun along with a quartet of other passengers. Emily huddles in a corner and withdraws into herself, and I mentally review my conversation with Florence Pineo.

I keep trying to see the situation from her point of view. Like many social workers, she's no doubt overworked and understaffed, burdened with too many disadvantaged children and too few places to house and care for them. The fact that she already has a home lined up proves that she's making a special effort in this case, and I suppose I should be grateful. Nevertheless I feel increasingly apprehensive, fearing that the agency may treat Emily more as a statistic than as an individual with unique needs and problems. Two days ago I wouldn't have cared, but that was before I began to see her as a person and not just an annoyance.

My watch reads nearly five past two, and I'm wondering how soon the bus will arrive when Emily suddenly clutches my arm in a death grip and shrinks down beside me. She's staring at a new arrival, the man she called Ben, who is approaching the shelter from the ticket office. He enters the enclosure and takes a seat at the opposite end, paying no attention to us, but I know it's no accident that he's waiting for the same bus. We've probably been followed since we left the marina.

"Stay cool," I whisper to her.

"Let's go back," she begs, tears in her eyes. "Please?"

"If we do that he'll just follow us, maybe all the way to the island. That'll be worse. We have a better chance of losing him once we get to the city."

"No. He'll tell Lucas where we are. He'll get me!"

"Just take it easy. I won't let that happen."

The bus arrives and discharges half a dozen passengers. The driver steps down and enters the ticket office, and the four who are waiting with us queue up near the door. Ben lounges nonchalantly in place, waiting for us to make a move. The driver returns and lets the others get on board.

"Come on," I tell Emily, and she clings to my arm as we make our way onto the bus. The right hand row of seats nearest the door is vacant and I steer her into it, sliding the duffel bag onto the floor at my feet. Ben waits until we're settled, then rises indolently and saunters over to board. He passes us without a sidelong glance and heads down the aisle close to the back, taking a seat next to a window on the left side.

"What're we gonna do?" Emily whispers urgently.

"I've got an idea," I tell her. "Be ready to move fast when I say so."

The driver is sorting through some papers on a clipboard, making notes. I check my watch again—nearly ten after two—as a late-comer rushes from the ticket office to join us, laden down with a large backpack. He drops into a seat halfway to the back and stows the backpack on the floor, partially blocking the aisle.

The ticket agent emerges from his office and climbs the steps to speak with the driver. I glance over my shoulder and find Ben gazing out the window to his left. As the agent steps down and the driver reaches for the handle to close the door, I seize Emily's hand and the duffel bag and plunge down the steps, dragging her behind me and squeezing through the narrow opening.

Inside the bus Ben rushes forward and stumbles over the backpack in the aisle. The driver glares at me and yanks the door shut, and pulls away from the curb abruptly. The bus joins a stream of traffic and I hold my breath, expecting it to pull over again, but it continues on its way.

"Is he gone?" Emily asks, peering around the wall of the enclosure.

"Yes. The driver wouldn't stop to let him off."

"What're we gonna do now?"

"We can't take the next bus," I tell her. "Ben might expect us to do that and be waiting for us in Halifax. I think we'll have to see if we can find a taxi that will take us that far instead."

"God, I'm so scared."

"I know, but you're safe now. And I think we'd better get something to eat before we go. You'll feel better if you get something inside you."

"I'm never gonna feel better."

"Come on, we'll head downtown and find some fast food. We'll have better luck getting a taxi down that way, too."

We leave the bus station and find Corbett Street, heading for the string of fast food restaurants a block north of Lower Water Street. The McDonald's franchise seems to be the least crowded, and we place our order and take our trays to a seat near the window.

Emily eats in silence, picking listlessly at her food and glancing nervously at the crowds of late-afternoon shoppers passing by outside the window. Suddenly her face turns deathly pale, her eyes wide and her lips bloodless. She's staring at something over my shoulder. I'm about to turn and look when she claps her hand over her mouth, scrambles out of her chair, and bolts toward the ladies' room.

Lounging against a lamp post in front of the restaurant is a flashily dressed macho type who can only be Lucas the pimp, holding a cell phone to his ear. He and Ben are apparently comparing notes. Six feet tall, indolent and supremely confident, he grins at me as he snaps the phone shut, then tosses me a sarcastic kiss with his obscene Mick Jagger lips.

He straightens up and adjusts the lapels of his sports jacket as I approach the window for a better look, memorizing his face. He's almost a caricature of a big city gangster, inspecting his fingernails casually and slicking back his hair, John Travolta in *Grease*. He glances at his watch, waves to me sardonically, and saunters off down the street.

My appetite is gone. I dump the remaining half of our meals in the nearest waste bin except for Emily's Coke, and hoist the duffel bag onto my shoulder. Over the next five minutes several customers move in and out through the ladies' room door, but there's no sign of Emily. People come and go, and when it seems the room is just about empty, I stop a woman on her way out.

"Excuse me, did you happen to notice a young teen in there? Blue shorts, lots of dark hair?"

"I didn't see her," she says. "I was alone, unless she's in one of the stalls."

She walks off and I open the door part way and call in softly.

"Emily? It's okay, he's gone."

There are scuffling noises in the stall farthest from the door. A half minute later she peers around the edge of the door, her face pasty and her eyes red and terrified. She creeps toward me.

"Lose your lunch?" I ask. She nods. "We'd better go, then."

She shrinks part way back into the rest room. Two young girls, about eight and ten, shoulder their way past her. Once they're inside one of them says, "Shut the door." I reach out and take Emily's hand and draw her into the corridor.

"Shake it off," I tell her. "He wants you to be scared. Show him you're not."

"I am! He's gonna beat the shit out of me!" She swallows convulsively, the sour smell of vomit on her breath.

"What, right here? With all these people around? No way! You're with me, and I won't let him." I hand her the Coke. "Here, drink a little of this. It'll take the nasty taste out of your mouth."

She sips a bit through the straw, chokes a little, then drinks some more.

"You don't know him," she says, panicky. "He's..."

"I know his type. He's a coward. Thinks he's a big shot because he beats up on girls and children."

Her eyes dart desperately around the room. "No, he..."

"Yes!" I say sharply. "Look at me!"

Her head snaps back, trembling, eyes dilated.

"Nothing is going to happen to you," I say calmly and deliberately. "You're in charge now, not him."

"No I'm not!"

"You are. *We* are. You're not alone, and you don't have to be afraid. You're never going back to him. I'm going to make sure of that."

She heaves a great sigh. "We can't go out there."

"Sure we can. I'll bet he won't even try to bother us. And if he does, I can handle him."

I'm a lot less confident than I sound. I'm no street fighter and Lucas probably is, but with so many people on the street I don't expect him to try anything violent. The main problem is how to keep him from following us to the boat.

Emily is still shaking with fear. "Oh my God! I can't..."

118

"Hey!"

"What?"

"It wasn't you he had before. It was Bambi. Emily is someone different, and she has a friend now."

She gulps down the rest of the Coke, struggling to bring herself under control. Through the front window of the restaurant we can see up and down the street for a block in either direction. The pimp is nowhere in sight.

"Coast is clear," I tell her. "We can go now."

She drops her empty cup on a table and clings desperately to my arm as we head for the door. She cringes fearfully as I push it open.

"You're letting him win," I say.

She stares at me, terrorized.

"Let go of me and stand up straight. Stick your chin out. Show him you're not afraid."

Her eyes dart wildly. She's almost in shock, panic-stricken and close to collapse. I lean down close and whisper in her ear.

"Okay, you can hold my hand, then. We're going to walk straight out, and I'll show you why you don't have to be afraid of him. Okay?"

No response.

"Okay!" I say firmly. I pry her off my arm and take one fragile, ice-cold hand in mine, and we leave the restaurant. Traffic on Corbett Street is heavy and slow, and clusters of shoppers pass in both directions. There's still no sign of Lucas.

We try to blend in amid the tourists and bargain hunters that mill in and out of the shops. Emily stumbles along, craning her neck to peer into every storefront. At the next intersection the traffic light holds us up, and when the *Walk* sign flashes, we join the wave that starts across the street.

As we reach the opposite curb, Lucas steps out of a drug store on the corner. Emily blanches and tries to shrink back, but I hold her hand tightly, staring the man down as we walk past him, my heart pounding wildly in my chest. Emily ducks her head but can't help looking at him. He grins at her and puckers his lips.

"Hey, Bambi sweetheart!"

His hand snakes out, fingers rubbing together in invitation, and I feel her sag at my side. Her face goes blank, her eyes dull, and she sways away from me. If I let go of her hand, I know she'll go to him. She can't help herself.

Lucas and I lock eyes. Slowly and deliberately I shake my head back and forth, telling him silently that he can't have her. The crowds surge around and between us, oblivious to what's happening. He leans back against the wall of the drug store and regards me calmly. He points to Emily, and then to himself. Again I shake my head. He shrugs and taps his watch.

"Now or later," he says softly. "But it's gonna happen."

He pushes off and swaggers down Corbett, stopping a dozen paces later to stand idly next to the entrance to a convenience store. Emily is lethargic, resigned.

"We're going to outsmart him," I tell her.

"We can't get away," she says tiredly. "He's just gonna follow us."

"That's what he thinks."

I stride off down the street, ignoring Lucas as we pass him, Emily stumbling at my side. He slouches away from the building and falls in step twenty yards behind us. Back near the restaurant a taxi angles into the curb and discharges two passengers. The traffic light at Chestnut Avenue changes from amber to red and I hold back, drifting along among a small group of window shoppers.

The cab passes us and pulls up in line, third from the light. On the opposite corner a woman raises her hand to signal the driver, and he flips on his turn signal. The light begins to change again and I break into a run, dragging Emily along with me, the duffel bag bouncing crazily against my leg. We reach the cab as it starts forward and race across the intersection just behind it. The woman reaches out for the door handle, and I push rudely in front of her and wrench it open, shoving Emily inside and tossing the duffel on the floor. The woman shouts at me, and the driver stares at us suspiciously.

"Sick child!" I bark.

The woman steps back, momentarily confused, and I scramble inside and slam the door behind me. Lucas is running across the intersection toward us. I draw Emily in close against my side and shout at the driver.

"Hospital! For God's sake, hurry!"

He nods and jerks the car in gear. Lucas reaches for the door handle, half a second too late as the driver bulls his way into the traffic.

"Where are we going?" Emily whispers shakily.

"Just away from downtown." Behind us, Lucas is racing back across the intersection, waving wildly at another approaching cab.

"Why did you say the hospital?"

"Because it got us moving fast."

"I thought we were going to Halifax," she says.

"Not any longer."

120

Our cab threads its way through the traffic, heading for the intersection with Wilson Avenue.

"Take a left here," I tell the driver.

"The hospital's straight ahead, Mac," he says, driving through the intersection.

"I know. Take us to the waterfront instead. Down by the marina."

The driver pulls over next to the curb and turns to face me. "Listen, what the hell's going on here?"

I swivel around to look out the back window. Another cab is stopped at the light at Wilson.

"We're being followed," I tell the driver urgently.

"Says you. Nobody's gonna hurt no kid in my hack."

"Ask her!"

He looks at Emily. "What about it, kid? Is this guy legit?"

"He's my dad," she says meekly, clinging to my arm. "I'm in trouble. Some guys are after me."

"You're sure?"

"Please, can we just go?" she begs.

He looks back and forth between us, then makes up his mind and yanks the cab away from the curb, cutting off a delivery van. The light changes behind us, and the other cab spurts forward.

"Is that them back there?" the driver asks, looking in his rear view mirror, and I nod to him. "Hang on."

He floors the gas, and two blocks later whips the wheel and careens around a corner, north onto Armoury Boulevard. The other cab is still stuck behind the van as we take the next right and race down a one-way street.

Emily clutches my arm as the driver blasts his horn and bullies another car over to the curb. He runs an amber light, squirts between a parked car and a pickup, and brakes hard for a quick dash through a corner gas station parking lot, coming out going south on Holland Avenue. Another right, and we're heading back toward the harbour on Lower Water Street.

"We've lost him," he tells me, slowing to match the pace of the traffic. "Now how about some answers? This could cost me my license if anyone caught my tag number and reports me."

"We owe you," I say, looking anxiously behind for any sign of the other cab. There's nothing but a couple of cars and a pickup behind us, and a bus a block away.

"So what are you, some kind of James Bond?"

"Just a father protecting his daughter." I lean forward and drop a wad of bills on the seat beside him.

He glances at the money, then accelerates toward Wilson Avenue and slides to a stop opposite the marina. He swings around to look at Emily.

"You gonna be okay, kid?"

She's almost over her shock, beginning to rally. "I'm fine. I'm not scared any more. My dad will take care of me."

"Okay," he says reluctantly. I retrieve the duffel from the floor and we pile out and start running toward the dock, her hand firmly clasped in mine.

"You all right now?" I ask as we pound up to *Amy's Pride*.

"Getting there," she pants.

I toss the duffel over the rail and boost her over the side. I throw off the lines and jump into the cockpit. The diesel springs to life and I jam it in gear and crank the wheel hard, hauling us away from the pier and out into the bay. Emily peers over the transom, nervously watching for any sign of Lucas.

"Guess we made it," she says at last.

"He won't know where to look for us. Ben probably told him about the boat, but he doesn't know about the island."

"What're we gonna do now?"

"Take some time to think," I tell her. "We don't dare go back because he'll be watching for us."

"How am I gonna get to Halifax, then?"

"By boat, I guess. Takes longer, that's all."

She slumps into one corner at the transom, dishevelled and worn out from the wild escape.

I try to cheer her up. "Good acting back there."

"Huh?"

"That 'He's my dad' routine in that cute little voice. The cab driver would have had the cops on us if you hadn't pulled it off."

" 'Desperate times call for desperate measures'. "

I stare at her in disbelief. "What did you say?"

"I know lots of quotes. You think I'm dumb, but I'm not."

"I never said that."

"I read a lot."

"Obviously."

"Not much else to do during the day when you work nights," she mutters.

"Stop saying things like that!" I shout at her. "Damn it, that's all over now!"

She recoils and shrinks back against the rail. I grip the wheel tightly, knuckles white on the rim, and set a course for the east end of Farrell Island. Emily slips off the locker and edges around me, heading for the hatch. She climbs over the sill and disappears down the ladder.

My stomach is churning, my heart racing and adrenaline still pumping in my veins. I'm sickened to be living in a world that could do to an innocent child what has happened to her, but instead of supporting her after a gut-wrenching experience, I'd turned my rage into a weapon to further shatter her self-esteem. Abruptly the anger drains out of me, replaced by guilt over my outburst. I throttle back and turn the boat into the wind. No sound comes from below, and I lean in through the hatch and call down.

"Emily? I'm sorry I yelled at you."

No answer.

"Can you come up here, please?"

In the dim light below she shuffles into the galley from the forward berth, lost and lonely and miserable. She reaches the ladder and climbs up slowly, her face ravaged by tears. As she steps over the sill, I gather her up in a close hug. She sobs wretchedly, burying her face in my shirt.

"I'm sorry," I whisper softly, stroking her hair. Her shoulders heave, and her breath sobs in her throat.

"It wasn't really you I was mad at," I tell her. "I guess it just hurts me to think about what happened to you when you were with Lucas. I was angry at him, and I took it out on you."

She pulls away from me. "It's okay."

"No, it's not. I'm ashamed of how I acted, and I'll try not to let it happen ever again."

"It doesn't matter." She wipes her eyes on her sleeve and stares off across the harbour. "Are we gonna take the boat to Halifax now?"

"No, it's too late. We're going back to the island. Anyway, we need a new plan."

She seems to accept that, accept whatever is going to happen to her, her spirit almost crushed. I put the boat in gear and swing back toward home.

"Want to steer?" I ask her.

"Man the helm," she says softly.

"Right."

She steps in beside me at the wheel and I put my arm gently around her shoulders. Loneliness shared, but not halved.

* * *

The cabin is warm when we arrive back at the cove, the last rays of the sun still above the hill to the west, but Emily shivers inside her sweatshirt. Her face is drawn and pinched. I throw some kindling and a small log into the wood stove and light them. We skip supper, our stomachs still upset from two narrow escapes.

"Anything you'd like to do this evening?" I ask her as she sinks into a corner of the daybed and pulls a blanket over her knees. "I've got some cards, and there's a Scrabble game around here somewhere."

"No thanks. You're not going anywhere, are you?"

"Of course not."

"What if he comes here?"

"Lucas? No chance. He doesn't know where we are."

She turns away from me. "I just want to stay here forever, then."

"Remember what I told you before? You can't hide from life. We have to solve your problem once and for all, so you won't have to be afraid to go places again."

"So are you gonna try to take me to Halifax again tomorrow?"

"That didn't work out so well the last time, did it?" I'm disgusted with my own failure, and the danger I put her in.

"You sound mad," she says quietly.

She's right, of course, and I soften my tone. "I am, but not at you."

"So what's gonna happen to me?"

"Let me think about it for a while, okay?"

I make some coffee for myself and offer her some cookies and milk, but she refuses them. I try to tempt her with a card game again, but she just huddles miserably against the cushions, staring blankly into space.

"Long day," I say at last. "Want to head for bed?"

"I guess."

"Shower first. You stink."

I'm hoping the insult will provoke some response, but she merely pries herself off the daybed and pads into the bathroom.

"Want me to heat up some water?" I call after her.

Muffled, from behind the door: "Doesn't matter."

"It won't take long."

She shuffles out again and sits down at the table, arms folded against the chill within her despite the heat rising from the wood stove. I take a large iron

124

kettle from under the sink, fill it three-quarters full, and put it on top of the stove. Then I carry half a dozen bucketsful from the pump to top up the shower barrel, leaving just enough room for the hot water to come.

While we wait for the water to boil I retrieve my journal from the bedroom and sit down opposite her at the table. Halfway through is a poem I especially like, hopeful lines of sunshine and rainbows, written on that rarity of days when some small measure of optimism pushed aside my despair for just a moment.

"Want me to read to you?" I venture.

She shrugs. "I probably wouldn't understand it."

"I thought you were a genius."

"I don't feel too smart tonight."

"Okay. Maybe some other time." I let the journal fall shut, my own interest waning. "Sure you don't want to play Scrabble?" A small head shake. "Arm wrestle?" She looks at me quizzically. "We could go outside and wash an elephant."

She's in no mood for humour. "Is the water hot enough yet?" she asks listlessly.

"I'll see." Steam is beginning to curl from around the cover of the kettle. "By the time you get undressed and brush your teeth, it'll be ready."

She rises and wanders into the bathroom. A few minutes later I lift the kettle and knock on the door. She opens it, wrapped in a towel, and I enter and pour the hot water into the barrel.

"This should feel pretty good," I tell her. She nods wearily and I leave her to bathe, shutting the door behind me. A few minutes later she emerges and drifts into the bedroom. Not long afterward I hear her call my name, and enter the bedroom to see what she wants.

"What's up?"

"Still want to read to me?" she asks. She's buried deep beneath the blanket, her hair fanned out on the pillow and a hint of colour back on her cheeks.

"Sure. Hang on." I retrieve the journal from the table, pick up one of the kitchen chairs, and carry it in so I can sit beside the bed.

"What do you want to hear?"

"Anything. Another poem."

"I've got one about a cat I used to own. Her name was Socs."

"Did she have white feet?"

"Yes, and that's in the poem, but that's not the reason for her name. She was S-o-c-s, not s-o-c-k-s."

"I don't get it."

"Amy named her after Socrates, the Greek philosopher. Because she was so smart."

"That's weird."

"Want to hear it?"

"Okay, sure."

"Her name was Socs," I begin.

> *Not socks for feet,*
> *as would befit a cat with paws of white,*
> *but Socs for Socrates, of course,*
> *fine feline fountain pouring forth*
> *the wisdom of her kind.*

I finish the poem, thirty-seven lines of speculation about the ancient lore all cats must pass along to each new generation of kittens. Some of the images make her smile and one even provokes a small giggle, which was my intent.

"Again, please?" she asks when I finish. I repeat it, then move on to some of the others, sharing them with another person for the first time, but carefully avoiding the ones that cry out of pain and loss. At last I reach the final page.

"Time to sleep," I tell her, closing the journal and standing up.

"Stay with me?"

"I'll be right outside your door."

"I mean in here. Please? I'm scared."

Dragons in the closet, monsters under the bed.

I collect my blanket and pillow from the daybed and spread them out on the floor next to her, risking a stiff, sore back in the morning for the sake of helping her feel secure. She wants to talk at first, but quickly gives in to the exhaustion of the day and drifts off. I'm not so lucky.

Twice during the night I hear her cry out, restless with dreams, her brow a wrinkled frown. The demons are back, Ben and Lucas and six months of confinement with an assortment of amoral freaks using her body to satisfy their own sick appetites. So far I haven't come close to breaking through the shell of fear that holds her captive.

13
Saturday

The sun is well above the trees when I finally awake the next morning. Emily lies as still as death, exhausted both physically and emotionally from the day before. A few hot embers smoulder in the stove and the air is dense and stuffy, so I open a window to admit the cool morning breeze. I have the coffee brewing and breakfast set out before she finally emerges, drowsy and pink from the overheated cabin and somewhat groggy. Her tee shirt is wrinkled and creased, her hair tousled.

"Hi," she mumbles, sliding onto a chair at the table.

"Hi, yourself. Feeling better this morning?"

"A little."

"Good. Want some breakfast?"

"Okay."

Just for a change from the cereal, I toast some bread over the open flame of the propane stove and spread it with strawberry jam. The meal seems to lift her spirits a bit, and she asks for seconds.

"Are we going someplace today?" she says as she carries her dishes over to the sink.

"If you want another boat ride, I've got a couple of ideas."

"I really want to stay here."

"That's okay too. We could both use a day's rest while we try to figure out what to do next." There will be no talk of Halifax or foster care today. She needs a breather, time to herself to get over yesterday's fright. I can afford to give her that much; it's not as if I have anything better to do.

"I thought I might go in swimming," she says. She pumps some water into the kettle for washing up and puts it on the propane burner to heat. "Come in with me?" she asks shyly.

"Okay. But we didn't find you a swimsuit."

"Oh, yeah."

She scrapes the dishes and stacks them, ready to be washed.

"I've decided something," she says at last.

"Tell me."

"I'm going to have fun today."

"Okay."

"What I mean is, I'm not going to just sit around and be scared, like last night."

"Good."

She gathers up my empty plate and silverware, adding them to the small pile in the sink. She dribbles liquid soap over everything and checks the kettle to see if it's hot enough, hiding worries in a basket of busy-ness.

"Not ready yet," she says, sitting down across from me. A short pause. "I didn't say thank you yet."

"For what?"

"You know. Saving me yesterday, and staying with me last night. That kind of thing."

"I didn't do much. You stood up to Lucas."

"No I didn't."

"A little bit, maybe. And you sure bluffed that cab driver. It's a first step."

"I was really scared."

"And now?"

"Still scared, but maybe not so much."

" 'What does not destroy us will make us strong'."

"Is that a quote?"

"Just a little valuable philosophy from an old reprobate named Nietzsche. Understand it?"

"I think so. Lucas didn't get me after all, and I'm still here. So maybe if there's a next time, I'll be able to get away then, too. Think so?"

"I'm sure of it."

* * *

We spend a quiet morning. She sits in the cabin reading, exploring my meagre library and puzzling over the entries in my journal. Several times she asks the meanings of words, and I can hear her mumbling to herself. Finally she approaches me with the book in her hand.

"Want to hear what I can do?" she asks.

"Okay."

" 'Jenny knows. She knows when I'm not well, or lost in Hell...' "

She finishes the poem, her rhythm precise and every word carefully pronounced, then looks to me for approval. My eyes are scratchy and at first I can't trust myself to speak, but I smile and reach out to squeeze her hand.

She looks pleased. "I guess that means you liked the way I read it, huh?"

I manage to find my voice. "It was beautiful."

After lunch we explore the island, wandering among the scrub pines and clambering over the huge jumbled rocks that keep the ocean from eroding the land. We pluck barnacles from driftwood logs, find a fallen bird's nest with pale blue eggshell fragments beneath the maples that grow near the foot of a hill, and wade in the frigid water of a spring that tumbles down a miniature chasm to form a perfect bowl-shaped pool.

A gentle, peaceful day...

After supper I challenge her to a contest at the Scrabble board. She demonstrates a surprising aptitude for the game, and a vocabulary that I would have thought to be far beyond the norm for a young teen. I don't hold back and beat her two games to one, but her single win is honest and decisive.

When at last she's in bed and asleep, I sit up mulling over our situation. Where once I had only wanted to be rid of her as soon as possible, each crisis has dumped her back into my lap. Somehow I have acquired a temporary daughter, and I have to stop thinking in terms of sending her away until I can be sure she'll be safe. She's beginning to trust me, probably the first time she has trusted any man in a long time, and I have to justify that faith.

There has to be a permanent solution. Common sense says I should take her to the authorities and wash my hands of the whole matter, the sooner the better. By letting her stay with me I'm probably in violation of half a dozen child protection laws, but I can't consign her to the establishment without getting some guarantee that she wouldn't become just another lost cog in the welfare machine. At best she'd be shifted around among foster homes, possibly returned to jolly old Uncle Frank. Worst of all, if she's placed in the Halifax area she might fall into Lucas's hands again, and he'd make sure she never got away from him again.

What she's been through should have hardened her, aged her prematurely and instilled in her a cynical hatred for humanity in general. It hasn't happened. She still delights in picking out new clothes, still blushes at the attention of a normal, good-looking boy her own age. Still feels the pain of others.

I have to believe she can still learn to love.

I also have to admit that I'm beginning to enjoy my new role as surrogate father, even if only a little. To my immense surprise, while the lonely emptiness that followed Amy's passing is still oppressive, especially in the hours before dawn, the days are marginally less bleak now. If I can help Emily to reclaim a place in the world, perhaps there's even some reason for me to consider doing the same. The problem is, how to do it.

14
Sunday

Sleep comes late, and flees far too early. I'm sitting outside with my coffee in the early warmth of a bright summer morning when Emily bursts through the door and out onto the deck, grinning like the Cheshire Cat. She wears a pair of Amy's oldest shorts, the cuffs rolled up and the waist cinched in with a safety pin. The tails of Amy's oversized tee shirt are tied in a fat knot beneath her tiny breasts.

"I feel good today!" she bubbles. "Let's go swimming!"

"Let me finish my coffee first. It's barely daylight. Did you have any breakfast yet?"

"Nope. Later. Let's go." She grabs my hand and tries to pull me upright.

"Is this the latest style in beachwear?" I tease.

"Best I could do. Come on!"

"Give me a minute," I tell her, and carry my mug inside and set it next to the sink.

The change in her from the day before is remarkable, and it takes some thought to determine what caused it. Finally I conclude it's the feeling of security that being on the island offers. As long as we stay here, she won't have to face the terror of an uncertain future, and a possible return to virtual enslavement.

I change into trunks and go back outside to find her hopping up and down impatiently on the dock.

"Race you out to the boat!"

"Who wound you up this morning?"

"Carpay something. 'Seize the day!' Right?"

"Right. And it's 'carpe diem,' my literary genius."

"That's what I said. Come on." She whirls and plunges off the end of the dock.

"Hey! Wait a minute!" I run out to the end as she surfaces. "There are rocks in there. Don't go jumping in like that."

"I checked it out while you were changing. It's deep right here. Don't be a wuss."

"A wuss, am I?" I execute a rusty but serviceable dive and come up beside her, ducking her under. She breaks the surface, sputtering but gleeful.

"Race you to the boat!"

She takes off in a flat, powerful crawl and I try to keep up, badly out of practice. She reaches the stern a dozen yards ahead of me and scurries up the ladder.

"Wuss!"

"You're shark bait!" I mount the ladder too quickly and slip on the top rung, stumbling into the cockpit and landing hard on my right knee. She squeals and jumps back out of the way. I haul myself up and sit on the locker, kneading my battered joint.

"You play too rough. I'm an old guy, remember?"

"Are you okay?"

"As if you really care."

"I do." She regards me seriously, not sure whether I'm really hurt, and steps closer.

"Gotcha!"

I jump up and grab her around the waist, tossing her over the side in one quick motion. She vanishes out of sight. I count the seconds, too many of them, and when she doesn't reappear I climb over the rail, about to dive in after her.

"Wuss!"

Her face is shining at me over the transom, two dark eyes alive with mischief.

"Truce," I say. "You're too much for me."

She climbs back into the boat and we sit down side by side.

"I bet you're having fun," she says.

"I bet you're right."

"Did you and Amy go swimming a lot?"

This time the mention of her name doesn't hurt quite as much. "All the time. She loved it out here on the island."

"I figured. What else did you do?"

"We did just about everything together except work. She was a teacher. University. Before that, ninth grade for two years."

"That's where I should be next year. Guess I'll have to repeat eighth."

"That's one of the things we'll have to sort out."

She seems to be thinking in a positive direction again, looking beyond the immediate future and the threat she faces. After minor victories over Lucas and Ben she seems more upbeat and optimistic, but I can't forget his apparent power over her. When confronted by him at close quarters, she leaned away from me, seeming to accept that she belonged with him. That could prove to be dangerous.

She stands up and pirouettes around the cramped cockpit floor, showing off for me. "What'll we do today?"

"Stand still."

"Huh?"

"I said, stand still. You're making me dizzy."

"I've got lots of energy. Let's go swimming again."

"You go. Let me sit here and nurse my wounds."

"You're okay. Let's race again. Bet you can't catch me." She spins around toward the rail, trips, and falls sideways into my lap, laughing.

What in the hell am I going to do with you?

* * *

Around noon we sit at the table eating sandwiches. Her shorts and tee shirt are rinsed and hanging outside the cabin on my makeshift clothesline, and she's changed to the yellow sundress. She's parading around the cabin a little too ostentatiously, and I'm beginning to see that my problem has more layers than I realized at first.

Amy had told me of the crushes that students sometimes developed on their teachers, and how hard they could be to deal with. Something of that sort now seemed to be happening between Emily and me, and I had no idea how to go about keeping things cool. Everything about our forced companionship contributed to a growing emotional attraction that could too easily move in the wrong direction.

Halfway through lunch she leaves the table and disappears into the bedroom. I'm staring out the window, trying to figure out how to approach the problem, when her voice intrudes on my thoughts. She stands hipshot just inside the hallway, consciously provocative.

"You got a trash barrel someplace?"

"Out back. I bury the food waste and collect the rest of the trash to take back to the mainland when it gets full enough. Why?"

"I want to throw some stuff away."

"What?"

She concentrates on her shoes.

"Okay, *don't* tell me. Just don't forget to put the lid back tight on the barrel. Otherwise the racoons get into it."

"My clothes..." she says finally.

"Come again?"

"The stuff I came in. Bambi's stuff."

"Good idea," I tell her. "She doesn't need them any more."

Talking about her past in the third person seems to help. She comes back to the table head high and finishes her sandwich, then carries our plates and glasses to the sink. She stacks them quickly and neatly and comes back to stand beside my chair. She moves in too closely and bumps her hip against my arm, resting her hand lightly on my shoulder. She begins to knead it. Her leg presses against my thigh, sliding gently back and forth.

I turn my head to look at her, my expression serious. "You don't have to hang on to me. I'm not going anywhere."

She jerks her hand back as if burned and retreats to the sink, seizing the pump handle. Water splashes onto the dishes, and some cascades out onto the floor. I get up to take the kettle off the stove, and pour some of the hot water into the sink.

Her back is rigid, her posture tense. She adds some detergent to the water and begins to wash the plates, rubbing them hard and fast, each one too many times. As she rinses them I take each one from her and wipe it dry. It takes less than five minutes to stack everything in the cabinet, five silent, uncomfortable minutes.

As she pulls the stopper from the drain I say, "Ever run across the quote 'Know thyself' in your extensive reading?"

She crosses the room and sprawls on the day bed, staring out the window. "Nope. Must have been written by some *old* guy."

"Who said it isn't important. What does it mean?"

"Who cares? I'm not in the mood for school."

"No, and the mood you're in is partly my fault. Cut me some slack."

She meets my eyes. "Okay, what about it?"

"Everybody's got feelings. Sometimes those feelings make us do things.

Like if you get angry at me, you say things like 'who cares' in that sarcastic tone of voice."

"So? You get mad at me sometimes, too, like a couple of nights ago on the boat. You scared me, yelling at me like that."

"That's what I mean. I lost control of myself and took it out on you. But when I realized what I'd done, I tried to make it up to you."

"I still don't get it."

"What I'm trying to say is, once I understood *why* I was mad, I could control it. 'Know thyself,' see?"

"What's that got to do with me?"

"You're feeling something new right now, mostly because you and I are stuck here together on this island, all alone with just each other."

She blushes and turns her head away.

"Me, too," I say quietly.

Surprised, she snaps her head back quickly.

"It's nothing to be embarrassed about," I go on. "I'm not ashamed of how much I like you. The problem is to figure out the best, safest way to show it."

She looks down and toys with the sash on her dress. I put my finger under her chin and lift gently.

"Look at it this way. Both of us are hurting, but for different reasons. You because you've had a rough six months, and me because I've lost the most important thing in my life. And while we're getting to be friends, it's natural that we want to help each other. But we can't let that turn into something else."

Her face shuts down. "I don't want to think about it." She rises angrily and hurries toward the door, pulling it open and rushing out onto the deck. The sound of her running feet crunches the gravel in front of the cabin, then fades away toward the west.

I seem to have handled it all wrong.

When I wander out onto the deck, she's nowhere in sight. *Amy's Pride* bobs in the middle of the cove, beckoning me to spend some time on a few neglected chores: airing out below decks, straightening up the equipment lockers, a couple of minor repairs. Busy work.

Once on board, I haul out the bumpers and lay them on the gunwale. I dip a bucket in the bay and splash water over them, then squat down to scrub them with a stiff brush. Bits of seaweed and other debris flake off, and I sluice it out of the scuppers.

As soon as the bumpers have dried I coil their lines and stow them neatly.

The next chore is to repair a small tear in the mainsail's canvas cover. I thread a thick needle and climb up by the mast and set to work. I'm about halfway done when I hear a small splash in the direction of the dock.

A few minutes later Emily's head appears above the transom. She climbs over the rail, once again in her makeshift swimwear. She stands behind the wheel, unnecessarily studying the motionless compass.

"You took the tender," she accuses me. "I had to swim out."

"You could have called to me. I would have rowed back to get you."

"You were busy."

"Not that busy."

She circles the console and picks up one of the jib sheets, looping it loosely and rearranging it on the winch. She notices me sewing the sail cover.

"Want some help with that?"

"Almost done," I tell her.

"What else needs doing?"

"What doesn't? Boats never leave you alone."

I tie off the thread and refasten the end of the sail cover. "Want to do some housekeeping?" I ask her as I return to the cockpit along the gunwale.

"I guess." Her voice is flat and colourless.

"There's an icebox down in the cabin, port side next to the ladder. Amy and I used to sail down the coast for three or four days at a time, and we kept our food cold with two or three bags of ice in it. I haven't used it much lately, and it's still dirty from the last time."

"How do I clean it?"

"There's detergent on the shelf overhead, and a small brush. Use fresh water."

She turns morosely and disappears down the hatch. A half minute later she sticks her head back out.

"There's no water," she complains.

"You have to turn the battery on. It's the same switch you turned off for me the other day."

She vanishes again, and shortly afterward I hear the pump start up. After a few minutes I ease my way through the hatch and climb down the ladder into the galley. She's leaning over the edge of the icebox, scrubbing the corners at the bottom.

"Messy job, isn't it?"

She doesn't answer, deliberately ignoring me as I slide onto the bench behind the table. She scrubs down the sides and rinses off the remaining detergent with some fresh water. Then she sponges out the bottom, leaving the lid open so it can dry out completely. She puts the detergent back on the shelf along with the sponge, then finds herself with nothing else to do. She won't look at me.

"Nice work," I tell her.

She shrugs.

"Deserves a reward."

She stares out the starboard porthole.

"Want to take her down the coast for a couple of days?"

Panic sweeps her features.

"Not to Bournemouth," I tell her quickly. "The opposite direction. It'll give us a little more time to figure out what to do to keep you safe."

She heaves a sigh and rotates her head and shoulders, working the stiffness out.

"Well? What do you say?"

She mutters something, and I have to ask her to repeat it.

"I'm not Amy!" she says, a little too loudly.

"No, you're not. And I wouldn't want you to be. But that doesn't mean I wouldn't enjoy doing some of the same things with you that I did with her. If you want to, that is."

She slides onto the opposite end of the bench, shoulders hunched and features pinched.

"I'm all confused."

"Because you have feelings you don't understand, right?"

She nods slightly, eyes lowered.

"Welcome to the human race."

That startles her.

"We all have that problem, no matter how long we live. And sometimes our feelings hurt us." I smile gently. "Good friends understand that."

She picks at the knot in her tee shirt. "I just wanted you to like me."

"Not hard to do."

"But I did it wrong, didn't I?"

"Not really. It's just that you don't have to do anything. Just being you is enough."

"God, I feel so weird!"

"You're a kid. Of course you're weird."

"Hey!"

"So are we friends again?"

"If you want to be."

"Duh!"

She smirks at me. "Limited vocabulary, huh?"

I get up off the bench. "Come on, squirt. Let's go back to the cabin and plan a little adventure."

She follows me to the ladder, and we climb out into bright sunshine.

"I'm all dried off," she says. "Can I go with you in the tender?"

"Sure. Want to row it?"

"I don't know how."

"Good time to learn."

Half an hour later she has blistered hands and a happy smile. We're all right again.

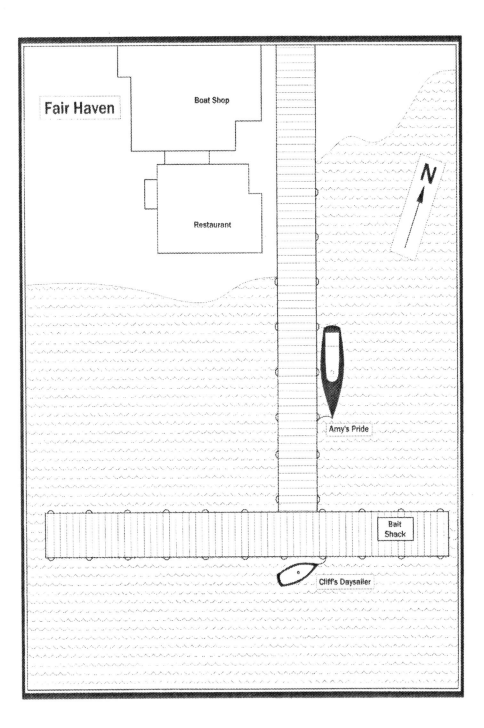

15
Monday

The next morning we motor southwest and stop for supplies at Fair Haven, a luxury marina a few miles down the coast that caters to wealthier sailing enthusiasts. We buy a couple of bags of ice and charge the cooler, then walk to the small convenience store at the head of the dock for some chicken and wieners to barbeque. Emily collects a package of hot dog buns, tubs of coleslaw and potato salad, and drinks and snacks.

After stowing the groceries on the boat we head for the main building of the big marina complex to treat ourselves to an early lunch. It's still too early for much of a crowd. Near the door, two roughly dressed men in their late twenties huddle in hushed conversation at a narrow table. A family of four occupies one of the booths lining the window wall. The rest of the seats are empty.

We find a place near the inside wall at a small table opposite the door, me facing out, Emily across from me with her back to the room. She casts a sidelong glance into the occupied booth, at the two adults and two children sitting there. The parents are involved in animated conversation. A girl of about seven draws geometric patterns in the ketchup on her plate with a French fry, and a boy of eleven or twelve peers at us over the top of his drink.

"Interested?" I tease.

"Nah," she says, picking up her menu. "He's cute, but too young."

"I wish someone would say that about me."

"You're pretty cute!"

"But definitely not too young, right?"

She giggles. The men at the other table look up at the sound of her laughter. One of them stares openly at her for several long seconds, then hunches forward and mutters something to his companion. They both laugh nastily. They ignore my glare.

The waitress arrives and takes our order. The family in the booth finishes their lunch and heads out onto the pier. They climb aboard a substantial yacht, a thirty-six foot Nonsuch, and soon afterward I hear the sound of their engine faintly through the restaurant walls. The big boat eases out of the slip into the channel.

The dock is now nearly deserted. On such a beautiful day most boat owners lucky enough not to be working are no doubt enjoying the sun and favourable winds, not sitting in some harbour. In addition to *Amy's Pride*, only a small Cape Islander and a stubby open cockpit sailboat lie against the end of the pier, partly hidden behind a shabby and deserted shack where the marina once sold bait.

Our sandwiches and drinks arrive. As we're eating, another CS yacht comes in and ties up, almost a twin to mine but a couple of feet shorter. Emily watches with interest as a man and boy rig their spring lines and walk off the dock.

Before we finish our meals, the two men near the door pay their bill and leave. A second Nonsuch, more modest than the last at thirty feet, approaches the dock. We're the last customers in the restaurant. As Emily sits finishing her Coke, I notice her sunburned nose.

"We need to stop in next door," I tell her.

"What for?"

"Let's put it this way. Another few hours on board and you'll be able to lead Santa's sleigh in the fog."

Her hand flies to her face and she fingers her nose.

"It hurts a little."

"Told you. We need some sun block, and you need another hat to replace the one you lost. It'll be pretty hot out there today. Maybe you can find a swimsuit too. They sell sportswear in the boat shop."

After paying the cashier, we escape out the door and around the corner of the building to the entrance to the marina's retail complex. Down the pier one of the men I'd seen in the restaurant is getting aboard the Cape Island boat. A fancy Great Lakes cruiser aims for the mouth of the harbour. Half a dozen triangular white sails dot the horizon, a subject worthy of an artist.

Inside the shop, Emily immediately spots a floppy-brimmed fisherman's hat and tries it on. It falls down over her ears like Amy's souwester, and she turns and crosses her eyes comically in my direction. She lifts it off and picks up a blue and white baseball cap instead.

"How's this?"

"Should do the trick. Want to go back where the clothes are?"

"Can I really get a swimsuit?"

"Sure."

The shop has a huge selection, and Emily paws through the racks, taking one after another to hold up in front of her. Most of her choices are dark-coloured competition tank suits. I ease myself down onto a hard chair beside the sales counter, trying not to be bored or impatient.

"Which one should I get?" she asks.

"I'm no expert," I tell her. "Get what you like."

She fingers a dark brown suit with a high neck and a Nike logo. "This is what real good swimmers wear."

"Get that, then."

She frowns and puts the suit back on the rack. The next one she pulls out is dark green but otherwise almost identical. After turning it this way and that, she discards it too.

"Look, short one, this will take all day unless you try something on. Take the plunge. You won't know what you want unless you start making comparisons."

She sighs. "I guess so." She picks out another high-necked tank suit in navy blue and drags her feet toward the fitting room. A salesclerk has been watching her and comes over to offer some advice.

"Is your daughter having trouble making up her mind?" she asks.

Daughter again!

"I'm not much help," I tell her.

"Is she a competition swimmer?"

"No. This is just for sailing."

"Then why doesn't she look over here?" She motions toward a rack of brightly coloured two-piece affairs.

I smile helplessly. "You're asking me to understand the female mind?"

"She just needs a little encouragement. Excuse me for a minute. I'll be back."

She leaves to help another customer, and my attention wanders to the fitting room area as Emily straggles out, looking dejected. The tank suit trails limply from her hand.

"Not so good?" I ask her.

She shrugs. "It kinda hung on me."

"Need a smaller size?"

She shrugs again.

"Look, why not live dangerously. Try on something with a little colour to it. Stripes? Maybe a Hawaiian print."

"I can't."

"Why not?"

"Because."

"That's no answer."

"You won't like it if I tell you."

"How do you know? Try me."

She glances around to be sure the sales clerk can't hear her, and drops her voice almost to a whisper. "Because every time I start to say anything about 'before' you shut me up."

I know what "before" means. I lower my voice to match hers. "Bad connotations, right?"

"Right."

"You can tell me. And I'll really listen this time."

"On the boat, the night I escaped?"

I nod, encouraging her to go on.

"The other girls, that's what they had on."

"Bikinis?"

"Uh huh. Real bright, and skimpy like underwear. Cheap and sleazy."

I'm getting good at theatrical sighs. "What am I going to do with you?" I ask rhetorically.

"I can't help it. I hate them, and I don't want to look anything like them."

"That's fine. I can't argue with that. But there are a lot of styles that won't look 'sleazy,' as you put it, and still put a little fun in your life. It's just a matter of exercising some good taste."

"I don't know anything about that."

"Want to get a little expert help?" I incline my head toward the clerk, still busy with the other customer.

"God, no!"

"Why not? I bet she'll have some good ideas."

"I'd be too embarrassed."

"So get over it." I smile at her. "Either that or you'll spend the rest of your life looking like Old Mother Hubbard. Think David would like you then?"

Her face flushes a bright pink, surprising me.

"Oops. Struck a nerve, did I?"

She glares at me, seizes the nearest swimsuit off the end of the rack—another tank suit, black this time—and stalks off into the fitting room. I'm batting zero.

Five minutes later she stomps back out, still glowering and clutching the suit in her fist.

"This one," she says, eyes flashing.

"Emily, I'm sorry I teased you."

"No you're not!"

"Hey, give me a break. I've never had kids, you know. I said the wrong thing, and I admit it."

She softens a bit. "It's okay. You just..." The words die in her throat.

"So is this the one you really want?"

It isn't. She's close to tears. I feel completely helpless, and just then the sales clerk glides over to us, all helpful smiles and enthusiasm. Emily pivots away, wiping at the corners of her eyes.

"Having a little trouble, are we?" the clerk says. "Can I help?"

"What do you say, sweetheart?" I ask gently. "Shall we get some of that expert advice I mentioned a few minutes ago?"

Her shoulders rise and fall, a sigh both visible and audible. It may have been the "sweetheart" that broke through to her, or just that her resistance is wearing thin, but she turns around with one last swipe at her eyes and says, "I guess."

"Let's take a look at this rack over here." The clerk crosses to the opposite side of the aisle, away from the competition suits. "Come and see."

Emily wanders over reluctantly.

"This is a new line this year. How about a bikini?"

"No!"

The sales clerk frowns at her abrupt reaction and looks over at me. I shrug, playing dumb. She turns back and sorts through the rack.

"You've got a cute little figure, sweetie," she says. "You ought to show it off some."

Emily ducks her head, crosses her eyes and mouths "sweetie" at me. I give her a tolerant parent look. The clerk tries again.

"How about this? A brand new style, and just your size too."

Emily glances briefly at the sleek one-piece suit she's holding, bright orange with a cut-out front panel and laces up the sides, spaghetti straps at the shoulders. She shakes her head.

"This one's nice." The clerk sweeps another off its hanger, a backless

144

modified tank style in an iridescent metallic blue with the legs cut almost to the waist. I know what Emily's reaction will be. She shakes her head politely, her eyes sad and discouraged.

"Maybe something a little more conservative," I suggest.

"I know just the thing!" the clerk says, professional enthusiasm undampened. She pulls out a modest two-piecer in a vivid red with white trim. "See, it's low on the hips, and the legs are squared off like a guy's suit. Covers your whole bottom, but shows off that tiny waist of yours. Real cute. And look at this." She peels a square of cloth from the hanger and shakes it open. "This makes a little wrap-around skirt to go over it, for when you're out of the water." Expertly she flips it over the swim pants. "Elegant! Grown up!"

Emily's eyes appeal to me: *Save me!*

"Why don't you try it on?" I suggest.

She glares at me and mouths "traitor." Then she turns back to the clerk and forces a smile. "I guess so."

She takes the suit and shuffles reluctantly to the fitting room. The clerk stands beside me, slowly shaking her head.

"Is she always this self-conscious?"

"You don't know the half of it. My guess is, she'll eventually settle for a tank suit a size too big, black or dark blue."

The clerk shrugs, knowing when to admit defeat. "Well, let me know if I can be of any more help." She hurries away to wait on yet another customer. After a few minutes Emily's face appears around the corner of the dressing room door.

"I don't like it."

"Let me see."

"No."

"Okay. We'll pick out something else."

I expect her to vanish back inside but she lingers uncertainly, all but her face and one bare shoulder hidden behind the doorjamb. "It just isn't me," she says hesitantly.

"Which you?"

"Don't start in on me again."

"Don't ask for my advice, then."

"I wasn't!"

"Fine!"

"Fine!"

We glare at each other, and then a trace of a smile reappears. She steps out

145

of the fitting room and walks pigeon-toed across the aisle to stand in front of a mirror.

"Bright!" she says.

"Pretty," I counter.

The suit is well matched to her age and slight form, the bra top generously cut and softly structured. The little wrap skirt divides modestly at the side to show one squared-off leg of the pants. She unties the skirt and lets it dangle in her hand, twisting sideways to catch the rear view in the mirror. She looks at me over her shoulder and waggles her hips sarcastically.

"Do I get to have an opinion?" I ask.

"Nope."

The salesclerk starts toward us, and I wave her off. Emily reties the wraparound skirt and studies herself critically. "Do I look cheap?" she asks me.

"I thought you didn't want my opinion."

"Well, I do."

"Okay, then, I think you're beautiful."

She colours slightly. "It's too flashy. People will look at me, and maybe they can tell what I've been doing for..."

"Emily, come here," I interrupt. She turns from the mirror, brow furrowed and the corners of her mouth drooping.

"Come on."

She edges over closer, eyes down.

"Can you look at me, please?"

Her head comes up slowly.

"Now listen to me very closely, all right? All of us carry some baggage around with us, things that have happened in the past that we can't shake off. You just have more of it than most of us, more than anyone your age ought to have. Sometimes we just have to set some of it down and walk away. But nobody can do it for you; you have to do it for yourself."

"I don't know how," she whispers.

"I know. But you have to keep trying. And the first time you succeed will make the next time easier. Do you understand what I'm saying?"

"Not really."

"'What does not destroy us will make us strong.'"

"That again?"

"Sweetheart, I can't even begin to imagine what you've been through, but it's in the past. From now on you have to think about nothing but the future."

146

"You don't understand."

"I think I do. Look, it's like my sadness over Amy. I used to think I'd never get over it, and in some ways I never really will. But that can't be my whole life. I know that now. And guess what? You're part of what helped me to realize it. You're going to get over most of your bad feelings, too. I know you will."

Her eyes are wet and glistening. "You called me 'sweetheart' again."

"I did? Must be because that's how I think of you now."

"I'm not..." She stops.

"Not what?"

She looks down again.

"Never mind," I tell her. "I think I know what you were going to say. Now how about this swimsuit? We can make it a symbol of something, a first small step toward putting down that baggage I was talking about. You have to get comfortable with yourself again, that's all. You have a right to look pretty, and you *do*. Not cheap. Pretty. You just have to learn how to accept it."

"You called me 'sweetheart'," she says again.

"You really don't understand what I'm talking about, do you?"

"Maybe a little. You want me just to forget about the way I feel inside, and I can't."

"Not yet. It's hard, I know that. But do you trust me enough to give it a try and see if I'm right?"

"Are you still sad about losing Amy?"

"Of course, and I always will be. But not all the time. Like when we're out on the boat and you're having fun, I am too. For the first time in a long time."

"This isn't really about my swimsuit, is it?"

"No. And I'm so glad you figured that out for yourself. Come on, let's go look in the mirror again."

She follows me reluctantly and gazes into the glass. I stand behind her, one reassuring hand gently on her shoulder. A deep, shuddering breath ripples through her, and she wipes her eyes.

"Now," I tell her, "just try to imagine that the last six months never happened, and look at yourself through new eyes. How do you feel?"

She sways back and forth, and a shy smile touches the corners of her mouth.

"Like with my dress. I feel pretty."

"Sounds like a song cue," I said.

"Huh?"

"Never mind, you're too young to remember that one. So what's the verdict?"

"I guess I like it."

"I like it, too. Let's pay for it and get out of here."

She heads for the fitting room, a new lightness in her step. It takes her longer to change than I expect, and when she comes out again, looking dejected, the suit hangs loosely from her hand.

"What's the matter?"

"I changed my mind."

"How come?"

"I just did."

Now what?

The clerk hurries over again, smiling brightly. "Is this the one, then?"

"No," Emily says sadly.

The clerk raises her eyebrows, no doubt feeling as helpless as I do. I had thought the problem was solved. She takes the suit and begins putting it back on the hanger. Then she fingers the tag, considering.

"This is a designer suit, you know," she tells Emily. "Hand made, the only one like it in the whole world, and it fits you perfectly. I could take twenty per cent off for you."

"Sounds good to me," I say. "How much would that be?" She shows me the tag.

"Holy…! Is that right? What does that work out to per square inch?"

The clerk tries not to take offence, not sure whether I'm joking. "Did you look at the label, sir? It came from Paris."

"It should come *with* Paris at that price."

"See?" Emily says. "You can't spend that much on me. Even on sale."

"Is that what's bothering you now? Forget it! I can always sell Jenny to pay for it."

She can't stifle a giggle. "Who'd buy Jenny?"

"You've got a point. However…" I turn back to the clerk. "Consider it sold."

"But…" Emily stammers.

I bend down to her as the clerk walks off to the register.

"No arguments. You like it, I like it, and I can afford it. It's something very special, okay? You deserve it."

Her eyes fill. "No I don't."

"Are you arguing with me?"

She grins through her tears. "Yes."

"You lose. We're getting it."

"Thank you."

"Don't thank me. I just hate to lose an argument."

We pay for the suit, then spend another fifteen minutes looking around the shop. Emily is drawn to the boat clothes, and finds a navy blue halter top with red and white anchors embroidered on its wide straps, paired with brief, white-cuffed boat shorts. She holds the top up in front of her.

"That's cute," I tell her. "Matches the new hat."

She starts to hang it up again.

"I think you need it. It's getting hot out there, and it'll be a lot cooler than what you've got on now."

"You've spent enough money on me," she says.

"It can be your birthday present, then. You can't turn that down. It's not polite."

That surprises her. "You remembered."

"Of course I did. Fourteen today, right? Go try it on."

"Can I really?"

"Sure. The more clothes you have, the longer it will be before we have to do laundry."

A rack of navigation charts and an assortment of flags capture my attention while she's gone. I consider getting a new pennant to replace the faded one that flies from my boat's stern, but decide against it. Amy chose the one I have now, the day we signed the papers and *Amy's Pride* became our own.

Emily comes looking for me, wearing the new outfit and a grin a mile wide. The top is a little too big, emphasizing her youth, but it looks good on her, leaving a broad band of her tummy bare. The little shorts flare cutely from a couple of inches below her narrow waist.

"Anchors and everything," I tell her, looking at the straps. "Now you look like a real sailor."

She spins around. "I love it." We've taken a giant step forward in the way she feels about herself.

"Keep it on, then. I'll pay for it, and then you can take the price tags off. And happy birthday."

She stretches up and throws her arms around my neck, pulling my head down.

"Thank you, thank you, thank you!"

149

"Ouch! You're welcome. Don't break my neck."

We settle up for the outfit and hat, and she disappears into the fitting room to gather up her other clothes. I'm becoming uncomfortable in my heavy jeans and decide to treat myself to something, too. I find a pair of cargo shorts that look to be about my size. On my way to try them on, I pass her coming back.

"Give me a minute," I tell her. "I want to see if these fit."

"Can I go out to the boat?"

"Sure. I won't be long."

"See ya."

She skips out of the shop while I enter the changing room. It occurs to me that I haven't bought any new clothes for myself since before Amy's accident. There hasn't seemed to be any reason to. I'm puzzled to discover that the mundane things of life, buying clothes and sailing for pleasure and having someone to talk to once more—someone to look out for—are beginning to take on some meaning for me once again. My sadness doesn't seem quite as oppressive as before.

The shorts fit well, and I pay for them and a tube of sun block and head back out to the pier. The Cape Islander is gone. The big Great Lakes cruiser sits idle with no one aboard, moored to a buoy twenty yards off the end of the pier. Aside from two young boys loading some fishing gear into a skiff near the shore, the area is deserted. *Amy's Pride* tugs on her spring lines against the outgoing tide, the bumpers chafing and groaning against the pilings.

And something else… A muffled cry comes from behind the ramshackle bait shed, feet scraping, a loud slap.

I toss the bag containing my shorts over the rail and hurry around the corner toward the sounds. Emily lies sprawled on the dock, the coarse-looking man from the restaurant standing over her. He reaches down and hauls her roughly to her feet. She tries to kick him and he slaps her face, snapping her head back. I let out a roar and run toward him.

"Back off, Jack!" he shouts. He yanks her up against his chest like a shield. She kicks and struggles weakly as he edges toward the little daysailer next to the dock.

"Get your goddamn hands off her!" I shout.

"Stay out of this!" he snarls. He twists her arm cruelly and she screams. I skid to a stop. "You're not taking her!"

"The hell I'm not! This little bitch and I are old friends. She belongs to Lucas Brady, and he wants her back."

"She's with me now."

"You're her new sugar daddy, huh? Well, screw that!"

Emily goes limp, dead weight in his arms, and he drags her toward the edge of the dock. I'm outsized and outclassed, nothing going for me but some pretty good reflexes from years of competitive sports. It's probably not enough, but I'm sure as hell not letting him put her in his boat. I go at him again, and he clamps his left arm across her thin chest, digging his fingers into her ribs. She whimpers.

"You want to see her get busted up?" he growls.

I swallow hard, trying to keep control. "You're chickenshit, you know that? Can't handle anything but kids!"

His arm snakes out and backhands me hard across the jaw. Emily ducks her head and buries her teeth in his forearm, and he howls and drops her. She scuttles away and cringes up against the side of the bait shack, her eyes wide as dinner plates.

He thrusts his hand into his jeans. Cold steel glints in the sunlight, a six-inch switchblade. He jabs at me as I hop backwards. He spreads his arms wide for balance and comes at me, a street fighter's stance, blade angled upward for a gut thrust. We circle around each other, bobbing and feinting, and the blade whistles past my face. Instinctively, my hands fly up. He whips the knife back and slices my palm, then aims a wicked roundhouse slash at my chest, tearing the front of my shirt.

I lash out with my foot and slam it into his kneecap, knocking him off his feet. He comes out of an awkward crouch off balance with the knife straight out, and I get lucky. The blade goes wide, and I catch his wrist and spin to my right. His momentum carries him past me and he stumbles head first over the edge of the pier. The knife flies from his hand as he hits the water. He breaks the surface swearing.

I wave Emily toward *Amy's Pride*, and she scrambles to her feet and races up the dock. She clambers frantically over the rail and drops into the cockpit. The man swims to a wooden ladder bolted to the pier and starts to climb up. Seizing the advantage, I tower over him at the top, and he pauses halfway up.

"You're dead, you cocksucker!" he shouts.

"And you're a worthless piece of shit!" I want him mad and careless. "Can't even manage sex with anyone but children."

He bellows and rushes up the ladder, and as he grabs the top rung I stamp down hard on his hand. He howls and lets go, tumbling backward into the water. I trot down the pier to his boat and yank the bow rope off the piling.

"Get your goddamn hands off that!" he yells from the water.

I toss the line into the cockpit and shove the hull hard with my foot. The boat drifts out into the channel.

"You son of a bitch!" he screeches.

I stride back to the ladder, still mad as hell but icy calm. "Here's an idea for you, baby raper. Call the cops and complain about how I set your boat adrift. Then we'll all have a nice long talk about your sexual activities. Ought to be good for at least a ten year sentence."

He glares at me, treading water, then flips me the finger and rolls over into an awkward crawl stroke. The tide has caught his boat, carrying it toward the mouth of the bay. He's in for a long swim.

My hand is dripping blood, and I wrap my handkerchief around it and tie it off. Emily's clothes, the ones she'd been wearing that morning, lie scattered on the dock. I gather them up and head for *Amy's Pride*. She's huddled against the bulkhead, peering around the edge of the canvas dodger.

"Holy shit!" she says as I climb over the rail, her voice raw and strained. "How'd you do that?"

"Wasn't hard. You didn't do so bad yourself, biting him like that."

She's trembling in spite of the hot sun. I sit down next to her and gather her in close.

"Holy shit!"

"You said that already. Are you hurt?"

"Not much. But you are! You're bleeding!"

I check my hand, then look down and find my shirtfront stained a deep reddish brown, torn and gaping open over a long shallow gash a couple of inches above my navel. It oozes thickly, already beginning to clot.

"It's not bad," I reassure her. "I'll put a bandage on it in a minute. Do you know who that guy is?"

She rallies a bit. "His name's Cliff. One of the johns. Where'd he come from? Was he following us?"

"No. He was sitting in the restaurant when we walked in. I guess you didn't notice. It's just bad luck that he spotted you."

"Oh, God, I knew something like this was gonna happen. I want to go back to the island."

She burrows into my side for comfort. It's time for this cat and mouse game to be over. Something has to be done so her old customers won't be able to recognize her so easily.

"Maybe there's another way to handle it besides hiding out," I tell her.

"This Cliff, is he buddies with Lucas?"

"He works for him sometimes. He's always hanging around, looking for free ones."

"Nice guy."

"He used to slap us around, too. He likes it, acting tough all the time. I never saw anybody take him out before."

"He's just a bully and a coward. Guys like that aren't as tough as they look. All you have to do is stand up to them."

"I couldn't do it. I'm too little."

"I know. He counts on that."

"He's gonna tell Lucas where he saw me."

"So what? We're not staying here. We've got some sailing to do."

She studies the slash in my shirt, the soggy handkerchief wrapped around my hand. The blood flow has almost stopped.

"You're not scared of anybody, are you?" she says at last.

"Oh, yeah. Plenty of things scare me, like that knife he had. But I don't run away from a fight, either."

"Know what?" she says softly.

"What?"

"I like having you for a father. Even if it's only pretending."

"Me too," I tell her, surprised to discover I mean it.

16
Monday Afternoon

*A*my's Pride glides down the coast, a light wind off the stern to starboard driving her at a little more than four knots. With my wounds bound up and not too painful, I'm feeling comfortable and cool in the new shorts, relaxing in the stern and happy to let Emily handle the boat.

After the victory over Cliff, however temporary, her confidence in me is at an all-time high. She poses at the console, her long dark ponytail flying out behind her, enjoying the sunshine and eager to put some distance between herself and her troubles. The baseball cap shades the upper half of her face, but not the broad grin that plays across her lips. Her nose shines with greasy sun block.

With nothing to do except watch her having fun, I turn my mind to the problem of the next few days. The trip down the coast is a stall, a minor postponement of the moment we both know is coming. She has to move on. She needs a permanent home and a normal family to take care of her, the kind of safety and stability that a lonely widower can't provide. Even though I've assumed the role of her protector for the short term, it isn't my call to decide her future.

But I know I'll miss her when she's gone.

What to do with her? I've almost ruled out turning her over to Family and Children's Services, at least for now, despite the best intentions of Florence Pineo and her colleagues. I know the foster care system to be overloaded, the number of caseworkers pitifully small, and the options open to them severely limited. They might mean well, as most of them undoubtedly do, but the reality is that too many kids get lost somewhere in the system, fall through the proverbial cracks, and grow up unloved and emotionally stunted.

There has to be some other way, some alternate approach to the problem. Emily has suffered too many cruel blows already, first the loss of her parents, then Uncle Frank's abuse, and worst of all her sexual enslavement. Perhaps she needs a different kind of advocate, someone with the kind of legal clout that a reclusive ex-architect can't muster.

"Hey! What's that?"

Her shout snaps me out of my reverie. She's pointing over the stern where another yacht is bearing down on us, a huge and brightly patterned sail billowing out over her bow.

"Spinnaker," I tell her. "It's a lightweight sail with lots of area to catch the wind. Makes you go faster on relatively calm days like this."

"Have you got one?"

"Somewhere." I haven't used the big sail since my last trip down the coast with Amy the previous autumn.

"Let's get it out!"

"Too much trouble. And it makes the boat ride rough."

She bounces up and down with excitement. "They're gonna catch up to us! They're gonna *pass* us! Come on!"

"So what?" I tease. "Let them go. We aren't in any hurry."

"*I* am!"

Competitive, just like Amy. Feigning reluctance, I haul myself off the locker and go below. After a brief search, the spinnaker turns up under the forward berth, and I drag it out and lift it up through the bow hatch. By the time I get back to the cockpit the other yacht is closing fast on our stern, bearing off to port in order to pass us. Emily is nearly frantic with excitement.

"Hurry up! They're coming!"

"Keep your shorts on."

By the time I run the sail up the mast, she's in a frenzy. I secure the lines, and as the second boat draws abeam of us, the huge triangle balloons out over our bow. *Amy's Pride* tosses her skirts in the air, and we're off.

The other boat looks familiar, the near duplicate of mine that tied up in the marina while we were eating. At the helm a teenaged boy stares at us keenly, his mouth set in a taut line, daring us to take up the challenge. A man about my age, by appearance no doubt his father, stands ready at the traveller. He grins across the expanse of water that separates us and tosses me a snappy salute, and I return it.

The race is on. With virtually identical rigging the boats are almost evenly matched, the extra length of my waterline giving us only a slight advantage.

155

Nevertheless our opponents begin to pull away, skilled sailors who know their gear. My crew member is new to the game, but what she lacks in skill she makes up for in competitive enthusiasm.

"Do something!" Emily yells, bouncing up and down at the helm. "We're losing."

The sails are working hard in the freshening wind, not quite in trim. I let out the main and haul the traveller to port, and the knot meter jumps a fraction.

"Bear off a little!" I shout to her.

"Huh?"

"The main isn't helping the spinnaker. Turn the wheel a little."

I waggle my hand in the air to show her which way, and she twists the wheel too far. The main roars and the bow mushes down.

"Too much! Bring her back! Keep the main filled!"

I release the traveller a bit to compensate, and the boat finds the sweet spot. Emily grips the wheel fiercely, and we stop losing ground. I tweak the trim, and within a few minutes I can see we're gaining a little. The boy in the other boat stares back over his shoulder, then turns and shouts something to his dad. The man plays the lines.

I'm suddenly caught up in the fervour of an impromptu race, surprised at how much I've missed such juvenile contests. Amy and I had played like children, ramming up and down the coast. Privateers, game for any challenge.

How she had loved our boat!

I give the sails my full attention, adjusting the lines and shouting instructions to Emily. It takes us fifteen minutes, but we finally come abeam once more, racing on bow to bow until the first of a string of small offshore islands blocks our way. Both boats bear off and I see my chance. I jump behind the wheel and give *Amy's Pride* her head. She heels over and puts the other boat in her shadow, stealing their wind. Their spinnaker flutters and the main luffs, and we squirt ahead of them into clear air.

"We did it!" Emily shouts. "We passed them!"

She's hopping up and down in the stern, waving in delight at the other boat where a disconsolate teenaged boy stares glumly ahead, trying to ignore her. I can almost read his mind: beaten by a *girl!*

"Mind your manners," I caution. "Good winners don't boast."

"Huh?"

"They were worthy opponents. They put up a good race."

I wave to the other boat and give them another smart salute. The man

156

returns it, then says something to his son. The boy follows his example, although not too cheerfully.

"See? Good manners make good friends. We might see them again. And next time they could be the winners."

She spins around and drops happily onto the starboard locker, her long slender legs splayed out in abandon, arms flung back over the rail.

"But not this time, right?"

"No. Not this time."

* * *

We haul in the spinnaker and cruise among the islands for the rest of the afternoon until hunger drives us to find an anchorage. The nearest cove on the map shelters another fair-sized marina, and we drop the sails and motor in to find the bay crowded with boats of almost every description. There are no slips available at the dock and every buoy is occupied, so we settle for a stretch of open water in the lee of a headland. I set the anchors fore and aft to keep us from swinging when the tide turns.

Emily goes below to explore the ice chest while I inspect the cylindrical barbecue that hangs from the stern rail. It hasn't been used since the previous summer, but it takes me only a few minutes to scrape the grill clean before lighting the briquettes. She comes back up bearing hot dogs and chicken legs, and we set out buns and styrofoam cups of coleslaw and potato salad next to the rail, ready to enjoy an outdoor meal as the sun goes down.

While we wait for the fire to get hot enough for cooking, Emily prowls restlessly around the cramped cockpit, chattering non-stop about the day. With the resiliency of youth, she's already bounced back from Cliff's attack and is revelling in being far, far away from Lucas and all that he represents.

"Will you please settle down?" I beg. "You're driving me nuts."

"I can't help it, this is so much *fun*. I've never done anything like this before. We won a *race*, my first one *ever!*"

"Speaking of races, here come our opponents now."

Off the port bow, the other yacht is just entering the mouth of the bay. Its diesel growls and the sails come down. They head for the dock, only to discover as we had that there's no room at the inn.

"They'll probably look for a place to anchor out here," I tell her. "Shall we invite them to dinner?"

"Think they'll even talk to us?"

"Why not? It's not like we cheated or anything. We beat them fair and square."

The sleek CS weaves among the buoys in our general direction, and as soon as they're within range I hail them. The other skipper waves back and changes course to come alongside. Emily clings to the rail, anxiously watching them come. The boat drifts past slowly and I call out to them.

"We're about to start the barbecue. Care to join us?"

The man turns toward his son, who is eyeing Emily suspiciously but with curiosity. I can almost read his mind, torn between embarrassment over the lost race and the chance to get to know a pretty girl. He nods to his father.

"Thanks," the man calls back. "We'd like that. Can we tie up alongside?"

"We're solidly anchored," I tell him. "Rig your bumpers and toss me a line."

Letting the engine idle, they begin tying bumpers to their starboard rail, and I open the locker to take out our own. Emily leans in to help, then stops dead.

"Oh my gosh!"

"What's the matter?"

"*Look* at me!" she exclaims in a stage whisper, staring down at her shorts and halter, just a bit of tomboy in her jaunty ball cap. She scrubs the oily cream from her nose.

"You look fine," I tell her. "Super cute, in fact."

"I do not!"

She bolts toward the hatch and disappears below. I finish hitching the bumpers to the rail and throw them over the side, and flash the other boat an "okay" sign. The man waves back and the diesel's note deepens. He comes about in a sweeping curve and tosses me his stern line, and I make it fast. The boy crosses over amidships and carries a second line to the bow.

"Welcome aboard," I greet the man as he steps into the cockpit, giving him my name. He's about my age, lanky and fit, with the kind of pleasant, open face that speaks of both modesty and confidence.

"Ken Curtis," he says, extending his hand. He gestures forward to where his son is returning from securing the bow rope. "This is Alex."

The boy drops down into the cockpit from the cabin roof, taking my outstretched hand somewhat shyly. I figure him to be close to Emily's age, taller than average but still bearing the soft facial features of early puberty, and just beginning to acquire some muscle definition. He has his father's square chin, dirty blond hair and wide-set, grey-green eyes.

"My first mate's around here somewhere," I tell them. "Her name's Emily."

"This is a real treat," Ken says. "All we packed is sandwiches."

"Glad to have you. We have enough for an army."

They settle down on the starboard locker while I open the lid on the barbecue to arrange the wieners and chicken legs on the grill. I call down to Emily to bring up the paper plates and plastic knives and forks. Her muffled reply drifts up to me, the words indistinct, and I sit down across from our guests.

"This is a thirty-footer, isn't it?" Ken asks. I confirm it.

"You sailed a fine race," he continues. "I thought we had you for a while there."

"We got lucky. The wind came around at the right time, that's all."

"It wasn't luck. You played it just right. Even Alex said so." He claps his son on the shoulder and the boy smiles uncertainly.

"You're a hell of a sailor," I tell him honestly. "You were getting every last knot out of her."

"Thanks." This time his smile is more open and friendly.

Emily picks that moment for her grand entrance, filling the hatchway with a vision in yellow. The ponytail is gone, brushed out to fall softly below her shoulders and caught back at the temples to frame her small pale face. Somehow she has even managed to dull the shine on her sunburned nose.

She steps delicately over the sill and into the cockpit, her knees flashing cutely below the short skirt of the sundress. Alex, slack-jawed and tongue-tied, can't take his eyes off her. We make the introductions and she sits down shyly on the port side beside me.

I raise my eyebrows at her. "And the paper plates are..."

"Oops!"

"That's okay. The meat isn't ready yet."

"I'll get them," she says, bouncing up. "Can I show Alex the galley?"

And so it starts.

"Sure. Don't forget the knives and forks."

"We won't."

We!

The two of them disappear down the ladder, and Ken and I grin at each other, no doubt experiencing similar emotions.

"Your daughter is a knockout," he says. "Alex looks stunned."

"Thanks. But she's not..."

159

I catch myself, thinking it better to leave our connection a question mark. That relationship, Emily's and mine, is not something to share with strangers.

"She's not too secure herself," I recover. "Handsome boys throw her a little. Do you sail out here often?"

"Every chance we get," Curtis says. "Usually my wife comes with us, but she's on call today. She's an RN. I've got a law practice in Bournemouth, but when the weather turns as nice as this, I let the associates sweat the details. How about you?"

"Extended leave. I'm an architect by trade, and right now a loafer by inclination."

"Does your wife sail?"

"I'm a widower."

"I'm sorry," he says. "You're lucky to have a daughter to share things with, then."

"And speaking of her, we'd better roust them out." I raise my voice: "Supper's almost ready!"

A minute later Emily emerges carrying the plastic cutlery, followed closely by Alex with the plates. We pass things around, and I spear the meat out of the barbeque onto a platter so they all can choose what they want.

"Forgot the drinks," Emily announces, and vanishes below again. A minute later I catch sight of her at the top of the ladder, waving for me to come close. When I reach the hatch, she leans out to whisper in my ear.

"Who am I this time?"

"Well, Mr. Curtis already thinks you're my kid," I whisper back, "and I didn't tell him any different. I guess we better leave it at that."

"So should I call you 'Dad' then?"

"If you want to."

What can it hurt?

She drops down to rummage in the icebox and hands me half a dozen cans of pop, assorted flavours. I carry them back to our guests and she follows me and sits down again.

Familiar pleasures, too long neglected, bring back bittersweet memories. Amy and I had entertained frequently aboard the boat, often finding kindred souls at overnight stops like this one to share our food and fun. The last time had been in October, an Indian Summer sail off Lunenburg that netted us four new friends—friends I've left behind in my flight from memories of Amy.

Such a simple thing, sharing a meal and the pleasure of someone's company, but too much trouble to pursue when the light has gone out of your

160

life. But it's funny how much better the food tastes tonight, compared to my solitary dinners in the cabin.

The sun is still above the horizon when we finish eating, but chased by a cloudbank that mutes and finally hides its glow, although not its heat. Dusk descends unnaturally early. As Ken and I talk, the children become restless.

"We've got a TV," Alex tells Emily. "It works off the battery. Can we go over to our boat, Dad?"

"Okay by me, as long as Emily's allowed."

"Can I, Dad?" Her eyes sparkle with mischief.

"Sure."

They scramble over the rail and disappear below decks.

"Think they'll behave themselves?" Ken jokes.

That shakes me, sudden conflicting emotions chilling my spine. My lovely surrogate daughter, seemingly a normal, outgoing teenager, is barely a week away from a life that would make this man snatch up his son and run far, far away. Then I remember her shy flirtation on the dock that night in Bournemouth, and her confused uncertainty over how the new Emily should act.

"They'll be fine," I tell him honestly. "Just fine."

* * *

The clouds climb the sky, blotting out even the reflection of the setting sun, and the lights in the marina office dim as people retire to their boats for the night. After more than half a year with almost no one but Jenny for company I'm somewhat rusty in the conversation department, but soon began to feel at ease, sensing both integrity and decency in my guest.

We cover the usual masculine topics, cars and sports and the like, and trade stories about our college days and careers. He seems genuinely interested in the art of architectural design, and we're both surprised to learn that his law firm occupies a floor in one of the first commercial buildings my company put up in Bournemouth. Hoping not to show my general ignorance of things legal, I ask him if his practice specializes in any particular branch of the law.

"I do mostly corporate work," he tells me. "The money isn't bad, and there's a lot less strain to it than some other fields. Criminal law, for example."

"Must be interesting," I say, trying to sound positive but sure that it would bore me stiff. It seems doubtful that contracts and such could do much to satisfy the creative urge.

"Actually, it can be fascinating," he says. "We deal with some real high rollers sometimes, and get to funnel chunks of foreign money into the local economy. And it's gratifying to help people find the right kind of backing for their pet projects. We've funded half a dozen start-up businesses in Bournemouth this year alone, and so far they're all holding their own. One of them, a website designer and all-around computer whiz kid, even has a branch office in Halifax, and he's good enough to make the big boys nervous."

"Ever do any family law?" I hazard. "Divorces, custody cases, that sort of thing?"

"Not me personally. We aren't known for that, and to be honest, I don't find much challenge to it, just a lot of headaches. Once in a while a case will walk in the door, and we either refer it to another firm or one of my younger associates handles it for us. No cloak and dagger stuff, though. No snooping around motel rooms with a camera to catch cheaters in the act."

"Why not? I would think that sort of thing would pay well."

"It does, but to me it's a matter of dignity, I guess. I've always tried to avoid being associated with the shadier law firms, the ambulance chasers. Not that I'm not sympathetic toward people's problems, but domestic disputes can get a little messy sometimes. I shy away from angry confrontations, spouses screaming at each other across the conference table and so forth."

"But you like to help people, right?"

"Every chance I get."

My next question requires considerable courage. "How would you feel about giving me a little free legal advice?"

He laughs. "I'm totally against it. Got to keep up the mercenary reputation of the law profession, you know."

My face must register disappointment, and he sits back and stretches his arms out along the rail, sensing that I'm serious.

"I'm kidding," he says. "After eating such a great meal, I'm at your beck and call. What do you want to know? You aren't having a problem yourself, are you?"

"This is just hypothetical…"

"Names will be changed to protect the innocent. Or guilty, as the case may be. Shoot."

His gentle sense of humour helps to put me at ease. "Suppose, for example, I had personal knowledge of a case involving an abused child."

"A relative of yours?"

"No."

"Then you report it. I can give you a number you can call that…"

"Hang on," I interrupt. "Suppose this child means a lot to this hypothetical non-relative. A whole lot. In fact, suppose it was a kid *you* knew and liked. Would you just turn her over to some social agency?"

"Her?"

"Or him…"

"Well," he says quickly, "at least I know you're not talking about your own daughter. Never have I seen a more delightful kid."

That almost stops me.

If you only knew…

"You're not in some kind of jam, are you?" he continues. "Because if you are, I have an obligation…"

"No, it's nothing like that." If there's a God, may he forgive me for the lies I'm starting to tell. "I know how the police feel about people who have knowledge of a crime and try to conceal it. But sometimes the law perpetuates a crime, or the consequences of it, without meaning to."

"I don't follow."

"Okay, let me give you an example. Suppose a kid gets picked up for something, break and enter, car theft, something like that. Third offence. He gets sent away to a juvenile facility for six months where he learns how to be a better burglar or car thief from the other inmates. Then he gets dumped back onto the streets, supposedly supervised by some welfare agency that has ten times more kids than it can look after. A week later he's back to stealing again and better at it this time, thanks to all that jailhouse education."

"So you know of a boy who…"

"No. That's just an example. I'm talking about what happens to kids who get lost in the shuffle."

"Okay," he agrees, "probably the system loses more than it can save. But there are good people out there trying to make it work better."

"I know that. But let's suppose there's someone who really cares about this particular kid, this car thief. Takes a personal interest and is willing to assume responsibility for him."

"Sure. That happens all the time. An older brother, an uncle…"

"No relation, remember?"

"That's a little stickier. Normally there would have to be some kind of court-approved formal arrangement, like a foster home."

"So are you saying most troubled kids just end up living with strangers?"

"Not always. Sometimes a clergyman who knows a family's situation will take in a troubled child, although with all of the scandals in the Catholic Church lately, they have to be pretty careful with that, too. I once knew of a doctor who took a boy into his home with the blessing of the courts after his mother died. The kid was a real troublemaker at first, but it worked out okay. He's in college now, and doing well."

"But that's rare?"

"Pretty infrequent. Mostly the system has to rely on routine foster care and group homes. I know sometimes it doesn't work out, but you'd be surprised how many people are willing to make room for a child who needs help. An approved foster home is the best solution anyone has come up with yet, and the safest."

"Safest?"

"It's mostly a matter of ensuring protection. There are pretty strict rules governing the custody of minors. There have to be. The authorities bear the final responsibility, so they have to check out a person's motives for offering to take a child in."

"Some people are just in it for the money, I suppose."

"Not as many as you might think. For one thing, the stipend is pretty low. I'd say most foster parents, the sincere ones, end up spending a lot more than they make."

"So in order to take in a troubled kid, you have to have some sort of official stamp of approval?"

"Right. Now how about telling me what's really bothering you so I can give you more specific advice."

"I wish I could," I say sincerely. "Maybe sometime soon I can. If I do, it will be a professional consultation, a paid one."

"We can do that now. Just give me a dollar for a retainer, and anything you tell me from now on will be privileged."

"I'm not quite ready for that. I have to think things through a little longer before I'm sure what's the right thing to do. There's another problem, too."

"And that is…?"

"Suppose the abuse is sexual. How would you go about getting the child checked out medically without the authorities getting involved?"

"You mean, what if they find some sexually transmitted diseases?"

"Right. Would a doctor be obligated to report it?"

"Almost always. It depends on what turns up, and how it was contracted. I can refer you to a clinic that would keep things as confidential as possible, but in the case of HIV or any of the other serious STDs, they'd have to report it. It's standard procedure to demand a list of all known sexual contacts. Otherwise there's no hope of keeping it from spreading."

"Would the child's name have to become known to the public?"

"In the case of minors it's unlikely, same as the way they protect the identities of juvenile offenders. But you know how that works. Plenty of people inside the system have access to that kind of information, and people talk. Is this hypothetical kid likely to be infected?"

"I hope not, but there's a possibility."

"Then you have an obligation to..."

"Ken, please. I've been struggling with what my obligations are for almost a week now, and I can't come up with any answers that won't make matters worse than they already are."

"So this isn't really hypothetical. Who is this child?"

I shake my head.

"At least tell me this," he says. "Is he or she still in the abusive situation?"

"No."

"In any kind of imminent danger?"

"No. Absolutely not."

"Sexually active?"

That shakes me. "No," I tell him simply.

Not any longer.

"I won't press you, then," he says. "But let me give you my phone number and address. When you get back home, check out my firm. I think you'll find our reputation is pretty good, and we're fanatical about protecting the confidentiality of our clients. I'll be ready to help whenever you decide to call on me."

"Thank you. It may be sooner than you think."

He flips over a paper plate and scrawls the information on the back. I fold it twice and slip it into my back pocket.

He glances up at the sky. "That's a storm front, I think. Have you heard a weather forecast?"

"Not since morning, but they were just predicting light rain then. Winds are supposed to pick up, though."

"Then we'd better cast off and anchor out away from you. And we'd better separate those two from the TV. And maybe from each other."

He straddles the rail and calls down into the cabin of his own boat. "All hands on deck! We've got a ship to move."

17

Tuesday, Very Early

Shortly after midnight the erratic motion of the boat tugging on its anchor lines wakes me. The wind is gusting noisily through the rigging and Emily is having the same problem, tossing restlessly in the forward berth. I'm about to make a pot of coffee and try reading for a while when she wanders out into the galley.

"Can't sleep?" I ask her.

"Nope. It's too hot in here." Her face is puffy, her hair disarranged, damp and stringy. Amy's oldest worn tee shirt hangs limply from her shoulders, wrinkled and trailing halfway to her knees.

"Want to go out on deck? It's probably cooler up there."

"Do I have to get dressed?"

"You're decent enough. There's no one around to see you, anyway. Bring a towel or a blanket to lie on."

She leans into the head and finds a big beach towel. I grab my blanket from the bunk beside the engine and lead the way up the ladder. The air feels heavy and dense in spite of the wind, but a change is coming, most likely a cold front from the west.

"Pick a spot," I tell her.

"Same as last time? Top of the cabin?"

"You're on."

The boat pitches uneasily as we make our way forward and stretch out forward of the mast. Waves slap the hull and curl into breakers on the rocks framing the mouth of the harbour.

"Wind's hot," she says.

"Uh, huh."

"No stars."

"Cloudy. Rain coming later."

"That'll feel good."

We lie still for a while, quiet and contemplative. She gazes out toward the Curtis boat, fifty yards to starboard. It's little more than a dark and silent outline, just barely visible in the dim light reflected from the marina's distant lamp posts.

"I had fun today," she tells me. "Thank you."

"Me too."

"Alex is nice."

"I bet he can't sleep either, thinking of you in that beautiful dress."

She pokes me in the ribs. "Never thought I'd ever like wearing one. I used to hate them. But now it makes me feel good."

"Good how?"

"Like a girl, I guess. Is that okay?"

"That's very much okay."

The wind shifts slightly, coming around off the bow and carrying a hint of cooling moisture. Emily sighs and sits up, clasping her arms around her knees.

"I wish we could do this forever," she murmurs softly.

Silence from me.

"No 'me too' this time?" she prompts.

"I could say it, and I could even wish it, but we both know it won't happen."

"I guess not." She picks at the edge of her towel, then idly smoothes it out again. "Why does everything have to hurt so much?"

"Like what?"

"Like I'll probably never see Alex again."

"What makes you so sure? He lives in Bournemouth."

"But I don't. I don't even know where I'm gonna end up."

"Maybe we can find somewhere for you to live near there. How would that be?"

"No good. Now that they've seen me, Lucas and his buddies are gonna keep looking for me there."

"I know, and we have to do something about that, get some help from somewhere. You'll never be safe as long as he's on the loose."

"So what'll you do, sic the police on him?" she asks worriedly, still fearful of anyone in authority, afraid that her past will become known.

"I'm not sure. I would if I thought it could help, but it probably won't."

"The cops don't care about kids like me," she says sadly.

"I think they do. It's just…"

My voice trails off. Eliminating prostitution is like trying to control any other human appetite. You can attempt to drive it underground, but you can't eradicate it. There's too much money to be made. The best the police can do is throw up barriers, and keep it out of nice neighbourhoods. As long as nobody complains too loudly, they turn a blind eye to the problem. Once in a while they make a few arrests for show, but it doesn't do much good.

"I wish they'd just lock him up in jail," she says.

"That wouldn't help for long. He'd get a lawyer and be out on bail the next day."

"You mean if Lucas gets arrested, they'll just let him go again?"

"That's how the system works."

"Some system…"

"Justice is an ideal, not a reality. Human nature keeps getting in the way."

She sighs. "It won't do much good anyway," she says sadly, gazing out toward the Curtis boat again. "Somebody else'll recognize me, all those johns from before. They always do."

"I've been thinking about that too, and I've got an idea."

That sparks her interest. "What?"

"You'll see."

She stretches out again and rolls toward me, propping herself on one elbow. "Come on! Tell me!"

"Nope. You'll have to wait at least until tomorrow. It'll be a surprise. Another birthday present, just a little late."

She flounces back down on the blanket. "I hate secrets! Are you gonna go beat somebody up or something?"

"Not me. I'm a peace-loving guy."

"Yeah, right. I bet Cliff doesn't think so. I wonder if he ever caught up with his boat?"

"That wasn't my fault. I was just defending myself."

"He cut you, though. I thought he was gonna kill you with that knife."

"So did I."

"So how come you didn't run away?" she asks seriously.

"I couldn't just leave you there. And running away never solves anything. You have to face your problems sooner or later."

"But…"

"Look, sometimes you just have to have confidence in yourself. If I thought I had no chance against him, I would have gone for help, but I figured if I could make him mad he'd get careless, and it worked. Besides, if I had left to call the police, he'd have taken off."

"And taken me with him, too."

"Right. That's the main reason why I had to stay."

"You sure surprised him. He flew off that dock like a soccer ball." She giggles. "And I bet you broke his hand when he tried to climb out."

"I doubt it. And as I told you, it was self defence. Violence isn't the answer to a problem like this, at least not permanently."

"I'm still glad you hurt him. He hurt me enough times…"

Amy's Pride shifts to port and tugs gently on her bow anchor line. The wind is definitely dropping, the lines now barely ticking against the mast. The thickening clouds press down, nearly filling the sky and only occasionally parting to reveal a wan moon fleeing before the storm.

"Rain for sure by morning," I tell her.

"Can we stay out here?"

"It'll be cold when it comes."

"I don't care."

The boat has taken on a gentle side-to-side sway, the waves lapping the hull musically. Cradle and lullaby. Emily's small hand brushes mine, tentative and unsure. She retreats, then touches me again. I reach out and take her hand gently, giving her a little squeeze. Her breath catches, then sighs. She says something, too softly for me to hear.

"I didn't get that."

"I said I wish you were really my Dad. Then I could stay with you forever."

Forever… Amy and I had said those words once, when what lay before us was a landscape filled with endless possibilities, a future now bleak and cheerless without her. But Emily's outlook might still be made bright, salvaged from the wreckage of accident, abuse and slavery. The world owes her more than the comfort of holding my hand, the temporary reassurance that someone cares, and I have to find a way to make it happen.

"I talked to Mr. Curtis about our problem last night," I say quietly.

"What?" She drops my hand and sits bolt upright, eyes widening alarmingly. "You didn't tell him about me, did you?"

"Of course not. All I did was ask some questions about how the law works for runaway kids, but he doesn't know I was talking about you."

"God, if Alex ever knew…"

"He won't. Anyway, I was trying to find out if there's any way other than foster care to help kids who don't have any place to live."

"What did he say?"

"He's a corporate lawyer and this kind of thing isn't his specialty, but he thinks that's the only way. He promised to look into it, though, and to help us if we need him."

"No. Then he'll find out about me, about what I've been doing."

"We won't ever tell him that. We can tell him why you ran away from Uncle Frank, and that's all."

"You really think he can help me?"

"We have to trust someone. I think it's worth the risk."

There isn't anything more to say. She lies down again and her hand creeps back into mine, soft and warm and trusting. The air has cooled and I draw the edge of my blanket over her. Eventually I feel her hand relax as she drifts off to sleep. Toward morning, as the first faint promise of dawn touches the sky, light rain begins to fall. I wake her enough to climb down the ladder, and she falls asleep again almost before she reaches her bunk.

* * *

Lulled by the rain's soothing music on the deck, I manage more than an hour's sleep before the weak, cloud-shrouded daylight penetrates the portholes. Emily sleeps until well after nine. When she finally wanders out of the bow compartment, eyes dull and skin blotchy from the warmth of the cabin, she slumps in the corner seat of the galley barely awake. I make breakfast for her, and gradually she begins to come to life.

"No sailing today," I tell her. "The radio says light rain until noon and no wind all day, so we'll have to use the engine."

"What'll we do, then?"

"A good day for your surprise, I think."

"What is it?"

"Wait and see."

She scrunches around and kneels on the seat cushion, looking out across the harbour.

"Alex's boat is gone."

"I know. I heard their engine start up about an hour ago."

She flops down on the bench, sombre and pensive.

171

"I know right where to find him, though," I say offhandedly.

She brightens. "You do?"

"Sure. His dad gave me their address and phone number."

"How come?"

"Remember I said he offered to help us? Maybe he'll have some ideas on how to find a place where you can live. Get you back in school again, so you can have a normal life."

"I've been thinking about that, too. Why can't I just stay with you?"

"We've already been over this. It's not possible."

"Why not?" She sits up stiff and straight. "I thought you said you liked me."

"I do, but that's not the problem."

"What is, then?"

"You can't go to school by boat. We'd have to move back to the mainland."

"So?" she persists.

"Think about it. Here's this burned-out architect who lets his career go to hell, goes off and lives on an island, and all of a sudden he shows up back home and there's a fourteen-year-old girl living with him. No school records, no birth certificate, nothing. You think that wouldn't cause talk?"

"You can get all that stuff from Uncle Frank."

"From what you've told me, I think he'd want to get you back. And legally, he probably could."

"No way! I'd run away again!"

"And go where? That didn't work out so well the last time."

She slumps in the corner. I carry our plates to the sink, then return to the table and slide onto the bench beside her.

"We can't cut corners," I tell her. "If we're going to get you safely back into the world, we have to work with the law, not against it."

"I still don't see why I can't live with you."

"Because you're a minor. You come under the jurisdiction of the child protection services, and I doubt that they give young girls away to single men."

"Boy, they don't know much, do they? Where were they when Lucas had me?"

"They do their best."

"Didn't help me much." She folds her arms and shrinks down within herself. "I might just as well go back to him, I guess."

172

"You don't mean that."

"Why not? You don't want me!"

"I never said that."

"You didn't have to!" she says angrily. "You keep making up all these excuses why I can't stay with you, so that means you don't want me to!"

"They aren't excuses. It's the law…"

She squirms out from behind the table and stamps off toward the forward compartment. I let her go. There doesn't seem to be any way to make her understand.

As I wash and dry the breakfast dishes, assorted noises echo from the forward berth, an occasional thump and the soft swish of clothing. I'm sitting at the table again with another cup of coffee when she comes out, dressed in a simple top and shorts and her old sneakers. She flops down on the bench across from me, glaring defiantly.

"I thought you threw those away when you tossed Bambi's clothes in my trash barrel," I say, pointing to her feet.

"We left them here on the boat the day we went shopping. I'm ready to go now."

"Go where?"

"Back. I left all the stuff you bought me in there. Except these." She indicates the clothes she's wearing. "I'll get them back to you later somehow." She sits sullenly, idly playing with her fingers and avoiding my eyes.

"All those clothes belong to you," I tell her.

"I don't want them."

"Why not?"

She shrugs, eyes cast down to the floor.

"Slide over here," I say.

"What for?"

"You need a hug."

"Not from you."

"Would it help if I said I'm sorry?"

"It doesn't matter."

"To me it does."

"You don't want me. Nobody wants a kid who's been a whore. What other reason is there?"

There it is, out in the open.

"I told you before, that wasn't you. It was some other person named

173

Bambi. I never knew her. I've only known you for a few days, but I like you. Nothing that happened before makes any difference to me."

"Yeah, sure."

"Can you look at me, please?"

Her eyes flash angrily.

"Try to see it from my angle, just for a minute, okay? I don't know anything about how to look after a teenager. I haven't even got a career any more. My cabin is no place for you. You need a nice place to live, go to school, have friends. I can't make that happen. The authorities won't *let* that happen."

"You could do it if you wanted to. You just don't want to try. You only want to get rid of me."

"That's not true."

"Where did you live before, anyway?"

"Just outside of Bournemouth. The house is closed up now."

"See? All that stuff about the cabin is just an excuse. If you really liked me, you could move back there and take me with you."

Could I?

I had hired a security company to look after the house until I could force myself to put it on the market, too unhappy to live in the midst of all the memories Amy and I had shared together. I saw her around every corner, felt her in the shadows and reached out for her, only to grasp intolerable emptiness. Unable to stand it any longer, I had flown.

It had been a happy house, far more than merely walls and a roof, because Amy had been with me. There had been such promise, a lifetime stretching ahead of us with a child to make us complete, and then the sudden, violent end to all our dreams.

A child...

"Would you like to see my house some time?" I ask her.

She cocks her head and the frown softens for a moment, then drops back in place. "What for? I'm never going to get to live in it."

"If things work out, maybe you'll be staying someplace close by. You can visit."

"Where is it?"

"Northwest of town, about a kilometre over the county line. It has a big yard, lots of open space. There's even a duck pond close by, and woods to explore. There's skating on the pond in the winter."

Her face closes down again. "Nothing to do with me."

"Sweetheart, I'm so sorry, but even if we could make it happen, I just don't know where I'm going from now on. In fact, I'm planning to sell the house this fall. I can't make any kind of life for you. I haven't cared about much of anything since my wife died."

"I thought for a while that you cared about me."

"I did. I do."

"Well? I wouldn't be any trouble!" The words tumble out desperately. "I'd stay out of your way, and I could help you take care of your house and everything. I'm good at that, cleaning and stuff. Didn't I do a good job on the ice box?"

"Yes, but…"

"You wouldn't even know I was there."

She just doesn't understand. "The social worker…"

"I'll tell her about Uncle Frank!" she blurts. "What he did to me, maybe even about Lucas if I have to. She'll see I haven't got any other place to go, and she'll let me stay with you. She *has* to!"

"Take it easy. That isn't the only problem."

"Then what is?"

I look away. "I don't know."

But of course I do know. I'm desperately afraid to let anyone get close to me again, afraid to have anyone to care about. Afraid to risk a repeat of that terrible feeling of loss if…

And then I realize how selfish that is. I have something to give, a role to play that no social agency, perhaps no one else in the world can fill. Emily trusts me, and I can't turn her away. Equally important, I can't go back into my shell again, hiding from the world as if I have nothing more to offer.

I once told Emily to face her problems, not to run away. Maybe it's time to take my own advice. Could she be the one to help me to fill those barren rooms, a child like the one Amy and I had planned for but now would never have? Not a replacement for what I had lost, but someone to give my life a sense of purpose again.

A reason to get up every morning.

How long have I known her? Just a week, but in some ways a lifetime. Someone else watched her grow up, first the parents who were torn away too soon, later the perverted uncle to whom she was nothing but a target for his sick obsessions. Then came her captivity, the unimaginable horror of sexual exploitation that should have destroyed her innocence.

But I've been the one to see her transformed from abused and scornful hooker back into the shy, ingenuous child she must once have been. It's a remarkable recovery, but no more extraordinary than the change she's wrought in me. Since Amy's death I've become a self-absorbed and reclusive hermit. Now once again I have someone who needs me.

Someone I need, too.

She breaks my reverie. "If I end up in some foster home, I'll never see you again."

"I've been thinking about that just now. That would make me very sad."

"Me too."

"And foster parents are just ordinary people, right?"

"I guess."

"Like me?"

She stares at me in wonder. "You mean...?"

"What if Mr. Curtis can fix it so I can be your foster dad? Legally, I mean."

"Can he do that?"

"I'm not sure. He says foster parents have to be approved somehow. But if you want me to try..."

"You really want me to stay with you?"

"That's what I'm trying to tell you."

Her expression is a turmoil of hope and distrust. I've made a commitment, perhaps the most important one in my life since Amy and I said "I do." Now I have to find some way to honour it.

"Suppose we give it a try," I tell her. "We'll ask Mr. Curtis to represent us, and we'll do whatever it takes for you to stay with me."

"What if they won't let me?"

"I don't know. All I can do is try to make it happen. But if they won't let you stay with me, no matter where you go, I'll always be somewhere close by and watching out for you. That's the most I can promise. And I've still got that hug to give away."

She slides over and wraps arms around my waist, burying her face against my chest.

"We'll make this work somehow. You'll see."

She mumbles something into my shirt front. I tilt her chin up. There are tear tracks on her cheeks, but she's smiling.

"Come again?"

"No matter what happens, you're stuck with me."

18
Tuesday

We sit playing cards at the galley table until after eleven o'clock. The rain slackens to showers, then stops completely, but clouds hang low over the mainland. I open up the cabin to air it out and we climb up on deck. In the distance the dock is two-thirds empty, many of the slips having been vacated earlier in the day.

"Let's tie up over there so we can go ashore," I tell her. "I want to find out if this town is big enough for your birthday surprise."

"What is it?"

"You'll see."

"You keep saying that! Tell me!"

"Whoa. A little temperamental, are we?"

"I told you, I hate secrets!" She stamps her tiny foot ineffectually, making little noise on the fibreglass deck.

"You've still got your old sneakers on," I say. "Scruffy. I'm not taking you anywhere in those."

"Don't change the subject! Where are we going?"

"Sneakers..."

"You make me so mad!"

"I work at it."

"Suppose I just won't go with you?"

"Then you'll miss out on some fun."

She collapses onto the port locker. "I give up."

"Come on. See if you can remember how to start the engine, and we'll put this thing next to the pier."

She scampers below to get her good sneakers, and I go forward to haul up the bow anchor. There are very few boats next to the dock and lots of room to manoeuvre, so I decide to let her pilot the boat in. I hand her the ignition key when she comes through the hatch, and haul up the stern anchor as she brings the diesel to life. As soon as it's running smoothly, she turns to me impatiently, hands on her hips.

"Well? Let's get going."

"Be my guest."

"Huh?"

"You've seen me do it often enough. Put her in gear and take her in."

Her jaw drops. "What if I smash into the dock?"

"You won't."

"But what if I do?"

"Just go slowly, that's all. Practice with the wheel a little before you get too close. If you get in trouble, I'll tell you what to do."

"If I get in trouble, you can take over!"

"Nope."

"I don't get it. This boat must be worth like a million dollars, and you're trusting me to…to…"

"Uh, huh."

She stamps her foot again. "But what if…"

"You're missing something," I interrupt her.

"What?"

"You just said it. I trust you."

That stops her cold. She stares open-mouthed, trying to process such an amazing concept, then edges over behind the wheel.

"Tell me what to do."

"No, you tell me. What do I always do first?"

"You look over the transom at something. I've never figured out what."

"You see? You're more observant than you realize. I always check the water discharge to be sure it isn't clogged up. If it is, the engine can overheat."

She bends to look over the rail. "There's a whole bunch of water coming out."

"So it's working. What's next?"

"I can't remember."

"Okay, there are two main controls besides the wheel, the throttle and the gear shift."

I explain how everything works, and for the next few minutes she practices moving *Amy's Pride* forward and backward with the engine barely above an idle. I leave her to it and rig the bumpers on the rail. Gradually she gains confidence, getting the feel of how the engine affects the rudder.

"Two things to watch out for," I tell her. "There isn't any wind, so you don't have to worry about that, but the tide is pretty strong, running at an angle to the dock. It'll push you toward the pilings, so you'll have to compensate."

"How?"

"Come in slow and a couple of yards out, and the tide will carry you in sideways, nice and gentle."

"What's the second thing?"

"Remember that when you take it out of gear, the boat won't stop right away. It'll keep drifting forward, so you have to aim for where you want to be after the propeller stops turning."

"I can't do this."

"Sure you can."

She advances the gearshift but not the throttle, and we creep across the expanse of open water at a snail's pace, aiming for the side of the pier. The tide bears against the side of the hull, and before we've covered half the distance the bow is pointing directly toward the blunt end of the dock.

"What happened?" she asks.

"The tide. We're going too slowly to counteract it, so you have to leave extra room. Swing out and line it up with that building on shore," I tell her, pointing to an old fisherman's shed. "That'll give you enough room."

She twists the wheel, and with so little headway *Amy's Pride* responds sluggishly, the idling engine grumbling. She cranes her neck in fierce concentration to see beyond the dodger as we approach the dock. Once again we lose the battle with the tide, and the pilings loom up in front of the bow, too close to pass safely.

"Shit." She spins the wheel and comes about for another try.

"Sailors don't say 'shit'," I tell her.

"What do they say?"

"How about 'shiver me timbers'?"

That earns me a grin. She manoeuvres the boat into line for another try, another failed attempt to come in safely.

"Help me!"

"You're doing fine. You just have to practice. And you're being too cautious. Give it a little more throttle."

"Suppose I hit the dock too hard? I can't do it!"

"You'll have to."

Time for a little play-acting. I squint my eyes shut and throw my hand to my forehead, palm out, a dramatic silent movie gesture. "I've been struck blind! I've fallen overboard! You're out here all alone with no one to help you, so you have to save yourself."

"Stop kidding around. I can't do this."

"You did once before."

"Huh?"

"Saved yourself. When you found my island."

"Shit!"

"What?"

She gives me a 'stupid parent' look. "Shiver me timbers!"

"That's better. And I'm hungry, so you'd better get us ashore darn quick."

She eases the throttle forward a notch and grips the wheel tensely. It isn't a pretty approach. The bow waggles back and forth as she coasts by the dock too far out, then overcompensates and bounces against the pilings, squashing the bumpers almost flat, but before long we have *Amy's Pride* safely and securely tied on spring lines.

"Did I hurt it?" she asks anxiously, peering over the side at the hull.

"No damage done. The bumpers did their job. And you did better than I did on my first try. You should have heard Amy laugh at me. Next time will be even better."

There's a hint of pride in her stance, a stiffer spine, as we close up the hatchway and fasten the padlock.

" 'I can't'," I whisper softly as we hop over the rail onto the dock and head for the marina office.

"Leave me alone," she mutters, but there's a tiny grin on her face. Step by step, each little accomplishment is helping to rebuild her confidence and self esteem.

We go inside to pay the dockage fee, and I ask the attendant to recommend somewhere for lunch. He suggests a bayside place north of the marina. Emily wanders over to a display of ship models, and I lean in close and ask the man where I might find the kind of services I need for her surprise.

"You'll have to go up the line into town," he tells me. "There are three places you can try, but in my opinion this is the best one." He writes a name and address on a slip of paper.

"How far is it?"

"About four or five klicks. You could walk, but it's gonna get hot pretty soon. There's a bus that comes through about quarter past one." He tells me where to find the bus stop.

"Should I phone for an appointment?" I ask.

"Wouldn't hurt. They're usually pretty busy during the summer."

He writes the number down for me, and I get through to a woman named Tanya who says she can accommodate us at 1:30. Emily joins me and we leave the marina and head off down the narrow road that skirts the bay.

"Hungry?" I ask her.

"Shiver me timbers!"

"I gather that means yes this time. The man in the office said the Seaside Shack is the best, unless you want McDonald's or Burger King."

"No. I've got bad feelings about fast food places now. Let's try the seafood one."

"I hear they're having a special on squid soup."

"Can I have a squid burger, too?"

"Sure. Or squid pizza."

"A squid shake!" she squeals delightedly.

"You win. I can't top that."

The sun begins to break through the clouds, dappling the waters of the bay. After walking half a kilometre we arrive at a tiny restaurant, perched upon a ramshackle wharf that sits high above the water. Rippling wavelets wash the rocks below, and gulls fight over scraps and the clam shells that litter a narrow expanse of sand beside the road, a scene right out of the tourist brochures. The birds are probably on the Board of Trade's payroll.

Half a dozen tables crowd each other inside the small dining room, fighting for space. Beyond a tall glass window we can see another seven or eight outside on the wharf, each one shaded by a large fringed umbrella.

"In or out?" I ask her.

"Out," she says happily, and we push through the screen door into sea breeze and sunshine. A young man in a captain's hat hands us our menus. His tailored jacket sports gold braid on the shoulders.

"Is he for real?" Emily whispers as he retreats to the kitchen.

"Tourist stuff," I answer. "He probably doesn't know a gaff from a gopher."

She giggles and opens the menu. "No squid."

"Let's leave, then. This is obviously a second-rate establishment."

We both order a rich lobster chowder, and enjoy a pleasant twenty minutes of good food, easy banter, beautiful scenery and incomparable weather. Emily is good company. It's a little past one when we finish.

"We have to hurry," I tell her as we leave the restaurant.

"Why?"

"We have an appointment."

"Where?"

"Come on." We hurry inland and locate the bus shelter a few hundred yards along the busy coastal highway. Half a dozen others are waiting inside, out of the hot sun. One-fifteen comes and goes, and I'm beginning to worry that we'll be late.

After such a great lunch, Emily's spirits are high. Being far away from Lucas Brady is no doubt the main reason. She's eagerly anticipating the prospect of an adventure, whatever it turns out to be, and pesters me to tell her where we're going. Finally the bus arrives, and we pay our fare and take seats near the front. Three stops later we get off at a busy intersection.

"Now what?" she begs.

"This way. Hurry up. The man at the marina told me it's just about half way down Commercial Street."

"What is?"

"You'll see."

"Will you please *stop* that?"

"It's not much farther. Come on!"

In the middle of the next block we come to a stop in front of the entrance to a prosperous looking salon. Oversized glass windows flank the door, revealing plenty of activity inside. At twenty minutes before two, every chair inside is full but one.

"This is it," I tell her. "I called ahead from the marina. They're expecting you."

"What for?"

"Whatever you want. A cut, a perm, even a dye job. Something that will turn you into a new Emily and leave the old one behind, somebody that most people won't even recognize."

"I don't want my hair cut."

"That's fine, just get a trim then. They'll do whatever you want. But they'll probably have some good ideas, and you might want to listen to them."

She hesitates in the doorway. "I've never been inside a place like this."

"Come on. It'll be fun. I guarantee it."

"I take care of my own hair."

"And you do a good job, too. But what's the harm in getting a little advice from a pro?"

She opens the door and steps through uncertainly, and a blue-smocked woman in her mid thirties comes over to greet us. I give her Emily's name and tell her we have an appointment with Tanya.

"That's me," she says, leading us toward the second chair from the back. Emily boosts herself up reluctantly. The stylist snaps a protective sheet across her chest and ties it around her neck. Then she moves to one side and meets Emily's eyes in the mirror. She fingers the substantial ponytail. "Wow! You've been growing this for quite a while, huh?"

"Sorry we're late," I say.

"No problem. I was running behind anyway. Are you from around here?"

"No, we're down from Bournemouth. Just out for a sail, and thought we'd get spruced up a little."

"*You* did, not me," Emily mutters. Tanya looks puzzled.

"The man at the marina recommended this place," I tell her.

"That's Todd, my husband's brother. He steers me some business sometimes. What is it you'd like me to do?"

"Talk to Emily. I'm just along for the ride."

"What do you think?" Tanya asks her.

"This wasn't my idea."

Tanya raises her eyebrows at me and I shrug, the very picture of an ignorant, helpless father.

"A lot of girls would kill for hair as thick as yours," she says, sliding the elastic ring from the ponytail, "but it's taking away from your best features. Your pretty eyes, for example. And it's not right for the shape of your face this way."

"I like it like this," Emily grumbles. She's anxious and uncertain, and a little bit defiant. So far my surprise isn't working out the way I figured.

"We can leave it this way if you want. Just a little trim, maybe. But look at this."

She separates Emily's hair into fat skeins on either side of her head, folds it under and fluffs it out on either side of her heart-shaped face. She draws the ends back and hides them behind her hands.

A different child stares out of the mirror at me, the contours of her face now softly rounded and much less overwhelmed by the masses of hair. Emily opens her eyes wide, and their deep brown colour seems to leap out into the room. Her mouth slackens in surprise.

"Holy sh... Cow!"

"See?" the woman says. "And that's just one idea. We could do this instead."

She coils the mound of hair into a fat swirl and piles it on top of Emily's head, adding five years of sophistication to her youthful profile.

"Or this…"

She skins the hair back severely at the temples, loops it over her fingers, and lets it hang down in a wide fall. Then she releases it, and the old Emily snaps back into focus.

"Well?" Tanya prompts. "Just a trim, or shall we experiment a little?"

Emily's eyes plead with me. She's overwhelmed.

"Your choice, sweetheart," I tell her. "But I say, go for it."

She grins. "I liked everything but the second one."

"Okay," Tanya says, "let's go over it all again. I've got some other ideas, too."

"How long?" I ask her.

"Give us at least two hours."

Taking a seat by the door, I watch them for a few minutes. Indifferent and resistant only a few minutes before, Emily is leaning forward eagerly, staring at the mirror as the stylist performs magic for her. Once it seems certain that things will go well, I head for the door and push through into the street. She doesn't even see me go.

I find myself in a typical South Shore town, the main street lined with cafés and an assortment of craft and souvenir shops that tempt the tourists to stay longer. Their specialty seems to be imported woollens. Scottish tartans crowd the display windows, along with fully rigged ship models and diminutive lobster traps. There are rows of neat miniature wooden lighthouses and beautifully hand-carved decoys, the best that Nova Scotia folk artists have to offer. Not a sign of imported plastic junk anywhere.

I wander down the street, taking in the sights and finally ending up in front of that staple of every prosperous Maritime town, a Tim Horton's coffee shop. A vending machine beside the door gives up a weekly newspaper. The shop is more than half full, and I order an extra large black and carry it to a table tucked away in one corner, out of the flow of traffic.

Not much in the local paper interests me. I find myself watching the other customers come and go, people I don't know, will probably never know, all with myriad goals and desires and responsibilities. Not one seems to be in retreat from life as I am.

A quartet of young matrons enters, three of them pushing strollers. They choose muffins and fancier drinks than mine, iced cappuccinos and designer teas, and crowd around a table across the aisle from me. A bright two-year-old turns his solemn face in my direction.

I smile at him and return to my paper, but he continues to stare at me, frowning. His rosebud mouth puckers and he furrows his brow, threatening tears. I cross my eyes and give him a wide Joe E. Lewis grin. He ducks his head and tucks his chin into the collar of his shirt, peering at me from beneath tiny blond eyebrows.

My specialty is sucked-in cheeks and fish lips, and he breaks into a wide grin. I stick out my lower lip and try to touch my nose with it, and he laughs out loud. His mother looks down, then over at me, but I'm once again studying the newsprint.

When she looks away I cross my eyes at the little guy again, and he crows delightedly. This time his mother catches me. I smile and wave to her and she smiles back. I make a few more faces at the child until he loses interest. Growing sleepy, he sticks his thumb in his mouth and scrunches down in the stroller.

I've missed a lot, not having a family of my own. During the last few months of her life, Amy had talked of little else but starting a baby. My life was fairly settled by that time and I liked it that way, but achieving tenure at the university guaranteed her some permanence and stability, and her contract included excellent maternity benefits. She was in a hurry to experience everything life had to offer, and motherhood was high on her list.

She was an only child, never having coped with the battles of sibling rivalry as I had, and I suspected she had a somewhat idyllic view of parenthood. I also thought that the constant strain of dealing with other people's offspring in the classroom might have discouraged her from wanting her own, but apparently that isn't the way things work. She had enjoyed her two years of public school teaching as much as her work at the university, and seemed to relate well to students of any age. I was confident that she would become an excellent, caring parent.

Just a week before the accident, the home pregnancy kit tested positive.

Our last day together was very special. We spent an entire afternoon window shopping at Mic Mac Mall, examining nursery furniture, car seats, strollers and the myriad equipment necessary to give a newborn a proper start in the world.

Amy lingered in a children's clothing store, fingering the outfits for infants and toddlers. Finally she came upon the cute little dresses for two-, three- and four-year-olds. I was getting impatient and was about to try to hurry her up when she turned to me with tears in her eyes, but a huge smile on her face.

"What's the matter?" I asked, concerned.

"I'm so happy!" she said. "We're going to have our own baby."

I'm on my own now and will never have that baby, hers and mine together. Instead I've acquired an awkward child-woman who now commands my full attention and fills, at least in part, a terrible void in my life.

Shaking off the daydream, I turn my attention to the newspaper's crossword puzzle, a challenge I haven't faced in more than six months. Seldom buying a paper during all that time, I've mostly ignored the news too, only occasionally listening to the radio. The world has gone by without my input, and I haven't cared.

Now I have to care.

Fifteen down, "modern day gladiator" in eight letters is probably pugilist. Twenty-three across, "of domes and brushes" has to be Fuller, for Buckminster and the venerable door-to-door vendor. Eleven down stumps me for a minute: "Fantine" in ten letters. Then it hits me, the sad, reluctant prostitute in *Les Misérables*, condemned by a callous society that cared little about the implacable forces that put her on the street.

Too close to home. Someone else can finish the puzzle.

Three older teenagers saunter in, the essence of cool. The two girls sport numerous punctures, out of which sprout rings and studs and shiny stones. Their tops and jeans come nowhere near to meeting. The boy's pants could hold a pro wrestler, with room left over for an entire peewee hockey team. What's keeping them up I can't imagine.

They order cold drinks and pastries and sit at the central table closest to the window. See and be seen. How often at that age the search for identity results in slavish imitation of one another. How important it must be for them to advertise their desperately sought individuality by becoming indistinguishable from the herd.

Will this be Emily in a year or two? Somehow, after what she has been through, it seems unlikely. To her, the world will never seem that superficial.

Two elderly men limp unsteadily through the door, one with a cane, the other hunched and trembling, bearing the burden of early Parkinson's disease. They order coffee in china mugs and find an out-of-the-way place to sit. I suspect they will nurse their drinks as long as management permits, probably until the supper hour puts table space at a premium.

Come and go. Once important cogs in the machine of society, many such as these eventually become sadly unnecessary ones, outliving their usefulness. Drop them from among the living and others quickly fill the void. Like burned-out architects, their presence or absence scarcely makes a difference.

I wonder who's building my houses now.

According to my watch less than an hour has passed, and Tanya wanted two as a minimum, assuming she's been able to convince Emily to throw caution to the wind. There's little doubt of her success.

The street outside Tim Horton's is mostly empty in the heat of afternoon, and I wander along the row of shops, looking into windows and watching the people go about their routines. I feel strangely disconnected, and suddenly realize why. For a week I've been trailed by a constant companion, rarely away from my side except to sleep, and even then no more than a few metres away. Thanks to her my loneliness has begun to recede, and I miss her.

I really miss her.

There's a cluttered used bookstore down a side alley, all but invisible among more prosperous stores. Its windows are streaked and a patina of dust covers much of the stock strewn about the sills. The heavy old oak door swings open to reveal a wonderland of ceiling-high shelves, each one crammed to bursting with colourful jackets, rich leather bindings and ancient texts. Broken spines attest to loving perusal by many scholars, most probably long gone.

The shop is much deeper than it appears from the street, the shelves seeming to stretch endlessly toward the back. Torn scraps of lined foolscap are thumb-tacked to the uprights, identifying the categories of the collection in carelessly scrawled pencil notations. Lazy fans turn beneath an ornate nineteenth century pressed-tin ceiling.

I'm surprised and pleased to discover an astonishing array of construction and architectural volumes in a distant corner, embracing everything from ancient monuments to contemporary urban planning. Familiar names, Wright and Pei and other icons, jump out at me from the dust jackets, side by side with the new young lions. Cutting edge stuff!

One oversized paperback attracts me, a pictorial essay on significant developments in mid-priced residential housing for the nineteen-eighties, already well out of date. The world has passed it by with astonishing speed, and I suspect that in my brief absence, I too am a relic, no longer relevant.

Another aisle rewards my restless exploration with a host of esoteric tomes, privately printed volumes by writers to whom fame and income meant little. They created knowledge, or manipulated it, and it was enough that their thoughts and conclusions would survive them in print.

What will I leave behind?

I decide to buy the book on residential design to justify my dalliance in the store, and find an elderly clerk poring over a volume of eighteenth century philosophy behind the front counter. He barely notices me, seeming almost to resent the time stolen from Voltaire and Kant to change my twenty. Had I simply tucked it under my arm and walked out, I doubt that he would have noticed.

There's more than one way for a person to hide.

The lateness of the hour surprises me, after four, and I retrace my steps to the salon. Tanya is just beginning a shampoo for another customer. Emily's absence makes me nervous, and I'm about to interrupt the stylist when she notices me and waves her hand toward a chair near the door, indicating a small figure I had barely noticed.

Two impish eyes sparkle over the top of a magazine. She lowers it slowly, eager to see my reaction. Gone is the massive overabundance, replaced by a sculptured cap that curls inward to tickle her jaw line on either side. Every rich brown strand shines, overlaid with just a touch of auburn.

"Well?" she says, wearing a coy and sophisticated smile.

"I beg your pardon, mademoiselle, but have we been introduced?"

"Isn't it great?" She bounces out of the chair and spins around to show me the back. She shakes her head and the waves swirl around her ears, then fall back perfectly into place.

"Who are you, anyway?"

"I'm *me!*"

"You sure are. And is that a new colour you're sporting?"

"Just a few highlights. That's what she called them. I love it!"

"You're too young for that!" I tease.

"I am not! Tanya said so!"

She bounds over to the mirror, turning her head this way and that. She's apparently become a celebrity. One of the stylists calls to her by name, and beckons her to the back of the salon where a twelve-year-old sits nervously under a protective sheet, dwarfed by the chair. Emily hurries over and I watch as she preens, happy to serve as an example to another reluctant customer.

Tanya wipes the shampoo from her hands and motions me toward the cash register. "I'm afraid it comes to quite a bit," she says. "We got a little carried away."

"It's worth it just to see the change in how she feels about herself. How long will it stay that way?"

"She has wonderful hair. We just followed the way it wants to grow, and that's how it turned out. It won't take much care, and I explained to her what to do."

Form follows function. This woman might have been a successful architect, had she not chosen her current profession. I pay the charges and add a generous tip, along with my thanks.

A different child leaves the salon with me, transformed into a confident young woman whose appearance I hope will go unnoticed and unremarked by those who have known her under other, less wholesome circumstances. Maybe, just maybe, we're going to pull it off.

19
Tuesday Evening

A short bus ride takes us back to the marina for another good meal from the barbeque aboard *Amy's Pride*. The harbour is a portrait out of the nineteenth century, a dozen or more graceful boats returning under full canvas before a warm and gentle southerly breeze.

"It's nice here," Emily says as we clean up the leftovers. "Do we have to go back tomorrow?" The spectre of a return to the Bournemouth area is making her uneasy.

"I'm afraid so," I tell her. "Old Jenny will be running out of food, and she'll need her water freshened up."

"Can she get out?"

"Sure. I built her a little cat door, but she doesn't use it much, mostly just for sanitary disposal. She's a homebody, and a world-class coward."

"What's 'sanitary disposal'?"

"You figure it out."

"Oh." Another thought occurs to her. "If she can go out, what's to keep other stuff from getting in?"

"Good question, and that was a major problem when we first started going to the island. The cat door was down low near the floor, and we used to find squirrels inside sometimes when we'd come back late in the day. Once a racoon tried to get in, but the opening was too small and it got stuck. That was a circus, let me tell you."

"What did you do?"

"Nothing. Those guys have teeth. We just waited him out, and eventually he worked his way free. That wasn't the worst, though."

Her eyes sparkle, twice as big as before with all that hair gone. I have her undivided attention.

"Late one afternoon we came home and found Jenny on top of the chest in the bedroom with her fur standing straight up. We couldn't figure out what was wrong. I lifted her down and took her out into the kitchen, but she wouldn't stay on the floor. She kept jumping up on the table. Later, while we were having supper, another cat came waddling out of the bedroom."

"Another cat?"

"A nice fat one, mostly black with a white stripe down its back. What some people call a wood pussy."

"Uh, oh."

"'Uh, oh' is right! Amy and I stood up very slowly and backed up out the door. Then we took off really fast, didn't stop running until we were halfway to the trees. I left the door open, and fortunately that old skunk decided to leave. But I nailed the cat door shut that night and made a new one the next day, halfway up the wall."

"What good did that do?"

"There's a little shelf on each side, and Jenny can jump up on it to go in and out. She's a good jumper, but skunks aren't. We haven't had any trouble since."

We! I suddenly realize I'm speaking as if Amy still shares the cabin with me.

"I never noticed it," Emily says. "Where is it?"

"Next to the wood stove."

"Don't the squirrels still get in?"

"I put a spring on it. Jenny is strong enough to push it open, but the squirrels are too little."

"If we don't get back in time to feed her, won't she catch a mouse or something?"

"She might try, and that wouldn't be good. Wild rodents have all sorts of parasites, worms and things. They could make her sick."

She sighs. "I had a cat once."

"You told me. What happened to it?"

"I don't know. My aunt and uncle gave it away when I went to live with them."

"Jenny can be yours now. You can feed her when we get back if you want to."

"Okay. But I still wish we could stay out here longer."

"We can do this again sometime. Besides, we have to make a stop at the laundromat on the way home tomorrow. Can't have you looking scruffy, especially with that new coif."

"New *what?*"

"Hairdo. I thought you had a good vocabulary."

"I do. You talk weird sometimes."

Always eager to help out, she scrapes the leftovers from our meal over the rail to feed the fish, and dumps the paper plates into a trash bag before disappearing down below. The difference in her is amazing. No longer overpowered by that huge mass of hair, her face has lost the waif-like appeal that Lucas must have traded on. Equally important, the defeat in her eyes is almost gone, that haunted look that sees no future worth living.

The transformation is probably radical enough to fool anyone who doesn't know her well, including most of the degenerates who paid to molest her. I have no real hope of deceiving Lucas, however. I'm beginning to think that the only solution is to move her completely out of the area, to another part of the province.

Wondering what she's up to, I go below decks and find her sitting at the galley table, repacking the duffel bag.

"Are you coming back up?" I ask her.

"I'm just looking at some of my stuff. You're right. Some of it needs to be washed."

She fingers the blue halter we bought at the boat shop, examining the embroidered anchors. She puts it in the bag, then smoothes out the little cover-up skirt to her swimsuit and folds it neatly in quarters.

"I never had so much nice stuff," she says. "Know what?"

"Tell me."

"Everything's new."

"Well, sure."

"What I mean is, I threw out my old stuff, and you bought me these. There's nothing left from before."

I know what "before" means. "You are too," I tell her gently.

"What?"

"New."

She toys with the zipper on the duffel, then pulls it closed. "Where's the laundromat we're going to?"

"In Bournemouth. Right near the harbour."

A sad expression crosses her face, and I'm wondering if the old fears are eating at her again. Instead, she surprises me.

"Think we could go see where Alex lives?"

"I don't see why not. If not tomorrow, at least real soon. I bet he'll be glad to see you."

She stands up and carries her duffel to the forward compartment. She comes back looking serious.

"Do you think I'll ever meet someone?" she says shyly as she eases herself down on the seat. She plays with the button on the waistband of her shorts, avoiding my eyes.

"Someone like what?"

"You know, someone special. Somebody who would like me."

"Probably lots of somebodies. You'll get to pick and choose."

"Lucas says I'm..." She stops.

"What?"

"He called me 'damaged goods.' He said I have to stay with him because I'm no good for anything else, ever again."

"And you believe that load of crap?" My abrupt tone startles her. "Listen, little buddy, everyone does stupid things in their lives, or things happen to them that they can't help. It isn't permanent. We don't have to live with our mistakes forever, or with the things other people do to us. We move on."

"But who'd want me, after what all those guys did to me?"

"That was Bambi, remember? You're Emily."

"She's still inside me."

"Come over here. You need another hug."

She slides around on the cushion and I gather her in close.

"First of all, you're not broken."

"I feel like I am."

"Bull! Your biggest problem won't be other people from now on. It's going to be learning to live with yourself, and you can get some help with that. There are people you can trust, people to talk to who can teach you to get beyond all this."

She drags in a deep breath and rests her head against my shoulder. She traces the outline of my belt buckle with one finger.

"You haven't met very many nice men up to now, have you?" I suggest gently.

"You've got that right!"

"Everyone isn't like that. Most people are pretty decent, in fact."

"Yeah, right. Lucas, Ben...Uncle Frank..."

"And do I fit in that category, too?"

She turns her troubled face quickly up to mine.

"No! Of course not!"

"So your experience has been a little bit slanted for the past six months. From now on it will be different. And you can learn how to relate to other people, especially boys, in all the right ways."

"How do I find somebody to help me?"

"We'll look for someone. Probably a psychologist who knows about kids' problems."

"I need a shrink, huh?"

I can't help laughing. "You watch too much TV."

"What else is there to do when you…"

"Don't say that!"

She falls silent.

"That's the first thing you have to do. You have to look ahead, not back. And that means no more comments about what you used to do. Put it behind you. Move on."

"You said that before."

"And I meant it."

A long pause.

"Thank you."

"What for?"

She shrugs. The light coming through the portholes is dimming as the sun slips toward the horizon, casting a gloom over the galley. The lost, discouraged look is back on her face. She needs a lift.

"You feel up to another little adventure?"

She stirs. "What?"

"We could head back tonight instead of tomorrow morning."

"In the dark? Is it safe? How will we see where we're going?"

"I know these waters pretty well. You'll be amazed how beautiful the ocean is at night, and how much you can see. The stars seem even brighter out here than they do in the cove, and there ought to be a good-sized moon later on."

"Have you done it before?"

"Many times."

Amy had loved our night cruises the most, lying back against the rail amid the incredible silence and splendour of the open sea after dark. More than once we had given the boat her head, only to find ourselves miles from the harbour by dawn. We'd made love on deck, slept a little, and revelled in the joy of just being with each other. Now it seems like a lifetime ago.

"What are you thinking about?"

Her voice tugs me back from memories. "Nothing."

"You look kind of sad. Amy again?"

"Come on. Let's go up on deck and see if the sky's still clear."

I release her, and she straightens up but makes no move to leave, serious eyes searching my face.

"Why don't you like to talk about her?"

My throat tightens and my eyes fill. I rise from the table and start toward the ladder, hiding my face from her. Once up on deck, I start the engine and cast off the lines. The tide has turned, and *Amy's Pride* drifts out from the pilings, leaving space for the last of the yachts that are returning for the night. I put her in gear and she glides gracefully out toward the mouth of the harbour.

Alone in the cockpit, I thread between the mooring buoys and enter the channel, and as soon as we pass the headland I throttle back and let the engine idle, heading for the mast to uncover the mainsail. Emily still hasn't come out on deck.

"I could use some help up here," I call down to her.

I unsnap the sail cover and fold it back, dropping it into the cockpit, and turn to attach the halyard. When I climb down again, she's standing next to the traveller.

"I'm sorry you're sad," she tells me.

"It's okay. It just happens once in a while."

Only every waking moment of my life.

"I wish you had kids to make you feel better."

"I've got one. A nice one."

"But not for real."

"Not yet maybe, but we'll keep working on that. Remember how to set the jib?"

"Sure." She uncoils the lines from the winches. "Which side?"

I check the wind direction. "The wind has shifted to a little bit south of east, so what do you think?"

"Left?"

"What?"

"Sorry. Port?"

"Try it and we'll see."

She hauls on the jib sheet and the big triangle rolls out. She hangs on to it while I crank the main tight on the port winch and clamp it off. I clear the winch, and she wraps her line around it and draws the jib in tight.

I return to the console and kill the ignition. The sudden silence is disturbed only by a quiet murmuring of water beneath the drifting hull, and the soft rustling of slack sails. With the bow aimed directly into the light wind, *Amy's Pride* slows and rocks gently in the ebbing tide.

"Think you know how to get us moving?" I ask her.

She steps behind the console and looks up at the big mainsail. "Which way are we going?"

"Let's take her out to sea, away from the lights on the shore."

She twists the wheel a half turn to port and the bow comes slowly around. The jib fills first, then the main, and the hull cants and starts to slide forward.

"Did I do it right?"

"Perfect. Now look behind you."

She sights over her shoulder toward the distant marina.

"Line up our flagpole with the end of the pier back there."

She makes minor adjustments of the wheel and the stern slips sideways a few degrees.

"Now take a compass reading."

"It says about a hundred and ten."

"Bring it back to eighty degrees."

She turns the wheel to starboard, and *Amy's Pride* points up and gains speed. She looks at the compass again.

"Oops. Wrong way."

She brings the wheel back, and the boat falls off the wind and slows down. She studies the dial and shifts the wheel by millimetres, lining up the numbers with fierce concentration.

"Eighty degrees!" she announces triumphantly.

"Check the knot meter."

"It says about three. Kinda slow."

"We aren't taking the wind at a good angle, but now we're heading in the right direction. And we aren't in any hurry. Just hold her steady."

Gradually we pull away from the shore. The wind is freshening from the south, washing us in tropical warmth. I pull out a life jacket from the starboard locker and toss it to her. "Put this on."

"What for?"

"You'll see."

She braces the wheel with her knee and slips her arms through the straps, and I help her buckle them securely.

"I'm going below," I tell her, heading for the ladder.

"Hey! Don't leave me!"

"Why not? You're doing fine."

"But suppose something happens?"

"Handle it."

* * *

It feels good to stretch out on my back for a few minutes, and my mind turns to trying to sort out what has to be done. Medical attention for Emily is high on the list, to be sure she hasn't contracted anything serious and to try to cure it if she has. That's as important as her legal status, and I have to decide just how much I can tell Ken Curtis. I'm hoping I can stick to the abuse angle and leave the prostitution out of it. Other than that, I'll tell him everything.

Next I have to check up on Uncle Frank. Before talking with Ken, I want to clarify whether he's her legal guardian. It might take some doing, but I figure the man can be persuaded to revoke any claim on her. The threat of public exposure as a child molester should guarantee that.

But that still leaves Emily in a kind of limbo, unless I can convince the authorities to let her live with me instead of in some sort of foster home. Despite the outward signs of recovery she's still emotionally fragile, and turning her over to strangers is likely to undo everything we've accomplished so far. The problem is to convince the Florence Pineos of this world that I can provide the best environment to allow her to continue to heal.

Overriding it all is the ever-present problem of Lucas, but as I wrestle with what to do about him, my mind grows weary. I close my eyes for what seems like only a few moments, and Emily's frightened face floats before me. Menacing figures threaten her with vague and incomprehensible dangers. A medley of confused, angry voices ricochets around inside my head, and I hear her scream.

"Hey! I need help up here!"

I awake with a start and check my watch, surprised to see that I've slept for almost half an hour. I stretch my cramped joints and head for the ladder. Emily clings anxiously to the wheel.

"Where were you, anyway? I've been calling and calling."

"I fell asleep. What's the problem?"

"Look!" She points over the starboard side of the bow. A rusty coastal freighter is chugging slowly northward toward Halifax, too close for comfort.

"Whoa! Where did he come from?"

"He's gonna hit us if we don't do something."

"What do you think we should do?"

"Me?" Her voice quavers.

"Sure. You're the one standing the helm."

She studies the freighter's progress, steadily bearing down on us on a collision course. "Go behind him, I guess."

"Okay. Come up to about one-ten."

She turns the wheel, concentrating on the compass, and with a more favourable point of sail we pick up a couple of knots. Emily is apprehensive and excited.

"Now we're aimed right at him!"

"Think about it."

She studies the narrowing gap between the two boats. "I get it. By the time we get there he'll have moved ahead, out of our way."

"So you don't need me after all."

"I was scared."

"And if I hadn't been here, would you have kept on the way you were going and hit him?"

"Duh!"

"So you could have handled it all by yourself."

"I guess so."

"Fine. I'm going back to my nap."

"Don't you dare! It's getting dark!"

The disk of the sun is gone, leaving behind a pale glow over the land to the west. The sky is streaked with nursery pink and blue, reluctant to give way to the first bright stars of evening. The lights of the freighter glow dimly as it passes close in front of us, her engines a basso counterpoint to the gentle song of our sails.

"Let's follow him," I tell her. "As soon as we pass behind his stern, bear off and fall in behind."

She grips the wheel with intense concentration as the freighter ploughs on up the coast. *Amy's Pride* plunges through the wake, dipping her bow and tossing her stern high in the air. Emily rises to her toes as the hull settles back, weightless as in a fast falling elevator.

"Neat! When do I turn?"

I'm getting an idea for some fun. "Wait a little longer, until you can't see the sides of the hull, only the stern. Then you'll be directly behind him."

Several minutes pass. The ship towers above us.

"Now," she says firmly. "Coming about!"

She twists the wheel and I man the winches, hauling the jib across as the boom swings by over our heads. *Amy's Pride* heels over and comes up on a broad reach. I check the wind and adjust the sails, then sit down by the port rail.

"How'd you like being in command all by yourself? Was it fun?"

"Yeah, it really was. Peaceful, too, until that boat showed up. And it was really pretty, watching the sun go down."

"Now you see why I like being out here so much."

"I'm getting kinda tired, though."

"We're on an easy track now, and the winds are steady. We'll let her sail herself."

I take over the helm. The boat wanders a bit to port, and I make small adjustments to bring her back on course and engage the autopilot.

"Want to go forward for a few minutes?"

"Okay. I like it up there."

We climb to the top of the cabin and make our way around the mast. In front of us the freighter churns the sea to froth, whipped cream beneath our bow.

"Want to see where Amy used to ride?" I ask.

"Sure."

"Sit up there on the point, with your legs on either side of the bowsprit. Only take off your sneakers first."

"What for?"

"You'll see."

She kicks her shoes off and scampers forward and perches on the bow, looking back at me over her shoulder. "It's bouncy up here."

"Grab on right there," I tell her, pointing to the bow cleats on either side. I unhook a safety line from the base of the roller furling and loop one end around the rail, clipping the other end to a ring on her life jacket.

"What's that for? I'm not gonna fall in."

"You never know…"

Amy's Pride is drifting slowly to port once more. I sit down on the sloping roof of the cabin as we approach the turbulent crest of the freighter's wake.

"What's the big deal?" Emily calls back to me, just as we begin to cross the wake broadside. The bow dips and plunges and the hull rolls to starboard.

"Yeow! Help!"

"Hang on!" I shout.

She clings desperately to the cleats as a gout of spray fountains upward and soaks her shorts. She jerks her legs up and squeals. The hull wallows to port and tosses her sideways, and the backwash crashes over her head.

"I'm gonna drown!"

"Nope. The sharks will get you first."

The bow drops out from under her and she bounces on the deck, scared and thrilled as on a first-time roller coaster ride. We clear the wake and the hull rises back up to starboard, then plummets once more and flings her several inches off the deck. Her bottom slaps down again like a gunshot.

"Whee! Let's do it again!"

Pure delight, so much like Amy.

"Hang on, then. I have to bring us back on course, and we'll cross the wake again."

Back in the cockpit I step behind wheel and turn it a few degrees, aiming for the crest of the wake, then spin it hard. The sails luff and the boom centres as I cross at right angles. The hull digs in and pitches forward, a sounding whale tossing her flukes at the sky.

Emily rides the bow, screaming at the top of her lungs. Another yank on the wheel and the boom crashes over to port. The sails snap full as the bow rises, and we heel over and take the waves broadside. At the point of the bow every twist and turn is magnified, a bucking bronc, a parachute ride.

Twice more we cross the wake, but the freighter is pulling away and the waves are receding. I retie the wheel and head forward again. Emily is soaked. Beneath the life vest her top clings to her in wet, splotchy patches, and her hair is plastered to her forehead. She grins at me insanely in the glow from our running lights.

"You've been properly initiated," I tell her. "You're a real sailor from now on."

I unsnap the safety line and pluck her off the bowsprit. She shakes her head and runs her fingers through her hair.

"Wow! That was *great!*"

"I thought you'd like it."

"Did Amy really do that?"

"All the time."

"You guys had fun."

"We did."

She retrieves her sneakers and we climb back down into the cockpit. I help her out of the life jacket and chase her below to change out of her wet clothes, then set a course that will bring us back toward the mainland. The wind is dying as the sky darkens to velvet, and we're making barely two knots on the sails.

Emily comes back on deck in one of Amy's long tee shirts, no shorts, her feet still bare.

"Thanks!"

"For the ride? You're welcome."

"Not just that. For everything."

"You're welcome again."

"And for telling me something about Amy, too. It wasn't so hard, was it?"

"No, it wasn't."

"I bet I'd have liked her."

"I know you would."

She gazes out over the rail. The stars of the Milky Way are a misty blanket, cradling a crescent moon and washing the deck with silver. She turns back to face me, her face now drawn and serious.

"Can we do this again?"

"Whenever you want."

"Even if I don't get to stay with you?"

"Don't give up on that. We're going to give it our best shot. We just have to be prepared in case the law says no, that's all."

She falls quiet for several minutes. Then: "Can I ask a question?"

"Sure."

"Does it still hurt much?"

I know what she means, and I can't lie to her. "Yes. But it gets a little better every day."

"Does having me around help, or make it worse?"

"Nothing about you makes anything worse. Not ever."

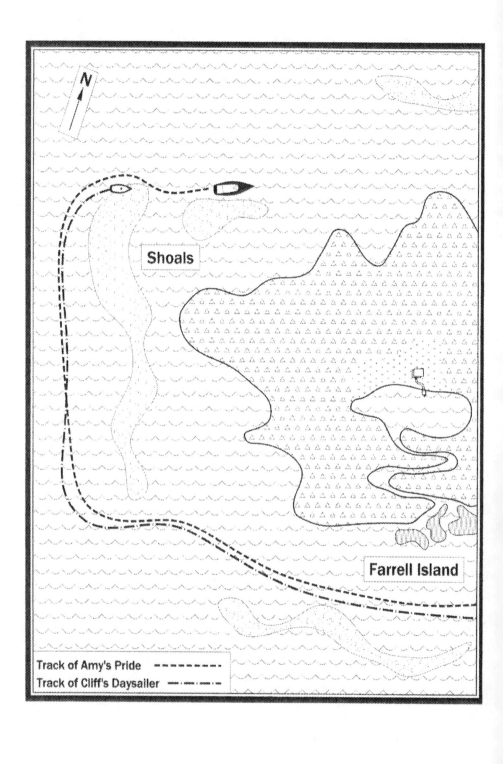

N

Shoals

Farrell Island

Track of Amy's Pride   - - - - - - -
Track of Cliff's Daysailer   — · — · · — · · —

20
Wednesday

The wind dies to a sporadic breeze shortly after midnight, then fades completely to dead calm. Not wanting to use the engine all the way back to Bournemouth, and figuring we both can use some sleep, I find a peninsula on my chart that promises shelter from onshore waves. Emily helps me set the anchors, and *Amy's Pride* rocks gently on her lines in the lee of a headland.

We secure the hatches, and she curls up quietly in a corner of the galley, nestled into the bench cushions behind the table. I try to convince her to go to bed but she wants to talk, idle chatter about nothing to keep her fears at bay. Finally she drifts off in mid sentence, and I cover her with a light blanket and leave her there.

As the stylist promised, her hair has fallen back neatly into place after drying, and now frames her peaceful, unlined face like a halo in negative. The boat is her sanctuary, its limits not confining her, but instead setting her free. She is beautiful in sleep.

I lean back against the cushion in the opposite corner, intending to rest a moment before going to my bunk, and the next thing I know, sunlight is slanting into the cabin. My neck feels stiff and my shoulders ache, and there's an unfamiliar weight on my right leg. Emily has crept over during the night to rest her head on my thigh, her knees drawn up and one hand slipped in behind my back.

Pins and needles attack me when I try to stretch my leg. I lift her head carefully and slide out from underneath, but when I set her down again, she stirs. She yawns and stretches.

"What time is it?"

"Getting late," I tell her. "The sun's pretty far up."

She rubs her eyes and sits up, looking suddenly embarrassed. "Are you mad?"

"About what?"

"I got lonely last night."

"What's there to be mad about? Kids are allowed to cuddle."

She smiles sadly, and I cuff the back of her head lightly. "Come on. It's your turn to make breakfast."

The winds are light, and it takes us until early afternoon to reach Bournemouth under sail. We tie up near Mussel Beach for lunch. Both of us are a little jittery, examining every boat that pulls in at the dock, every tourist who strolls past the restaurant. There's no sign of Lucas, Ben or Cliff, and since we've been away almost three days, I dare to hope that they've given up watching for us.

After lunch we retrieve our duffels from *Amy's Pride* and leave the pier to find the laundromat. An hour and a half later we have everything washed and dried, and Emily does a great job at the ironing board. We fold it all neatly and repack the bags.

"Think we could go see Mr. Curtis now?" she asks as we leave the building.

"It's not Mr. Curtis you want to see." That earns me a poke in the ribs. "It'll be supper time soon. We have to go back and feed Jenny, too. How about tomorrow instead?"

She looks disappointed.

"It's just too late in the day to impose on them without warning," I tell her. "Suppose I give him a call and ask if we can come by tomorrow morning. We'll leave early and spend the whole day in town."

She brightens. "Let's do it!"

We find a phone and I call Ken's office number. The receptionist puts me through, and I explain our plans for the following day.

"Be glad to see you," he says cheerfully. "Does this mean I'm about to get a new client?"

"Could be." I look down at Emily's eager face. "And somebody here wants to see Alex again."

She stamps her foot angrily and whirls away from me.

"Shall we meet in your office?" I ask him.

"Why not come to the house instead? I'll take the day off."

"No need to do that."

"I want to. And speaking of Alex, he's been moping around the house like a lost sheep ever since we got home. I can't imagine why."

I can't help laughing, and Emily glares at me. "Are you sure we won't be any trouble?"

"Not at all."

"There's something else. I have an errand to run, and I can't take Emily with me."

"We'll keep her busy while you're gone. We've got a pool, so tell her to bring her swimsuit."

"Better put a leash on Alex, then."

"She looks that good, huh?"

"Gives me nightmares."

"Can you find our place? We're the last house out on Chestnut Avenue, next to the park."

"We'll find it. Is sometime after nine okay?"

"Any time. We're always up early."

Emily glowers furiously beside me as I hang up. "I can't believe you said that!"

"What?"

" 'Somebody wants to see Alex again!' What'll he think of me? God, I'm so *embarrassed!*"

"It's true, isn't it?" I tease. "Anyway, it's all set. They've even got a pool."

"I'm not going!"

"Oh, yeah. I bet."

"He'll hate me!"

"Who, Mr. Curtis?"

"Stop it! You know I mean Alex!"

"According to his dad, he can't wait to see you again, too. Come on, let's go home. Jenny will be trying to eat the furniture."

We carry the laundry back to the boat and cast off. Emily finally forgives me, and chatters in growing animation as we pull away from the dock and approach the mouth of the harbour. We pass half a dozen sailboats going the other way, large and small, as well as a cabin cruiser and two open skiffs coming in for the evening. A lone windsurfer coasts across our bow, vainly trying to coax one more good ride out of the diminishing wind. I debate using the engine, but there seems to be enough breeze to fill the sails for a short, leisurely trip to Farrell Island.

"What time are we going in the morning?" she wants to know.

"As early as you can get ready."

"How big is their pool?"

"I have no idea."

"Is Mr. Curtis gonna tell Alex what you said about me wanting to see him?"

"Probably."

"Dad!" she exclaims, exasperated, then claps her hand over her mouth.

"I'm just teasing you," I tell her. "I'm sure he won't say anything."

Her face flushes bright pink. "I'm so sorry…"

"What for? Calling me 'Dad'? That's about the nicest thing I've ever heard you say."

We sail on quietly while she gets over her embarrassment. Finally she says, "Are we going to stay there all day?"

"You are. I have to go into the city for a while."

"What do you…?" She breaks off in mid sentence, staring across the port gunwale at a small open daysailer that's heading for the dock.

"Problem?" I ask.

"Cliff," she whispers.

She's right. It's the same boat I shoved away from the pier at Fair Haven a few days earlier, and despite a recent scraggly growth of beard, Cliff's malevolent gaze is unmistakeable.

"Stand your ground," I tell her. "He may not recognize you with your hair cut."

He doesn't seem to, but he remembers me, pure hatred spilling out across the water as our boats pass each other.

"Got yourself another little piece, asshole?" he snarls at me. "You're no different from the rest of us."

I turn away, dismissing him, and the boats draw apart.

"God, that scared me!" Emily says.

"But he thought you were someone else, so your new look is a success."

"Hey, yeah!" She brightens. "Think we can fool Lucas, too?"

"Why not?" I answer, but I don't really believe it. She'd been with him for too long, and he must know her features well.

Circling Farrell Island to the Atlantic side, I bring the boat off the wind. Emily climbs up around the dodger, ready to fold the sail against the boom. I'm about to drop the main for the trip into the cove when the sound of an engine echoes off the hill, and I stop to listen.

Cliff's little craft comes around the point, the sail down and his small outboard pushing her through the water. As soon as he catches sight of us he throttles back, keeping his distance.

Emily slips down beside me in the cockpit. "He's following us," she says anxiously.

"Uh huh."

"You think he figured out who I am?"

"I doubt it. He just wants to see where I'm going. He's carrying a grudge against me for the dunking in the harbour, and he's looking for a way to get back at me."

"What'll we do?"

"We'll leave the sails up and go on. I don't want him to know where the cabin is, so we can't risk letting him find the channel."

Not only do we have to keep Cliff away from the island, it would be good if we could teach him a lesson, something that would discourage him from trying again. I could attempt to run him down, but his little boat is much more manoeuvrable than *Amy's Pride*. He can play cat and mouse with us for a long time. My best option is probably to lead him around the back of the island where the worst of the shoals lie just beneath the surface, and try to run him aground.

"Want to work the winches for me?" I ask her at last. She nods and pulls the handle out of its cradle as I turn the wheel and point up. The wind fills the main and we bear off toward the western end of the island. Cliff's little outboard whines as he gains speed to follow us.

Once past the headland we sail on southwestward into open water, skirting the windward shoals that cup the island like an outstretched hand. The tops of the rocks are submerged and almost invisible in the dwindling light. I can spot them only because I know where to look, and it's unlikely that Cliff will know exactly where they are.

"Ready to come about," I say, and Emily takes up her post by the winch. "Coming about!"

The boom drifts across and the jib follows, smooth as clockwork, and Emily cranks it in tight. We head north-northwest, closely following the edge of the shoal. Well back off our stern, Cliff's boat tracks our wake as if on rails, avoiding the rocks.

"He's still coming," Emily tells me.

"I know. He's smarter than I thought, letting me show him safe passage."

Our little procession sails on, dangerously close to disaster. If my reckoning is off I'll lose my keel, or maybe even hole the hull.

"This will be the tricky part," I tell Emily. "I'm going to make a sharp turn up ahead, right at the end of a shelf of underwater rocks, and loop back toward the island. I'm betting he'll try to cut the corner and hit them. That should put him out of action."

"You're gonna try to sink him?"

"If I can. We won't let him drown. I just want him to learn that it's not smart to mess with us."

"What can I do?"

"Stay by the winches in case we have to tack, and be ready to release the main halyard. Know which one that is?"

"I think so." She steps beneath the dodger and lifts the end of the rope that raises the mainsail. "This one?"

"Good girl."

We wait tensely, our progress slow in the light air. Just off the starboard rail I can make out vague shadows of jagged points sticking up within a few inches of the surface of the waves. I've never been so close to them before, and don't dare take my eyes off the water. Emily is keeping watch behind us.

"We don't have to tack this time," I tell her. "Can you still see him?"

"He's right there. Closer now."

"Good. Hang on."

I twist the wheel and *Amy's Pride* heels over slightly and takes the wind astern. I let the main billow out, and she sweeps off to the east and bears down on the back of the island. Emily keeps her eyes on Cliff while I divide my attention between the sails and the treacherous water beneath us, playing the wind. Suddenly the boat shudders and stumbles, the keel brushing the top of something below the surface, then rights herself and sails on. Too damn close.

"What's he doing?" I ask her. She stands up on the locker beside the dodger for a better look in the fading light.

"Still coming. He's gonna do it. He's gonna cut the corner."

"Good. Keep watching."

We plough on, a miniature two-boat parade, and just as I'm beginning to think he may have cleared the shoal safely, we hear a loud thump. I spin around and see the little craft canting to port, the top of the mast dangerously close to the water. Another loud bang, high and metallic, and the outboard screams and races, then falls silent as Cliff shuts her down.

"Let go the jib and release the halyard!" I shout. Emily yanks the line off the winch and flips up the clamp that holds the main aloft. The big sail luffs and the hull settles and slows.

"Let's get her down." I start the engine while she scrambles up next to the mast, ready to fold the sail as I lower it. I haul the jib onto the furling and tie it off.

"He's kinda low in the water," Emily says as she straps the sail to the boom. Cliff is bailing frantically as the little boat wallows in a following sea.

"He's in big trouble," I tell her. "We'd better go check it out."

I put the boat in gear and swing about, keeping well off the rocks. Within minutes we're abreast of him, ten yards off his port bow. He hurls a string of curses at me as he tries to keep up with the flow of water coming in through a tear in the hull.

"Shut up and listen!" I shout to him. "Your best chance is to make a run for the harbour before you fill up!"

"I can't, you dumb bastard, the outboard's busted. The shear pin broke!"

I ease off on the wheel to let *Amy's Pride* drift in closer, halving the distance between us. "We'll tow you in then."

"Why the hell would you want to do that?"

"Let's just say I don't want shit like you polluting the ocean. Tie something on the end of your bow rope to weight it, and toss it to me."

"I'll go under before you can get me to the harbour."

"Not if you keep bailing. Shut up and throw me that line."

He loops the bow rope through a life ring and heaves it toward us. It falls short, and I fish it out of the sea with a boat hook and drag it aboard as he resumes bailing. Emily cleats it off at the stern and I shove the gearshift forward. The line tightens, taking up the slack, and we begin to tow the stricken boat toward the harbour.

It's a slow trip, the rapidly filling hull acting as a sea anchor behind us, and my engine labours to keep us moving. Despite his best efforts, Cliff can't bail fast enough. We're still a hundred yards from the dock when the boat swamps, turns its bow toward the sky, and slips beneath the waves. I quickly release the line. Cliff is sucked under, then breaks the surface a half dozen yards away, and I swing the wheel to bring us around and throttle back.

"You can swim in from here," I call out. No answer. "All you lost this time was your boat," I continue. "There better not be a next time."

Cliff glowers and strikes off for the dock, swimming strongly. As soon as I'm sure he'll make it, we come about and set a course for the southwest, away from Farrell Island in case he decides to watch where we're going.

"That was scary," Emily says as we pull away. "Think he'll come after us again?"

"Maybe. He's that stupid. But he hasn't got a boat any more."

"Do you suppose he recognized me?"

"I don't think so. He'd have said something."

"What are we gonna do now?"

"Get some help," I tell her. "We'll start tomorrow with our visit to Mr. Curtis, and see what advice he gives us."

"Are you gonna tell him all about me?"

"I told you before, no. I promised."

"Then how will he know what to do to help us?"

That's the sixty-four dollar question. "I'll figure something out."

We travel down the coast and out of sight of the marina before doubling back to the island, and enter the cove as the last of the daylight is fading. Both of us are worn out. Emily makes a fuss over Jenny and pours some cat food into her dish while I change her water. I start the coffee maker while Emily makes sandwiches, and we eat our meal in silent exhaustion.

"You can leave the dishes for me to do," I tell her when we finish, and she wanders off down the hallway and tumbles into bed. I look in on her just a few minutes later and find her already sound asleep. After cleaning up I try to read for a while, but my eyes keep closing too, so I spread my blanket on the daybed and call it a night.

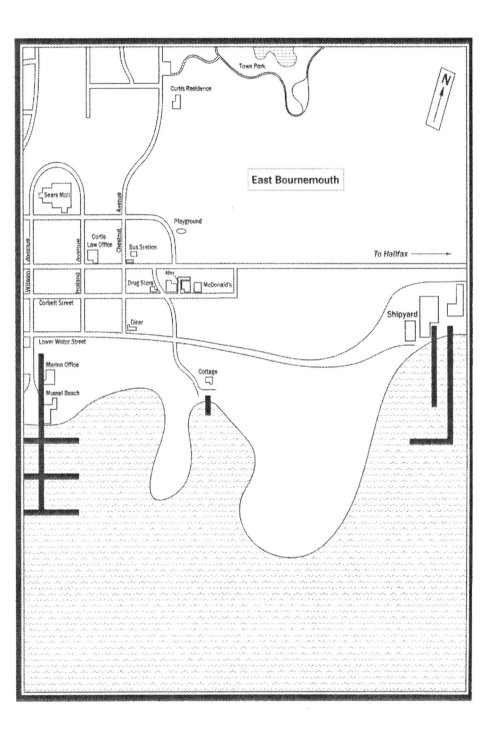

21
Thursday

Emily is up before me the next morning, rested but conflicted. She's eager to get back to Bournemouth to see Alex again, but afraid that Cliff will be watching for us, and maybe Lucas too.

"We'll go ashore someplace else," I tell her. "There's a private shipyard up the other end of town where we can rent a berth. If we stay away from the public marina, they won't see us. And the Curtises live way out at the edge of town. We'll be okay."

I'm not as confident of that as I want her to believe.

After breakfast and a shower, I rummage in a trunk and find a backpack that Amy had used when we explored the island. "You can stick your swimsuit in here," I tell her. "Better bring a towel too, and an extra change of clothes."

"How come?"

"You never know what the day might bring."

"Should I bring my dress?"

"Wouldn't hurt."

"This'll be so *fun!* What are you going to do all day? You said you had to go somewhere."

"I've got an errand to run before I talk to Mr. Curtis about our problem. I don't know how long it will take. It depends on where I have to go."

"What kind of errand?"

"I have a little business to discuss with your Uncle Frank. Where does he live?"

She gives me the address, on a rural road in western Hants County. "But he won't be there," she says. "He drives into Halifax every day. He sells cars,

Pontiacs and Buicks. Why are you going to see him?"

"It's like I told you, we have to get your legal status sorted out. School and medical records, birth certificate, that kind of thing. We have to start somewhere."

"Do I have to go with you?"

"No."

"Good! I never want to see him again."

"You might have to somewhere down the line, but not today. And you won't be going back there to live. That's one of the things I'm going to get settled with him."

"He's an asshole!" She picks up the backpack and stomps off into the bedroom, her face a mask of disgust.

After refilling Jenny's food and water dishes, I pack some extra clothing for myself and hunt around for my wallet and the boat keys. Emily comes out lugging her overstuffed backpack, looking a little happier. We row out to *Amy's Pride*, sail out of the cove, and tack around the eastern end of the island to go up the coast from the harbour.

The sky is bright and clear, the temperature just right, and according to the radio it's expected stay that way for the next several days. To be approaching a weekend without a storm predicted is a rare bonus. A standing joke the natives tell tourists about Nova Scotia's weather asks, "What follows two days of rain?" The answer is "Monday."

We sail eastward and well out to sea to approach Bournemouth's small commercial shipyard from the opposite direction. After paying for dock space, we walk up the Lower Water Street extension to find a cab. Ten minutes later we're standing in front of a spacious Tudor home tucked in among the tall pines that border Bournemouth's extensive northern parklands. Emily hangs back as we start up the path.

"What's the matter?" I ask her.

"I'm scared."

"What of?"

"Maybe he won't like me this time."

"Who, Mr. Curtis?"

"You know who I mean," she says, annoyed at my teasing. "I don't know how I should act."

"Relax. You don't have to act any special way. Just be yourself, the same as you were on the boat. Alex was practically drooling over you then."

"He was not!"

"Want to bet?"

The door opens before we reach the porch. Someone has been watching for us. Alex stands uncertainly on the threshold, looking eager and shy all at the same time.

"Hi."

"Hi."

"Nice hair."

"Thanks."

"Come on in."

Close encounters of the adolescent kind.

* * *

Everything about the Curtis home evokes modest success and good taste. The den is warmly panelled in rich honey oak and dominated by a huge and ancient pine desk, heavily constructed of broad boards with handmade nails. A stack of file folders next to the telephone suggests that Ken does at least some of his work at home.

"My wife's gone down to the mall," he tells me as we settle down to talk. The children are off exploring the house and grounds. "She'll be back before lunch. What's this errand you have to run?"

"It has to do with the child I was telling you about," I answer him.

"You didn't tell me much."

"I'll get to that, after I find out a few things from you. First, I want to retain you, if you'll agree to represent me."

"Give me a buck."

I dig out a dollar.

"That seals the bargain," he says. "I'll have my secretary draw up the papers tomorrow. Now what's this all about?"

"Just let me go at it slowly, okay? First, how far does this confidentiality thing extend?"

"You're not planning to commit a crime, are you?"

"Not if I can help it."

"Good, because that would fall outside of our agreement, and I'd be obligated to report it."

A bank of tall windows overlooks the back lawn, where Alex is showing Emily the pool. I'd have had trouble sliding a sheet of newsprint between their shoulders. Conscious of my promise to keep her past a secret, I choose my words carefully.

"Well, to be honest I guess I am kind of skirting around the law right now. A crime of omission, I would call it."

"Is it covered by the criminal code?"

"Not as far as I know."

"Is anyone likely to get hurt because of it?"

"No. Just the opposite."

"In that case anything you say is strictly between us."

"This child I've been talking about, she's a runaway. Her parents were killed on the highway, and she ended up living with an aunt and uncle. A funny uncle, if you know what I mean. She took off right after Christmas."

"Where is she now?"

"Safe. But if she's going to stay that way, I have to settle a few things with the uncle first."

"What's your interest in this? You say she's not related to you?"

"That's right," I tell him. "But I'm sort of responsible for her. It's complicated."

"Why not let the RCMP deal with the uncle for you?"

"I want to keep them out of it if I can. If the police get involved, I'm afraid I'll lose control of the situation. Suppose the man turns out to be plausible, or has connections somewhere? A judge in his pocket, maybe. She could end up back with him again."

"Sounds like you've had some experience with the system."

"My wife was a public school teacher before she moved on to university. She told me some stories."

"So you know what can happen. Okay. First, how serious was the abuse? Was it sexual?"

"Primarily physical, beatings and so forth. She ran away when it began to escalate into something more."

"And how old is the child?"

"She just turned fourteen."

"Where has she been since Christmas?"

"That's not really relevant. Let's just say it wasn't a good situation, not something she should go back to."

"All right, we'll leave that for now. Do you want this uncle arrested? He could be facing serious charges under the criminal code. It shouldn't be too difficult to make a case for some kind of assault."

"That wouldn't do the child any good at this stage. What I really want is to keep him away from her permanently."

"So you don't plan to press charges?"

"No. I just want to make sure she never has to live with him again."

"You can still hold the threat of legal action over his head," he tells me. "If you insist on confronting this jerk yourself, that is, which I still don't recommend."

"I just want to size him up. What I need to find out is whether he's her legal guardian. If not, the hell with him, but if he still has custody, I want to know it."

"I can dig out that information for you."

"Don't take this personally, but I'm not ready to give you her name yet."

"Damn it, if I'm going to be your lawyer..."

"Please, Ken, do it my way for now. You'll see why later on."

"Forgive my candour, but you're acting like a damn fool."

"I know..."

A door slams, and the two kids come running into the room. Emily is glowing like a beacon.

Alex is breathless. "Can we take the bikes out, Dad?"

"Okay," Ken tells him. "Give Emily Mom's mountain bike. It's a little big for her, but I bet she can handle it. And stay off the streets."

"We're just gonna go around the park."

Ken looks at me. "Is that all right with you?"

"It's public property, right?"

"The town owns it."

"Should be okay." I turn to Emily. "Keep your eyes open," I caution. She nods solemnly.

"Thanks!" Alex says, grabbing Emily's hand and pulling her along into the back hall. She hasn't said a word.

"I'm not ready for this," Ken says, chuckling. "Last week all he talked about was soccer and hockey."

"Happens overnight, doesn't it?"

"Oh well, you're her father. I'll let you worry."

I sit silently. He looks at me closely. A puzzled expression crosses his face, then dawning realization.

"Emily's not the..." he begins, then stops.

I stand up again and walk over to the window to watch the children going into the garage. Through the open door I can see Alex showing Emily which bicycle to take.

"What have you gotten yourself into?" he asks quietly.

I turn to face him. "Up to now, you didn't question who she was, did you? Everything about us says she's mine."

"Yes."

"Then let's leave it at that for now. If we've fooled you, we'll keep on getting away with it, at least until I figure out what to do."

"I never would have suspected. She seems so normal…"

"She is. She's going to survive what's happened to her."

"Let me help you."

"I will. I'm counting on you to backstop me down the line. Just don't rush me."

He shakes his head. "If you do anything stupid, I can't help you cover it up."

"I won't ask you to."

His eyes bore into mine, making me uneasy. His mouth is drawn in a tight, disapproving line. I would not want to challenge this man in court.

"Have you got a map of Halifax?" I ask, trying to break the tension between us.

"What do you want to know?"

"The uncle works at a car dealership there."

"What kind?"

"Pontiacs and Buicks."

"I can help you find it. Why don't I run you out there once my wife gets back from shopping?"

"I need to do this alone. I can call a cab."

"If you won't let me go with you, at least take my Jeep. But two of us would probably have a better chance of getting some results. If he needs his arm twisted…"

"Thanks. I really appreciate it, but I want to keep this low key. And if I have to do anything you wouldn't approve of, it's better that you aren't a witness."

"I just told you, anything criminal…"

"I know," I interrupt. "But you won't have to cover up what you don't see. And I appreciate the use of the car."

Resigned to my stubbornness, he gets up and heads for the door. "I'll get you the keys. You can get the street address from the phone book, and I'll give you directions. Look in the top right hand drawer of my desk."

* * *

The midmorning traffic on Highway 103 is relatively light, letting me make good time going into the city. I'm not looking forward to dealing with Uncle Frank, and only hope I can control my temper. It disgusts me that people like him can get away with crimes against their own families, and especially against helpless children. For a species that can write symphonies, paint masterpieces and travel to other worlds, humanity has a damned rotten underbelly.

Halfway around the Armdale rotary a sign directs me to the route that Ken suggested. The auto agency occupies a corner lot, festooned with pennants and signs proclaiming zero percent financing, a sure sign of a seasonal slowdown in sales. A smiling receptionist greets me just inside the door and I ask for Frank by name, as if he's an old friend.

"He's outside with a customer," she says brightly. "Can someone else help you?"

"Thank you. I'll wait."

A big plate glass window overlooks the crowded used car lot. A young couple stands next to a three-year-old Chevrolet four-door, examining the paint job. A florid, heavyset man gestures to them enthusiastically. The woman seems interested in the car, but her companion keeps glancing over his shoulder at a low-slung red Firebird that squats in powerful potential at the far end of the row. She appears to be at least eight months pregnant, a condition sure to put an end to his dream of a sports car. I see a bloated sedan or a minivan in his future.

Frank is a stereotypical car salesman, big and jolly and given to talking with his hands. Despite his considerable girth, he seems agile and light on his feet as he circles the car, extolling the virtues of a large trunk and spacious back seat. A sincere smile plays across his open, honest face. If it comes to an official investigation of his relationship to Emily, I have no doubt he'll mount a credible defence.

It looks as if he's losing the sale. The customer helps his wife into their elderly Toyota and drives off. Uncle Frank walks toward the building, waddling slightly under the weight of an impressive beer gut. He stops at the receptionist's desk and she gestures in my direction.

"What can I do for you?" he says jovially, his hand extended.

I decline his offer to shake hands. "Is there somewhere we can talk?"

"Right over here." He leads me toward a thinly partitioned cubicle at the back of the showroom, one among four where the salesmen conclude their deals. Two of the booths are occupied, and sounds of persuasive conversation drift through the walls, every syllable easy to understand.

"I think you might want to go somewhere a little more private when you hear what's on my mind," I tell him.

"What's going on?" His professional salesman's smile is growing a little strained.

"Suppose we look at a few used cars."

I trail him outside, and we walk down the first row of vehicles until we reach the Firebird. Its brilliant crimson paint shines richly in the sun.

"You look like a man who can appreciate this baby," he says enthusiastically, falling naturally into his spiel. "She's a steal. Got some years on her, but she's cherry. Low mileage, non-smoker had her. And she'll hold her value. They don't make them any more, you know."

"This is about Emily," I say quietly.

He freezes.

"Let's not waste time," I tell him. "How hard have you been trying to find her?"

"Who are you?"

"Doesn't matter."

"What makes you think I'm going to talk to you, then?"

"From what I hear, you've got busy hands. How will your wife and kids feel if that becomes public knowledge?"

He looks around furtively. There's no one within earshot.

"Where is the little bitch?" he growls nastily.

My fists tighten unintentionally and I stare him down, waiting him out. He begins to sweat.

"Okay, so you've been talking to her. So what?"

"She isn't going back to live with you."

"The hell you say! When I find her…"

"It's up to you whether all this stays confidential. Did you adopt her after her parents died?"

"No, but I'm her legal guardian. That makes her my kid, just like my own two. We've got custody, me and the wife."

"Not any more. You're giving her up."

"Screw that!"

"Listen, you sick bastard! You aren't fit to have children of your own, but that's not my business. Emily is, and you're going to sign her away for her own good, just like the fine, upstanding, loving uncle you are."

"Bullshit!"

"Okay, then we'll do this the hard way. How do you think your boss will react when your name ends up all over the front page for child molesting?"

"Jesus Christ!"

"Your choice."

"Listen…"

"My lawyer will be in touch," I tell him, "and when the time comes, either you sign on the dotted line, or I pay a visit to the police. And the press."

I turn abruptly and walk away, leaving him standing open-mouthed beside the plush sports model. Probably rusted out underneath, just like his miserable soul.

22

Thursday Afternoon

It's a little after two when I pull into Ken's driveway and stop in front of the three-car garage. Sounds of happy children echo from the direction of the pool, and I find a gate in the fence and push through. Ken's wife is sitting beneath a sun umbrella, keeping an eye on the action in the water. Emily stands out in her red Paris creation, with Alex hovering close by amid half a dozen other young teenagers.

"Hi, I'm Katie," the woman greets me. She gestures toward a chaise as I reach the concrete apron, and I introduce myself and sit down.

"Ken had to go into town," she tells me. "Some sort of a minor emergency at the firm. He said he won't be long. Can I get you something to drink? Have you had lunch?"

"I picked up something on the way home. Thank you for the use of the Jeep. And for letting Emily ride your bike."

She gestures dismissively. "A pleasure. Your daughter is a gem, by the way. My misogynistic son is ready to renounce bachelorhood forever."

I've been apprehensive over Emily's ability to get along with ordinary kids once again, but it looks like she's having no trouble. She seems to be perfectly at ease, as if she's known the others all her life. They play like sleek young seals, ducking each other, tossing a Frisbee, and engaging in quick, short races up and down the pool. She's definitely fitting in, well on the road back to normality.

"It's good of you to let us visit," I tell Katie.

"Do you live here in town?"

"I have a place just over the county line, west of here." I describe the area, avoiding the fact that the house has been empty for months, and that my only home at present is an isolated island cabin, my only companion a timid and reclusive cat.

"I hope we'll see more of you," she says. "Emily's welcome to use the pool any time. And you too, if you swim. We keep it filled and heated almost until the snow falls."

"This looks like a nice neighbourhood for raising kids," I note, just making conversation.

"It is. And most of the young people around here are pretty well behaved, too. We haven't had much trouble with vandalism, the way some towns do. Are you thinking of moving in closer to your work? Ken says you're an architect here in town."

"Not since last year. I'm semi-retired, I guess you'd say. Taking a sabbatical, actually. I closed up my office soon after my wife died."

"I was sorry to hear about that. How is Emily handling it?"

"We're fine," I tell her, not exactly lying, but skirting the subject.

"Must be hard, a man alone with a daughter that age. Lots of trials ahead."

"Got any advice?" I'm trying to keep things light.

"I'm no help with girls. We just have the one boy, and they're supposed to be different. I remember what it was like for me, though. I was very close to my father. Mom helped with all the female stuff, but it was Dad who kept me straight and sane. He always said it was his duty to keep me away from boys like him."

She laughs musically, an attractive woman secure in her world, thanks no doubt to the kind of upbringing every child should have.

"He was kidding," she continues, "I knew that. But it was nice to know that he understood what boys are like, and what kind of pressure I'd be up against."

"Sounds like he gave you some good advice. Does he live in this area?"

"He's retired now, and he and Mom moved to Florida. I miss them every day."

Emily climbs out of the pool and pads over to me. She reaches for my hand playfully.

"Come in with us!"

"I'm too old."

"Sure!" She turns to our hostess. "He's a good swimmer, Mrs. Curtis." She leans down and tickles my ribs. "Almost as good as me."

"Go! Leave me in peace!"

"Okay. But you're missing out."

She bends forward spontaneously and kisses my cheek. Suddenly embarrassed by what she's done, she blushes prettily, whirls around, and sprints toward the pool. Her neat dive splits the water with barely a splash.

"It looks like you don't need much advice in the parenting department," Katie says. "I'd say she loves you very much."

I can't trust myself to respond.

The kids engage in a frantic game of dodge ball, and the noise level rises alarmingly. Above the din I hear the sound of an engine on the other side of the fence, and presently Ken comes through the gate into the pool area. He drops a big box of donuts on the table.

"Anybody drown yet? It sounds like they're killing each other."

"Just having fun," Katie tells him unnecessarily. "Did you get your work done?"

"Do I ever? Anyway, we averted the crisis, and I left the details to the rest of the gang." He turns to me. "How did you make out? In general terms, that is."

"He never lets me in on anything he's working on," Katie says. Then to Ken: "Do you want me to go inside?"

"Please don't," I tell her. "It went well," I say to her husband.

"I take it he was amenable to your suggestions?"

"Let's say the prospect of reporters inquiring into his sex life didn't sit too well with him. I'm pretty sure that once he's thought it over, he'll sign the papers when the time comes."

"He has legal guardianship then?"

"He claims to."

One of the children spots the donut box, and they all swarm out of the pool and surround us. Emily trails the pack. She collects her little wrap skirt and covers up with it, if only slightly. A china doll.

"Hi, I'm Jay," one of the boys tells me around a mouthful of donut. "Are you Emily's dad?"

I tell him I am, and my name. Another lie; they're beginning to pile up. The other children introduce themselves, a nice group, respectful of adults but open and friendly. I briefly imagine having them visit my home, coming there to be with my daughter. The house full of laughter again.

Emily chooses a donut as the rest of them head off toward the chairs and lounges at the far end of the pool. She lingers beside me, apprehensive after seeing Ken and I talking. I smile and gave her a tiny, discrete nod and a wink. She hesitates, looking pointedly at Katie and Ken, then chooses her words carefully.

"Did you see him?"

"I did."

Our hosts begin an animated conversation and appear to be ignoring us, although I'm sure Ken isn't missing anything we're saying. Most lawyers I know can divide their attention when the situation warrants. Katie has no frame of reference about our situation, but her husband must be curious about my encounter with Emily's molester.

"What did he say?" she asks me.

"If I told you, you'd have to go and wash your ears out."

"That bad, huh?"

"Good, actually. I think he got the message."

"How did you do it?"

"Told him I'd shine a spotlight on him, that's all. He wasn't too keen on his name getting in the newspapers. I guess he's more concerned with his own reputation than with seeing you again."

"Good! Now can I stay with…?"

She stops short and her eyes fly toward Ken, who is still talking with Katie.

"We haven't discussed that yet," I tell her quietly. "That comes later. And aren't you missing out on some of the fun?"

She looks over her shoulder at the others. Alex is pretending to pay no attention to her, but his eyes keep shifting our way. I catch Ken's eye and incline my head, and he gives me a quick nod. He and Katie stand up and walk over to a large gas grill next to the fence, unnecessarily inspecting the propane lines. Emily moves to the foot of the chaise and sits down by my feet.

"Something else on your mind?" I ask her.

"He's really nice," she says, looking toward Alex.

"I'm not surprised," I tell her.

"Can I come back sometime?"

"Mrs. Curtis has already invited us both. She says they swim until the snow falls."

Emily stiffens and squirms restlessly on the chaise. "I'm getting scared again."

"Of what?"

"Hoping too much."

"Don't you *ever* stop doing that! That's what I did last winter, and it's no fun. Doesn't help, either."

"What does?"

"Good friends," I tell her. "You taught me that."

She stares at me for a long moment. Then she grins and, in one graceful fluid motion, bounds off to join the others.

Ken and Katie wander back from the grill.

"Is she okay?" Ken asks.

"I think so. She's developing a major league crush on Alex, and that's helping her to forget her problems a little."

"She told you that?" Katie asks in surprise.

"She tells me just about everything," I laugh. "Sometimes I wish she'd just shut up."

"Don't do that. You're lucky. Some kids who lose their mothers can't transfer their confidence to anyone else, even their fathers. *Especially* their fathers. It can leave them lonely and insecure, even lead to major adjustment problems. I've seen it happen with some of our friends."

I glance at Ken, his face drawn in a concerned frown. It may have been a mistake to confide in him about my true relationship to Emily.

"We wanted a big family," Katie continues, "and especially a girl, but I almost died when Alex was born. The obstetrician said we didn't dare try again."

"Looks like you hit the jackpot the first time," I tell her. "Alex seems like a fine young man."

"So far, so good," Ken says, "but we keep our eyes open. There are too many dangers and temptations out there. Worse than when we were kids, with drugs everywhere and so much sex on TV."

The pool games resume, and we watch the ebb and flow in amusement. Alex moves as if tethered to Emily by an invisible bungee cord, constantly shifting position to be next to, in front of or just behind her. Not only is she aware of it, she tests its limits constantly, enjoying a sense of power she never knew she possessed.

"You see what's going on?" Katie says in amusement.

"How the hell do women know how to do that?" I ask. "It must be genetic."

"Girls sure are different from boys," Ken observes.

"Your wife was just saying that a while ago."

"And vive la différence!"

The rest of the afternoon passes pleasantly, and I'm feeling more relaxed than at any time since Emily first arrived on Farrell Island. The children spend the whole time in and around the pool, and Alex's guests linger until shortly after five, finally leaving for home and supper.

Emily is sporting a pink nose and shoulders and a perpetual happy grin as we enter the Curtis house. I call her aside and whisper in her ear. She nods eagerly, and I straighten up to address the others.

"We'd like to say thanks, the two of us," I tell them, deferring to Emily.

"May we take you out to supper?" she says shyly. Her eyes slide sideways toward Alex.

"That would be lovely, dear," Katie says.

"Mussel Beach, Dad?" Emily asks me.

Dad again. It was coming almost too easily to her now. I catch Ken's quizzical look out of the corner of my eye.

"Maybe someplace a little fancier?" I suggest. I'm apprehensive about being seen by the wrong people.

"I love it there!" Alex exclaims. "We can watch the boats while we eat."

I raise my eyebrows at Ken, and he nods.

"That's settled, then."

"I have to change," Emily says.

"You can use our room, dear," Katie tells her. "Alex will show you where it is."

She finds her backpack lying beside the door. The boy reaches for her hand and they run off up the stairs.

"Where did she ever find that swimsuit?" Katie asks. "It looks like it was sewn right on her."

"The Fair Haven Marina complex. The label says 'Paris' and the price tag spelled bankruptcy."

"Worth whatever you paid. She looks lovely, and I'd say it makes her feel good about herself."

Twenty minutes later we all pile cosily into Ken's sports coupe, myself in front and the two young ones squeezed in with Katie in the cramped back seat. Emily is resplendent in her yellow sundress. I make a mental note that my little social butterfly will need some additions to her wardrobe.

The thought jolts me. *My* social butterfly. Emily isn't the only one thinking about our relationship in ever more permanent terms, but I'm still not sure what the outcome will be.

* * *

Mussel Beach is crowded. The only available table stands in a corner far away from the windows, much to Alex's disappointment and my relief. He's hoping to be able to watch the boats come and go, but I'm grateful to be out of sight of anyone passing by. Ken promises him enough time on the dock after dinner to examine everything in port, and that's when I'll have to be on alert.

We study our menus until the waiter comes back with pad in hand. "Something to drink?" he asks.

"Coffee with my meal, please," I tell him. Ken requests the same and Katie declines. The children order Cokes.

"An appetizer?"

"Spinach salad," I tell him.

"I'll have the calamari," Ken says. "Katie?"

"No, just a garden salad for me."

"My God," Emily mutters.

"What, dear?" Katie asks.

"I didn't know people really..." She stops short and blushes, afraid she's being rude, and I can't help laughing.

"What's going on?" Ken asks.

"Will you let Emily sample your appetizer?" I'm watching her expression out of the corner of my eye.

"Of course." He turns to her. "Have you ever had any?"

She tries to say no, and a fit of coughing takes her.

"I'm sensing a private joke here," Katie says.

"I hate squid!" Alex exclaims decisively. "It tastes like an old rubber boot."

"And how many old rubber boots have you eaten?" Ken says.

"You know what I mean. It's all chewy and gross."

"Manners, please," his mother cautions.

"Well, it is!"

"It's an acquired taste," Ken observes. "Most people don't like it the first time they try it, but maybe Emily will be an exception."

The waiter brings the drinks and appetizers, and takes our orders for the main course. Emily can't take her eyes off Ken's plate. He cuts a thin strip of the squid and places it in his mouth with obvious enjoyment.

"Want to try it?" he asks Emily. She looks petrified but manages a tiny nod. He slices a tiny morsel and transfers it to her plate, and she pokes it with her fork and lifts it close to her nose.

"Take the plunge," I tell her. "It won't bite back."

She squeezes her eyes shut and pops the bite into her mouth, wrinkling her nose. I wait expectantly, surprised when her brow smoothes out.

"That's not bad!"

"Yuck!" Alex mutters.

"My mother always told me," Katie says, "never close your eyes to a new experience."

"I'll bet Gram never tried squid," Alex says.

Despite having avoided almost all social occasions since Amy's death, I'm completely at ease with these new friends. The meal passes quickly, topped off with rich desserts that strain our waistbands. We leave the restaurant to find the evening air soft and warm, the dock crowded with camera-toting tourists. Most of the slips are full, and several boat owners are washing down their decks after a day on the water.

We meander toward the end of the pier, and Alex is anxious to show off his knowledge of the various types of craft. Emily acts the eager audience, as if by instinct knowing how that particular game is played. As we turn to go back they skip on ahead out of our hearing, heads close together. Her infectious giggle echoes back to me. Secrets...

"This has been my best day in a long time," I tell Ken and Katie honestly. "Thank you."

"It's you we should thank," Ken answers. "The meal was wonderful, and Alex is on top of the world."

"I trust his intentions are honourable," I joke.

"Takes after his father," Katie laughs, "so you may be in trouble."

"Sorry to talk business," Ken says finally, "but are you ready to pursue your problem a little further?"

"What's your schedule like?"

"I'm in court all day tomorrow, but I can give you most of Saturday morning. Will that do?"

"That's fine. I need a little time to..."

The words die in my throat. On a short stretch of beach off to one side of the pier, the marina provides half a dozen cradles for owners to use when working on their boats. One of them supports the unmistakeable lines of Cliff's daysailer, forlorn and battered about the keel, her splintered mast lying on the sand. Her owner is standing beneath her, hammer and chisel in hand, but he isn't working on the hull. He's staring at the dock, watching Emily and Alex as they walk along.

"What's wrong?" Ken asks.

I shake my head, waiting to see if Cliff will make a move. Something about Emily, maybe her laugh, seems to have jogged his memory in spite of her new hairstyle. Abruptly he drops his tools and trots swiftly across the sand. He vaults up onto the dock, less than a dozen paces behind the children.

I break into a run, startling Ken and Katie and nearly tripping over a baby stroller in my path. Cliff strides up behind Emily and clamps his hand on her shoulder. He spins her around before I can cover half the distance between us, and she screams.

Alex hesitates only a fraction of a second. He lands a well-placed kick on Cliff's left shin and the man stumbles, cursing. Emily scrambles backward and trips over a loose plank, falling against a piling just as I reach them. I skid to a stop in front of her to fend Cliff off.

He backs up a couple of paces, hands raised protectively in front of his face. Behind me, Alex grabs Emily's hand and helps her up. They run down the dock to Ken and Katie, who are hurrying toward us.

"That's her, ain't it?" Cliff says nastily.

"Leave her alone!" I threaten him. "You got off easy last time."

"Next time I ain't gonna be alone. Lucas wants her back, and I'm gonna help him get her." He twists around and drops off the dock onto the sand, and strides off toward his boat as the others come running up beside me.

"What the hell was that all about?" Ken exclaims. "That wasn't Uncle Frank, was it?"

I shake my head. "Just some unfinished business that won't quite go away."

Emily is trembling, her face ashen, and I wrap my arm around her shoulder in a warm hug.

"Round four," I whisper to her, trying to smile. "The good guys win again." She manages a weak grin.

"Thanks for the help," I tell Alex. "You took on a nasty character there."

"What'd he want?"

"He's a creep!" Emily mumbles.

"He won't bother us again," I lie, meeting Emily's eyes. She isn't fooled. The battle is escalating and will soon come to a head, but I'm beginning to believe she has the strength to see it through. The biggest problem will be to keep others from discovering the facts about her past, and the true nature of the threat to her.

23
Thursday Evening

Your nose is sunburned."

"Again?" She touches it gingerly. We're back in the cabin.

"And you're going to have sore shoulders in the morning," I tell her. "I think I've got some stuff here somewhere to make them feel better. Didn't you put on any sun block this afternoon?"

"I forgot to take it with me." She looks around the room. "Where's Jenny?"

"Where she always is, probably. Under the bed. I think she's still annoyed at being left alone so much."

She picks up her backpack and disappears into the bedroom. I wait until she's out of sight, then bend down to examine the area in front of the cabin door. A shrivelled leaf clings to the threshold and there are faint traces of dirty footprints, a couple of sizes larger than my own. We've had visitors.

With its hidden cove and protection from the offshore shoals, I've come to think of the island as virtually impenetrable. Amy and I had gloried in the privacy and solitude. Only on very rare occasions had anyone stumbled upon us. Once, years before, a yacht was blown ashore in a storm and we offered the crew shelter. On another occasion we found an ancient skiff half sunk near the mouth of the inlet. But as far as I knew, until Emily arrived, no one had made it to the clearing on their own.

It's almost certain that Lucas and his pals have managed to find us, however, probably by checking the tax rolls in the town office. Both Ben and Cliff have seen my boat, with her name clearly painted on the transom. It would have been simple for them to check the boat registry for the owner, a little more difficult but not impossible to trace my connection to the island.

Emily reappears in one of Amy's tee shirts, the collar stretched out over the points of her reddened shoulders.

"She's not in there," she says.

"Jenny? She must be outside then."

"What can I put on my sunburn?"

"The sun block won't do much good now. Let me see what else I can find."

The first aid kit yields a tube of antiseptic cream. "This should help for now. We can pick up some kind of lotion on the next trip to Bournemouth. I'm not used to thinking about such things."

"That's okay. Put it on for me?"

She turns her back, and I squeeze a dab out of the tube and work it gently into her shoulders. They're hot to the touch.

"Mmm. Feels good," she says.

"Hedonist!"

"What's that?"

"Greek for 'annoying teenager.' Turn around."

I squeeze out another small bit and wipe it on her nose. "That tickles!" she giggles. She shrugs the neck of the tee shirt up onto her shoulders again.

"Come over here so I can talk to you," I tell her. She pulls out a chair and sits down at the table across from me.

"What's up?"

"We had a visitor while we were gone."

"How do you know?"

I point toward the dried leaf and scuff marks on the floor.

"Any idea who?" she asks.

"Could have been somebody who got lost. I always leave the cabin unlocked in case someone is in trouble or needs shelter when I'm not here. Like you did."

"Does that happen much?

"Not often. In fact, it never has until you."

"Are they here now?"

"I didn't see any boat. The only place to come ashore is the cove, and we'd have seen one when we came home."

"So somebody just stopped by for a drink of water or something?"

"Maybe…"

Her face clouds over. She's thinking of Lucas too.

The hinge on the cat door squeaks and Jenny pokes her nose inside, surveying the cabin for intruders. Finally satisfied that the danger is past, she squeezes through and drops to the floor, heading for her food dish. Finding it empty, she stalks off in annoyance toward the bedroom.

"Somebody scared her into going outside?" Emily asks.

"Looks that way."

"Who? Lucas?"

"I think so."

"How'd he find us?"

"Ben read the name off my boat, probably Cliff too. I figure they asked around and someone told them who owns it. All they had to do was check with the town office for my address."

"This address? The island?"

"No, but the deed is in the public records under my name. Cliff has seen us circling the island more than once. If they're smart enough, the three of them could have snooped around the coast and found the entrance to the cove."

"Oh, boy!"

"So we have to be careful from now on. We have an appointment with Mr. Curtis at his law firm for the day after tomorrow. Until then, we can't stay here."

"Where are we gonna go?"

"We can sleep on the boat. I really don't think they'll be back tonight. It's too hard to get through the channel in the dark, but we won't take any chances."

She stands up from the table, thoroughly alarmed. "Can we go right now?"

"Take it easy. I'll go out and take a look around, and then we'll move the boat around behind the island."

"You think Jenny's okay?"

"I'm sure she's fine. She'd never show herself if a stranger came in here."

"I have to go see." She hurries into the bedroom. A couple of minutes later she reappears with the cat cuddled in her arms.

"Can we take her with us?" Her face is pinched and pale under the sunburn.

"She hates the boat," I tell her. "She'll keep us awake. She prowls around and cries if I keep her down below, and I'm afraid she'll fall overboard if I let her out on deck. She'll be better off here."

"What if Lucas comes back? He might hurt her!"

"If anyone comes in she'll hide. Even if they see her, she'll be out the cat door in a flash if they try to catch her."

"Can we go now? Please? I'm so scared!"

"Just give me a minute to look around. Go get dressed."

Outside the cabin the moon is a day larger, and between that and the stars I can see signs that someone has been walking around the perimeter. The woods are dark and opaque, but it's unlikely anyone is hiding there. They'd have come after us by now.

When I go back inside Emily is standing close to the door, trembling. She's pulled on a pair of shorts under the long tee shirt, and has her sneakers back on. The backpack is clutched tightly in her hand. Jenny lies curled up at the foot of the daybed, recovered from the invasion and no longer threatened by it. I add some pellets to her food dish and replace her water, and she jumps down for a meal.

Emily is nervous and jittery, eager to be off the island. It takes me just a few minutes to put some things in my own backpack.

"Ready to go?"

She nods anxiously. We leave the cabin and I padlock the door behind us. I can hear the wind kicking up outside the island, waves crashing along the shore. We climb aboard the dinghy and row quickly out to the centre of the cove.

"Might be a little rough out there," I tell her as we mount the ladder over the transom.

"Can't be worse than staying here. I'm really scared."

"We'll be okay."

We stow our gear, and I start the engine and release the bow rope. It takes a while to get through the channel in the dark, picking our way carefully among the obstructions, and as soon as we clear the barrier islets, two-metre-high waves set us rolling. Leaving the sails covered, we circle around to the leeward side into the shelter of the highlands and set the fore and aft anchors, bow on to the wind.

The waves are less powerful and a little more regular in the strait off the mainland, blocked by the western head. With any luck the motion won't keep us awake, although I'm not sure if Emily will be able to overcome her fear enough to relax. Once we're safely down below in the galley, I bolt the hatch in place.

"Want to listen to the radio?" I ask her.

"No. Do you think they'll find us here?"

"Look, we don't even know for sure who it was in the cabin. It could have been anybody."

"It was Lucas. I know it was."

"You're probably right, but so what? Even an expert sailor wouldn't try to approach this island at night, especially with the sea running the way it is. We're safe."

"You're sure?"

"Positive. Want to play cards?"

"I guess so."

She stows her backpack in the forward compartment while I break out the cribbage board. I pour some potato chips in a bowl and take a couple of Cokes from the icebox, and we sit opposite each other at the table.

"Want to make it interesting?" I suggest.

She looks alarmed.

"What's wrong?" I ask her.

"Lucas used to say that. He'd make us play strip poker with the johns." She ducks her head, her voice a faint monotone. "First one to lose all her clothes got passed around to all the men."

One more addition to my list of things to make Lucas Brady pay for.

"What I was going to suggest was a small wager," I tell her. "Loser has to serve the winner breakfast in bed and wash the dishes afterward. How about it?"

She seems to relax a bit. I slip the cards out of their box, extract the jokers, and hand the rest to her. She shuffles lethargically and sets them down for me to cut, then deals out the hand.

"You've got a lot of memories to cope with," I say quietly. "I know that. But with every day that passes, they'll begin to seem less and less important."

"It's just that…" She swallows convulsively. "I know you don't like me talking about what happened then."

"It's okay. If it helps to talk about it, I'll listen. As long as you don't tell anyone else."

"Even Mr. Curtis? If he's gonna be our lawyer, doesn't he have to know about me?"

"Only about why you ran away from Uncle Frank. I've already explained that to him, and he doesn't think any less of you for it. He knows it wasn't your fault."

"Will he tell Alex?"

"No. He didn't even tell Mrs. Curtis. I'm paying him to represent us, and he can't reveal anything we tell him to anyone, even family, unless we allow it."

"Is this gonna cost a lot of money?"

"I think you're worth it."

That earns me a tiny smile. "So you won't ever tell him about the rest of it?"

"Not unless you say it's okay. And my advice is to keep that part to ourselves. All I want him to do is represent us when I try to get custody of you. He doesn't have to know about Lucas to do that."

"Is that what you want? Custody?"

"That's how the law works."

"Like I'm some piece of property…"

"Hey! It's only a first step."

She riffles her cards absentmindedly. "Guess I'll have to be satisfied with that."

I pick up my hand, ready to play, but she isn't looking at hers. She stares out the dark porthole.

"If Lucas gets me again, I'll kill myself."

"No you won't."

Her gaze shifts back at me.

"If he does," I tell her, "and he won't, but even if he does, you're strong enough to handle it. You got away once. You're tough. And look at how you managed the boat when that freighter crossed our bow. You can deal with anything now."

"I'm still scared."

"Shut up and feed the kitty."

"Huh?"

"The cards. It's your kitty."

"Oh."

She examines her hand and drops the discard. I add mine to it and slap down a card.

"Seven!"

"Fifteen for two," she says without enthusiasm, and reaches for her peg. I put down an eight to match hers.

"Hah! Twenty-three for two!"

She perks up. "Hah, yourself! Thirty-one for eight!"

"What?"

"Three eights in a row, that's six, and two more for thirty-one." She pegs the score.

"Where'd you get that other eight?"

"Don't blame me. You cut the cards. Go on, lead."

"Cheat!"

"I did not!"

I grin at her.

"What?"

"Nothing. You're fun, that's all. You take this so seriously, and I like to get a rise out of you."

"Pay attention. I'm ahead, ten to two. Your turn."

I lead a queen. "Ten."

"Fifteen for two!"

"You're definitely cheating!"

"How? You cut!"

"I don't know how, but you are. Twenty-five!"

"Yippee! Thirty-one! Looks like I'm going to get breakfast in bed tomorrow."

* * *

The weather forecast proves wrong; no surprise there. A storm blows up a little before four, just after the turn of the tide. Rain slashes the portholes, and lightning paints Halloween horrors across the walls. The boat pitches and rolls, and I stick my head out the hatch to check on the anchors. The stern line strains and thrums, bass guitar to the storm's wild brass, but the anchor stays solidly driven into the ocean floor.

Fighting for balance as I back down the ladder, I hear a soft whimpering beneath the wind's wild keening, a kitten's mew from the forward berth. Emily is huddled in one corner, eyes tightly shut and hands splayed in her hair, a silent scream on her lips. I lean forward and touch her arm to wake her, just as a tremendous clap of thunder shakes the boat. She jumps violently, lashing out to slap me away.

"Hey, wake up! It's only me."

She thrashes her head from side to side, moaning "No, no, no." I crawl onto the mattress and gather her up in my arms. She struggles, then goes limp, and I murmur to her softly, stroking her hair and rocking her gently back and forth. Gradually she comes awake as the nightmare retreats. As soon as she recognizes me she hangs on desperately, shivering in spite of the cabin's warmth and wracked by tiny hiccupping sobs.

"It's all right," I whisper, "you're okay now."

236

"Oh, God, I thought you were Lucas!"

"It was only a dream."

The tension drains out of her and she melts against me. The storm rages around us, and she burrows in for comfort against the tempest that roils inside her. When at last I try to separate us, she clings tightly and buries her face against my chest. Two years old again, afraid of the dark.

Finally she calms and rallies a bit. "That was so awful," she whispers.

"Dreams can seem pretty real."

"That one sure did!"

"You want to talk about it? Sometimes that helps you get over a scare."

"He was beating me, just like last time. He wears this thick leather belt, and he uses it like a whip." She's breathing hard again. "It hurts so *bad!* He just kept hitting and hitting…"

She's trembling fiercely again, eyes wild, drawn into the memory of the dream. I shake her gently and she comes back with a start.

"It wasn't real. You're still safe."

"It made so much *noise!* That big belt…"

"You were just hearing the thunder outside. It didn't happen."

Her skin is cold and clammy, her hands like ice. I lean back against the bulkhead and help her to stretch out with her head resting on my thigh. She shivers violently, and I pull the blanket up around her.

The storm is moving off to the east, the rain now tapping a moderate waltz-time cadence on the deck. The thunder drums distantly on the other side of Farrell Island's bulk, the lightning diminishing to a muted glow behind the hill.

"Think you can go back to sleep now?"

She grips my hand. "Will you stay here?"

"If you want me to."

She sighs deeply. "Sorry I'm such a baby."

"Forget it." She seems to shrink within the covers as I stroke her hair, small and scared and needing me close. I choose a simple melody and hum it softly in rhythm to the receding storm, and slowly her limbs relax, her breathing slows, her trip-hammer heart stops leaping in her chest.

My mind drifts back to my own childhood, a scene forever engraved in memory, the violence of another storm as real today as when I was seven.

* * *

We were camping in a state park in southern Illinois one summer, the year my father read for his Ph.D. at the university in Carbondale. Tornado country. We arrived late and pitched the tent in the dark, and my mother had just settled us down to sleep, my brother and I, when I noticed the floor of the tent was moving slightly, a distinct and animated bump. I touched it cautiously, and it slithered away.

"Something's under there!" I shouted, and my brother craned his neck out of his sleeping bag to see. He reached out and poked the lump, and the fabric wrinkled and bulged.

My father took a flashlight and went out through the flap. We felt him tugging on one of the pegs, and a corner of the tent sagged inward. We backed up into the opposite corner as he lifted the floor, and when he dropped it again, the lump was gone.

"Here's the culprit!" he announced, and deposited a large, squat toad through the flap. We had pitched the tent right on top of the poor creature, but he seemed to have survived intact. My mother declined to let him spend the night with us.

A simple event, but so important that it played in my mind like a well-loved movie for me thirty years later. The closeness of our family, my father's gentle humour...Time together, and fun. I was a lucky kid.

After Dad anchored the corner of the tent once more we finally fell asleep, only to come awake again a few hours later to incredible noise, the howl of a runaway freight train roaring past the tent. The canvas whipped wildly and great gouts of water buffeted the walls, penetrating the seams and dripping from the peak. Thunder and lightning deafened us, barely an instant's pause between them, and the whole world shook with fury.

Through it all, my mother was an island of calm in a turbulent sea, wrapping her children in the safety of her arms and crooning softly as my father fought to keep our shelter from collapsing around us. We knew we were safe. Mom and Dad were there.

In the morning we emerged to find the campsite drenched, our tent one of only three still standing, the rest torn and flattened. We later learned that the tornado had missed us by less than a quarter mile, ripping a wide swath of destruction through the forest and levelling a mobile home park on the outskirts. My father cursed himself for letting us stay there throughout the night, not realizing the danger we were in, but I knew it was all right. No storm would ever mess with my Dad.

* * *

For the first time in my life, I truly understand how my mother and father must have felt during that frightening night. Assaulted by forces beyond their control, they did what they could to protect us, and hid their own fear so we would feel secure.

Now their role is mine.

Emily lies close to sleep, eyes vague and unfocused, one delicate finger picking at the collar of my shirt. No barriers separate us now. The rolling of the hull becomes the swaying of a hammock, lulling us both in the sanctuary of each other's trust: mutual need and mutual confidence, hers in the promise of my protection and mine in the comfort of having someone to care about once more.

24
Friday

The rainstorm is over but the wind has risen again with the dawn, humming through the bare rigging as we circle the island under power and enter the cove. I leave Emily aboard and take the tender ashore to be certain we're still alone. Jenny meets me at the door, and everything looks secure.

Emily joins me for the second trip. After breakfast she helps me clean up the dishes, then prowls uneasily about the cabin, constantly glancing out the windows.

"What are we doing today?" she wants to know.

"Nothing planned. Mr. Curtis is in court all day, so we can't see him until Saturday."

"I know. But I don't want to stay here. I don't feel safe anymore. Please let's just go somewhere. Anywhere."

"We can take the boat up the coast again."

"Good."

"I need a shower first. How about you? You can go first."

"What if they come back?"

"I'll keep watch."

"Okay," she says nervously. She vanishes into the bathroom, and a few minutes later I hear the shower running. Jenny demands her breakfast, and after setting out a big dish of dry food and changing her water, I'm about to pick up my novel as Emily walks out, wrapped in a towel.

"Are we coming back here tonight?"

"Depends on where we are after supper. We'll sleep on the boat again like last night, but you'll probably want another shower in the morning before we go to see Mr. Curtis."

"So I don't have to pack all my stuff now?"

"No. Are you done in there? I need to wash up too."

"The water's cold."

"I'm tough."

A couple of seconds silence. Then, very softly: "I know."

* * *

An hour later we're well past Bournemouth on our way up the eastern coast, two reefs in the main and a hot dry wind driving us hard. With the island well behind us, Emily relaxes a bit, cute and animated in her little blue shorts and halter and with the rakish baseball cap sideways on her head. To her the boat represents safety, washing away her cares with salt spray and sunshine. She could be any normal young teen, standing the helm and delighting in the rush of the wind, not the same child I found the week before in my forest. Like her nightmare, her imprisonment by Lucas may finally be starting to seem like an impossibly bad dream.

Amy's Pride porpoises through a strong but not unpleasant chop, foredeck awash and heeled over on a close reach.

"Do you ever get seasick?" she calls out to me.

"Not so far."

"I guess I don't either, huh?"

"If you were going to, you would have by now."

"How far are we going?"

"You'll see."

"Don't start that again!"

"We're almost there." I point off the port bow. "See those masts sticking up behind that headland? There's another marina back there, a really fancy one just off the highway between Bournemouth and Halifax. You'll see some amazing boats. Huge!"

"I like this one."

"It suits me too, and I can run it by myself when I need to, although it's easier with both of us. And more fun."

She grins appreciatively.

"Some of the big ones need a lot more crew," I tell her. "Especially the sailboats. Instead of just the one mast, they each have two or even three."

"Think they'd let me ride the bow of one of them?"

"It wouldn't be as much fun. The bigger boats don't get tossed about like this one, and you'd be too far above the water. Want to try it again now?"

"No thanks. It's too rough today, and I don't want to get wet. What time are we going to see Mr. Curtis tomorrow?"

"It isn't Mr. Curtis you want to see," I tease. "Got a pretty serious crush on that boy, haven't you?"

"I do not!"

The wind gusts and *Amy's Pride* points up, her sails fluttering.

"Watch out!" I shout.

She freezes as the mainsail slams across the deck and the jib back-winds. She hauls on the wheel to correct but turns it the wrong way, and the hull rolls sharply, knocking me off balance. I grab for the stern rail and miss, my feet flying out from under me. My head cracks on the console and my leg twists beneath me, white-hot pain lancing through my left ankle.

"What'll I do?" she screams as the boat broaches, waves pounding the side of the hull. The keel rises and the mast dips, threatening a knockdown. Fighting the cant of the deck, I seize the wheel and haul myself to my feet, and Emily tumbles onto the starboard locker. The wind howls in the rigging as the rudder bites into the waves, hauling us back on course.

Amy's Pride struggles upright, sails flapping wildly until the wind fills the jib. I manage to grab the boom to keep it from slamming back across the cockpit again, and bring us about. The main snaps taut with a thump like a mortar.

Emily is terrified, clinging to the rail. "I'm so sorry!"

"It's okay," I gasp, straining to bring the pitching hull under control. We come off the wind and begin to slow, still buffeted by the waves but safe once more.

"What happened?"

"You let the wind get on the wrong side of the sail, that's all. I was teasing you and you got distracted."

"It scared the hell out of me."

"Didn't do me much good, either."

"Oh my gosh! Are you hurt?"

"Nothing serious. Two broken legs and a ruptured spleen."

Her eyes widen in horror. "Are you kidding?"

"Of course I'm kidding. Here, take the wheel again."

"Oh, no!"

"Oh, yes. I have to go put a bandage around my ankle before it begins to swell."

She huddles against the rail. "What if it happens again?"

"It won't if you pay attention. Just keep her steady on this heading. Come on, you can do it."

When you fall off a horse, get right back on.

Reluctantly she steps behind the console. My ankle throbs as I hop one-legged to the ladder and limp down below decks. My ankle is hot and puffy, and I wrap it tightly with an elastic bandage from the first aid kit. There's enough ice left to fill a plastic baggie, and I strap it over the bandage before returning to the deck.

"Here! You do it!" she calls out over the console as I come through the hatch.

"You're doing fine."

"No. I'm scared. I'll do something wrong!"

I try to hide my limp as I make my way to the port rail and sit down. "What's the big deal? It was an accident, that's all. And as much my fault as yours for picking on you like that. We got out of it okay, so there's no harm done."

"How about your ankle? And what if we'd..."

"Hold it! No 'what ifs' allowed."

"But suppose I do it again. You shouldn't let me steer any more."

"Do *what?*"

"Oh, shit! Man the helm, then!"

"Hey, calm down. Everything's okay."

I get up again and limp behind the wheel beside her. She lets go and backs off, shrinking into the starboard corner of the cockpit.

"What if I sank your boat?"

"That's another 'what if.' It didn't happen."

"But..."

"And you have to stop being scared. Of anything."

She leans miserably against the rail. I reach over and squeeze her shoulder to reassure her, and she recoils from my touch, a strange reaction.

"We'll talk about it later, okay?"

"Are you gonna...?" She hesitates.

"What?"

"Never mind."

"Right now I need your help to take us into the marina. We're getting close, and with the wind this strong I don't want to risk doing it by myself."

She rallies a bit. "What do you want me to do?"

"You steer. I'll take down the sails when we get nearer to the pier."

"Steer?" She manages a tiny grin.

"You got me that time. Can you do it?"

"I guess. If I have to."

"Keep it steady on this course."

She steps behind the wheel again and I turn on the ignition and start the engine, letting it idle. The jib disappears into the roller furling with a few quick overhand pulls. Then I release the clamp on the main halyard, keeping tension on the line.

"Now bring her into the wind," I tell her, "just until the sail luffs."

"What if the boom hits you or something?"

"What if?"

"Shit!"

"You've got some mouth on you today. Here we go."

She turns the wheel gingerly and I release the rope, letting the sail sag toward the mast. My ankle complains as I climb up to fold it against the boom and tie it off, and I make an effort to hide my awkwardness. There's no sense in adding to the load of guilt she's already feeling.

"You want to take her in?" I ask her as I ease myself down into the cockpit.

"No! I'll smash it up!"

She hands off to me and collapses onto the port locker. I put the engine in gear and advance the throttle, and we swing toward the entrance of the marina. The wind is approaching gale force beyond the bay, keeping most sailors ashore, and although most of the mooring buoys are occupied we find plenty of room to tie up at the dock.

The ice bag is sagging around my ankle, its contents mostly melted, and I peel it off and flex the joint: sore but manageable. Emily stares at me anxiously, no doubt imagining broken bones, but the ice and bandage have helped and I know I can walk on it. To distract her, I gesture toward the array of world-class pleasure craft filling the immense marina.

Many of the massive sailing yachts and cabin cruisers dwarf *Amy's Pride* by many feet. Towering masts scrape the sky, and a few of them, vintage craft trimmed in gleaming oak and teak, recall Nova Scotia's glory days, when the original *Bluenose* left every other racing schooner struggling in her wake.

"What do you think?" I ask her.

"Are you okay?"

"I'm fine. Forget it. Look around you."

She gives the boats little more than a cursory glance, still too concerned over my injury. I manage to climb over the rail and set the lines without limping so she'll stop worrying. We set off for the marina office to ask the attendant where we can get some lunch.

"All we've got is a snack bar here," he tells me, "chips and ice cream and candy. Nothing else close by, but there's a big mall up near the highway."

"How far?"

"Fifteen minute walk. Or you can use our shuttle."

"I'd appreciate that," I tell him, not wanting to push my luck with a weakened ankle.

"Go stand by the road and I'll hail the driver for you."

* * *

Emily is still subdued as we sit in the food court, and leaves half of her lunch uneaten. It puzzles me that the mishap with the boat has disturbed her so. After finishing my own meal and a single sip of the burger joint's weak coffee, I discard the rest in the waste bin and suggest a stop in the Chapters bookstore that dominates the centre of the mall. Emily wanders about the aisles while I linger over a decent cup of coffee in the Starbucks concession. She returns as I'm draining the cup, a strange sad look on her face.

"Was your coffee good?" she asks me.

"Brought me back to life. What's bothering you?"

"Nothing…"

"Don't give me that. You're not still worrying about the boat, are you?"

"No. I found something."

"What?"

"It's a sailing book. Somebody named Slocum wrote it."

"Joshua Slocum? I know that one. *Sailing Alone Around the World*, I think it's called."

"Do you have it?"

"No. I took it out of the library once, but never got around to reading it. Why?"

"I wanted to buy it for you."

"That's really nice. Thank you."

"But I can't. I don't have any money."

"So that's it…"

We leave the café and walk out among the stacks.

"You know," I tell her, "if we're going to make our arrangement permanent, you're entitled to some family privileges."

"Like what?"

"An allowance, for example. You've earned it."

"How?"

"Dozens of ways. Cleaning the boat, washing the dishes…Keeping me entertained."

"I'd feel funny taking it."

"No reason to. Why don't we start right now?"

"No. Then I'd just buy you the book, and it would be like you bought it yourself."

"Okay, I get that. But once I get cust… Once you come to live with me, we'll work it out so you have some money of your own."

"I could get a job."

"Not yet. Your only job will be school for the next few years. You'll need good grades to get into university later. Want to show me where you found that book?"

"University?"

"Sure."

"I never thought…"

"That was then," I tell her. "From now on, the sky's the limit."

She leads me down an aisle to a rack labelled "Transportation" and plucks a slim volume from a shelf. The old man stares out at us from the cover, hand on the boom and master of his world.

"He's a little like you," she says, "except for the beard." She giggles, the first sign of pleasure since the near accident on the boat.

"You know," I say, "a gift isn't about money. It's about the thought behind it."

"Yeah, I've heard that one before. 'It's the thought that counts.' Some greeting card company came up with it."

"Maybe, but even so, it's true. Giving someone a gift means you want them to be happy. So even if you can't afford to, it means something that you cared enough to think of it."

"But…"

"And I'd really like to have the book. It would still be a gift, because you thought of it."

"You're pretty good, you know?"

"What?"

"You know how to turn everything around and make it right."

Do I? If only it were true.

"You want to look around any longer?" I ask her.

"No thanks."

"Want to go down to the marina again and look at the boats?"

"I guess." She's subdued again.

"We can walk this time. My ankle feels pretty good now."

"I'm really sorry about that," she says.

"Will you please forget it? It was an accident, that's all."

We leave the mall parking lot and come out on the narrow coastal road that meanders down to the marina. The wind is dropping, chased out to sea by an approaching high pressure ridge. The air is soft and pleasant, but Emily doesn't seem to be enjoying it. She's still uncommonly reserved and nervous.

I keep trying to figure out what's bothering her. She acted so strangely after we got the boat back under control, upset and fearful all out of proportion to the seriousness of the accident, and still can't seem to shake it off. Whatever it is that's bothering her, it's probably best to get it out in the open.

"How come you were so frightened on the boat?" I ask.

"I could have sunk it."

"Not likely. You just made a mistake, that's all. You turned the wheel the wrong way, and that was mostly because we were talking."

"I made you hurt your ankle."

"Another accident. Not your fault. I told you so then, but that seemed to make you even more upset."

She shuffles silently at my side. We reach a bend in the road and I steer her off the pavement into a meadow to avoid the shuttle bus coming up from the marina again. The driver waves as it rattles past us, and I respond but Emily doesn't.

"Can't you please tell me what's wrong?" I persist.

"You'll be mad at me."

"No. Whatever it is, I just want to understand."

"I was afraid."

"I know."

"No, I mean I was afraid of *you*."

"Me? You're kidding!"

She won't look at me. I take her hand and lead her to a rise of land a couple of dozen yards from the road. We sit down on a flat-topped boulder. The marina spreads out in the distance below us, tall masts and colourful hulls tossing in the still powerful waves that crash against the pilings.

"Come on now," I say seriously. "I really want to know what could possibly make you afraid of me."

"It's about Lucas again. Whenever I used to do something he didn't like, he'd hit me. And if I didn't go along with whatever he wanted me to do for the johns, he'd beat me really hard. The worst was when he went after me with his belt."

"And you thought I'd punish you somehow, just because of a little accident?"

She squirms uncomfortably. "I'm all confused about it. Every time, after he got through hitting me, he used to say he only did it because he loved me."

"Did you believe it?"

"I guess so. I must have."

She sits quietly for a couple of minutes, watching a small skiff pounding the waves as it comes in too fast toward the pier. We both stare at it. It's easier for her to talk if she avoids my eyes.

"You're gonna be mad if I tell you what else I did," she says.

"I don't think so."

The skiff overshoots the end of the pier and swings out to come around again, slower this time. She crosses her right leg over her left and grasps her ankle. She stalls, concentrating on the little boat's struggle against the rough water.

"Come on, out with it," I urge.

"Sometimes," she says, her voice a timid whisper, "I used to act up on purpose, trying to get him to punish me."

"Uh, huh," I say softly. "So you'd know he loved you."

She fingers the lace on her sneaker. "But I hate him! I really do! I don't know why I felt like that. And it hurt really bad when he hit me."

"But you tried to get him to do it anyway." I reach out and squeeze her hand gently. "That's a little bit like what they call the Stockholm Syndrome."

"What's that?"

"With Lucas you were a prisoner, like a hostage. According to the theory, hostages begin to identify with whoever is holding them and try to get their approval. I think that's what happened to you."

"That sounds crazy. Anyway, that's why I got upset on the boat. And now you're really gonna hate me."

"Why would I do that? Are you saying you turned the wheel the wrong way on purpose?"

"Gosh, no!"

"But I suppose you expected me to punish you for it. Did you want me to?"

She flushes, her cheeks a bright crimson under fresh tears.

"It's okay. I understand."

"I don't."

"Think about it. Lucas hit you when you did something he didn't like, and then he said he loved you. You did something you thought was wrong and I *didn't* punish you, so you thought I didn't love you. Even though I do."

Her eyes widen. "You do?"

I smile at her. "Duh!"

She ducks her head. Her eyes are wet, and she wipes them with the back of her hand. "I'm really embarrassed."

"No need to be. And I want you to understand something. This is really important. Even if you'd crashed the boat, or if my leg had been broken, it wouldn't have mattered. When people care about each other, it doesn't change when one of them makes a mistake."

She stares at me in wonder. After Uncle Frank and Lucas, she's still a long way from believing in fairness and decency.

"And another thing," I tell her firmly. "Lucas doesn't love you, no matter what he said."

"I know that now."

"But I do, just as if you were really my own little girl, and no matter what you do, that won't change."

"I'm not a little girl."

"Sometimes you are." I take out my handkerchief to dry the tears on her cheeks. "Like now."

"I love you, too," she says in a tiny voice. "But I was afraid to tell you so."

"You don't have to be afraid to tell me anything. For example, I bet you'd like an ice cream cone right now, but are afraid to ask."

"You're teasing me again."

"Me? Never! Come on, let's go check out the snack bar at the marina."

"I have a question first." Her face is solemn and serious. "If I get to live with you, what'll you do if I do something wrong? Something bad on purpose, I mean."

"I'll ground you so fast your head'll spin," I tell her. "You won't be allowed out of the house until you're thirty-five! Now how about that ice cream?"

She picks up her shopping bag with the book from Chapters and we head for the road and start down the hill, happy in each other's company.

25
Friday Evening

We spend the rest of the afternoon sailing off shore. The galley yields some beans and a can of tuna, and we improvise a casserole for supper. There are still a couple of hours of daylight left when we enter the cove at Farrell Island and tie up to the buoy. The shore is deserted, just as we left it, but I'm not about to take chances.

"We're gonna sleep on the boat, right?" Emily asks nervously as I haul the tender around to the stern.

"I think we'd better, just in case. You can stay out here while I feed Jenny. It won't take me long."

"Come back quick, huh? I don't like being here any more."

"Want me to bring you anything?"

"Another long T-shirt. And my toothbrush."

A few minutes later I'm standing on the dock, searching for anything out of place. The cabin windows stare back at me blankly, and there are no signs of a boat being pulled up onto the shore. As I mount the deck and press down the latch, I suddenly remember too late that I had padlocked it that morning. The hasp is hanging loose, and the door swings inward easily. Lucas Brady is lounging on the daybed, a foreshortened shotgun resting casually in the crook of his elbow.

"Where is she?" he demands.

"I left her in Bournemouth."

"Bullshit! Is she on the boat?"

I don't answer. He rises off the couch in one fluid motion and rams the butt of the shotgun into my gut. The air explodes out of me and doubles me over. He slams the stock across my jaw and drops me to the floor, stunned.

He kicks the door shut and pulls a cell phone from his shirt pocket, flipping it open. I try to catch my breath as he yanks a chair out from under the table and sits down. He punches in a number and waits for the connection.

"Ben? He's here."

He shifts the shotgun in my direction. My stomach is throbbing and the blood is pounding in my temples as I struggle to pull myself upright and slump back against the wall.

"Bambi isn't with him," Lucas says. "I think he left her on the boat." There's a pause while he listens.

"Hang on." He stands up and strides to the window overlooking the deck. "It's tied up out in the middle of the cove. When you get here, go on board and drag her out. We're in the cabin."

He snaps the phone shut and faces me. "Get off the floor," he orders, pointing to the daybed, and I climb painfully to my feet and collapse onto the mattress. Thick bile chokes my throat.

"You're a pain in the ass," he growls nastily. "I'd have had her back a week ago if you hadn't stuck your nose in my business. She'd better be on that boat."

My mind is racing but I keep my face blank, trying to hide my fear, more for Emily than for myself.

"I took her to Family and Children's Services in Halifax," I tell him, my voice a jagged rasp. "They're putting her with a foster family."

"Where?"

"They didn't tell me."

"If Ben doesn't find her on the boat, you're gonna get her back for me. She's my property."

"Not any more."

"She's the least of your worries, shithead. Tom has a score to settle with you before this is over. Cooperate with me and maybe I'll keep him away from you. If not, I'll give him some help."

"Tom?" I haven't heard that name before.

"Tom Clifford. My girls call him Cliff."

His girls! Somehow I have to keep him from taking Emily back.

"You're pretty damn stupid, you know that?" he snarls. "I didn't really expect you to come back here tonight."

"So why are you here?"

"Just wanted to have another look around, maybe find something I can use for leverage."

"Where's your buddy?"

"He dropped me off and took the boat back out. He's been cruising around out of sight, waiting for my call."

"He won't find her," I tell him, knowing he almost certainly will.

"We'll see." He turns to the window and throws it open, then swings around with the gun levelled at my chest. "If he doesn't, you're sure gonna wish he did."

"It won't matter what you do to me. You'll never find her."

The faint sound of an outboard echoes among the trees along the inlet. Lucas bends down to peer out the window, the gun still aimed in my direction. The engine roars as the boat enters the cove, then drops to an idle and finally dies altogether. Emily will have heard it coming, but I can't think of anywhere on *Amy's Pride* that she might hide. Time passes, long anxious moments full of imagined horrors: Emily back in the hands of these thugs and me unable to do anything about it.

"Shit!" Lucas mutters at last. He turns from the window and drops into the chair by the table again, glaring malevolently at me. I hear the outboard start up once more. A few minutes later heavy footsteps cross the deck. The door swings inward and Ben shoves his way inside.

"Not dere," he says brusquely, a trace of northern New Brunswick French in the consonants.

"You sure?" Lucas snaps.

"I searched the whole damn t'ing, even the cockpit lockers. I know boats. Dere's no place I missed." He kicks the door shut behind him, waiting for orders.

Lucas regards me coldly. "Well," he says at last, "this changes things."

He joins Ben at the door. They argue in low tones, but I can't make out the words. Finally they seem to reach a decision, and Lucas turns abruptly and faces me.

"Ben wants to beat the shit out of you. I figure then you'll tell me what you did with her."

I struggle to stay calm. "You think so?"

"No, I don't suppose you would. But there are other ways. For example, be a shame if something happened to that nice house of yours."

That jolts me, and I show it.

"Drove out and took a good look at it yesterday morning," he says. "Worth what, half a mil? Sure hate to see you lose it."

"Won't make any difference," I tell him. "It's insured."

All but my memories, and my photos of Amy.

252

"We'll see." He crowds me, shoving the gun barrel under my chin. "There are worse things than a beating, asshole. You'll find out, unless I get Bambi back damn quick. Now where is she?"

"Go to hell."

He glares at me, then lashes out with the barrel of the gun. The sight rips into my cheek, spraying my blood against the wall.

"Let's go," he barks at Ben, turning toward the door.

"Lucas, let me…"

"Forget him. Sooner or later this piece of shit'll lead us to her. Then we'll deal with him for good."

He flings the door open and storms across the deck. Ben slams the door behind them. I take out my handkerchief and press it to my face, cutting off the flow of blood. My vision is cloudy, my head throbbing painfully.

The outboard roars to life, and I manage to get to the window in time to see them pull away from the dock in a big inflatable Zodiac, a rental from the marina with a vintage Evinrude engine clamped to the stern. They race across the cove and enter the mouth of the inlet, with Ben at the tiller. Gradually the sound of the engine fades away.

Where the hell is Emily?

My face feels raw and tender. I grab the first aid kit from under the sink and take it into the bathroom to inspect the damage in the mirror. The gun sight has torn a ragged flap of skin from my cheekbone almost to my ear, and I wash it as well as I can and pin it back in place with butterfly bandages. It isn't a pretty repair, but it will have to do until I can get it stitched.

My head clears a bit, and I leave the cabin and stand on the deck, listening to the receding sound of the outboard. As I try to decide what to do next, a quiet voice startles me.

"Are they really gone?"

Emily peers out around the southeast corner of the cabin, her clothes soaked and her hair plastered flat.

"Don't move," I tell her, and run out onto the dock, down to the very end. The mouth of the inlet is deserted in the gathering dusk, the sound of the engine a long way off. They haven't doubled back.

"Come on," I call to her, and she rushes toward me and throws her arms around my waist.

"Whoa, you're wet!" I say. "Come on inside."

She spots the bandages on my cheek. "Did they hurt you really bad? You're bleeding."

"It's okay," I tell her. I can feel blood seeping out around the edges of the gauze, but it's beginning to clot.

"Are they coming back?"

"Not likely. It's getting dark, and I think I convinced them you're still on the mainland somewhere. How did you get away?"

"When I heard that outboard, I climbed up on deck and flattened out on the top of the cabin with a blanket over me."

"Smart girl."

"While Ben tied up at the stern, I slid down next to the jib and went over the bow. I hung on to the buoy until he finished searching the boat. Then when he went to the cabin I swam in."

"Saved yourself again."

"Well, *duh!* I wasn't gonna let him get me."

"You're amazing."

"I'm scared to death. Let's go."

"We'd better not. They could be lying out there off the island, waiting for us. I'm pretty sure they think I'm alone here, but..." I was thinking about the threat to have me followed. "How much do you know about Ben?"

"His name's Eugene Benoit. He's got a car repair shop in Halifax, Agricola Street, I think. One of the girls told me he steals cars and strips them for parts. He's a pimp, too, in business with Lucas."

"Nice people. Prostitution, car theft..."

"And drugs."

"How do you know?"

"He sells them out of Lucas's place. They won't let the girls use, though. Lucas caught one of them smoking crack once, and after that I never saw her again." She's close to panic. "What're we gonna do now?"

"It's safest to stay here. I'll bet they're waiting for us out there, but if we don't try to run, they'll decide you aren't here and give up."

"Are you sure?"

"To be honest, no, but we have to play the odds. Lucas carries a shotgun, and I can't fight that, especially out on the ocean. He can outrun us in that inflatable boat of theirs."

"I'll go sleep in the woods!"

"You don't have to do that. They can't get back here without us hearing them. I'll stay up while you sleep, and if I hear them coming I'll wake you up. You'll have time to run and hide outside."

"They'll see me go out the door."

"We can go out the bedroom window instead."

"Where's Jenny?" she asks, suddenly concerned about something besides herself.

"I don't know. Let's look."

We check out the bedroom without results. As the minutes pass with no sign of the Zodiac's return, Emily calms down enough to ask to take a shower, and I heat some water for her. Afterward she sits by the window listening while I clean myself up and replace the blood-soaked bandages.

"Jenny's back," she announces as I come out of the bathroom. The cat is curled up on her lap.

"Was she outside?"

"Nope. She was under the daybed." She's rubbing her eyes, exhausted and emotionally drained.

"Off to bed," I tell her. "I want to be out of here by daylight, in case they decide to come back in the morning."

"You can't stay up all night watching," she says.

"Sure I can. Now scram."

I'm worried that fear and tension will keep her from sleeping, but when I check on her a few minutes later, her eyes are closed, her breathing regular. She lies on her side, one fist balled beneath her chin. Jenny lies plastered against her back.

She lies supine against my spine in silken, furry drowsiness, and purrs her song of comfort 'til comes my healing sleep.

I set up my tin can alarm system in front of the door once more and shoot the bolt home. With a blanket to keep me warm, I take up my post at the end of the daybed where I can see out the window, leaving it open to keep track of any unfamiliar sound from outside. There's nothing but insects and the soft rippling of water against gravel and rocks, a gentle and familiar lullaby. I have to fight to stay awake, and sometime after midnight I lose the battle.

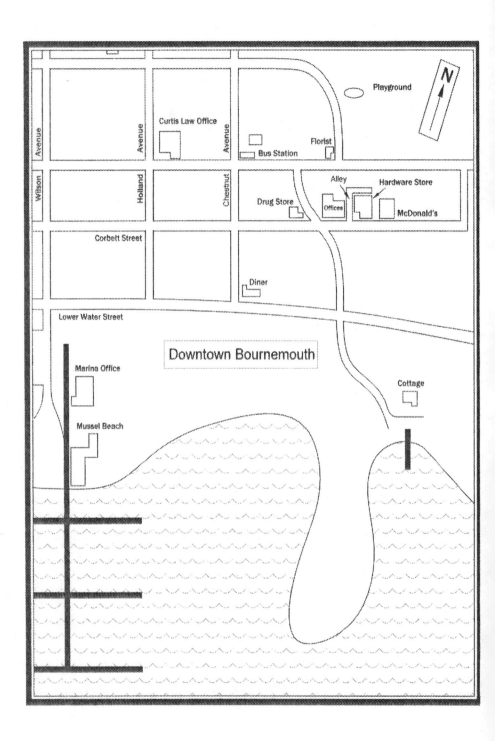

26
Saturday

Something wakes me, some small sound from outside that cuts through my dreams. The first hint of daylight outlines the trees to the east, and I light a lantern and inspect the room. Everything seems undisturbed, the door still bolted and the cans lying as I left them.

In the bedroom Emily sleeps on, buried beneath the blanket. Jenny stretches and pries herself away from her back, and follows me into the kitchen. I feed her and change her water, then fill an extra bowl with chow in case we don't get back for a day or two. I consider making breakfast, then decide we'd better eat ashore. We need to get moving as quickly as possible.

When I whisper her name, Emily comes awake reluctantly at first, then with a start as memories of last night flood back. She dresses quickly in her jeans and sweatshirt and stuffs a couple of changes of clothes in her backpack. She won't be coming back, at least until we resolve things one way or another. Except to feed the cat, I won't either.

I put a few things in my own backpack, and we leave the cabin and row out to *Amy's Pride* amid the first thin rays of dawn. Instead of leaving the tender on the buoy I hitch it to the stern, and we tow it behind us through the channel.

The sea appears deserted as we emerge from the island. There's barely enough wind to fill the sails, but I don't want to attract any attention by using the engine, just in case Lucas has posted a sentry somewhere along the mainland shore. Instead of heading directly for Bournemouth I tack off to the east, planning to find somewhere to land between the shipyard and the public marina.

The air stays calm as the skies brighten. Several times the sails collapse and flutter, leaving us all but motionless on a mirror-like sea. Emily fidgets restlessly, and once again I debate the wisdom of using the engine. Our appointment with Ken is scheduled for ten, leaving us plenty of time, so I decide against it and eventually manage to catch enough wind to get us in close to shore.

We find a shallow cove with a private dock just west of the shipyard, and anchor fore and aft and row the tender in to shore. There are no lights on in the cottage beyond the dock, and no car in the drive. If we're lucky, the owners are away and no one will notice *Amy's Pride* or the dinghy until we have a chance to reclaim them.

We gather up our backpacks and hurry across the lawn to the main road. We aren't far from the marina, but we have to avoid Mussel Beach, the first place Lucas might look for us. Within twenty minutes we're seated in a booth in a small diner on Lower Water Street, two among just a handful of early breakfast customers. No one takes much notice of us.

"What looks good?" I ask as Emily scans the menu.

"Squid pancakes."

If she can manage a small joke after the previous night's scare, I figure we're going to get through the day all right. The waiter brings two glasses of orange juice for us and coffee for me, tactfully ignoring my damaged face. Emily asks for milk. We both order a stack of blueberry pancakes and sit back nervously to wait for them to arrive.

Neither one of us feels like talking, and when the pancakes arrive we can only eat about half of them. Emily hoists her backpack and heads for the rest room to change. When she returns I'm pleased to see her looking summery, if not quite happy, in a light cotton top and the shorts that masquerade as a pleated miniskirt.

Amy always said I could tell her mood by the way she dressed, and if that's true for Emily too, she's beginning to get over her fright. There's a strange dichotomy to her outfit, making her look both very young and very sophisticated at the same time. A little girl poised on the brink of womanhood, and just about pulling it off.

"Very pretty," I compliment her.

She smiles shyly. "Do you think Alex will like it?"

"I'm sure he will. Not that it matters…"

She frowns at me, puzzled. "What do you mean?"

"Just that you should dress for *you*, not somebody else."

"How come?"

"Because you have to decide who *you* are, not what you think someone else might want you to be. Be yourself. Any guy who doesn't like what you really are isn't going to like you any better if you dress to please him."

"But…"

"I'm not teasing this time. I'm serious. 'This above all, to thine own self be true.' I really believe that."

"Is that a quote?"

"Yes. Do you understand it?"

"I guess so. But I want Alex to like me."

"He already does. He likes you the way you were when he first met you, and if you try to figure out what he might like instead, and try to change yourself, you might screw things up."

"How do you know all this stuff?"

"I was married to a very smart woman."

* * *

It's well after eight when we finally leave the diner and make our way along the waterfront. A couple of sport fishermen are sorting their gear at the end of the wharf, and a family of five swarms over a twenty-eight-foot Viking. An elderly couple comes strolling along the quay. Two men sit among piles of lobster traps, smoking and talking. Three teenaged boys stand disconsolately beside their windsurfing rigs, no doubt cursing the lack of a breeze.

All very innocent, and yet any one of them could be a plant, watching for us and ready to give us away.

As we head away from the shore I keep watch behind us, but no one follows. That doesn't guarantee our safety in an age of cell phones, however, so I hurry Emily along up Holland Avenue, toward the corner where Ken has his office. To kill the intervening time before our appointment, I suggest we might try to find a gift for Katie.

The law firm is close to the edge of the commercial section, a pleasant area a couple of blocks from the fast food joints and tourist attractions. Among the craft and souvenir shops to the east we find a small florist, not yet open. We walk on past and window-shop for a while, and Emily notices me checking over my shoulder, covertly inspecting every passerby.

"They won't dare try to grab me here on the street, will they?" she asks nervously.

"Of course not." Confidence, masking dread.

"What happens after today?"

"We can't sleep on the island any more. I think the best thing to do is for you to stay somewhere temporarily where no one can find you. Maybe Mr. Curtis will have a suggestion. Then I'll sail back and get Jenny and close up the cabin."

"How will you get her back, if she hates the boat so much?"

"We can buy a cat carrier. There must be a pet shop around here somewhere."

"How about you? Where will you go?"

"A hotel, maybe."

"I want to stay with you."

"We'll see what we can work out."

We reach the end of the commercial district, bordered by a well-kept park with playground equipment and a small wading pool, completely deserted at such an early hour. Emily settles comfortably onto one of the swings and I sit down next to her, awkwardly close to the ground. She pumps her legs a few times, then lets the swing coast to a stop.

"What if…" she begins.

"No 'what ifs,' remember?"

She twists from side to side, uneasy.

"I'm a lot of trouble to you, aren't I?"

"Damn right!"

That startles her.

"I'm kidding. Of course you're not."

"Kids are expensive," she offers.

"So I've heard."

"Do you have a job somewhere?"

"Not now. I closed my business when I moved to the island."

"What do you do for money, then?"

"I've been living on my savings."

"Do you have enough for the rest of your life?"

"Another year or so, maybe."

"Then what?"

To the north, a neat residential subdivision climbs a gentle hillside with a view of the distant harbour. It's an area of nice homes, well-cared-for lawns, backyard pools. Families.

"Go back to designing buildings again, I guess."

"Is that what you want to do?"

"To be honest, I'm not really sure. Why are you asking?"

"Because I don't want you to have to do anything just because of me."

"Sweetheart, that's a very nice thing to say, but you don't have to worry about that. I can take care of both of us."

"What kinds of buildings did you make?"

"All kinds. Houses for people to live in, offices. Even a school once."

"Was it fun? Designing houses, I mean."

"Yes, it was, especially when…" I stop.

"I know what you were going to say. When Amy was alive."

"Yes."

"Why did that make a difference?"

"I guess because I had someone to show my accomplishments to."

A long pause. "You could show me…"

"You know, you're right. I could. And I think I will, starting with the building where Mr. Curtis has his office."

"Did you design that one?"

"Uh, huh."

We pick up our backpacks and head back to the florist's shop, and Emily chooses a flowering plant for Katie, something that the clerk promises will last a long time with minimal care. Rather than carry it around with us we ask him to deliver, and we leave the shop to walk downtown for our meeting.

Ken's office overlooks the town from the fourth floor. He shares the building with a real estate firm on ground level, two CPAs and an income tax consultant the next floor up, and an import-export firm on the third. Emily cranes her neck as we enter the spacious lobby and head for the elevator, taking in the Italian marble floors and the tropical plants that grow lushly beside a ceiling-high cascading waterfall. Everything gleams in the filtered sunlight that slants through skylights in the atrium. The maintenance contractors are doing their job well.

"Wow!" she exclaims in wonder.

"Wow, what?" I ask.

"This place is beautiful!"

"I'm glad you like it."

The elevator lets us off directly into a panelled reception area that conveys the warmth and welcome of a private home. Ken's secretary announces us, then ushers us into his office. He meets us at the door, and his eyes open wide at the sight of my bandages.

"What happened to your face?" he exclaims.

"It's not serious. Tell you later."

He's about the press the issue, then changes his mind. He turns to Emily. "Somebody looks pretty sharp today."

She thanks him shyly.

"Special occasion?"

She blushes slightly and doesn't answer.

"Drop your backpacks by the door and have a seat," he tells us. He returns to his desk and spreads out the contents of a file folder on the blotter.

"Let's get to it," he says. "First, let me repeat that as my clients, both of you are entitled to complete confidentiality. Emily, do you understand what that means?"

"Yes, sir. No matter what we say, you can't tell anyone."

He smiles. "Hardly legal language, but you're dead on. I can never repeat anything you say without your permission. That means you can tell me all about whatever has happened to you, and I hope you will."

He pauses, waiting to see if she'll offer anything, but she holds her tongue. He turns back to me.

"My next question is, do you want to discuss this alone? Emily can wait outside if there's anything…"

"No," I interrupt. "This concerns her future, and she has a right to hear everything we say. For her own peace of mind, I want her to know we aren't keeping anything from her."

"I'm going to have to ask some very pointed questions."

"Doesn't matter."

"Fair enough."

"I guess we better start by telling you who she is," I offer.

"I already know," Ken says. "I did some digging yesterday, based on what little you've told me. I have a copy of the police report her uncle filed last January."

The man is more clever than I thought. Emily looks apprehensive, and I can tell she's worried about just how much information he's managed to uncover.

"What's in it?" I ask uneasily.

"Not much. The uncle reported her as a runaway, and the police conducted a search for a while, but they hit a dead end. The file is still open, but no one is looking for her very hard any longer." He turns to Emily. "Where have you been since then?"

She glances at me nervously.

"That's one of the things we're going to have to keep to ourselves," I tell him.

"If I'm going to help you…"

"I'm sorry. That's non-negotiable. We can go to another attorney if that isn't acceptable."

"All right, we'll leave it for now. How did you two get together?"

"She showed up last week on my island."

"Your island?"

"I've been staying off the coast on Farrell Island."

He looks surprised. "I thought that place was uninhabited."

"It's been in my family since the eighteenth century. I have a small cabin, but there's no one else living there. In addition to shutting down my business, I closed up my house and moved out there last March."

His eyes shift to Emily again. "How did you get there?"

She squirms uneasily. I'm afraid that in confusion she might blurt out something about her recent past.

"To save time," I suggest, "I'll answer for both of us. Emily will let me know if I get anything wrong. Is that okay with you, sweetheart?"

A tiny nod. She looks very small and vulnerable.

"To put it simply," I go on, "after she left her aunt and uncle, the people she was staying with didn't treat her very well, and when she had the opportunity to get away, she took it. My island was the closest place."

"In the middle of the ocean?"

"She jumped off their boat and swam."

Ken sits back and regards us both. "If you tell me who these people are, we can get the police to…"

"That doesn't matter now," I interrupt. "All we care about is the future, and what's the best thing for her from now on."

"You're making this difficult, but we'll play it your way for now. You told me she's just fourteen, and that coincides with the birth date in the police report. Has she been going to school?"

"Not since Christmas."

"And you say she's not related to you in any way?"

"That's right."

"Well, it shouldn't be too hard to place her with a good foster family…"

"No!"

Emily's sudden violent outburst surprises us both. She squirms forward off the chair, her fists balled up and her lower jaw quivering. "If you make me go someplace like that, I'll just run away again!"

"It's all right," I tell her. "We're only here to see what's possible and what's not."

She's up on her toes, feeling cornered and ready to run. I look to Ken helplessly.

"Please sit down, Emily," he says soothingly. "I'm on your side, remember? I just don't have a handle on what you want yet."

She turns to me desperately. "I'm staying with you, right? You promised."

"Is that what you want, too?" he asks me.

"Yes."

He leans back and taps his pencil on the blotter. "And I thought this was going to be easy."

I take her hand and urge her back onto the chair. "You see our problem?" I say to Ken.

"Not really. When you were talking to me about this two days ago, you didn't say anything about keeping her permanently. You just told me you wanted to get her away from her Uncle Frank, and help her get somewhere safe."

"I'm sorry, I didn't mean to mislead you."

He studies us for a long moment, considering. Emily is balanced on the edge of her chair, still clinging to my hand.

"Are you saying now that you want custody?" he asks me.

"It's what we both want."

"All right, I've brushed up on my family law a little since I saw you on Thursday. There are a couple of legal issues here, and they hinge on her age. In this country, kids acquire some specific rights at age fourteen. Even though she's still a minor she'll be allowed to make certain decisions for herself."

"Such as?" I ask him.

"Children this age are consulted about custody matters. If there's a dispute between divorced parents, for example..."

"That doesn't apply to us, since her folks are dead. Are you saying that Uncle Frank...?"

"Forget him. We'll deal with him later."

"So?"

"Believe it or not, social workers have a fair amount of latitude in cases like this. If we get a good caseworker, one who decides to look beyond the fine print, there's a pretty good chance they'll take her wishes into consideration without making us go to court. In other words, as long as the situation appears to be safe and positive, Emily can probably choose who she'll live with."

She grips my hand tightly, clinging to every word.

"Even though we aren't related?" I ask.

"It may not make any difference. But that isn't the only issue here."

I wait for the other shoe to drop.

"You realize this isn't going to look good. She's a runaway, and you've let her hide out with you a week."

"I wasn't hiding her!"

"That's how it's going to look. Someone's likely to question your motives."

I sink back into the chair, deflated. Emily swivels back and forth between us, not quite understanding.

"Ken, all I want to do is take care of her. She's been through a really bad time, and I'm willing to look after her. More than that, I really want to."

"I accept that. But you're just getting over a major loss yourself," he says. "Are you sure you're thinking straight?"

I shrug helplessly.

"There's another law you need to know about," he says carefully, looking at Emily, "another choice she's allowed to make now."

"What's that?"

He hesitates.

"Go ahead," I tell him. "She has to hear everything."

"Okay. Sexual consent."

"What about it?"

"At age fourteen, a child can elect to have sex. With adults, if she wants to, and it's not against the law."

"That's insane! That's statutory rape!"

"Not here. Most people think so because of American TV shows, but laws are different in the United States."

"Jesus Christ!" I mutter. "That's like giving kids a driver's license before they can see over the steering wheel. How is someone that age going to understand the consequences, physical and emotional?"

"Some can, most probably can't. And they shouldn't have to deal with that kind of pressure, but that's how the law reads. So when you step up and tell the courts you want her to move in with you, especially so soon after your wife died..."

"That's disgusting!"

"It's reality."

"You can't honestly believe…"

"It isn't what I believe that's important."

"Jesus Christ! And if I were female, I suppose nobody would bat an eye."

"Not necessarily. Things have changed. For example, years ago no one would have questioned it if a man offered to take responsibility for a troubled boy. But after all the church abuse scandals, same-gender pairings are no longer considered automatically safe."

"How the hell could anyone think I'd…" I stop short. Emily is looking terrified, probably only taking in half of what we're saying. It never occurred to me that I could be accused of exactly the kind of abuse I'm trying to protect her from if I try to get custody of her.

"So it's hopeless then?" I ask him.

"Maybe not. Got any skeletons in your closet?"

"Jesus Christ! Not that kind!"

"Then it's not impossible. It looks to me like you two have a healthy relationship, and we just have to make sure it's apparent to a caseworker, too. But you'll be like a bug under a microscope for a while. They'll turn over every rock you ever stepped on."

"I have nothing to hide!"

He regards Emily closely. She's digging her nails painfully into my palm. "Are you up for a fight?" he asks her.

"Whatever it takes," she says.

" 'Whatever it takes'," he repeats softly. Then he nods as if coming to a decision, smiles at her, and addresses me again.

"What are your long term intentions?"

"What do you mean?"

"You tell me. You must have thought about it. Do we just go after legal custody?"

"I know it probably isn't possible," I tell him, looking directly at Emily, "but I'd like it to be more than that. I'd like to adopt her."

"Emily?" Ken says softly. "If there's any way to do it, is that okay with you?"

She can't answer him. She clings tightly to my arm.

"I guess I have my answer," he says.

266

27
Saturday, Lunch Time

For another hour we explore the problem, and in spite of Ken's probing I manage to conceal Emily's recent past. He covers several sheets of paper with detailed notes, including information about her aunt and uncle, the school she last attended, and the names of every other relative she can remember. There aren't many, and none nearby. According to Emily her grandparents are dead, two from natural causes and the others in the same accident that claimed her parents. Her mother had been an only child, and her aunt Margaret was her father's only sister.

By eleven thirty we've developed a comprehensive outline of the situation, and Ken is prepared to do some research into applicable legal precedents. Emily has calmed down and is tired of the topic. When Alex arrives at his father's office, she jumps up happily to greet him.

"I guess it's lunch time," Ken announces. "Where shall we go?"

"Can I take Emily to McDonald's, Dad?"

"I take it we're not invited?"

"Well..."

"I know. Parents are a drag. Suppose you two go ahead and find yourselves a table. We'll come along in a few minutes and sit as far away from you as possible. We'll pretend we don't even know you."

"That's not..." Emily begins.

Alex grabs her hand and tugs her toward the door. "Let's go before they change their minds."

The last thing we hear as they disappear through the reception area is Alex's voice: "You look cool!" Ken and I both stifle our laughter so they won't hear us.

"That boy of yours is working on his line," I tell him. "He's going to worry a lot of fathers some day."

"Tell me about it."

"So what's the bottom line? Is there any hope she'll be able to stay with me? If not, I have to find some way to look after her that won't make her run away again."

"I think you've got a good chance, but a case like this attracts a lot of attention. You'll be under close scrutiny. It would help if you'd give me some more information, especially about where she's been since Christmas."

"I can't. I promised her, and I honestly think it would do more harm than good. How does she strike you, anyway? Seem normal to you?"

"Better. She's a real sweetheart."

"If you knew what I know, you'd be amazed at that. She's been through absolute hell."

"And you're never going to tell me about it, right?"

"Right."

"What if some judge asks you that question?"

"I'll play dumb and pretend I don't know. She'll never tell either."

Ken leans back and studies me closely, and finally comes to a decision. "I think I'd better investigate you personally, and not leave it up to some caseworker. If I work up a comprehensive file on you, and can prove that you're above reproach, maybe we can forestall anyone probing too closely into *her* past."

"If you can do that…"

"May I assume you don't have a criminal record of any kind?" he interrupts.

"No."

"Are you listed with the Child Abuse Registry?"

"The *what?*"

"It's an official record. The authorities maintain it. Schools and sports teams have access to the information when choosing chaperones or coaches. Scout and Girl Guide leaders too. If you've ever been charged with a crime against children, or even if you've been under suspicion…"

"What the hell kind of world are we living in?"

"You tell me. You're the one keeping Emily's past a secret."

That settles me down a bit. He's in my corner now, and I don't want to antagonize him. "What else?" I ask him.

"Financial problems? An old divorce?"

268

"No and no."

"Pure as the driven snow, I suppose."

"Lost my driver's license for a week when I was nineteen. Other than that, clean as a whistle."

"You're going to have to prove it to me if I'm going to swear on your behalf," he says heatedly. "Full disclosure. I'm Emily's lawyer too, and if you're hiding anything about your own past, you can forget about custody or adoption or anything else. I'll have your head on a plate myself."

"Just tell me what you want to know."

"I'll need access to your whole past for starters. School records, names of people who've known you all your life, previous employers. If you can't stand the heat, tell me now."

"Do it."

"Fine!" He glares at me for a moment, and then his face softens. "Sorry to come on so strong, but it's better coming from me now than from some cop or social worker later."

"It's okay," I tell him. "If you care that much about her welfare too, then we're on the same team."

He stands up and walks around the desk. "Let's get some lunch. Then we'll come back here and start taking you apart, piece by piece."

We leave the office and take the elevator down. We're halfway across the lobby when Alex comes flying through the revolving door.

"Dad, help!" he hollers. "He's got her!"

"What's wrong? What happened?"

"Where's Emily?" I shout.

He's gasping for breath, words running together. "Some creep grabbed her and dragged her down an alley. Come on!"

"Slow down. Who? What alley?"

"He came out of nowhere and smacked me, knocked me down and grabbed her! Come on!"

"Show me!" I'm trying to stay calm, my heart pounding like a blacksmith's hammer. Alex turns and plunges through the door, Ken and I close behind. Three blocks later he skids to a stop and points to a narrow alleyway between an office building and a hardware store.

Halfway down, a sleek black Lexus squats with its lights on and the engine idling. Eugene Benoit lounges against the front fender, a cigarette hanging out of the side of his mouth. He stands up lazily as Ken and I approach.

"Reinforcements this time, asshole?" he says sarcastically. "Won't do you any good."

Out of breath, I fight to keep my voice slow and even. "Where is she?" I demand.

"Gone where you'll never find her," Benoit says with a self-satisfied smirk. "She's not your business any more."

Ken pulls out his cell phone and flips it open.

"You touch that t'ing and you'll find her floating in the harbour in the morning," Benoit growls at him.

I struggle for control of my emotions. "Ken, you and Alex give me a minute, okay? Don't call the police."

He flips the cell phone closed. "What the devil's going on?"

"I can handle this."

"The hell you can."

"Just cut me some slack for a few minutes, but stay close in case I need backup."

"You're crazy!" he tells me.

"You're probably right. Just do it, okay?"

Ken nods to Alex and they back up toward the mouth of the alley. Benoit drops his smoke and grinds it out under his shoe. He's calm and relaxed, knowing he holds all the cards.

"Got a message for you from Brady," he says once the others are out of range. "You can walk away now and it's over, but keep screwin' wit' us and see what happens."

I take a few wary steps forward. He tenses and stands up straight, Goliath to my David, four inches taller and outweighing me by at least fifty pounds of muscle. He wipes his arm on his shirt, leaving a broad streak of blood.

"What happened to your arm?" I ask him.

"The little bitch bit me," he snarls. "She'll pay for that tonight."

Good girl! She's fighting back. But I have to find her quickly.

"You don't need her," I tell him, stalling and trying to manage my fury. "With all the whores you're running, what's one kid more or less?"

"She's a money-maker, but that's not the point. Nobody takes our property. Not good for business. We keep the tail in line, and dey know what happens if dey cross us."

"She didn't cross you. She's just a baby."

He snorts. "Some perverts pay big for babies like her. We'll get a few more good years out of her from the schoolgirl freaks, den put her on the stroll."

"You bastard! That'll kill her!"

"Hell, no. Little ones like her are tough. We run a clean shop, too, keep 'em nice and healthy. We know our clientele, no sickos, ever'body wears condoms. A clean operation."

"No sickos? What do you call that boat party? They were going to beat the hell out of her."

"Shit, that's just a little family fun. Dey whip the kid's ass 'til she's good and tender, that's all. Some guys get off on that, and it pays double. Gets ever'body in the mood for a good screw."

White-hot rage nearly blinds me and I lunge forward, ready to take a swing. He puts up his hands and steps back, grinning.

"Touch me and she's a dead little whore. And you too."

We lock eyes for a few long moments, and I have to back down. He opens the car door and rests his hand above the window.

"Cut your losses, shithead," he sneers. "She's not worth it."

He bends his leg to slide in, and I throw myself forward and slam the door hard on his wrist, leaning my full weight on the door and trapping him against the frame.

"You goddamn son of a bitch!" he screams, trying to wrench his arm free. I whip the door open and slam it again, mashing the bones in his wrist, and he lets out a high, girlish shriek. I grab his hand and yank it upward, pinning it against the roof of the car. Behind me, a few people have stopped on the street and are looking down the alley. Ken is starting to run toward me, and I wave him off.

I bend down close so Benoit can hear me clearly. "Where is she?"

"Shove it, asshole!"

I hammer his wrist against the roof and he turns white. Sweat breaks out on his forehead. When he finally speaks, it's barely a whisper.

"Lucas took her."

"Where?"

He moans pitifully. "You broke my friggin' hand! And you just killed her, you dumb shit!"

The blood is pounding in my ears, and my gut heaves. I kick the door hard and hear the bones in his arm grind together. He screams again and writhes in his seat.

"Look at me," I snarl. He turns his head and I slam my fist down on his arm. The jagged end of a bone tears through the skin, splattering blood all over the roof.

"Last chance," I tell him. "Where did he take her?"

He gasps for breath, his face deathly pale. His jaw is sagging and saliva soaks his shirt. His bowels let go, filling the car with the stench of blood and shit and fear.

"The boat," he says weakly.

"Which boat? The Zodiac?"

"Charter..." he gasps.

"The Hunter?"

He nods feebly.

"Where's he taking her? Somewhere in Halifax?"

"North...Northwest Arm."

I'm not likely to get much more out of him, nothing important anyway. A curious crowd fills the mouth of the alley. Sickened by my own violence, I drop his wrist and stride off to join Ken and Alex.

"Show's over," I say to the onlookers, trying to sound casual. "We're making a movie here next week. Just rehearsing."

I motion for Ken and Alex to follow and we hurry up the street, back toward the law office. A police siren cuts through the noise of the traffic, heading our way. We break into a run.

"My God!" Ken exclaims, fighting for breath. "Who was that? You damn near tore his arm off."

"Did you call the police?" I ask urgently.

"No. Some guy with a cell did, though."

"Don't talk to them. Emily's life depends on it. Anybody back there recognize you?"

"I don't think so."

"Is your car here?"

"Behind the office." He slows to a walk, panting. "What the hell's going on?"

"I'll tell you as soon as I can. Get me down to the harbour. Fast!"

"Listen..."

"*Move*, for Christ's sake!"

An engine roars behind us, and the black Lexus bursts from the alley, scattering the onlookers. It careens across the street, sideswiping a parked car and narrowly missing an oncoming bus, then rights itself and tears off.

We sprint in the opposite direction.

28
Saturday Afternoon

After dropping Alex at Ken's office, we tear around to the parking lot and pile into Ken's coupe. He whips the car out into the street and runs a red light at Corbett, careening onto Lower Water. I'm out of the car and racing along the boards as he slams on the brakes at the foot of the pier. The charter company's slip is empty, and the Hunter 33 is just clearing the first buoy at the mouth of the harbour. Her sails are down, and two figures are standing in the cockpit, the charter captain in his distinctive hat and Lucas Brady. There's no sign of Emily.

Ken comes pounding up to me, and I swing back and shout to him. "Is your boat here?"

"No. We keep it in Chester."

"Damn! Get back in the car!"

He spins around and we jump aboard. "Which way?" he asks.

"East. Coast road."

He guns the engine and rockets off down Lower Water, flying through the noon hour traffic with his horn blasting. Pedestrians scatter as we cross Holland, narrowly missing a taxi in the intersection.

"What the hell's going on?" he says, gripping the wheel tightly and mashing the gas.

"They've got Emily aboard that big Hunter."

"Who? Why'd they take her?"

"Pull in there!" I shout, spotting the lane to the cottage where Emily and I left *Amy's Pride*. Ken brakes hard and skids up onto the grassy shoulder. I leap out and run for the dock, and hear his door slam behind me. He catches up as I'm unhitching the dinghy.

"I'm going with you," he pants, breathless.

"This isn't your fight." I drop onto the thwart and unship the oars, and he grabs the transom and leaps into the stern.

"Whatever you're planning to do," he says, "you can use some help running your boat."

It's hard to argue with that. I lean hard on the oars and we pull up next to *Amy's Pride* and scramble aboard. Once the anchor is up I jam the key in the ignition, and the little diesel comes to life.

"The wind's up." I tell him. "Get the cover off the sail."

"What about the dinghy?"

"Let it go. It'll just slow us down."

He drops the tender's painter and clambers up on the cabin roof to unsnap the sail cover. He bolts on the halyard as I throw the transmission in gear and swing toward the mouth of the cove.

"Get her up!" I shout as he jumps down into the cockpit. The wind is southerly, twenty knots or more, and I have a better chance of keeping up with the big yacht with the sails than with the engine. Ken hauls away on the main and winches it in tight, then yanks the jib off the roller furling and sets the sheet.

Amy's Pride heels over hard under the full force of the wind as we clear the headland southwest of the cove, overpowered and bucking. With no time to take a reef in the main, I swing the wheel and point up, all the time searching the sea. If Lucas is heading for Halifax, he has to be somewhere among the dozen or more yachts between us and the horizon. Finally I spot the distinctive outline of the Hunter, off to the east and heading for deeper water.

"That's her," I tell Ken. "Get my binoculars, will you? They're over the map table."

I toss him the padlock key and he opens the hatch and drops down into the galley. He reappears a moment later with the glasses in his hand and mounts the rail to peer out over the bow.

"Two men on board," he tells me.

"Any sign of Emily?"

"Not that I can see."

"Let go the traveller." Ken ducks beneath the dodger and releases the clamp. I'm trying to coax an extra half knot out of the hull. We're making better than six on an outgoing tide, and it looks like we're closing the gap. The Hunter's sails are furled and she's running on the engine. With her longer waterline and a decent captain, she could easily outrun me with her canvas flying, but it looks like they're in no hurry.

The minutes drag on, but we soon pull close enough to see the two men clearly, deep in conversation. They haven't noticed us. Finally Lucas turns away from the helm and weaves around the console to the companionway, then vanishes below.

Where Emily is!

"What happens when we catch him?" Ken asks anxiously.

"Depends on how soon he spots us. If we can get close enough, I'm going to try to board her."

"What? How the hell…?

"Rig the bumpers on the port side. We'll come up astern to starboard and bear off, then come at him. When we're close enough, I'll jump across."

"You'll kill yourself!"

"I've got to try. He's got Emily on there somewhere."

"Suppose they're armed?"

"I can't worry about that now. Get the bumpers, will you?"

Ken hauls them out of the locker and ties them to the port rail. We're less than a hundred yards off the Hunter's stern, her diesel growling at half throttle. Lucas is taking his time getting to Halifax, and it's likely that Emily is suffering for it.

The captain glances back and sees us bearing down on him. He waves me off, and I acknowledge and spin the wheel to starboard, coming off the wind and losing a knot. The man turns his attention back to his boat, and I point up slightly to edge up on his stern.

"Take the helm," I tell Ken, and he moves in beside me. I hand off and climb onto the port gunwale, hanging onto the rail.

"Don't tip him off," I caution. "Wait until I signal, then come over on him hard. Don't hit him if you can avoid it. As soon as I jump, bear off quick but stay close."

We draw even with the big yacht. The two boats are only a dozen yards apart, and the captain looks over angrily and waves me off again. I drop my hand and Ken hauls on the wheel. *Amy's Pride* rears up, sails roaring, and heaves to port. At the last second I let go of the rail and launch myself across six feet of open water, falling heavily into the cockpit and knocking the captain's legs out from under him.

We collapse together in a heap beneath the wheel, but the man is faster than I am. He aims a punch at my face and I slip it, but he hammers his fist down hard on my collarbone. I grapple with him and take another blow to the shoulder, then manage to bring my knee up into his gut. He grunts and doubles over, and I jerk my clenched hands up hard under his jaw, rattling his teeth.

He rolls away and springs to his feet, and I'm half a beat too slow. His boot crashes into the side of my head, sending me reeling against the starboard gunwale. He comes at me again, and I try to duck and catch my foot in the jib sheet. He rams his boot into my kidneys, sending me sprawling on the deck.

The boat flounders broadside to the tide, and he stumbles to the helm and brings her back on course. Dizzy and disoriented, I lunge and tackle him below the knees. He buckles and staggers against the rail, but shakes me off and aims another kick at my head. This time I manage to catch hold of his boot and yank hard, knocking him off balance. His head smashes down on the binnacle and blood spurts from his forehead. His eyes roll back and he topples over onto his side.

I struggle to my feet and search for Ken. *Amy's Pride* is off the wind and keeping pace astern. I wave to him to stay away, then mount the rail and run forward along the gunwale, stopping at each porthole to peer inside.

Lucas is in the forward compartment, standing just inside the doorway and cursing. Emily huddles in the far corner of the berth, an angry red welt splayed across her left cheek. As I watch, the man unbuckles his belt and yanks it out of the loops, then reaches for her. She shrinks back but he catches her arm and drags her to the edge of the berth.

I run back to the cockpit, stumbling heavily against the console, and the boat lurches to starboard. I jam the throttle forward and the hull heaves and shudders. Spinning the wheel hard aport, I knock the throttle back again and the bow settles abruptly. The big boat broaches and wallows in its own wake.

"What the hell's going on out here?" Lucas roars. He bursts through the hatch and trips over the captain's body as he rounds the console. I kick out and connect with his kneecap. He yelps and scrambles back, and I come up from a crouch and butt my head into his gut, sending him sprawling to the deck. His hand flies back and grabs the winch handle from its pocket on the console. Before I can get to him he's on his feet again, brandishing the handle like a baseball bat.

I back off, circling the binnacle and searching desperately for some sort of weapon. His eyes are slits, glowing with hatred. He skirts the wheel and comes at me, a contest I can't win as long as he has that piece of steel in his hand.

I feint to my right and head for the companionway, and he backs up and

276

circles the console to port. Another feint, left this time, and I make another dash for the hatch, skidding to a stop when he cuts me off. I reach back and haul on the wheel, and the big boat lurches and rears up on her stern, twisting in mid air. The captain's body rolls to port and knocks Lucas's feet out from under him.

I spin around and fall on top of him, grappling for the winch handle, and he smacks his elbow into my jaw. My head rings and I fall back dazed, just as Emily's terrified face appears at the top of the ladder, pale as a whitecap.

Lucas bellows and dives for her, but she's two steps faster, leaping over the coaming and sliding to a stop behind the wheel. She shoves the throttle forward and the stern dips. Lucas scrambles after her, and she screams and heaves the wheel hard to starboard, knocking him off balance. He loses his footing and sprawls against the locker, howling with rage.

As the hull settles in the trough of a wave, Lucas struggles up onto one knee and grabs for Emily's leg, and she yanks the throttle back and whips the wheel the other way. The deck falls out from under him and he cracks his head on the console, losing his grip on the winch handle. I manage to snatch it as it slides across the deck. Lucas clutches the binnacle and hauls himself upright, and Emily lets go of the wheel and scurries to the port rail. He stumbles after her and I fire the winch backhand into his crotch. He screams and crumples to the deck again.

Ken is bearing down on us, driving *Amy's Pride* through the cascading sea. Lucas writhes on the deck, cursing and clutching himself and trying to regain his feet. I reach out and grab Emily's arm to pull her up onto the port locker.

"Get ready to jump," I holler, and she scrambles over the rail onto the gunwale and hangs on as I lunge for the throttle once more. I slap it home, then whirl to dive over the side as the big boat shoots forward. Emily hits the water a half second ahead of me and surfaces a dozen yards out.

The Hunter speeds off in a wide, sweeping arc to seaward, and Ken sails past us, close but too fast for us to catch the line and life ring he tosses overboard. He comes about for another try. I'm expecting the other yacht to turn back and make a fight of it, but it seems that Lucas is no sailor. The Hunter grows smaller and smaller, it's diesel still whining at full throttle.

Amy's Pride wallows between crests, sails loose with the wind dead on her bow. Emily's head bobs beside me, and I grip her arm and point to the boat.

"Think you can make it?" I yell.

She barely nods, her eyes vague and an ugly bruise already forming under the welt on the side of her face. She's nearly spent, disoriented and unable to see above the crests, and when she rolls over and begins stroking feebly, it's in the wrong direction. She flounders and goes under.

A wave catches me full in the face as I plunge after her, burying me in foam. The salt stings my eyes, blinding me. I thrash through the waves and dive beneath the surface into a dark and tumultuous maelstrom, and by pure dumb luck run into her. She grapples for me, wrapping her arms around my neck and nearly choking me, and I can no longer tell which way is up.

Suddenly Ken is in the water beside me, grabbing my elbow and tugging me upward. He drags us both to the surface, coughing and spitting. I manage to pry Emily's hands from my neck and flip her over onto her back. She chokes and spasms, flailing her arms weakly, and Ken braces his hand under her neck and lifts her head above the waves.

"Where's the boat?" I yell to him.

"Grab the line!" he shouts, thrusting a rope into my hand. A breaker slaps him and he goes under, taking Emily with him.

Amy's Pride is rolling and pitching in the roiling sea, her slack sails buffeted by the wind. She climbs the crest of a wave and nearly jerks the line from my grasp. I wrap it twice around my wrist as Ken and Emily bob to the surface again, ten yards away and caught in a rip. I thrash through the water and come up beside them, and he grabs my belt.

"Haul us in!" he yells, struggling to keep Emily's head aloft. I grapple with the line, hand over hand, towing them painfully toward my floundering boat. As I come alongside, a wave lifts me and smashes me against the stern, tearing Ken loose. I manage to hang on to the ladder and toss the line back to him. It lands across his shoulders, and he grabs for it desperately and misses.

Another wave lifts them both and sends them crashing toward the hull. I drop down, my body a buffer, and as they smack into me I catch Emily's arm and haul her out of the water and thrust her over the transom. Ken clutches the ladder, and we scramble up and into the cockpit.

Emily is gasping and choking, and I roll her over on her side. Seawater spills from her mouth, and she coughs violently to clear her lungs. Ken reaches the console and grasps the wheel to bring the boat about, bow on to the waves, and the sails fill with a resounding thump. He points up and the violent pitching eases as the hull cants to starboard and sprints off in the direction of the mainland.

I lift Emily's limp body and struggle toward the hatchway. She's almost dead weight, her eyes closed and her face ashen against the angry red imprint of Lucas's hand. She clings to my neck weakly, helping as much as she can as I climb awkwardly down the ladder into the galley and sit her down on the bench. I grab a towel from the overhead bin and wrap her up, and she whimpers when I touch her back.

She slumps down on the cushion, and I ease her gently onto her side and lift the back of her shirt. Bloody welts from Lucas's belt criss-cross her back, but only two, all that he could land before I sent the Hunter on its wild ride. There's a tube of antiseptic ointment in the first aid kit, and I coat the wounds gently and cover them with loose strips of gauze.

She's beginning to recover, her eyes more alert. I ease her into a sitting position and examine the swelling on her cheek. The skin there isn't broken.

"Are you hurt anywhere else?" I ask her softly.

"Uh-uh," she says feebly. "God, you got there just in time. He was gonna kill me."

"You're okay now."

"How'd you know where to find me?" she asks.

"You can thank Alex for that. He ran and got us real quick. What happened?"

"They were watching for me, I guess. Lucas and Cliff stuck me in a car and took me to that boat."

"Was Cliff on board too?"

"He went back to the car, I think."

"You were something else back there," I tell her sincerely.

"Huh?"

"The way you horsed that hull around after he smacked me down? If you hadn't kept him busy, he'd have finished me off. You handled that wheel just right."

"I had a good teacher," she says, hurt and exhausted but smiling with pride.

"I have to go up on deck," I tell her. "Want to stay down here for a while?"

"No. Is he coming after us?"

"Lucas? I doubt it. I don't think he can run the boat, and the captain is out cold."

She struggles to her feet, and I help her over to the ladder. "Is this ever gonna be over?"

"Soon. I promise."

Ken has *Amy's Pride* on a close reach as we emerge on deck, and I offer to take the wheel.

"You take it easy," he says. "I can manage."

Emily leans heavily against my side, and I ease her down onto the port locker. I put my arm high around her shoulders to avoid the belt marks and hold her close. My own head throbs agonizingly, and my jaw and temple are sore and swollen.

"Is she okay?" Ken asks.

"A little beat up, but nothing too serious."

"You don't look so hot yourself. Are you going to tell me what this is all about?"

"I guess I'd better," I answer him. "We've been running from a couple of Halifax pimps."

Emily tenses against me, and I squeeze her hand reassuringly.

"Jesus!" Ken exclaims. "What did they want with her?"

"Guys like that are always on the lookout for runaways. They thought they could get away with taking her, I guess."

"How long's this been going on?"

"About a week."

"Why the hell didn't you call the police?"

"It's complicated. I thought I could protect her myself."

"You damn near didn't! Did they...? I mean, before you found her..."

"She's fine." Emily's eyes are boring into mine. After all the other lies, one more won't hurt. "They roughed her up some, but nothing else."

He looks at me sceptically. "You're not telling me everything, are you?"

"We owe you a lot," I counter. "If you hadn't been with me, I could never have gotten her away from them, and I nearly lost her in the water."

"So they never..." He pauses, looking at Emily.

"No," I say quietly. She sighs and relaxes against me, her secret safe at least for a while. "We got there in time, thanks to you."

29

Saturday, Late Afternoon

We leave *Amy's Pride* dockside at the Bournemouth marina, and after a quick stop at Ken's office for our backpacks, we pull into the Curtis driveway a few minutes before four, shaken and emotionally drained and close to exhaustion. I turn Emily over to Katie's nursing expertise, and she bundles her upstairs to examine her injuries. Afterward she leads me to the bathroom to check the knife wound on my belly and the tear in my cheek from Lucas's gunsight.

"Too late for stitches to do much good," she tells me. "I can clean up the edges some, but you're going to have scars. What's been happening to you two?"

"Tell you later," I say. "How's Emily?"

"She'll be fine. You said someone beat her with a belt?"

"Started to. I managed to stop him pretty quick."

"He broke the skin a little, but it's just on the surface. She'll heal okay. Ken said he was some kind of pervert?"

"A pimp," I tell her. "He kidnapped her for the sex trade."

"My God! Took her right off the street?"

"Not a safe world, is it? I better go check on her."

"She might be sleeping. I gave her a sponge bath before I changed the bandages and then had her lie down in the spare room. You want something to eat?"

"No thanks. Maybe later."

"I'll put on some soup and make sandwiches. You can eat whenever you're ready."

"Do you know where Ken is?"

"In the den, I think."

In the spare room two doors down the hall, Emily is buried beneath a comforter, clutching an ice bag to her face. Two dark and sleepy eyes peek out at me. I cross over and sit on the edge of the bed.

"Rough day, eh?"

"I've had worse," she says ironically.

"Try to go to sleep for a little while," I tell her. "We'll wake you up when it's time to eat." I lean over to kiss her forehead, and she reaches out and wraps her arms around my neck.

"You came after me," she whispers in my ear.

"Of course I did."

She releases me reluctantly, and I tuck her in carefully. One small hand sneaks out from under the comforter, just the tips of her fingers waving to me as I back out of the room. I head downstairs to find Ken just hanging up the phone.

Alex sits nervously in a chair across from his desk. "Is Emily okay?" he asks me.

"She's fine. Your Mom took good care of her."

"How about you give Mom some help with supper while we talk," Ken says. Alex stands up half-heartedly and goes toward the hall.

"I just got off the phone with Linda, my secretary," Ken tells me once the boy is out of the room. "She said one of our associates called in a few favours and managed to get a little information from the RCMP."

"And?"

"There are no leads to the guy in the Lexus. Somebody took down the plate number, but it turns out it was stolen."

"Any suspicion that you were involved?"

"Apparently not. When we left Alex at the office, he told Linda what happened. She said the cops canvassed every business on the street, trying to find someone who saw something, but they didn't ask specifically about me."

"She'll keep on playing dumb, I hope," I said.

"She's been with me for ten years. I'd trust her with my life. But I can't keep on hiding this."

"What do you mean?" I ask.

"The kidnapping. I have an obligation to report any crime I have knowledge of."

"Can't we just let it go?"

"Why do you want to? Jesus Christ, those slimy bastards should be in jail!"

"I told you, it's complicated. Emily will be worse off if they're arrested."

"I don't see why. And I could be disbarred if any of this comes out."

"It won't. They won't bother her again."

"That's bullshit and you know it!"

"I can handle it."

"Sure. You did this time, but how about later?"

"Look, Ken, if we report this, Emily will have to testify. At the very least she'll face a barrage of questions, and the police won't let up until they get the whole story. Once that happens, they'll slap her in some foster home for sure. I can't let that happen."

"You may not have any choice," he says. "I still don't get it. Why did those bastards pick her in the first place?"

I decide on a half truth. After so many lies, it feels strange to come so close to the facts.

"She was trying to catch a bus, and one of them spotted her for a runaway and tried to grab her. That's how guys like that operate. She got away but they kept after her."

He isn't buying it. "And then she just swam out to your island and asked you for help, I suppose."

"Ken..."

"I know," he says angrily. "That part of the story is non-negotiable. I'm about ready to cut you loose, you know. Maybe you can find another lawyer who'll be willing to operate in the dark."

"If that's what..."

"Damn it! Talk to me! What makes you think you can protect her? I can't help either of you unless you tell me."

Emily appears in the doorway to the den, wrapped in one of Katie's robes. Her eyes look like two holes burned in a blanket.

"I thought you were asleep," I tell her.

"I heard you talking." She crosses the room and sinks into one corner of the sofa. Her face pleads with me: *Don't tell!*

I stare at her helplessly, then turn back to Ken.

"I have to go it alone," I tell him. "I'm her best chance."

The anger drains out of him. "You're a damned fool," he says, subsiding against the back of his chair. "So what do you want me to do next?"

"Are you still my lawyer?"

"I suppose so, but for her sake, not yours."

"I'm keeping her close from now on. Start your investigation of my background, so we can make it legal."

"I must be out of my mind," he mutters. "All right. I'll get on the phone from here and have one of my associates open a file on you. I also want to track down some expert advice from a friend who knows family law. That will start the ball rolling on the custody issue. But if those bastards come after her again, I'm calling the RCMP."

"It shouldn't come to that. I'm going to close up the cabin and move back to the mainland, back to my house. We'll be safe there."

He's about to argue when Katie and Alex come in from the kitchen and sit down. "The soup'll be ready in a couple of minutes," she says.

"Thanks, dear," Ken says. Then to me: "You shouldn't keep her with you."

"Why not?"

"It's likely to compromise your chances for custody. Once we contact Family and Children's Services, I think they'll want her to stay somewhere neutral until they can evaluate her situation. That almost certainly means a temporary foster home."

"No," I tell him, looking into Emily's tear-reddened eyes. "I promised her."

We sit silently. Then Katie stirs. "How about here?"

We all look at her.

"We've got plenty of room," she says. "She'll be safe here, won't she? These people who are after her, do they know anything about us?"

I shake my head.

"That's the answer, then." She turns to her son. "How about it, Alex? Would you like to have a sister for a while?"

The boy blushes bright red, but we manage not to embarrass him further by laughing. None of us feels like laughing anyway.

"Ken?" Katie asks.

"I suppose it could work. I can't think of anything better. But I still don't know how I'm going to explain her to the authorities."

"No," Emily says softly.

We all turn to look at her, small and sad in the corner of the big sofa.

"Why not, sweetheart?" I ask her.

"You know why."

And of course I do. The narrow escape from the yacht has left her badly frightened. In spite of the Curtis family's kindness to her, I'm the one who's managed to save her every time so far, and I represent the only safety she trusts. I know she won't let me out of her sight if she can help it.

"I guess we'll have to do it our way," I tell them, "and just take our chances."

* * *

We sit by the pool in the warm evening air, eating soup and sandwiches and talking. Alex and Emily are side by side on the apron, dangling their feet in the water. He hovers protectively, looking as if he'd fight lions for her.

We've been invited to spend the night, and although she puts up a fight, I finally convince Emily to stay with Katie while I return to the island in the morning to pick up Jenny and whatever belongings I can ferry out in the dinghy. I have to get in and out again before Lucas and his pals have time to regroup and come after me.

There's no doubt that they'll be back. It's no longer just a matter of taking Emily from me. They have to save face, but I expect the next attack will come later, when they figure my guard is down.

I watch her sadly, so pretty in her red swimsuit in spite of the bandages across her back, and so vulnerable in the limbo of her interrupted life. She's in grave danger, and I came too close to losing her this time. I had been on the verge of telling Ken the whole story, and might have if she hadn't appeared in the doorway when she did.

Ken could bring to bear the kind of official clout necessary to have Lucas and Ben and Cliff arrested and charged, but that would forfeit Emily's only chance at a new identity. If the men are arrested now, there's little hope of keeping her past a secret. Even worse, I'm unsure that people like Ken and Katie can accept the situation and forget how she spent the last six months, her innocence torn asunder. At best our new friends would be uneasy over any continued friendship with Alex, especially the possibility of any sort of future relationship. Emily needs a fresh start, with no shadows hanging over her head.

She glances over her shoulder and catches me looking at her. She levers herself up from the side of the pool and pads over to me, putting her empty plate down on the table. She takes mine from my hands deliberately and sets it down next to hers, then leans forward unselfconsciously and eases herself onto my lap.

"Hey," I tell her, "you're getting me all wet!"

She tucks her head into the hollow of my shoulder and looks over at Ken and Katie with a soft, sad smile.

"My Dad's the best ever," she tells them quietly.

And right then, I make up my mind. No one is going to split us up, no matter what.

30
Sunday

I'm awake a long time on the Curtis's sofabed in the den, trying to devise some plan to keep Emily safe. Aside from confiding in the police, I have painfully few options. One possibility would be to hire a bodyguard, although that would be impractical in the long run. I could sell the house and take her somewhere far away, to the Annapolis Valley or Cape Breton or even out of the province. I could even step outside the law and try to find someone to take care of Lucas permanently, but that would be hard to live with. One criminal act doesn't erase another, and if I were caught and sent to prison, there'd be no one to look after Emily.

In the morning we decide to have an early breakfast at Mussel Beach as a special treat for the children, and Ken drives us to the pier. Surrounded by friends, Emily is feeling a little more secure, and doesn't give me an argument about staying behind while I go back to the island alone. After we finish eating, Alex and Emily stray to the window to watch the boats while the rest of us linger over coffee.

"I still don't think it's safe for you to go out there by yourself," Ken says for the fourth time. "Let me come too."

"Thanks, but I'll be okay. I'll feel better if you're here to keep watch over Emily until I get back."

"Suppose they're waiting for you."

"Not likely. One of them is out of action with a smashed arm, and we're not even sure the guy on the boat made it back to shore anywhere near here. He didn't seem to know how to run it, and the charter captain was unconscious. The slip where they keep it is still empty. My guess is it'll be at least a few days before they try anything again."

287

"You can't be sure of that."

He's right, but it makes sense. Ben would have a rough time handling the Zodiac with his smashed arm, and I'd given Lucas something to think about with the winch handle. The danger would come later. Nevertheless I'm planning nothing more than a quick snatch and grab at the cabin, clothes and Jenny and not much else.

And then I realize I haven't bought a cat carrier, and that no pet shop will be open because of Nova Scotia's ban on Sunday shopping. I'll have a caterwauling feline on my hands for the sail back to the mainland. I'll have to shut her in the head.

"I should be back no later than mid morning," I tell them. "I'm not going to clean out the cabin this time, just pick up my cat and enough stuff to get us started at the house. I'll go back in a week or so for everything else."

"I'll come back down here to meet you," Ken says. "Ten thirty or so?"

"That's fine. I really appreciate it."

"Glad to do it."

After paying the bill, the five of us walk outside and head for the marina office so I can deal with the mooring charges. Katie and the two kids wander down to the end of the pier to watch a big Catalina enter the harbour, and Ken and I go inside.

"Have you got a cell phone?" he asks as we wait for an attendant to come and take my money.

"I cancelled the contract when I closed out my business."

"Mine's at home. Otherwise I'd leave it with you."

"Thanks, but I won't need it."

The desk clerk appears and I settle up. Then I remember that we left my dinghy behind the night before in the mad dash to follow the Hunter.

"Have you got a spare boat tender I can borrow for a couple of hours?" I ask him. "Mine's out of action."

"Gotta charge you a deposit," he tells me.

"That's okay. I'll have it back in a couple of hours."

I hand over some cash and we follow him out onto the dock and down to the end where the others are watching the harbour traffic. Emily runs up to me.

"Are you going now?" she asks me.

"Just as soon as this man finds a dinghy for me."

"What happened to yours?"

"Lost it last night. It'll probably turn up. Don't give Katie a hard time

288

while I'm gone."

She gives me a hug, then turns toward the marina office. "I gotta go pee," she says. "See you when you get back."

"Hang on," I call after her. "I don't want you going off alone."

"I'll be okay."

"I'll go with her," Katie offers, and the two of them head toward the public washrooms. At the end of the pier, the dockhand is unhitching an eight-foot pram from the stern of a rental yacht. He stows a pair of oars aboard and hands me the painter.

"Thanks," I tell him. "I'll take good care of it."

Alex offers to row the boat around the end of the dock and back to where *Amy's Pride* is tied up, and Ken and I stand talking as he fits the oars in the locks and pulls away. We turn back to my boat as he hitches the tender to the stern, and Ken helps me cast off the spring lines. I start the engine and head out from the dock. Katie and Emily are still in the washroom, but the other two wave to me as I clear the end of the pier and aim for Farrell Island.

A stiff breeze comes at me straight over the bow, and black clouds promise a gale to come. Rather than take the time to tack, I leave the sails down. The little diesel makes an honest four and a half knots against the wind and incoming tide, and I quickly leave the last of the mooring buoys behind and set a course for the eastern end of the island.

It's quarter to nine when I round the headland and thread my way through the channel into the cove. As soon as the cabin comes into sight, I throttle back and drift broadside to study the clearing. There's no sign of another boat, although I know it's possible for someone to have been dropped off and be waiting in the cabin.

It takes me just a few minutes to tie up to the buoy and row the borrowed dinghy to shore. Next to the dock there are fresh scuff marks in the gravel. It looks as if a skiff has landed and been hauled up onto the grass, although it's no longer in sight. The meadow is empty and Amy's violets lie undisturbed, but the tall weeds to the right of the dock show traces of something having been dragged off down the beach.

A storm is coming. The cabin squats quietly under the lowering sky, empty windows staring back at me blankly. If anyone is inside, he knows I'm here and is biding his time. No one could have missed the sound of my engine. Keeping low, I follow the trail eastward through the bent grass and come upon the marina's big Zodiac, lying partially concealed just behind a gravely sand dune. The same antiquated Evinrude outboard is tilted up on the stern.

Lucas is waiting for me.

The odds are against me. With his injured arm, I figure Ben has probably stayed behind, but Thomas Clifford would be looking to avenge the damage to his boat. I won't have a chance against two of them and Lucas's shotgun. I bend low and scurry back toward the dock, but a crackling noise from the cabin stops me short.

Thick black smoke curls out from under the eaves at the northeast corner. The front door bursts open, and Lucas strides onto the deck with the shotgun in his hand and fires at me. The pellets scream over my head and send me sprawling on the ground. Cliff lumbers out next, swinging a red gasoline can and splashing liquid on the walls and deck. He runs down the steps and around the far side of the building, Lucas close on his heels.

Fed by the wind, the fire gains ground rapidly, centred in the back. Thin tongues of flame dance on the roof as I scramble to my feet and race north across the clearing. The rear wall is smouldering, and the shingles on the roof over the propane tanks are beginning to curl. Lucas comes around the corner of the deck and fires over my head again, not really trying to kill me but pinning me down and keeping me away from the cabin. He wants me alive to lead him to Emily.

Cliff trots around the back on the far side, still splashing gas on the wall. He empties the can and pulls up a dozen yards from the propane shed. Ignoring Lucas's gun, I leap to my feet and shout a warning, just as the first tank explodes in a sheet of white-hot terror.

The concussion knocks me on my back, and I roll and bury my face in the grass as flaming debris rains down around me. The second tank erupts. Shards of wood and burning shingles cascade down around me, and I scramble to my feet and race for the shelter of the trees. The heat engulfs me like an avalanche. The back wall of the cabin bulges outward and collapses in a shower of sparks, and the roof sags and caves in. The rest is a raging inferno. Thick smoke billows skyward, blanketing the clearing.

My clothes are scorched and hot ash burns my skin, and I tear off my shirt to brush away the cinders that are eating holes in my jeans. I sprint toward the water just as Lucas stumbles out of the smoke onto the dock, his face blistered and his hair singed. His shirt is shredded and charred, and his left arm flaps loosely at his side, the skin flayed and blackened. He swings the gun toward me and I skid to a stop.

"What happened?" he barks, his voice rasping.

"The propane exploded!"

"Where's Cliff?"

"He was next to the tank when it went off."

"Jesus Christ!" He jumps off the dock and limps toward me, waving the gun. "Show me!"

The wind is blowing the smoke toward the southwest, out over the cove, and I lead him around the eastern end, staying well back out of the worst of the heat. Cliff's charred and dismembered body lies tumbled among blazing boards and shingles, his clothing still in flames.

"God DAMN it!" Lucas snarls. "Let's get the hell out of here."

We skirt the fire and sprint for the shore. With a tremendous crash the front of the cabin implodes, showering sparks toward the cove and igniting the dock and dinghy. Lucas jams the barrel of the shotgun into my spine shoves me toward the Zodiac. I manage to heave it stern-first into the water and climb aboard, with him right behind me. He collapses into the bow and trains the gun on me.

"Start it up!" he shouts.

Counting on his ignorance of engines, I yank the choke out all the way and hit the starter, and it coughs raggedly to life and spits black smoke.

"What's the matter with it?" he yells above the noise.

"Damned if I know!" I pretend to adjust the controls and jam the throttle forward. The engine floods, stutters and dies.

"Get it going, goddamnit!" he bellows. I press the starter again and the engine catches, backfires twice, and sputters into silence.

"Jesus!" He aims the gun at my face. "We'll take your boat then. Get us out there!"

I unship the oars and haul away, and as soon as we reach the yacht's stern he drags himself painfully up the ladder and falls over the transom. Before I can react he regains his feet and points the gun down at me. "Move your ass!" he barks, and I climb up and swing my leg over the rail into the cockpit.

He slumps down on the port locker, cradling his burned arm in his lap. The shotgun lies across his knees, too easy to reach. I don't dare try to take it away from him.

"Get us moving," he growls, wincing and gesturing toward the helm. I start the diesel and release the stern line from the buoy.

"Where are we going?" I ask him as we head for the channel.

"Shut up!"

Behind us the fire rages on, and a towering column of smoke trails off to the south, a beacon to anyone on the mainland. Someone will be out to investigate, but by then we'll be far away. I can't think of any way to get the upper hand.

We clear the mouth of the inlet and enter the Atlantic. I head east, broadside to the waves, hoping that someone coming from the mainland will spot us. Driven by the rising wind, a nasty offshore chop roils the surface, and *Amy's Pride* dips her bow as a rogue wave smashes into the hull and rolls us hard to port. Lucas falls heavily against the bulkhead, mashing his injured arm.

"Goddamn it!" he shrieks, waving the gun at me wildly. "Keep this thing steady!"

I bring her around, heading out to sea into the teeth of the approaching gale. The bow leaps and plunges as it cuts through the waves. At full throttle we're making barely four knots, and the hull is pitching fiercely. As we pull away from the island, the first boats leave the Bournemouth dock to investigate the fire.

Lucas sits clinging to the rail, grimacing in agony. Painfully he lifts the gun and stands up, spreading his legs against the frenzied tossing of the hull, his back to the hatchway.

"I oughta shoot your friggin' nuts off right now," he mutters.

"Think you can run the boat by yourself?"

"Shut up! Take this thing to Halifax."

"We're heading the wrong way."

"So change course."

I swing the wheel onto an easterly heading, and the sea comes at us broadside again. Lucas steadies himself against the console, his face less than a yard from mine and the gun hanging loose from his right hand. I'm about to make a grab for it when a movement in the hatchway catches my eye. Emily is creeping over the sill, head down low. She reaches out cautiously for the winch handle and raises it high to bring it down on Lucas's head.

The boat rolls in the trough of a wave and Lucas stumbles sideways just as the handle smashes down, shattering his left collarbone. He howls and whirls around, and Emily drops the handle and catapults herself over the rail onto the narrow starboard gunwale. She runs off toward the bow, and Lucas heaves himself across the cockpit and sets off after her.

At the bow she swings around and clings to the forestay, and as he bears down on her she tries to run down the port side. He hops across the deck to cut her off and drops the gun, clamping his right hand down on her arm. She screams and batters her small fists on his blistered flesh, and he cries out and loses his grip. He grapples for her again, and she throws herself over the side into the churning sea, disappearing in the froth of the wake.

I haul back on the throttle and shove it out of gear, and the bow drops out from under Lucas's feet. He stumbles against the jib stay, hooking it with his right elbow. He scrabbles for the gun and fires a wild shot at my head, narrowly missing me as I duck down behind the binnacle.

The boat wallows in a trough, and I yank the wheel to come about as he fires again, the pellets screaming past an inch from my ear. The gun's recoil sends him staggering backwards, and he bounces off the forestay and falls heavily, cracking his head on a cleat. He seizes it and clings desperately, trying to regain his feet as we lurch into another trough. The hull plunges to starboard and tears his hand from the cleat, and he slips under the rail and plummets into the water.

Two to rescue, and no real choice as to who comes first. I jam the engine in gear and slap the throttle, whipping the wheel into a tight turn and heading for the spot where I last saw Emily go in.

There's no sign of her, the sea so huge and her head so tiny among the waves. I try to estimate how far I've drifted since she fell and set up a grid pattern, making right angle turns at the end of each pass. Nothing but empty water.

The minutes drag by. Torn between the need to hurry and fear of missing her, I keep the engine at half throttle, trying to see between the roiling crests. Whitecaps toss spray high in the air, and great breakers crash against the hull, turbulent and fierce. Off to the west a squall line bears down on us, spears of lightning slashing the clouds.

On the fifth circuit I'm sure I've drifted too far. I tie the wheel and scramble up on the cabin top, trying to see down into the troughs. There's a fleeting glimpse of something in the water two hundred yards off the bow. It vanishes in the chaos of the waves as I leap into the cockpit and free the wheel, spinning it to port and gunning the engine.

Blinding spray and gouts of white foam soak the cockpit. Standing on the stern locker, I strain to see above the crests. The boat plummets deep into a trough and struggles up the other side, and as the bow plunges through a breaker I spot a slender arm and hand, waving frantically almost dead ahead.

As I come abreast of her I seize a life ring and fling it over the side and throttle back. It sails over her head and she splashes toward it, but the sea snatches it away. I drop the stern line overboard and come about. She grabs it on the second pass, and I yank back the throttle and haul away on the rope, hand over hand. A surging whitecap tosses her against the stern, and she seizes the ladder and clings desperately as I turn into the teeth of the wind and lean over the transom.

The pitching hull tries to tear her loose and she slams against the hull, one tiny hand grasping for mine. I manage to grab hold of her wrist and she lets go of the ladder and clamps onto my arm, her legs splayed out and windmilling in the air. Another wave tosses the stern to port, giving me the momentum to haul her to the edge of the transom. She scrambles for purchase, banging her knees on the rail, then vaults upward and throws herself into my arms, knocking us both to the deck.

"Oh, God, I thought you'd never find me!" she exclaims as we disentangle ourselves. Her soggy clothes are plastered to her body, her arms and legs trembling with fatigue and gooseflesh.

"Where the hell did you come from?" I yell at her. "I left you in Bournemouth!"

"I'm a stowaway."

"Jesus Christ, what did you jump overboard for?"

"To get away from Lucas. What did you expect?"

"What if I couldn't find you?"

"I can swim."

"Not ten miles you can't! My God, Emily, another five minutes and you could have drowned!"

"Tell me about it! Where is he?"

I've almost forgotten about Lucas. "He lost his balance and fell in. We have to go back for him. Go get dried off."

Fighting to stay upright on the pitching deck, she staggers to the hatchway and disappears below. I set up another grid pattern, but there's not much hope of saving him. I've lost my bearings during the search for Emily, and have no idea where he fell overboard. Nevertheless I have to try, just in case he's on the surface and by some miracle still alive, but with his burns and useless left arm, the odds are stacked heavily against him.

I'm on my third pass when Emily comes back on deck in dry clothes, rubbing her hair with a towel.

"Find him?" she asks.

"Not yet. Are you okay?"

"I'm fine," she says, "just sore from smacking into the boat. I'm tough like you. And I'm glad he's gone!"

"No one should ever be glad when someone dies."

"I don't care. He was going to kill you, right?"

"I don't think so."

"He shot at you, didn't he? I heard it. Anyway, it was his fault he fell in, not ours."

We spend another twenty minutes weaving back and forth, fighting the waves and looking for any sign of Lucas's body. Finally convinced that the man can't have survived both his injuries and the violence of the sea, I give up and head back toward the mainland.

"Think you can handle the wheel while I go below for a minute?" I ask her.

"It's pretty rough."

"All you have to do is keep the bow head on into the waves. Don't drift broadside and you'll be okay."

"I'll do my best." She takes the wheel so I can change out of my singed jeans into a dry shirt and shorts. On my way back up I find the wet-weather slickers that Amy and I kept in the locker across from the head. We'll need them when the squall hits.

"Are we going back to the cabin?" she asks as I climb back up on deck.

"The cabin's gone. Lucas set fire to it."

I step behind the console and take over the wheel. She sinks down on the starboard locker, shivering, and I toss her Amy's slicker. She squirms into it as the first raindrops begin pelting the deck, and backs up under the dodger.

"I heard a couple of big bangs, but I couldn't see without going up on deck. Was anybody else there?"

"Cliff," I tell her as I pull my own slicker on and tie the hood under my chin. A sudden blast of cold, wind-driven rain washes the cockpit.

"What happened to him?"

"He was next to the propane shed when it exploded."

That sobers her. "All that noise scared the shit out of me. It was so *loud!* I was hiding in the front berth and didn't know where you were. Is he dead?"

"He won't bother us again."

"I'm not sorry!"

We plunge on through the boiling sea and rain, the little diesel fighting to keep us on a steady course. Emily perches on the edge of the port locker under the dodger, her feet braced and her still sore back arched away from the rail.

"Now how about telling me how you got here," I insist. "How did you get away from Mrs. Curtis?"

"I didn't really have to go to the washroom. When she went into a stall, I sneaked out. Are you mad at me?"

"I should be, but you swing a pretty mean winch handle, so I guess not."

"I did good, huh?"

"You did, but your grammar's still lousy. Now how the hell did you get on this boat?"

"When you were watching Alex in the dinghy, I climbed over the rail. Nobody saw me."

"The Curtises'll be frantic by now."

"I guess. I'm sorry."

"It's done. We'll just have to get back as quick as we can so they'll know you're all right."

"What happened to Jenny?" she says suddenly. "Is she okay?"

"I didn't see her. She must have been inside the cabin. Maybe she got out, but it's more likely she hid under the bed like she always does."

She bursts out crying and runs across the cockpit into my arms. I try to comfort her as best I can. She clings to my side, sobbing and staring out over the water as the rain pours down on us.

Amy's Pride ploughs on.

* * *

Farrell Island looms up off the port bow, shrouded by the squall that thunders up the coast. We bear off to the east to get a better look and spot an RCMP patrol boat anchored near the inlet to my cove. A dozen or more pleasure boats stand off beyond the shoals, rubberneckers risking the storm for a chance to witness the aftermath of some disaster. Smoke barely rises from the interior of the island, dampened down by the rain.

A police Zodiac emerges from the inlet and approaches the RCMP cruiser. Two figures climb out and clamber aboard the larger craft. Garbled words from a bullhorn echo over the water. I know it won't be long before the authorities come looking for me.

"We have to decide what to do," I tell her. "The police will have found Cliff's body by now, but they probably won't be able to tell who he is yet. If we go back and tell them we were there when the fire started, they'll want to know who was with us. I don't want to have to explain any of that."

"Because of me," she says.

"Right. Once they identify Cliff's body, they'll start looking for some reason why he was out there. They'll discover that he's a pimp and try to find some connection between him and me. We don't want to give them any reason to think about you, now or later."

"So you're going to lie?"

"Not exactly. Just not say any more than I have to."

She considers that for a moment. "That's the same thing, isn't it?"

"I suppose."

Her eyes search mine. "Don't we have to tell them what happened to Lucas?"

"I've been thinking about that. Maybe it's best if we just keep quiet. Do you think you can live with it?"

"After what he did to me? I *guess!* What do you want me to say to the police?"

Not "What are *you* going to say?" Her sense of self-preservation has kicked in, and I have a co-conspirator. She's showing surprising strength, despite the shock of the last few hours. Something within me rebels at asking a child to lie, but I can't think of any other way to protect her.

"We'll keep it as simple as possible," I tell her. "How about this? We were up the coast toward Halifax, heading back to get ahead of the storm. Then we saw all the boats heading for the island, and put in at the marina to find out what was happening. Sound okay?"

"I suppose."

"Think you can pull it off?"

"Sure. Anything's better than somebody finding out about me. But what'll we tell Mr. Curtis?"

"I haven't got that figured out yet. Maybe just about the fire and that we escaped. If we tell him what happened to Lucas, I think he'll have to report it."

"Why?"

"He's a lawyer. He has to report any crime he knows about."

"Holy shit! Are we criminals?"

"Not really. We didn't kill him. We even tried to save him. But if we come clean about it, we'll never be able to hide what's happened to you for the past six months."

"So we don't tell Mr. Curtis," she says decisively.

"It's the best way."

"I don't want him ever to know about me."

"I know that."

"It would kill me if Alex…"

"I know."

She sits silently, watching the activity among the boats near the island, a curious blend of satin and steel. To me she's the toughest, bravest kid in the world.

"When do we go?" she says at last.

"Right now, if you're ready. Think you can pretend we're only a couple of cautious sailors, just trying to get out of the weather?"

She sighs. "Let's do it."

31

Sunday Afternoon

Ken is pacing up and down at the end of the pier as I guide *Amy's Pride* into the harbour, and we both wave to him. The rain has begun to slacken and a crowd mills around the dock, but almost everyone ignores us, distracted by the police activity. An RCMP cruiser backs out of a slip and roars off in the direction of Farrell Island, with a boatload of groupies chasing after it.

When we reach the dock, Ken catches my stern line and Emily jumps down onto the dock as he wraps it around a cleat. He gathers her up in a big hug, careful not to chafe her sore back.

"Thank God you're all right! I'm so glad to see you!"

"I'm sorry I sneaked out on you," she tells him. "Did I scare you?"

"What did you do, stow away while we were down at the end of the dock? And what happened out there?"

"We'll fill you in later," I tell him as I tie the bow line to a piling. "Where are Katie and Alex?"

"I took them home. When we discovered Emily was gone, I almost called the police, but Katie wouldn't let me. She was sure you were both on the boat, and that you could take care of her."

"We took care of each other."

Emily gives me a tired smile and reaches for my hand as we head off up the dock. I'm still trying to flesh out the details of a plausible story in my mind, one that will protect her from the uproar that's sure to ensue when the body on the island is identified, or if the sea ever gives up Lucas's remains. An RCMP officer is standing just inside the office, talking to the marina's manager.

"I'd better tell him who I am," I say to Ken. Then to Emily, in a whisper: "Don't say a word unless he asks you a direct question, okay?" She nods.

We open the door and move off to one side of the cramped office, waiting patiently for the officer to notice us. When he does, I introduce myself. "That's my island out there," I tell him. "Can you tell me what happened?"

For the next ten minutes he peppers me with a barrage of questions and takes notes, and I pretend to be a surprised and very unhappy landowner. Ken listens to my lies carefully, but keeps his mouth shut.

The Mountie's radio crackles to life, and I catch enough of the conversation to know that Cliff's body has been identified. That sets off a new round of questioning, but I play dumb and eventually the inquiry grinds to a halt. I ask to go out to inspect my cabin, but he tells me it's been declared a crime scene, and therefore off limits. He agrees to let me tour the island with an official escort sometime within the next week.

It suddenly occurs to me that I'll likely be under suspicion of arson myself for a while, but since the cabin wasn't insured, the police won't be able to prove motive. As long as no one can link me up with the corpse of Thomas Clifford, it should all blow over eventually. Besides, I have a good lawyer if I need one.

"Where can we reach you?" the officer asks me at last.

"I'm an attorney," Ken tells him, handing him a business card. "He'll be staying with me."

"Don't leave the area," he cautions, and dismisses us with a curt wave. He strides down the pier toward his patrol car.

The storm has eased. More curious onlookers are crowding the dock, and I'm anxious to get Emily away from all the excitement. The marina offers me a temporary mooring, and I leave the boat keys at the office and follow Ken off the dock to his car. During the ride to his house he pumps me for details. After all the help he's given us, lying to him is difficult for me. I tell him about the fire and the explosion, and about finding Emily hiding below decks on the boat, but nothing about Cliff or Lucas being there. He looks dubious but doesn't press me about it.

"I'd better get my house opened up," I tell him as we pull into his driveway. "We need somewhere to stay."

"You're bunking with us tonight," he says firmly, "and longer if necessary. After what you've both been through, you need someone to take care of you for a while."

Emily is exhausted as we enter the house, and I'm not faring much better, but between Katie's good lunch and Alex's attention, she soon revives. We have an immediate problem to address, our lack of spare clothing. Most of what I owned and more than half of Emily's new things were lost in the fire. Ken drives us to the mall for a fast round of shopping, lifting Emily's spirits immensely, and we arrive back home a little past six thirty.

After a quick supper, Katie takes Emily upstairs for a hot bath while Ken and I sit in the den over cups of coffee. He spends nearly twenty minutes on the telephone, and from hearing his side of the conversation, I gather that one of his associates has pried some information out of the police. Although I know there will be few details released to the press until the investigation is well under way, it appears that members of the bar are granted special privileges.

At length he hangs up and sits back regarding me gravely. Hard questions are coming, but just then Emily appears in the doorway of the den to say good night, barely able to keep her eyes open. Alex hovers in the background. Among her purchases are some lightweight summer pyjamas and a pretty blue cotton robe, and despite the harrowing day and the deepening bruise on her cheek, she looks adorable. A kiss and a hug and she's off back up the stairs, and Alex joins his mother in the kitchen.

"She's really beautiful, isn't she?" I say after they leave.

"One of a kind," Ken answers. "Is she going to come through all this okay?"

"I'm not worried. She's one tough kid."

"Seems like it." He pauses a moment. "The corpse on the island is someone named Thomas Clifford. The police aren't saying much beyond that."

I nod noncommittally.

"Someone you know?" he asks pointedly. I shrug. I've never mentioned Cliff's name to him, nor Lucas's. If I'm lucky, he'll never connect the badly burned body with the man who waylaid Emily and Alex on the dock a couple of nights before.

"They're launching a thorough investigation into the fire," he continues. "I expect you'll be less than forthcoming with them?"

"What's to tell?" I say. "Simple vandalism, that's all."

"As my son would say, 'Yeah, right!' And I suppose I have to go along with that."

"Isn't that what a lawyer is for? Besides, what do you know for sure? I could be telling the truth."

301

"And you're just an innocent bystander," he says sarcastically.

"Look, I'd tell you more if it would help Emily, but it would only make things more difficult. Let it rest, okay?"

"Something else..." he begins. "A fishing boat hauled a body out of the water about two hours ago. Had some nasty burns, and his left arm was half torn off. Know anything about that?"

"Have they identified him?"

"Not officially, but according to my office staff his name is Lucas Brady." He pauses significantly, leaning toward me intently. "The man was a notorious pimp."

I can't trust myself to speak.

"No more bullshit, okay? Did you have anything to do with what happened to him?"

"If I were an American, I'd plead the fifth amendment."

"Damn it, tell me the truth! Did you kill him?"

"No." That's the truth, technically. "Have the police connected him to the fire?"

"Not so far."

"They probably will eventually," I tell him. "He and Clifford were running whores together."

"I still don't understand why he was so intent on taking Emily. Why did they pick on her?"

"Kids get snatched all the time. It's a damned filthy racket. I guess the pimps can sense which ones have no families or anybody who cares about them. Those guys figured wrong this time, that's all."

He's still sceptical. "If you're hiding something and it comes out later, it could be worse for both of you. Things like this have a habit of coming back to bite you in the ass."

"I'll face that if and when I have to. I'm more concerned about what happens to Emily right now."

He relaxes a bit and sits back in his chair. "I was wondering when you'd get around to that. Can you handle a little good news?"

"Long overdue."

"Well, thanks to a friendly judge who owes me a big favour, I'm going to be appointed Emily's temporary guardian as a friend to the court."

"You?"

"Keep your shirt on. It's the easiest way to handle it. We can bypass social services that way. And the good news is, as long as I approve, she can decide

302

who she's going to live with. I wonder who that will be?"

"You're kidding! It's got to be more complicated than that."

"The law's on our side this time," he continues. "She's just old enough to write her own ticket, provided there's some reputable individual willing to step in and supervise. That's me for the time being, until we can complete your background check. If you've levelled with me, once we establish your reputation you can file for legal custody."

"I trust you haven't found out about all those chainsaw murders I've been accused of."

He laughs. "You must have covered your tracks well. All my staff has turned up so far is a couple of speeding tickets."

"Fast car," I tell him. "The Mounties only managed to catch me twice."

"Just like Mary Poppins: practically perfect. Anyway, there's more good news. We have a formal release from good old Uncle Frank. It seems as if he's just as pleased as punch to let his precious little niece make her own way in the world. Practically fell over himself being cooperative."

"How the hell did you manage that?"

"One of my associates has been busy looking into him. You can expect a hefty bill for our services."

"Come on, Ken, spill it."

"It shouldn't surprise you that there's a file on him with the cops, although it's mostly a matter of unsubstantiated complaints. Getting too cosy with some of the neighbours' teenaged daughters, that sort of thing. No formal charges were ever laid, and the kids just laughed it off. He's a joke to most of them. Anyway, we just leaned on him a little, and he caved in pretty quick."

"Slimy bastard! How about his sons?"

"Perish forbid that Uncle Frank would be seen as anything other than a straight arrow."

"That's a relief. Is it really going to be this easy?"

"Should be. With so few good foster homes available, social services won't want another kid to look after, provided they're satisfied with the arrangements. She'll have to have a complete medical workup, though."

"I'll see to that right away, but I don't expect a problem." I thought back to what Ben had told me: *We run a clean shop.* In any case, I plan to choose the doctor carefully, most likely the woman gynecologist who treated Amy. I'm sure I can trust her to handle the situation discretely, and without causing Emily any more discomfort and embarrassment than necessary.

"So when you mentioned abuse before…" Ken begins.

"I had it wrong. Uncle Frank had roving hands, but that's the worst that ever happened to her."

"And the pimps?"

"Same thing," I say, hoping it's the last lie I'll ever have to tell him. "We got her back in time, and I have your seamanship to thank for that."

"That's great. I'd hate to think…Anyway, are you still thinking about adoption?"

"Isn't that too much to hope for? A single male parent?"

"Who can tell? The world's changing, what with gay rights, same sex marriages, and keeping the government out of the nation's bedrooms. You can thank Pierre Trudeau for that. And if gay couples are going to be allowed to adopt, which is already happening in some jurisdictions, why not someone like you?"

I can't think of anything to say.

"Well?" he prompts. "Not getting cold feet, are you? I thought that's what you wanted."

"Ken, I'm scared to death. Last week I was a recluse, didn't give a damn about anyone or anything. Now all of a sudden I'm thinking about taking on the toughest job in the world, with absolutely no qualifications. What if I screw it up?"

"You think my kid came with an owner's manual? Every parent takes on-the-job training. There isn't any other kind."

"But…"

"You love her, don't you?"

That jolts me.

"Well?"

"Yes. Now more than ever. I can't figure out how it happened, or why, but I really do."

"Then you're stuck with her, warts and all. Let me tell you, and I'm speaking from experience, all teenagers have warts."

I smile ruefully. *If you only knew.* Then it strikes me that I'm doing just what I had told Emily not to do, rehashing the past in my mind. If she's going to have a new beginning, I have to take her as I found her, with no excess baggage for either of us.

And then reality steps up and slaps me in the face. Eugene Benoit is still out there somewhere.

32
Monday

We gather with Ken in his office the following morning, Emily and I. He shows me the formal release from Uncle Frank, along with the various documents—school and medical records, birth certificate and her parents' death certificates—that will give her back her status. He also hands me a preliminary copy of the results of his investigation of my past and character. He has me sign some papers that I barely understand, then closes the file and sits back with a smile.

"I have to ask you this," he says kindly. "Now that the ball's rolling, are you both sure this is what you want? It's a big step."

Emily and I look at each other. "I'm sure," she says. Her face shines with joy and what I know to be gratitude, and I suddenly realize how much I owe *her*, too. She's given me a reason to put grief behind me and get on with life, and I don't believe I could have done it without her.

"Me too," I tell them both.

* * *

Ken takes Emily home for lunch while I remain downtown. I meet with an RCMP corporal and endure a detailed and probing interrogation about the events of the previous day. He keeps returning to the question of motive, especially why Thomas Clifford would commit arson against my property. I stick to my story, insisting that I've never met the man, and he finally agrees to chalk it up to random vandalism.

It's well past noon when we finish, and I ask if I can return to the island. Because it's still considered a crime scene, they've posted a cruiser to keep everyone away, and they won't allow me to go alone. I press the issue, and they finally agree to escort me so I can examine the damage in person.

I call Ken to tell him where I'm going, and Emily insists on coming along. He brings her to the dock a little after one-thirty, and the two of us board the RCMP cruiser for the short trip to the island. We anchor off shore and the officers launch a Zodiac to take us through the channel.

Although the clearing is devastated, the rainstorm has contained the fire and kept it from spreading. The danger of a forest fire is over, but the authorities plan to keep someone posted there until they're sure the entire area has cooled.

Cliff's remains are gone, and my once-beautiful cabin is almost levelled. Everything aft of the main living area is ashes and rubble, and the entire roof is gone. Just one corner post of the front wall remains upright, charred and sagging inward.

Emily wanders off to poke along the shoreline, reluctant to go closer to the fire, and I begin to wonder if she's regretting having come. It might have been better for her to remember the cabin as it had been when it offered her refuge.

Trudging toward the remains of the deck, I search the rubble to see if I can identify any of my belongings. Little is recognizable other than soot-covered pots and dishes, the latter tumbled about and shattered. The propane stove is distorted beyond repair by the intense heat, and only some twisted bedsprings offer any hint that the place had once been furnished. A few soggy scraps of charred fabric are all that are left of clothing, towels and bedding.

Around the back side of the foundation, the earth is torn and blackened by the incredible devastation of the propane explosion. Only where Cliff's body had lain is there any hint of green grass. I'm grateful that Amy will never have to see the massive annihilation of a place that brought her so much happiness.

Off to the west a single bit of colour struggles for attention amid the desolation of the clearing. A small crescent-shaped plot of Amy's violets has survived, their tiny purple faces turned bravely toward the sun. A little bit of her is still alive on the island she had loved so much.

A sudden shout from the edge of the forest rouses me from sorrow. Emily is hopping up and down, waving to me frantically. I trot across the meadow, and she plunges into the woods and brushes aside a tangled mass of undergrowth. Jenny lies cowering among the weeds.

"I heard her crying," she tells me excitedly. "She won't let me pick her up. Is she okay?"

I bend down and stretch out to her, letting her smell my hand. She emits a penetrating yowl and struggles to her feet, and I scoop her up gently and cradle her in my arms. Her eyes are huge, ears plastered against her head, and the fur on her back is slightly singed.

"Used up a few of your nine lives this time, didn't you?" I tell her. She sinks her claws into my flesh, hanging on desperately to someone familiar in the midst of chaos. I probe her body carefully, but she doesn't seem to have any tender spots. She yowls again, her normally musical voice a rough, unpleasant rasp from breathing in too much smoke. She'll need a trip to the vet as soon as possible.

"How did she get out?" Emily asks. She's hovering close, and reaches out cautiously to rub Jenny's chin.

"Hard to tell. My guess is she bolted for the cat door when they lighted the fire. Smart cat."

Emily turns around to look at the cabin. "It's all gone, isn't it?" she says sadly.

"No, the important things are still here."

"What?"

"Jenny. And you and me. Nothing else really matters."

There's no reason to stay any longer. We retrace our steps back to the Zodiac. Emily climbs in first, and I hand Jenny to her.

"Watch out for her claws," I caution, but she doesn't seem to care. She sits down on the middle bench, clutching the animal tightly in her lap. Jenny still seems terrified.

"Hang on tight so she won't fall overboard," I tell her. "She hates boats."

The RCMP corporal shoves us out into the cove as he steps aboard. He takes his place at the controls and starts the engine, and I watch Jenny apprehensively as he revs it up. She tucks her nose into Emily's tee shirt, hiding her eyes and trembling but showing no inclination to panic. We begin the slow and cautious journey out to the cruiser, then back to the dock at Bournemouth.

Another chapter of my life is over.

* * *

Katie installs Jenny in the back hall, along with a water dish and some canned tuna. I can't let her go outside in a strange neighbourhood, so a dishpan full of shredded newspapers fills in for kitty litter until we can get to a store. I make an appointment for her at the nearest animal clinic for the following day, but since her voice seems to be returning to normal, I'm not expecting any permanent damage.

Ken stays late at the office, and Katie presides over the barbeque while Alex and Emily play in the pool. I help out wherever I can, and we enjoy a pleasant meal in the cool of the early evening. The children try to coax me in for a swim after supper but I decline, preferring to watch their fun from a safe distance.

"Magic, isn't it?" Katie remarks.

"What is?"

"The resiliency of youth. She's a mass of bruises, been kidnapped and beaten and probably scared half to death, and she should be an emotional wreck. I suspect what you've told me is only a fraction of what that child has been through, but you'd never know it to look at her. How did you manage it?"

"It's not my doing. You and Ken have…"

"Oh yes it is," she insists. "How long have you known her?"

I think it over. So much has happened, it seems like years.

"Just about two weeks," I tell her.

"And what was she like when you found each other?"

"What has Ken told you?"

"Practically nothing. I thought she was your natural daughter until you started talking about custody and adoption. He let it slip that she just suddenly appeared on your island. But then those men kidnapped her, and…"

"Katie, can we just let all that fade away?"

"I'm sorry, I didn't mean to pry. Really, I try to stay out of Ken's business entirely. It's just that I'm getting to be very fond of her. I'll shut up."

"No, look…" I struggle to find the right words, afraid I may have offended her. "She's a very brave girl. She got herself out of a nasty situation, and I was just in the right place to help, that's all. She's fine now, no permanent damage done."

"You did more than help," Katie says softly. "You gave her love when she needed it most."

And she gave it back when I needed it most.

"But I warn you," she continues, "she's going to become a normal, irritating, exasperating, moody and difficult teenager any day now, and some days you'll wish you'd never set eyes on her."

My gaze drifts to Emily, perched on the lip of the diving board and posing for Alex as he shows off his powerful crawl stroke, a figurative peacock's tail high in the air. The first hesitant steps in humanity's oldest dance.

"Never," I tell her sincerely.

She laughs. "Well, maybe I'm exaggerating."

* * *

Later that evening, with the summer sun below the horizon and Katie and Alex back inside the house, I pry Emily away to take her for a walk. We have a little unfinished business.

"What's up?" she asks as we step off the Curtis porch and head for the entrance to the town's parklands next door. There's almost no wind, and the air is pleasant and cool, washed clean by the storm the day before.

"I just wanted a little time with my daughter," I tell her.

"Fine by me." She tucks her hand into the crook of my elbow. "My God, it's really gonna happen, isn't it?" She looks suddenly alarmed. "Are you still okay with it?"

"Very much okay," I say, smiling. "Did you have fun tonight?"

"Uh huh."

"Feel up to helping me open up the house later this week?"

"Sure!" She hesitates. "Alex says I can come back and use the pool sometimes. Is that okay?"

"Of course. And you can have him over to our place, too. And all the new friends you're going to make."

"Is it really gonna be *our* place? Mine too?"

"Of course."

"Do I get my own room?"

"Not a chance. Your evil stepsisters got there first, so you have to sleep in the cinders on the hearth."

Her musical laughter sparkles like fireflies in the night, echoing through the recesses of my heart. She reaches for my hand and we leave the gravel pathway and sit down on a picnic bench beneath a huge oak, a soundtrack of frogs and crickets singing our accompaniment. The light is nearly gone.

"Think there'll be any shooting stars tonight?" she asks me, looking up at the heavens.

"Could be."

"The last one worked out pretty good for me. I got my wish."

"Me too," I tell her.

"More than one, I guess," she says softly after a long pause. "Alex is really nice."

"I agree. And you'll meet a lot of other nice people from now on."

She scuffs her foot in the grass.

"It's okay, isn't it?" I ask her.

"What?"

"Being a girl."

She breathes a deep sigh and wraps her arms around me, burying her face in my shirt. I hold her gently and she begins to sob, all the terror of the last six months finally behind her. I let her cry it out, and when at last she tilts her head back, she's smiling through her tears.

"Is it really all over?" she asks. It's the question I've been dreading.

"Almost," I tell her.

"Ben..." she says softly.

"Yes, Ben."

She straightens up and wipes her eyes on her sleeve. "Am I ever going to be safe?"

"You already are. I won't let him near you again."

"You broke his arm, right?"

"Uh, huh."

"And I bit him."

I grin at her. "You sure did. Probably gave him rabies."

"Good! He's gonna be really mad, though."

"I know. But maybe now he'll have sense enough not to mess with us. We're tough!"

"But he knows me." She thinks that over. "Even if he doesn't come after me, he'll tell people about me."

"I'll fix it."

"How?"

There has to be a way.

"You're going to have a good life," I tell her.

"Maybe..."

"Believe it. We'll make it happen."

* * *

Ken is back by the time we return to the house, and Alex has the Scrabble board set up and ready to go. We play four handed, he and Emily as a team against the rest of us. It's the most normal evening I've spent in a long, long time. We chase the children off to bed at close to eleven, then sit quietly in the living room over coffee. Katie's flowering plant, the gift from Emily, occupies a place of honour on the coffee table between us.

"I'm never going to be able to thank you for all this," I tell them.

"Wait'll you get my bill," Ken says with a smile.

"Whatever it is, I'll pay it cheerfully. You really don't know how much you've done for me."

"For *you?*"

"It isn't just Emily you've helped. I feel like I've gotten back a little bit of my life again. After Amy died, I wasn't sure I ever could."

"Are you going back into practice?" Katie asks me.

"It's either that or starve. Actually, I'm looking forward to it. I've already got some ideas for rebuilding the cabin. After that, I guess I'll just hang out my shingle again and see what develops."

"Residential or commercial?" Ken asks.

"Either. Probably both."

"I might know of something that would interest you. We handle the town's contracts, and there's a tender due next month for a new municipal harbourfront complex on the east side. The town council has grandiose ideas, a marine museum, a recreation park along the quay, that sort of thing. Plus at least two dozen shops."

"How are they going to pay for it?"

"They've floated a bond issue, and they've leased out half the commercial space already, just by word of mouth. It should make us competitive with Lunenburg and Mahone Bay for the tourist trade."

"If they're that far along, they must have a contract for designs already."

"They did have, but the Halifax firm that gave them the lowest bid went belly up before submitting the final plans, so they're looking for someone to take over. If you're interested, I can put your name forward."

"Maybe…"

"You seem to have a gleam in your eye, my friend. I'd say this is just what you need."

"I'd say you're right."

Ken and Katie leave me and head upstairs, and I enter the den and switch on the eleven thirty ATV newscast, listening with half an ear as I make up the sofabed. Thoughts of a return to architecture fill my head. I have responsibilities now, a daughter to raise and educate. And for the first time since losing Amy, I want to go back to work again.

Something the newscaster says catches my attention, a report of a body found in a local business establishment on Agricola Street in Halifax. I freeze and pay close attention.

"Police have identified the deceased as Eugene Benoit, owner of Benoit Auto Parts. He was found by a brother in his apartment above the business early yesterday morning. An autopsy will be performed to determine the exact cause of death, which has tentatively been ascribed to loss of blood from a massive injury to one arm. Foul play has not been ruled out."

I'm a murderer!

The blood pounds in my temples, and my skin turns clammy and cold. I hadn't meant to kill him, but I had to force him to tell me where to find Emily. At best I could be charged with manslaughter, at worst first degree murder, and either would almost certainly mean a jail term unless I can prove self defence. On the other hand, there's nothing to connect me with the man, and I had never told Ken his name.

I've never believed in moral absolutes, although the prohibition "Thou shalt not kill" has always seemed to me to be close. But how can you balance one life against another? In this case, the answer is obvious. Every child's life carries the potential for greatness, and saving Emily was the greater good. Lucas and Cliff and Ben had chosen another path, and all three ultimately paid for it.

We may take something like a star...

Will I turn myself in? Not a chance! The world is better off without them. And most important, the last shadow has finally been lifted from Emily's future, and from my own.

Suddenly exhausted, I climb the stairs to check on Emily once more before going to bed. She lies peacefully on her pillow, a stuffed bear clutched between one small hand and her beautiful face. In the morning I can tell her the nightmare is over at last. For both of us.

33
A Few Days Later

E mily sets Jenny down just inside the door, and she sniffs the jamb and slinks forward to begin a careful inspection of the carpet, the woodwork, and all of the furniture. I'm hoping she'll remember it and settle in quickly. As Ken's Jeep backs out of the driveway we stand in the doorway waving, three shopping bags full of food and two borrowed suitcases on the floor behind us. Once he's out of sight I close the door. Emily stands stock still.

"This is it," I tell her.

No reply. I pick up two of the paper bags from the floor.

"Help me put the food away in the kitchen. Then I'll show you your room and you can hang up your stuff."

As if in a daze she lifts the third sack and trails along behind me through the living room. Her head swivels in all directions, taking in every wall, every window, every dusty sheet that covers the sofa, chairs, lamps and end tables.

"I know it doesn't look like much right now," I tell her, "but we'll get it cleaned up."

"It looks wonderful," she says softly, her eyes glistening.

"Put that bag down on the table," I say. "I want to show you something."

She deposits the sack and we go into the living room. I yank the sheet off the sofa so she can sit down. Half a dozen framed photos sit beneath hand towels on the mantelpiece, and I uncover the largest one and sit down beside her.

"That's Amy," I tell her.

"She's pretty," Emily says.

"Yes."

She looks at me seriously. "Would she mind me living here?"

"That's what I want to talk to you about." I settle back into the cushions, unsure of how to begin. "Remember when we were on the island? I told you that you couldn't keep on hiding, and do you remember what you said?"

"Uh, huh. That you were doing the same thing. And then you got mad at me."

"Of course I did. Because you were right, and I didn't want to face it. When I lost Amy I didn't want to face anything, ever again. So I ran away from everything that still had her in it."

"That was dumb."

"You've got that right."

"So what's that got to do with me living here?"

"I left here because I thought the house was empty, only it wasn't really. She's still here, in all the things we shared and in all the plans we made. And one of those things was to have a family."

"How can she still be here?"

"People are never really gone as long as someone remembers them. A part of her is still somewhere deep inside of me, and she wants you here as much as I do."

She leans against my arm and rests her head on my shoulder.

"I don't understand."

"That's okay," I tell her. "I do, and that's all that really matters."

"I know one thing," she says.

"What's that?"

"Coming here feels just like coming home."

I put my arm around her, my daughter, the daughter I thought Amy and I would never have. If Emily is coming home, I'm coming home again.

Printed in the United States
51495LVS00003B/157-216

9 781424 120109